THE
DIVE

www.penguin.co.uk

THE DIVE

SARA OCHS

bantam

TRANSWORLD PUBLISHERS
Penguin Random House, One Embassy Gardens,
8 Viaduct Gardens, London SW11 7BW
www.penguin.co.uk

Transworld is part of the Penguin Random House group of companies
whose addresses can be found at global.penguinrandomhouse.com

Penguin
Random House
UK

First published in Great Britain in 2023 by Bantam
an imprint of Transworld Publishers

A CIP catalogue record for this book
is available from the British Library.

ISBN 9781787636859 (hb)
9781787636866 (tpb)

Typeset in 12.75/16pt Minion Pro by Jouve (UK), Milton Keynes
Printed and bound in Great Britain by Clays Ltd, Elcograf S.p.A.

The authorized representative in the EEA is Penguin Random House Ireland,
Morrison Chambers, 32 Nassau Street, Dublin D02 YH68.

Penguin Random House is committed to a sustainable
future for our business, our readers and our planet. This book
is made from Forest Stewardship Council® certified paper.

1

To Mom and Dad,
for making anything, and everything, possible.

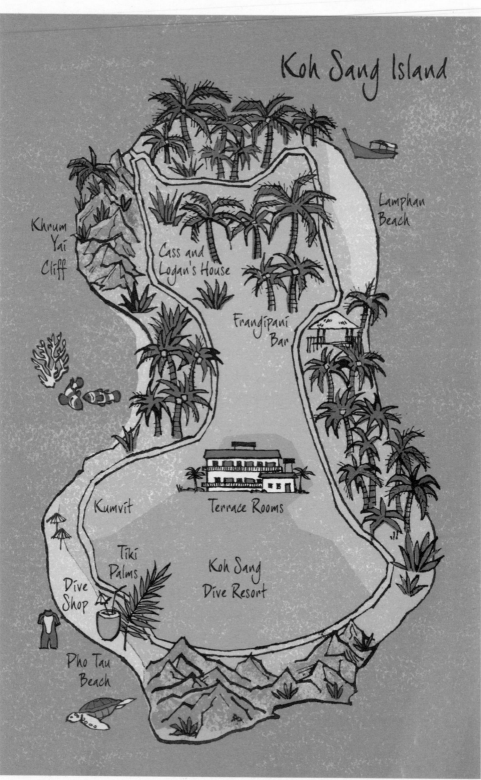

Prologue

Friday Night

The bass thumps from somewhere behind me, echoing the beat of the blood pulsing in my ears. I look back at the group I've left behind. Bodies painted in flashy greens and sickeningly sweet pinks rub against each other. Cheap beer froths out of gold and green bottles while friends sip collectively from fishbowls filled with noxious blue liquids. Further down, a dancer swirls a hula hoop of fire for the acclaim of an impressed – and extremely intoxicated – crowd.

Everything suddenly seems hazy, like I'm watching it all unfold from outside of my body. A neon cacophony of colour set to music that's become nothing more than one long, blurred note, deep enough and loud enough to shake my chest bones. My muscles are heavy, and I need to remind myself to breathe, like my body has forgotten to engage in its normal functions. Maybe they put something in my drink to make this easier. Or maybe I'm just intoxicated on the knowledge. The awareness that time is running out.

I call back towards the group, pleading for anyone to help me. But it's no use. The raucousness blasting from the party's speakers sweeps down the beach like an avalanche, picking up my voice and carrying it away into the silence.

I thought I could do this myself. That I was smarter than them, that I could figure out the darkness that lives on this island and stop it from hurting anyone else.

But I was wrong.

I made a mistake. I trusted the wrong person. I should have known better after everything that happened.

I feel a palm on my lower back. It's light, and I know what it would look like to any onlooker, even one who decided to walk this far down the beach away from the party. Two partygoers escaping the dancefloor for the romantic seclusion of the moonlight. It's so far from true it almost brings a smile to my lips, a bubbling euphoria that nearly escapes.

But it doesn't.

Because I know what that palm signifies. And I feel what the others down the beach don't. The thin prick of a knife digging into my lower vertebrae.

I hear a voice close to my ear, the tone hard and cold, the music doing little to muffle it.

'Move. Forward.'

I look before me, the ocean stretched out to the horizon, black waves glittering in the light from the moon – as round and full as a pregnant belly. I've looked at this view in awe several times since I arrived here, a beauty like nothing I've ever seen.

I do as I'm told and walk. What choice do I have?

The pulsing bass emanating from the bars' speakers recedes with each step, until I'm far enough away that the music becomes nothing more than a memory. This distance from the party, the beach is bathed in darkness, the shops lining this stretch long since closed. The only light comes from the smattering of stars over my head.

As I feel the water lap against my toes, I take one more

look over my shoulder. The people are only small blurs at this distance, but I can still make out their bodies grinding together, so many aching to make contact any way they can. Despite the sloppiness – the drugs and drink making them flop on to each other in lurid movements – there's a beauty to it.

For so long, I've felt nothing but coldness, even with the heavy humidity of the island cloying at my skin these past few days. People always talk about rage burning, but it sat inside my stomach, as hard as ice, freezing my veins. I couldn't think of anything besides revenge. A need to impose pain that I've never felt before.

But now, as the ocean water grazes my kneecaps and I watch the people down the beach from me dance in the glittering moonlight, so far removed from the rest of the world, it's as if that ice finally melts, the brief giddiness from earlier returning.

I wonder if she felt this way before it happened to her. An appreciation for life that comes only at its end.

Before I can think about it any more, my feet stop moving, and the single palm on my back turns into two, pushing me hard, face-first into the water. I gasp for breath as I fall, my forehead striking one of the rocks that litters the ocean floor. But it's not enough. The hands grip my neck tightly, holding my head under, legs now wrapped around my hips, pinning me down. Even though I fight back, the person barely moves. I lift my arms up, reaching for anything to grab hold of, but it feels as if I'm draped in a weighted blanket. My fingers finally grasp around wrists, and I drag my nails across flesh as hard as I can. But the water turns everything soft, and I barely make a dent.

My eyelids force open against the sting of the salt water. Small fish flick by me, deftly avoiding the bubbles erupting from my lips, seemingly unconcerned with the life seeping from my lungs.

My hands release, floating back downwards as if my muscles have realized the futility of the fight before my brain. And I picture her again, as I have so many times since she left. She's the reason why I'm here. Why I've sacrificed everything.

It's her I'm thinking of when the beauty of the water fades to black.

1

Fourteen Hours Earlier

Cass

The hotel room already smells like death. I know realistically it's too soon for that, that the body isn't anywhere near decomposing. But still the stench filters into my nostrils, cloying and visceral. A thick, wet substance smears through the cracks in my toes, and time seems to stand still as I see the blood seep into the carpet fibres. Each droplet holds little pieces of me that will stay long after I'm physically gone.

Suddenly, his body looms large in front of me. And then I feel the weight in my hand, the sturdiness of the knife. My eyes flick to it, the lamplight illuminating a rust-coloured substance that lines its sharp edge. Blood. My blood.

I try to pause, to take stock of what's happening, to piece it all together. But before I can, my arm plunges forward as if of its own volition, angry and desperate. And then it comes. The connection of the blade to the flesh. That satisfying feeling of contact.

I hear the scream erupt from my lungs as if it comes from someone else.

'Shh, shh.'

I clamp my hand over my mouth, and my eyelids snap

open. And then I'm staring into Logan's eyes, at the ocean waves he carries in his irises.

'Cass, I'm here. You're home. You're okay,' he soothes.

Slowly, I register Logan's palms on each side of my face, the sight of his concerned gaze, the sound of his deep Scottish brogue. I inhale a deep breath through my nose, the familiar scent of salt-tipped air flooding my nostrils. *In for two, out for two.*

'A nightmare?'

I can feel a headache forming at the back of my skull, and it takes me a moment to understand what Logan's asking.

'Yeah, I guess,' I answer noncommittally. He doesn't know about the terrors that haunted my dreams every single night for the first year after that day in the hotel room. My unconscious mind replaying the memory on an endless loop, every viewing becoming darker, more frightening. They'd stopped for a while, when I first moved to Koh Sang, but recently, as the third-year anniversary approaches, I feel my mind constantly returning to that hotel room, and the nightmares have returned, darker and more real than ever.

'What was it about?' he asks.

My heart is still beating erratically, and I swipe away a bead of sweat from my forehead. I force myself to breathe slowly, using the trick I teach my students. *In, two, out, two.* 'I can't remember,' I lie.

I realize with a start that my fingertips are tracing the line above my heart where my jagged skin has turned soft and stretched. Logan thinks it's from an accident. A car crash when I was in college. A piece of glass from the windshield piercing my chest. The accident I managed to survive, but which left me an orphan, my two remaining family members torn away in one fast movement of destruction. He thinks that because I've made him think that.

I pull my hand away from my chest, not wanting to draw more attention to the scar than necessary.

Logan's face slowly morphs from concern into his signature lopsided smile: his lips opened slightly, one side pulled up just a touch more than the other, a glitter reaching his dark blue eyes. A stray strand of curls has broken loose from his messy ponytail to graze his chin, and the sight of it sends a flutter to my abdomen.

He leans his face closer to mine. 'Well, whatever that dream was, it wasn't real. But you know what is?' he asks teasingly.

He lifts my left hand up to his mouth, his lips grazing my knuckles, giving me a clear view of the gold band that, as of last night, has taken up permanent residence on my ring finger.

The thought still sends a ripple up my spine. *He's mine. I'm his. We're all we need. No one else matters.*

My eyes travel downwards from his face to the identical ring hanging from the chain around his neck, perched upon his tattooed chest.

I think back to last night, letting the good memories replace the residual panic from the nightmare. Logan had gently pulled out that ring from where it lay tucked under his T-shirt moments after he'd held out a matching ring in a small red box in my direction. Time seemed to freeze, my brain temporarily glitching, nothing making sense until I watched him lower himself to the vinyl flooring of our patio, taking position on one knee. He timed it perfectly as the sun descended into the sea, a fiery ball drowning in the water that left the sky smouldering in pinks and shimmering blues.

I held the ring in my hand a moment before slipping it on my finger.

'Look on the inside,' Logan had instructed, and I did. There, engraved in delicate cursive, lay our words. The phrase we say to each other before bed every night or whenever we separate. Our version of I love you.

'Forever us two,' I managed through the emotion growing thick in my throat.

'Forever us two,' Logan echoed. 'It's official now.'

It was the moment I had been waiting for since the night I first met Logan, two years ago. Since the first time I saw him, I knew. He would be the one to save me.

Tears filled my eyes as Logan continued. 'You are everything to me, Cass Morris. When I was a young lad growing up, I dreamed I would find someone as loving and understanding as you, someone I could always turn to and trust. I can't believe I found you. I must be the luckiest guy in the world.'

All I could do was nod as I listened, the tears breaching the levies of my eyelids. I swallowed hard, and tried to enjoy that moment completely, tried to pretend I was really the sweet, shy, loyal woman he fell in love with and not the girl from the hotel room three years ago who would turn on anyone she could to survive.

I lean forward to him now in our bed, craving the feeling of his lips on mine. But just as they touch, a sound crashes into our bedroom.

Thud, thud, thud.

I feel my body go rigid, my muscles clench.

'It's only the door,' he says, frowning, his statement carrying a question.

'Of course,' I say in a rush, hoping he doesn't notice my embarrassment. 'That dream just felt so real.'

Logan rolls over, shifting his legs off the side of the bed as if making to get up.

'No, you stay,' I command. 'You don't work until the afternoon, and my alarm is about to go off anyway. It's probably just Greta with an engagement present. You know how she is.'

I can already picture her at the door, ready to wrap me in a huge hug and shout about how difficult it was for her to keep this a secret for so long. I feel a brief tinge of pity, thinking of Greta's recent breakup. The way Alice just up and left her and the entire life they built on this island without notice or apparent explanation. But I push it away. This morning is for celebrating. I deserve to be happy for once.

'Look at you. Already the best fiancée I could ever ask for,' Logan says. His comment sends a warm flush to my stomach, and I gently kiss his smiling lips before grabbing clothes that lie crumpled at the side of the bed – casualties from last night. As I slip Logan's T-shirt over my head, I pause briefly to look through the floor-to-ceiling windows that line our bedroom, giving us unbridled views of the sparkling, mountain-studded ocean.

Just like it always does, the beauty takes my breath away. We moved into this house a year ago, each of us fed up with our respective living situations – Logan crashing in an apartment in Kumvit with Neil and Doug, and me in one of the hotel rooms that Frederic rents out to resort staff at decent rates. As soon as we saw the house come on the market, we agreed we didn't have a choice but to put in an offer. It's one of the only buildings this far up the hill, situated right next to the Khrum Yai trailhead. But the view sealed the deal, the beauty of the island on display, as if it's ours for the taking. And in a way it is. Koh Sang is our home, nestled in the Gulf of Thailand, far enough away from all the other backpacking islands that it hasn't yet been tarnished by an overflow of tourists, like neighbouring Koh Phangan or Koh Samui.

Today, the sea looks placid. Good news, given that we're still very much in the rainy season. Every day is a gamble with the weather. But the sun is already well above the water, steadily ascending in the cloudless sky.

I walk through our living room and past the adjoining kitchen. With each step, I expect the knocking at the door to come again, but Greta seems to have given up for the time being. Either that or she's heard me moving around.

I pause when I reach the front door, smoothing my hair down, hoping it doesn't look like I've just rolled out of bed – which I have. No need to rub the engaged bliss in Greta's face more than necessary. As I open the door, I'm smiling, ready to feign mock surprise at Greta's presence.

But there's no one there.

I step out, the humidity instantly sticking to my skin. Could Greta have gone already, thinking that Logan and I were out? I look down the sharp hill that leads back to the rest of the island. If she'd left, I would at least spot her motorbike speeding down the hill, but the road is empty.

My forehead scrunches in confusion. I think about texting Greta as I step back into the doorway, but my foot brushes against something. It's small enough that I managed to step over it without noticing. A plain white envelope with my name – CASS – written across it in small capital letters in a handwriting I don't instantly recognize as Greta's. But it must be hers.

That explains it. She must have dropped it here as she knocked on the door, eager to make a quick getaway so as not to bother us. I find myself smiling again.

I pick up the envelope and take it inside, stopping at the kitchen table to open it. It's light enough to be a card, but knowing Greta it's likely something more. Maybe tickets to some new destination? She can be a bit over the top when it comes to gifts.

I rip the envelope greedily, not bothering to wait for Logan. I'm excited to surprise him with whatever this might be.

Once opened, I realize it's nothing more than a folded sheet of printer paper. I unfold it, curious.

Immediately, I drop it on the table, my fingers buzzing as if it's burned me. I instinctively step back, away from the unfolded paper, my heart rate accelerating, my thoughts racing. I stumble a few steps and grab at a chair.

The whole time, I keep my eyes trained on the paper, at the black-and-white photo of a girl staring up at me, wide-eyed and crazed, guilt splayed across her face. Reporters and cameramen rush at her from all sides, buffeting her in a media circus.

The photo sits in a sea of dense, black text, the sole image in the printed news page.

At the top sits a note, scrawled in red marker.

I know who you are.

Then, beneath the article and the photograph lies more handwriting.

And soon everyone else will, too.

I feel bile rise in my throat as the meaning of those words settles heavily around me. Everything I've accomplished in these last two years – this new identity, this new fiancé, this new life – comes crashing down.

'Was it Greta?' I hear Logan call from the bedroom.

It takes me several tries to answer. Each time I open my mouth, the sound sits trapped in my airway. My vision goes black and I'm back in that hotel room. The knife in my hand, my blood on the blade.

'No – no one there,' I finally manage, praying that Logan can't hear the strain in my voice. 'Greta must have given up waiting.'

'Good,' he says. 'Then come back to bed. We're not done celebrating.'

I walk as if in a trance, stopping in the kitchen to fold up the paper and shove it in our junk drawer beneath a pile of takeaway menus, somewhere I know Logan won't find it. I should destroy it, but part of me needs to see it again, with a clearer head. To make sense of how this could happen.

Even when it's out of sight, those words remain emblazoned on my mind. *I know who you are.* And the photo of that girl is everywhere I turn.

A girl I haven't seen in years, who I made sure no longer exists.

The version of myself I left behind a long time ago.

2

Brooke

I drag the cursor of my laptop inwards slightly, minimizing the size of my thigh to Barbie perfection. My smiling face stares back at me from the screen, my body contorted into the pose I've practised to precision: arm popped out to appear as thin as possible, torso slightly turned away from the camera, stomach tight.

Bored with the futility of the task at hand, I lean back in my chair with a sigh. There are a few guests milling about the Tiki Palms, but given that it's between the breakfast and lunch rush, the official open-air restaurant and beach bar of the Koh Sang Dive Resort is relatively empty. I take another sip from the iced coffee I've been nursing for the last hour. Despite how cheap things are here, I don't have the spare baht to spend on a second cup.

Unlike most of the clientele, I chose a seat in the corner of the restaurant, with my back towards the ocean. After two weeks on the island, I've become accustomed to the stunning aquamarine waters lapping gently against white sand, the colours oversaturated, like everything is draped in an Instagram filter. So, I face towards the resort, monitoring the guests coming and going. A much more interesting view.

The resort itself is carved into the side of a hill, as are most places that line the perimeter of the jagged island. From my vantage point, I can see the path from the beach sharply ascend to the main road. Perfectly trimmed palm trees and clusters of magenta flowers decorate guestrooms grouped in motel-style buildings. Two pools – one for lazing and one for training – dot the hill at the one place where an extended flat area makes their existence possible. Past the pools, one of the island's main roads bisects the resort, but the resort grounds continue even further on. Another, bigger, infinity pool – the resort's designated party pool – along with the spa, fitness centre and yoga studio, and even more guestrooms graze the northern half of the resort. All in all, the mile of landscaped grounds covers nearly a quarter of the island.

I watch as a group of divers descend the sharp incline, fins in hand and masks hanging from their wrists, evidently heading towards the dive shop, the resort's main draw. 'Koh Sang: a scuba-diving island with a party problem', reads the back of the T-shirts they sell in the resort lobby. But my eyes skirt over them to a small figure that follows about twenty feet behind. Unlike the divers, she's not carrying anything. She's petite with delicate features and fine, light brown hair.

Normally I wouldn't give her the time of day, except her eyes lock on mine. I hold her gaze for a second, convinced that she'll stop staring, but she doesn't. She's familiar in a way, reminding me of someone. I scroll through a mental list of past acquaintances, Instagram connections and even family members – but I come up empty.

I know what this must be: a follower who recognizes their favourite Instagram influencer in the wild. I've only been approached by my social media followers a few times in person, but it always makes me uncomfortable. I know what they expect from me: the bubbly, upbeat, slightly ditzy personality I post all over my @BrookeaTrip social media pages.

But Real World Me isn't the walking Barbie they expect. Unfortunately, Instagram still hasn't made a life filter that can permanently smooth away my rough edges.

I'm not in the mood this morning to plaster on my @BrookeaTrip smile. Hoping the approaching girl will take the hint, I divert my eyes, pretending to focus back on my laptop screen.

After a moment, I can't help but look up again. Unlike the divers walking in front of her, who veered right off the path to head to the dive shop, she continues towards the restaurant, her eyes still fixed on mine. Something in me tenses and my fingers curl into my palms.

'I figured I'd bring options.'

The voice close to my ear makes me jump.

'Jesus!' My pulse spikes until I turn around, realizing who it is. 'God, you nearly gave me a heart attack,' I scold, but I can't keep the smile from my voice.

'Sorry!' Neil smiles at me goofily. 'I didn't know what kind of drink you'd want so I figured I'd bring options.' He gestures towards the table in front of us where he's deposited three beverages: a green bottle of Chang beer, a pink cocktail topped with an umbrella, and a smoothie.

He's big, with a body more akin to a teddy bear's than the chiselled muscles most of the guys here spend hours in the gym refining each day. Freckles dominate the majority of his face, with a few stray dots sneaking on to his pink lips. His fire-red hair is wet and plastered to one side. I watch as a drop of water emerges from the end of one sodden strand, dangling before dropping on to my arm.

'Sorry,' Neil says with a chuckle as the water hits my skin. 'Just got out of a dive.'

That explains it. He must have dropped his stuff off at the dive shop and entered the restaurant from the beach side. I was so transfixed by the girl that I never even heard him order.

The girl.

I immediately turn back to the resort, but she's gone. That's strange. I could have sworn she was coming to talk to me. I look up and down the hill, even scanning the beach, but I don't see her anywhere. It's like she disappeared.

'I saw you up here and thought you could use some company.' The boldness of Neil's flirtation brings me back to the present, and, despite myself, I can't help but blush.

I met Neil last week when Cass dragged me to Frangipani Bar, an expat-dominated dive bar located a mile or so up from the beach that Cass's boyfriend – and apparently now fiancé, according to the text I received from her late last night – owns. Cass pointed Neil out as her co-worker, one of only three dive instructors at the resort. I tried to ignore the flutter in my stomach as he shook my hand in greeting and introduced himself in his British accent, but my disloyal face flushed every time I felt his eyes on me that night. It wasn't just his looks that set him apart, it was how he was so unabashedly himself, unconcerned with whatever anyone else thought. His originality radiated charm.

Every time I would steal a glance at him that night, he would look back, a glint in his eyes. I tried to hide the flush in my cheeks, drowning it out with irritation at my own naivety. I knew what Neil likely saw when he looked at me; the same thing every other guy did. A fit body, a perfectly made-up face, and absolutely nothing underneath. A person who morphs from beautiful to shrill whenever a guy realizes she actually has something to say. Believe me, I've read the comments on my Instagram page.

Since that first night, I've run into him on a few other occasions, whenever Cass would bring me along to a group event: karaoke at the Tiki Palms, an afternoon picnic and beach volleyball game in the gloriously empty Lamphan beach over on the opposite side of the island, where tourists don't bother to venture.

I would secretly dread those get-togethers, but I never had a good enough excuse to decline the invite. I had seen how that group of friends – the Permanents, they called themselves – interacted with each other. They were so close that it didn't seem like there was room for anyone else. Cass did the best she could to keep me involved, but eventually she would end up next to Logan, the two of them losing themselves in some romantic revelry. And I would always end up drifting off to the outskirts of the group. Alone.

But Neil would always be the one to save me. He'd drag up a seat next to me in the sand or at a Tiki Palms picnic table and pull me into conversation with one of his stupid dad jokes. Making me feel like I belonged, as if he actually wanted to get to know me. The real me, not @BrookeaTrip. It was a feeling I couldn't seem to shake for hours after we'd separate, a sugary hangover that filled me with a warmth that seemed lacking here, despite Koh Sang's blistering temperatures.

Something about this moment, though – us, here in the Tiki Palms – feels different than those other times. Without Doug somewhere behind us cracking dirty jokes to Greta, or Cass shooting me knowing smiles, silently taking the credit for us hitting it off, it's just the two of us. Neil and I have never been just one-on-one without the other Permanents. There's something oddly intimate about it.

'You do know it's barely ten a.m. right? Hardly happy

hour,' I say, gesturing to the drinks Neil's delivered and stifling a laugh.

He feigns a look of mock surprise. 'It's always happy hour on Koh Sang, has no one ever told you?'

I pull the smoothie close to me, deciding on the most innocent of the three options. I try to ignore the quick thrumming in my chest as I feel Neil's sun-warmed skin next to mine. Those kinds of thoughts are a distraction I can't risk now.

Undeterred, he slides into the seat across the table, gathering the cocktail and beer bottle in front of him. 'More for me,' he says with a wink.

He takes a large gulp from the pink cocktail, the paper umbrella rubbing against his freshly shaved cheek. I can't help but smile at how small the girly drink looks in his massive, freckled hand.

'Hey,' he says, noticing. 'Nothing shows that you're secure in your manliness quite like a pink drink.'

I laugh, meeting his kind eyes, the freckled skin around them crinkled in a smile. I force my gaze back downwards.

'Mm.' Neil smacks his lips together. 'Solid cocktail as always, Sengphet,' he shouts back towards the bartender.

Sengphet, who always seems to be manning the bar while simultaneously serving as the primary host, waiter and washer-upper of the Tiki Palms, nods back, his hands pressed in front of him in gratitude. I've only had a few short conversations with Sengphet since arriving here, during quiet moments between the breakfast and lunch rushes. He told me in broken English about how he'd come to Koh Sang so that he could send money to his family back in Laos in efforts to give them a better life. We talk about his son, barely three, and how Sengphet is reminded of him every time he makes a drink with bananas and coconuts – his son's favourite foods. Or about how much he misses playing *Sepak Takraw* – apparently some kind of mix between volleyball and soccer – with his friends and cousins back home. He fumbles through the new language he's been struggling to learn since he arrived on the island a few months ago with a toothy smile and a hopelessly endearing chuckle.

An up-tempo Mumford & Sons song plays from the bar speaker, a prelude to the raucous club beats that will take over as soon as the sun sets. I take a long sip from the smoothie. It tastes like a mix of papaya and dragon fruit and is absolutely delicious.

'So what were you doing here before I so rudely interrupted?' Neil asks.

My mind returns to the girl, and I scan the restaurant once more, but I don't spot her anywhere.

'Oh, nothing, just editing some photos I took from the hike Cass and I did on the Khrum Yai trail the other day so that I can turn them into a TikTok.'

'Ah,' he says. 'Cass is a good tour guide if she's taking you up there.' I nod, not telling him the real reason I asked her to show me the trail, my true intention in seeing the summit. 'It's nice that you've become so close,' he continues. 'You and Cass.'

I smile, silently remembering the day I met her two weeks ago, my first morning on the island. She was sitting next to me a few tables down from where Neil and I sit now, her back straight in that typical East Coast, upper-middle-class way I always envied growing up. I watched Sengphet smile at her as he took her order, the gentle way she touched his arm as she thanked him.

'You're American, right?' I asked after Sengphet walked away. Her eyes grew wide as if I was accusing her of something. 'I didn't mean to eavesdrop, but I heard you order. I've been in Thailand for a few days now and, strangely enough, I haven't run into another American yet.' I was surprised at how eager I was for her response. Even after travelling for years throughout Eastern Europe on my own without issue, there was something utterly foreign about Southeast Asia. Something I'd found oddly isolating.

She nodded politely but didn't respond.

'I'm Brooke.' I tried again.

'Cass,' she answered. Her voice was quiet, and there was a shyness to her that was refreshing given that most of my interactions lately came in the form of excited messages over social media with other extroverted influencers and eager followers.

'Where in the States are you from?' I asked.

'New York,' she said. And after a moment, 'You?'

'The West Coast.'

If Cass was curious about my intentionally vague answer, she didn't say. And it's not like she would have had any reason to suspect I was lying. I'd spent years moulding my harsh Kentucky accent, sharpening my consonants and shortening my vowels, so that I could leave my drawl behind with the rest of my upbringing.

I spotted the black polo she was wearing, her chest emblazoned with the label for the Koh Sang Dive Resort, the only hotel on the island. 'You work here?'

'Yeah, I'm a dive instructor,' she said, the hint of a proud smile on her lips.

'Wow,' I said, impressed. 'That's incredible. I can't imagine doing all that, spending all that time under the water. What's that like? Doesn't it make you nervous that things could go wrong down there?'

And with that it was like a switch had flipped. She began to tell me all about what it was like to lose herself below the water's surface, how it felt like an escape. Her quiet shyness melted as she opened up, her passion for diving evident. Eventually, I moved over to her table, and we talked for well over an hour, barely touching the meals in front of us. She told me about how she'd lived on Koh Sang for two years, and how she was in a long-term relationship with Logan, another expat who owned one of the island's bars.

She asked me questions as well, wanting to know all about the campaigns I'd established with hotels throughout Eastern Europe, how I'd created @BrookeaTrip, listening to it all attentively, without a shred of judgement. She leaned forward, eyes wide as I told her about the destruction I'd seen in Sarajevo, still unrepaired from war decades ago, and she nearly choked on her smoothie as I regaled her with the story of how I had reluctantly agreed to go on a first date with a guy in Croatia, expecting a casual meal, only to realize he had brought me as his plus one to his sister's wedding – an event I was severely underdressed and horribly unprepared for.

It felt good, this conversation, her interest. It was a type of female connection I hadn't felt in a long time, absent of the inherent competition that came with the shallow Instagram-based friendships I'd formed with other influencers. And I found myself disappointed when Cass eventually had to leave after an hour or so to get back to the dive shop. But we promised to meet up again, and we kept it, spending nearly every day together in the last couple of weeks. She was quick to introduce me to her friends, to welcome me into the life she had made here.

'Yeah,' I say to Neil now. 'I'm lucky to have met her.'

Neil nods knowingly, and we sit in silence for a few

moments. I expect it to feel awkward, but other than the nervous trill in my stomach, it's surprisingly comfortable. We watch a group of backpackers toss around a blow-up volleyball as they walk down the slope towards the beach.

'So, how are you liking Koh Sang so far?' Neil asks finally.

'It's great,' I say. 'I mean it's beautiful, obviously, and everyone is so nice.' Both statements are objectively true.

'Are we nice enough to get you to stay?' Neil's dark eyes are trained on mine, his eyebrows rising.

It catches me off guard, even though it shouldn't. I can tell the answer Neil wants, the one he's expecting. That I'll join him and the other Permanents who have made Koh Sang their home.

'Maybe,' I say finally, settling on as uncontroversial an answer as I can think of. 'Just taking it week by week at this point.'

I don't mention that I don't have much choice. That I've spent nearly all my savings on a one-way flight to Phuket, followed by a ferry ticket to Koh Sang. I have barely enough left to cover my expenses for the next two weeks, let alone to pay for travel out of here.

Neil nods. He looks as if he's considering saying something more, but I head it off before he has the chance. 'So, what brought you here? How did you know that this was the place for you to settle down?'

Neil takes another drink, apparently thinking over the question. He casually reaches down and starts playing with the bracelets that cover several inches on both of my wrists. Some beaded, some nothing more than a loop of string. Some purchased, some given to me, usually by kids, in the various places I've travelled. Neil shifts each bracelet one at a time, his skin brushing against mine. His touch is unexpected, but somehow it feels right. Even so, I pull my arm away, feigning an itch on my back that desperately needs to be scratched.

'Ah, you know, the usual story,' he says, pretending not to notice the sting of my rejection. 'Bit of a rough childhood, drunk dad, the whole lot. Took off travelling as soon as I finished school and didn't even consider stopping until I reached here. Discovered scuba, and kind of fell in love.' I feel a heat rise in my cheeks when he says that last word. 'Something about this place just felt right, I can't really put my finger on why. So, I worked it out with Frederic that I would serve as waitstaff here at the Tiki Palms to pay for my training. Once I finally finished my divemaster course, he took me on as an instructor. That was about three years ago now.'

He's right. It *is* the usual story. So generic it's almost laughable. But still, I can't help but feel a surge of compassion for Neil. My eyes keep drifting to his fingers, which have now retreated from my skin and are clasped around his glass, and I regret pulling away. I find myself craving human touch. His touch specifically. The feeling of his fingers on me.

Not now. I tell myself. This isn't the time, and it's certainly not the place.

He laughs lightly to himself. 'But I know the diving isn't what drew you here, Brooke. I think you're the only person I've ever met who's come to Thailand's most renowned diving island with no intention of even trying scuba.' He shakes his head slightly, as if he can't quite believe it.

I'd confessed my aversion to water sports to Neil the first night we met. I've never been athletic. When I was growing up, I always preferred to hole up in my bedroom with a book or sneak into the living room to turn on CNN, rather than join the other kids in our trailer park playing whatever kind of miserable game they'd made up that week. And it wasn't like we had the option of water sports in central Kentucky. Back then I didn't even realize scuba *was* a sport.

I've also never understood the desire to be that far below the surface. The claustrophobia, the water's pressure bearing down on you, relying on nothing but a tank and a small tube to keep you breathing. That's way more trust than I can put into anything, let alone any*one*.

'I still think I can convince you. I'll make a diver out of you one of these days. That's a promise,' Neil says, raising his glass.

'Sounds more like a threat to me,' I say, cringing at how flirtatious my words sound.

'So, what was it then?' Neil presses. 'If not the diving, then what brought you to this part of the world?'

'Well, I've been travelling for a while now,' I say, following my prepared script, 'and what kind of backpacker would I be if I never made it to Thailand?'

He nods, and something in his expression directs me to continue.

'I finished college early,' I explain, the best phrase I've come up with to avoid mentioning that I dropped out after only a few months, 'and I didn't really know what to do with my life. I had always wanted to travel. I started with backpacking through Eastern Europe. Thought I could pick up some freelance journalism jobs as I went, but that didn't really pan out. So, I made this Instagram profile, and then a TikTok, and then a website, and the whole thing kind of blew up . . .'

I trail off, glancing downwards as I feel the usual shame that comes with explaining my career. I prepare myself for Neil's response. An eye roll, or a snort of derision, perhaps. The typical response I get when I admit I'm an influencer, a profession that's come to be both envied and disdained.

But Neil simply sits there, completely quiet for a few seconds.

'Hmm,' he says finally, his lips turning into a smile, and for the first time, I notice a dimple piercing his left cheek.

'Hmm what?' I ask, a smile pulling at the sides of my mouth.

'I'm not sure I believe you, Brooke.'

Instantly, my smile freezes. My stomach tightens, and I force down a swelling panic. *He knows. He's figured it out. It's all over.*

But a glitter in his eye stops me.

'I feel like you're holding out on me,' he continues. 'A smart girl like you must have had tons of options after university. People like us – travellers, I mean – use travel either to find something or to hide from something. So, spill. What's your reason?'

I let my muscles unclench as I convince myself my fear was unfounded. Neil doesn't know – he *can't* know – why I'm really here.

'Oh, you know, just the usual twenty-something discovery phase. Travelling to find myself and all that. I heard a few other travellers raving about Koh Sang, so I knew I had to try it out.' Eager to change the subject, I hold my glass up, indicate for him to do the same, and clink them softly.

Neil smiles back at me, and we sip from our drinks in unison. I savour the taste of the smoothie, letting the sticky sweetness drown out the bitterness of my lie.

3

Cass

I know who you are.
The words have played on repeat in my head the entire morning, ever since I opened the envelope on my porch. I thought of them as I made love to Logan and as I clung desperately to him afterwards, wondering how long it will be until he knows the truth and refuses to touch me ever again. And I think of them now as I navigate my motorbike down the winding road that leads away from our house.

I wonder for the millionth time who could have recognized me. I'm not that girl any more. I replaced my mousy brown hair with blonde highlights, accentuated by hours spent in the sun, my pale skin turned tan from the same. I swapped out the round glasses for contacts, and I started going by my middle name when I got to Koh Sang. It wasn't much, but it was enough. No one expected to find that girl here on an island in the middle of nowhere, a place where news of the outside world barely infiltrates, so no one ever thought to look.

Until now.

I turn off my street and guide my motorbike on to the narrow lane of Kumvit, the closest thing our little island – home to only a few hundred locals and one resort – has to an urban centre. I pass open-air restaurants modelled fully in teak wood and locals pulling open the metal gates of their souvenir shops, each hawking identical versions of Thai beer-logoed tank tops, fake Nikes and knockoff Ray-Bans. The lane eventually opens up on to the beach road that leads around the entire perimeter of Koh Sang. The shops and restaurants become fewer and farther between until they disappear entirely, giving way to the untamed jungle on one side and the beauty of Pho Tau beach on the other. Wooden long-tail boats group together in front of dive shops in ad hoc marinas, and further out, paddleboarders struggle to remain balanced on the water. Back on the shore, a massive palm tree shoots out at almost a ninety-degree angle, parallel to the beach, so long that its coconut-bunched palms nearly reach the water.

But this morning I'm too distracted to even acknowledge the beauty. I need to get to the bottom of who sent me this envelope before they decide to make good on their threat.

After a few minutes, I pull into a small patch of pavement jutting out from the street, big enough to fit three motorbikes stacked next to each other, one for each full-time staff member of the resort's dive shop.

My skin sticks to the seat as I pull myself away from my bike, a painful reminder of the day's heat. Thankfully, it's only a few steps from my bike to the door of the shop, a small octagonal hut that has come to serve as my second home on the island.

As I walk, I pause, struck by the sudden feeling of being watched. I spin around, prepared to expose anyone who may be watching, but the road is empty except for a truck hurtling past. I stand there for a few seconds, long enough for a pinprick of sweat to form on my hairline, but I still don't see anyone. Trying to shake off the feeling, I head into the shop.

Doug's bright Australian accent greets me as I walk through the door. 'Well, if it isn't the future Mrs McMillan! Congrats!'

He steps out from behind the small desk that bears a stack of clipboards and an outdated PC and wraps me in a bear hug.

'Thanks,' I say, slapping him gingerly on the back, my fingers grazing his long, matted hair.

Doug got here a few years before I did. All I know from his past is that he's from Melbourne. It's somewhat of an unwritten rule that we keep talk about our lives before the island to a minimum. If someone wants to share, that's fine, but it's not expected. Which more than works for me. At the time I arrived, Doug was still a dive instructor, but Frederic, the resort's owner, has since appointed him to dive shop manager. This essentially means that Doug's my babysitter when Frederic is out of town on business, as he is now.

'Looking forward to tonight,' he says, handing me the clipboard on the top of the stack. 'We'll make it a ripper of an engagement party.'

I smile in return, forcing down the bile rising in my throat and silently hoping that whoever has found me doesn't choose tonight to expose me. I flip through the clipboard, totalling the number of clients in my head.

'Only four?' I confirm.

'Yup, Full Moon Party over on Koh Phangan tonight. Four's pretty good, considering.'

He's right. Once a month, the neighbouring island hosts an all-night rager on the beach, a party so raucous it's become legend in the backpacking circuit. It's popular enough that it draws guests away from the other islands, including Koh Sang. As sales began to decline in the last few months, Frederic started hosting our own Koh Sang version of the Full Moon Party, complete with neon body paint, fishbowl concoctions of juice and unidentifiable liquor, and fire dancers, but even so it pales in comparison to the original.

I should be annoyed. Fewer clients mean fewer tips, but I can't help but be grateful, particularly as the dull ache in my head has only grown since this morning.

With a nod to Doug, I head out of the shop, clipboard tucked under my arm. I walk down the beach, about fifty metres or so, to the pathway that leads up to the rest of the resort. Once I reach it, I peer into the Tiki Palms, spotting Brooke seated in one of the corner tables, her honey-coloured hair trailing down the side of her torso in a long, messy braid. She's talking with someone – a man seated across from her – and when he shifts, the sunlight glints off the unmistakable red of his hair. Neil.

Despite everything, I feel a smile form on my lips. It's no secret that Neil has developed a bit of a crush on Brooke – as have most men on the island – and given the way she's smiling at him now, it seems there's a chance it might be reciprocal.

I was a bit awestruck when I first met Brooke two weeks ago. She was extroverted and charming and beautiful – all the qualities you would expect in a travel influencer, I suppose, but everything I'm not. Her confidence was palpable when she struck up that first conversation with me at the Tiki Palms. She was so open, it felt like we had known each other for years. And indeed, there was something familiar about her that I couldn't quite peg down.

As soon as I got home that day, I looked up the Instagram handle she had mentioned – @BrookeaTrip – and once the first search result loaded, it flooded my screen with high-definition photos of beautiful mountains and cobblestoned city streets. Brooke was front and centre in all of them, of course, her dark-lashed blue eyes fixed on the camera, her body curvy and compact and always dressed in some fashionable – and usually revealing – outfit, her long hair perfectly styled. It felt masochistic, scrolling through the photos and videos of her travels, glossed with the perfection that only social media can deliver, as I lay there on my couch draped in one of Logan's old formless T-shirts. But I couldn't stop. I gorged myself on her beauty and the powerful captions she wove beneath each post, which confidently called out the corruption and autocracy in the countries she visited, speaking her mind in an easy way I could only dream of.

Since then, I've found reasons to seek her out, always drinking in her attention, revelling in the pride I feel when people see us together. It's the same feeling I get when I stand next to Logan, his arm wrapped tightly around my hips. Like I'm worthy.

I want to call out to her now, but I'm reluctant to interrupt whatever's going on between them. Instead, I continue hurriedly up the path, lined with carefully clipped shrubs and magenta flowers, up to the training pool. I immediately spot my students, huddled together near a group of lawn chairs under a beach umbrella.

I pause before heading over. The public-speaking anxiety I still get whenever I have to introduce myself to a new group is worse than normal. Because each new arrival on the island, every strange face, now feels like a threat. Could whoever left me that note be in my class? Or are they suntanning at the beach? Or partying over at the resort's main pool?

Koh Sang isn't that big. But someone here is trying to ruin me.

I take in a deep breath and try to force the thoughts away, as I walk towards the group.

'Good morning, everyone,' I call, hoping that my practised authoritative teacher voice drones out any wavers that may sneak in. 'I'm Cass, and I'm going to be your divemaster. Thank you all for choosing the Koh Sang Dive Resort for your Discover Scuba Diving course. By the end of the next two days, you will have learned everything you need to dive safely and effectively, and you will have completed two open-water dives.'

I pull up my clipboard, using it to minimize the slight tremble in my hands. 'Let me just take attendance real quick and have you all introduce yourselves.'

I scan the first sheet of paper. 'Ariel and Tamar Abramson.' I look expectantly at the pale couple standing before me. I peg them to be in their early thirties, on the older side for our clientele. The woman's short black hair is cropped bluntly at her chin, and she looks a bit anxious. But the man standing next to her draws my attention. He's tall and well built with a military-like buzzcut. His lips are pursed in a tight line, his eyes hard and cold. There's something discomfiting about him that I can't quite put my finger on. He doesn't respond when I say his name, although I see his shoulders tense.

'That's us,' the woman says. Her voice is clipped, in heavily accented English. 'I am Tamar. I am here with my husband, Ariel.' She points towards him, but he remains unmoving. 'We arrived yesterday. We are travelling from Tel Aviv.'

'Lovely to meet you two.' I look at the man again for a second too long before flipping to the next page on the clipboard. 'Daniel Ayad—'

'Yeah, all right,' says a guy in a brash cockney accent before I can finish pronouncing his name. An inch-long pink scar that runs along his cheek shifts up and down as he speaks. His swagger puts me at ease. I've dealt with thousands of travellers like him. 'That's me. Daniel Ayadebo. Yeah, I'm from London, on my gap year, and I'm starting off strong in Thailand. Gonna travel till the money runs out. Got here last night, and I'm loving it.' His eyes take in the girl next to him. She doesn't return his glance.

He looks older than most of the guests who come on their gap year, but I don't comment on it.

'Last but not least,' I say as I flip to the last page on my clipboard. 'Lucy Dupin.'

I turn to the girl next to Daniel. She barely reaches his biceps. Her hair is piled up on her head, mostly hidden under a light pink baseball cap, but wisps of light brown curls peek out from beneath it. She looks back, fixing her light blue eyes firmly on mine.

I swallow, forcing myself to keep the clipboard steady, to stay smiling.

It's her. She's alive.

Her name touches my lips, light with memory. *Robin.*

The last time I saw her – really saw her – she was lying in that hotel room. Her slender body was dwarfed by the queen-size bed, her face chiselled as if in porcelain, and those big blue eyes wide open, the brightness slowly leaking out of them. My sister, gone for ever.

It's not really Robin standing in front of me now, of course. The closer I look, the more obvious the differences become. Robin was taller than this girl, her cheekbones more pronounced, her hair a few shades darker and curlier. But the eyes are the same. Those big, blue doe eyes that belie an unexpected strength.

Still, I want to reach out and touch her. To hold Robin in my arms. But that's impossible. Robin is buried beneath six feet of frozen ground in a cemetery in Upstate New York, under a headstone that no one ever visits.

I can't seem to find my voice. My brain is devoid of any words to continue our conversation. Instead, I'm back in that hotel room, watching Robin fade away, the life evaporating from her face.

Thankfully, the girl takes the cue. 'I'm Lucy. I'm on a gap year as well.'

Her tone is confident, her words lilted. I scan through Lucy's guest sheet until I reach her country of origin. Australia. There's a flatness to her accent that distinguishes it from Doug's; they must be from different parts of the country.

'Okay,' I say, clearing my throat, hoping my temporary lapse in composure wasn't too noticeable. 'Nice to meet you. We'll be stuck together for the next two days, so it's best we all get friendly. We'll start with a few exercises in the pool to get you familiar with the equipment and the basics of breathing underwater, then we'll hit the classroom to work the science and practical instruction portion of the class, and then tomorrow, we'll move on to the fun part: the dives. But before all that, I want to start off with the most important topic I'll address in this entire course: safety.'

I ignore Daniel's groan. Most of these kids – or adults in Ariel and Tamar's case – want to jump over safety instructions and get right to the good stuff. They don't consider the risks inherent in breathing someone else's air through a tube while you are metres below the surface.

But unlike them, I know how close death is, leaving its phantom fingerprints on everything. How little it takes to breach that shadowy curtain between this world and the next. A broken respirator, a knife, small white pills.

I run through the many risks inherent in scuba. Everything from permanent lung damage caused by holding your breath underwater or a rushed, panicked ascent, to ruptured eardrums resulting from a failure to equalize upon descent, to the most obvious danger: running out of air while you are metres below the surface. Slowly, gingerly, my body starts to relax, forgetting the unpleasant surprises of the morning and easing back into the routine of the class, becoming familiar with the students' gaze on me.

The next few hours pass in a steamy haze of normality. Instruction on the basics in the shade, followed by exercises and equipment tests in the pool, and topped with a few hours of the classroom component – a lesson on the science behind scuba, complete with textbooks and quizzes – in the upstairs level of the Tiki Palms. The students seem to be enjoying themselves for the most part. All of them, at least, except for Ariel, whom I routinely catch staring into apparent nothingness, his body rigid, as if he's prepared to jump up and run at a moment's notice.

As the late-afternoon air hangs heavy around us, Daniel drops his head on the table in front of him and groans. 'I thought the point of a gap year was to avoid being in a classroom. Fuck, this is worse than uni, innit?'

That's my cue.

'All right, all right. I think we can call it for today. We'll meet at the shop tomorrow morning at exactly eight for our first dive. Make sure you're there early. We won't be able to wait for you if you're late.'

Daniel's already slammed his book shut and sidled up to Lucy, my words having no more effect than a mosquito buzzing in his ear. He loops his arm around her shoulder with a lazy confidence, and I see her spine lock in straight. As they start to walk away, I remember something.

'Stay away from the alcohol tonight, guys. I know it's Full Moon and all that, but a hangover makes for a miserable dive.'

Daniel and Lucy are already halfway down the stairs, giving no indication that they've heard me. I hear Tamar say something to Ariel in Hebrew before heading to the toilet. I bend over and busy myself cleaning up the books and pens left on the table, conscious of Ariel lingering near the stairs.

It all happens at once.

I register the toilet door slam shut with a loud bang. I'm making a mental note to remind someone to fix it when I feel something shift in the air.

I stand upright, momentarily forgetting my efforts at cleaning up, and survey the room. It's empty, everyone gone. Except for Ariel.

There's rigid intensity to him that was absent during class. His muscles are taut, and even from several steps away, I can see his breaths coming in short, rapid succession. Anxiety radiates from him.

'Ariel,' I say his name as I rush toward him, aware something is wrong. 'Are you—'

But he speaks before I can finish the question.

'It is not safe here.'

His voice is guttural, scratchy, as if it's been days since he last spoke. Which it very well could be, as I haven't heard him talk once in all the hours we've been together. His words snake in through my skin, gripping my veins, sucking the moisture from my throat and jumpstarting my pulse into an erratic, urgent rhythm.

'I – I don't know what you mean,' I say.

'It is not safe,' he repeats. 'There is something wrong about this place. *You* are not safe.'

Despite how quiet his voice is, his words take up all the space in the room. His grey eyes are glassy, yet they still bore holes into me.

I stare at him, unsure how to respond. His face is even paler than earlier, and his warning has sent shots of panic through my chest.

I open my mouth to say something, but another voice cuts through the room.

'Ariel!'

Tamar rushes towards us from the toilet. As soon as she's next to Ariel, she places her palms on each side of his face, peering into his eyes. She repeats a phrase in Hebrew until I see Ariel loosen, the anxiety physically leave him. His shoulders slump slightly, and his eyes shed their glassy sheen.

I watch as she pulls him in for a hug and his muscled frame slumps into her body. I realize Tamar must be stronger than her petite frame suggests.

Eventually, she pulls away, her voice gentle, soft enough for only Ariel to hear. As he begins to walk towards the stairs, Tamar turns to me.

'I am so sorry, Miss Cass,' she says in a hushed voice, apparently so that Ariel will not overhear. 'My husband, he is not well.' She glances over her shoulder towards the staircase.

I want to know more, to understand that stark shift in Ariel. To comprehend the meaning of what he told me. But it's clear that Tamar is eager to go after him. There's a desperation in her eyes that I can't ignore.

36

'It's fine,' I say. I consider resting my hand on her arm as a reassuring gesture, but she's gone before I can do so, already crossing the room to join her husband.

I'm left with that one word, echoing in her wake. Which couldn't be further from the truth.

Because I'm anything but fine. Ariel's words play in a jarring loop in my head. An ominous warning.

You are not safe.

4

Brooke

The sun is just beginning to set as I leave my room, a simple unit in the Coral Bungalows that Frederic, the resort's owner, begrudgingly agreed to rent out to me at the long-term rate he gives to resort staff, in exchange for a few Instagram posts advertising the resort. I start walking up the path towards the street where I park my rented motor-bike when I'm stopped by a single word shouted at my back.

'Hey!'

The voice is unfamiliar, and I whirl around, inhaling sharply when I see who it is. The girl from this morning, the one who looked like she was coming to talk with me at the restaurant. The one who I later saw in Cass's dive group. She's standing a short way from my door, almost as though she's been waiting for me.

'Uh, hi,' I say, quickly recovering from my surprise and plastering on the fake smile I save for my @BrookeaTrip pages.

'Brooke, right?' She asks. She's skinny enough that she looks like she could blow over in a strong wind, and her eyes carry that same wide, hungry look they had earlier. But her voice is stronger than I expected; there's a quiet strength to her.

I nod, expectantly, now certain that she must be an eager Instagram follower, preferring to ask for a selfie when I'm alone. Less chance of rejection that way. But her next question catches me by surprise, causing my smile to slip. 'You've only been here for two weeks, right?' she asks.

'Yeah, I guess,' I say cautiously. 'About two weeks.' I think back to what I've posted on my accounts. I remember sharing a TikTok when I first arrived, documenting the tuk-tuk ride from the ferry station to the resort. Still, it seems a bit strange that this girl would remember exactly how long I've been here.

The girl nods. 'So, you weren't here when that woman fell from Khrum Yai, then?'

I blink, surprised. The question is so far out of the realm of what I was expecting this girl to ask, this person I'd pegged for an overeager fan who just wanted to gush over my social media profiles.

Of course, I'd heard about it. The woman fell from Khrum Yai, the tallest mountain on the island, a few days before I arrived. She was twenty-one years old, like me. The few articles I'd seen posted online about it – all of which I'd found from setting up a Google alert on news of Koh Sang – said that this woman, Jacinta, had gone for a morning solo hike on Khrum Yai and fallen to her death. The articles withheld her last name for privacy reasons, but they did include a picture. Curly, chestnut-coloured hair framed her round, smiling face. Her nose was dotted with freckles, and her lack of make-up made her look several years younger than she was.

The Koh Sang police claimed Jacinta's death was an accident. She walked too close to the edge of the cliff. Something may have startled her, or maybe she just lost her footing. Either way, she tumbled to the rocky crevices below, her body left to rest there, broken.

Since I'd arrived, hushed stories of the woman's death had run like an undercurrent through the resort. I'd hear staff members gossiping quietly in rushed Thai; the topic of which would have remained unknown had it not been for their sharp pauses as they struggled to pronounce the English syllables of Jacinta's name.

But how does this girl know what happened? It wasn't like the woman's death made international news. Has she been researching the island as closely as I have? If so, why?

'No,' I say carefully, after a moment. 'I didn't know her. Why do you ask?'

She inhales deeply, as if she's thinking about exactly what to say. 'I know this is a lot, and I know you don't know me, but I don't think her death was an accident. I think there's more to—'

Whatever other words she tries to say are quickly drowned out by a voice from behind us.

'Lucy!'

We turn in unison to see a large guy, his chest bare and his face already smeared with neon-green paint, lumbering towards us, several others flanking him on both sides.

'We're going to Tiki Palms before the party kicks off,' he continues as he gets closer, clearly oblivious – or possibly indifferent – to our ongoing conversation. 'Come with!'

The girl – Lucy, apparently – opens her mouth as if to protest, but she's quickly stopped.

'Nope,' the guy says, 'I won't hear it. You're on holiday. You need to party, and I am appointing myself as your party facilitator.' He changes his voice to mock formality, as if he's impersonating a policeman. 'Ma'am, you're coming with us.'

He looks over, as if noticing me for the first time, and gives me a smile that I'm sure he intends as flirtatious, but which instead makes him appear uncomfortably constipated. 'Oh, hello. You're more than welcome to join as well.'

'Can't. Sorry,' I say, feeling anything but.

'Well, you know where we'll be if you change your mind,' he says with a wink. And before I know it, he's walking towards the path, his arm wrapped around Lucy, leaving me there with all the questions I didn't have a chance to ask.

What did Lucy want, exactly? What does she know about the girl who fell from Khrum Yai? And how? And why me? Out of all the people on the island, why seek *me* out to try to share whatever information she had?

I watch as the group heads towards the restaurant and briefly consider whether to follow, but a quick glance at my watch tells me I'm already late. I'm about to head to my motorbike, when Lucy glances over her shoulder, her eyes searching for me. They lock on mine with the same intensity as before, as if she's considering something. She lets them linger for a moment before she turns back, leaving me staring after her.

By the time I pull up to the party, the sun has just finished setting, leaving residual streaks of purple that bisect the night sky. I park among a dense cluster of palm trees that line the far side of the hill. Even though Frangipani isn't too far from a residential street, it feels like we're entirely secluded out here. The winding road on which the bar sits pushes up against a portion of the island that remains uninhabited jungle, and we're at least a mile from the bustle of Kumvit and Pho Tau beach. Trees form a dense canopy above, absorbing the sounds and draping the area in a blanket of quiet.

As I cut the engine of my motorbike, the murmur of excited voices floats over from the bar, which is little more than a chain-link fence enclosing a small area of waste ground. A hand-painted sign on a piece of wood tied to the fence identifies it as 'Frangipani Bar' in green block letters over a novice portrayal of the island's most common flower. White fairy lights throw a magical glow over the wooden stage in the far corner and a grouping of picnic tables arranged in no sensible order. Strung up among the lights is a large white banner, emblazoned with CONGRATU-LATIONS CASS + LOGAN. In the front and centre of the area sits a palapa with a thatched roof. The light from within reflects off a line of liquor bottles, and a peal of laughter erupts from the bar stools surrounding it.

From my vantage point, I'm largely hidden by the darkness, so I park my bike and take a minute to watch the group. Cass and Logan are standing behind the bar, his arm wrapped around her meek frame. Doug and Greta sit on adjacent bar stools opposite them, Greta's ice-blonde hair shimmering in the lights, her head tilted back in a full-bodied laugh. I feel a quick flood of relief when I see Neil standing beside them, leaning nonchalantly against the counter, wearing his usual goofy smile.

But this time, I can't attribute the flutter in my stomach to the sight of him. Normally, I wouldn't care about arriving at a party by myself, but there's something about this group, how strangely close they all seem. I've been dancing around their perimeter ever since I arrived. I seem to have won over Cass and Neil, but the rest seem somewhat aloof, as if they're not willing to welcome any newcomer who isn't committed to staying on the island permanently. I've seen how the other backpackers look at them, too, like they're an exclusive club that they can only hope to join.

I shake off the nerves and straighten my back, reminding myself that I have every right to be here, desperately ignoring the voice in the back of my mind, branding me as an outsider.

Almost immediately, I hear Neil shout in my direction, and a wave of relief crashes over me.

'Brooke! Come and join us!' he yells with a wide smile.

I watch the rest of the heads turn in my direction, and as if on cue, Cass hurries towards me.

'Congratulations!' I say, a touch too loudly as she wraps her arms around me.

'Thank you so much for coming,' Cass says into my ear, her voice a tad higher pitched than usual. She smells as she usually does, of tropic flowers and an undefinable sweetness that seems to perfectly reflect her persona, and I lean into her hug. Once she pulls away, I notice a glassy sheen covers her eyes. I wonder how much she's had to drink.

I grab the bottle I've carried with me here in my backpack, a strand of red ribbon looped around its neck, and hold it towards her. 'Figured this was as good a time as ever to pop some bubbly,' I explain.

I may be imagining it – it is quite dark where we stand in the street after all – but it looks as if Cass flinches at the sight of the bottle. I wait for her to respond, to explain, but she says nothing at first.

'Wow,' she says eventually, her voice slow and measured. 'Where did you manage to find champagne on the island?'

'That place, the Sunset Restaurant,' I say, referring to the nicest hilltop restaurant on the island, uncreatively named for its unbeatable view of the sunset over Koh Sang. 'I noticed they had a few bottles there. It's not much to split

43

among six people, but I mean, what's an engagement party without champagne?' I don't mention that I could barely afford the one bottle, let alone more. My wallet seems to issue a silent scream every time I open it now. But I didn't hesitate to buy the champagne, as overpriced as it was. Cass deserves this.

'Thank you, Brooke. You really didn't need to go out of your way like that. That's really sweet of you,' Cass says, apparently regaining her composure. I consider asking her about it, but before I can she grabs my arm, leading me towards the others, and everything is back to normal, any discomfort immediately forgotten.

'You remember everyone, right?' Cass asks as we approach the palapa. I follow her, impressed by how comfortable she seems around these people, all of whom turn to look at her with expressions of genuine fondness on their faces. I look at her in that moment, as well, seeing what they do. Her dark eyes, glassy but warm, her face painted in her usual sweet smile, reflecting her appeasing nature. Their little wallflower.

Despite my having met everyone several times by now, she starts the round of reintroductions.

'You know Neil, of course,' she says, setting the champagne bottle on the bar. She raises her eyebrows suggestively, and I nod. Subtle. She must have seen us earlier at the Tiki Palms.

'And then there's the resort's professional yogi, Greta,' Cass says, motioning towards the sinewy, blonde Swede sitting on the stool to Neil's right.

Apparently, Cass goes to Greta's yoga class every Monday. She's tried several times to drag me along, but yoga's never been my thing – the trailer park I grew up in surprisingly didn't offer many opportunities for *savasanas* or *namastes*. Even so, I've spotted Greta leading classes as I've walked by the fitness centre on the north side of the resort. She seems like she's in her element at the front of the studio, always warm and relaxed. But the few times I've spoken to her, once at Frangipani and once in the Tiki Palms, I've sensed a coldness running just below the surface. Even now, she waves at me with a smile that seems just a touch forced.

Cass has told me a bit about her, how Greta has been on the island for ever, at least for a few years before any of the other Permanents arrived, running the resort's fitness centre. And how Greta had lived in apparent bliss with her girlfriend, Alice, who had left her and the island seemingly out of the blue a few days before I got here. I suppose that's as good a reason as any for Greta to keep her distance.

'And the island's resident playboy, Doug,' Cass continues.

The face of the guy she motions to is a long, rugged landscape of jutting-out features. He has the nose of a rugby player, one that must have been broken so frequently that it never had a chance to heal correctly. His hair is matted against his head in mock white man dreadlocks, and he's wearing what I've gathered is his usual uniform of swim trunks and a Koh Sang Dive Resort tank top that accentuates his impressive biceps.

'She's only saying that because I'm her boss,' Doug says with a wink. 'How ya going, Brooke?'

He glides his eyes languidly up and down my body – stopping pointedly at two areas specifically – and even though I feel every one of my muscles tighten, I force the polite smile to stay glued to my face. I've met him once or twice, and each time he makes my skin crawl. Cass always speaks highly of him, how effective he is at running the

45

dive shop. And despite his creepiness, he seems relatively harmless with his whole easy-going Aussie vibe. But he reminds me of too many guys from my past. The ones who think they're owed something.

'And Logan, of course,' Cass says with a smile, heading back behind the bar to wrap her arms around his waist.

As if on cue, both Greta and Doug hold up their plastic cups in his direction. He smiles, and I understand what Cass sees in him. He's easily over six feet and built. His shoulder-length curly hair is pulled back in a manbun tonight, and I'm sure his charming Scottish brogue doesn't hurt him in the tips department. Cass has been pretty silent on his past other than a generic explanation that he moved here from Aberdeen about five years ago to avoid being forced into taking over the family carpentry company.

'Congratulations, Logan!' I say with a forced cheeriness.

'Thanks. Glad you could make it,' he says, although his tone suggests anything but. He looks at me briefly, his eyes seemingly wary, before turning away. As usual when I'm around him, I can't shake the feeling that something about me, about my friendship with Cass, bothers him.

It's not that surprising; I've met plenty of guys like him since I started @BrookeaTrip. Men who are quick to poke fun at my career, eager to puff up their own ego by pointing out how little skill my job takes, despite having absolutely no idea how much work it requires. Condescension filling their eyes whenever I mention landing a new campaign or securing a new sponsor. It's certainly not my dream job, but it's the best I can do under the circumstances. Circumstances Logan can't even begin to imagine.

'Certainly took the man long enough, didn't it?' Greta says with a wink. I temper down my irritation and force my attention back to the group's conversation.

'Hey,' Doug responds, barely pausing. 'He was just nervous. How many drinks did you have before you finally pulled the trigger and asked the question, mate? We're dying to know.'

'Well, if he made them himself, then he'd at least need double digits. I've never met a bartender who pours such weak drinks,' Neil jabs.

And just like that, it's like I'm not even there. I watch the friends banter back and forth and, for a moment, I'm flushed with a feeling of emptiness. It takes me a second to recognize what it is. Nostalgia, for a time and people I never had. I stand there transfixed at how easy it is for them, how they all seem to mould into each other like corresponding puzzle pieces.

'Well, what are we waiting for?' Greta's sing-song accent cuts through the noise. 'This is an engagement party after all. We need a champagne toast!'

All of us turn to Logan, the resident bartender, who raises his hands as if in surrender. 'I'm on it, I'm on it,' he says, grabbing the neck of the bottle.

I look to Cass, whose gaze doesn't move from Logan, not when he rips the foil from the bottle, not when he opens the cork with a loud 'pop' that echoes through the night air. A small smile decorates her lips the whole time, the adoration painted on her face. As Logan begins to pour the champagne into six plastic cups – Frangipani's apparent glassware of choice – he looks up at her and his eyes spark. Everyone else is distracted with their own conversation, but I catch him mouth 'Forever us two,' in Cass's direction. Her smile widens, turning into a laugh when Logan pours too much champagne into one of the cups, making it overflow.

The love between them is palpable. My heart should

47

warm at this display of affection, but the hollowness from earlier returns to my chest, tinged with something else.

When Greta starts handing out the glasses, I catch Logan return to Cass's side, his lips brushing lightly against her forehead. And that's when I grudgingly acknowledge the feeling I've been trying to ignore.

Envy.

'Okay, quiet down, quiet down,' Greta demands, and we all turn our attention to her. I've seen the crew together enough to understand the dynamic here. Greta seems to have leaned into the group's maternal role.

'Logan, Cass. I can't tell you how much love I have for you two,' Greta begins, before turning to face Logan. 'Logan, where would I be without you? Since you've arrived on this island, you've been my rock. Koh Sang would be an entirely different place without you in it.'

Logan gazes up affectionately at Greta as she talks.

'And Cass, you've been such a wonderful addition to our group. I can't imagine how we ever functioned without you. We always refer to ourselves as a family, and that's exactly what we are. The family we've chosen. And we're so lucky to have you be a part of it.'

Greta's voice catches briefly, and she clears her throat. Despite myself, the words pull at me, and I feel self-pity stab between my ribs. *I wish I had someone that would say that about* . . . I shake my head slightly, stopping the thought before it can fully form.

'Anyway,' Greta says, shaking her head. 'Neil, Doug and I got you a little something to show you how much you mean to us.' She pulls a gift bag from behind her, handing it over to Cass, who accepts it like an award. The group falls silent as Cass pulls a hardbound book from the bag, gasping when she sees the cover.

Her eyes fill with tears, and Cass flashes the book at the rest of us, revealing a photo of the five friends on the cover. Cass flips through it, the tears threatening to flow over as she examines the photos lying on the carefully constructed inner pages.

'We wanted to show you how much you both mean to us,' Greta says. I notice how careful she is to give credit to Doug and Neil, but the fact that this is her gift is lost on no one. It's incredibly thoughtful, especially considering the lengths she must have gone to to put it together. The island has no place to develop photographs, let alone the materials to create a scrapbook as intricate as this, and Amazon delivery isn't exactly an option out here. The gift must have involved at least one trip to the mainland. The pain in my ribcage returns.

'It's everything,' Cass says, wrapping Greta in a hug.

Logan follows suit, whispering something in Greta's ear before they separate. They do the same for Doug and Neil. I'm left, leaning against the bar, watching them. Alone. A voyeur peering in the windows of a perfect friend group. I look at the champagne bubbling in my cup, suddenly desperate to chug it all in one go.

When they finally separate, I breathe a sigh of relief. Greta raises her plastic cup in the air, the rest of us following suit.

'To the new Mr and Mrs Logan McMillan. Logan, Cass, we couldn't be prouder of you. The little brother and sister of our Koh Sang family.'

And I realize that's exactly what Cass is to this group. The little sister. Kind, sweet, dependable, someone for them to look after.

'I mean, that's a wee bit incestuous, isn't it?' Logan's eyes are light, but his voice is thick with emotion.

'Oh, you know what I mean,' Greta says, landing a playful punch on his arm. 'We're happy for you.'

Neil and Doug nod in agreement, and all at once, a flurry of '*skol*'s, 'cheers' and '*sláinte*'s erupts from around the table.

I take a sip of my champagne. Despite my best efforts at keeping it chilled, it tastes warm and overly sweet. But the others don't seem to notice. Everyone has downed theirs in one or two glugs. Everyone except Cass.

'Hey, what are you waiting for?' Doug teases her. 'You planning to make that drink last all night?'

Cass looks down at the champagne as if she's seeing it for the first time. Then she swings her eyes to take in the group. 'Bottoms up,' she murmurs and downs it.

Everyone erupts in cheers, and Cass smiles, but as the others begin to break into conversation, I watch as her smile abruptly fades.

Logan eventually suggests that we move the party over to the picnic table, and we encircle it, the six of us squeezing shoulder to shoulder. As I look around, the string lights that once sprinkled a magical sheen about the courtyard now paint a strange glow across everyone's faces.

Logan brings over six beers, and Doug pulls a bottle of Thai whisky seemingly out of thin air. It quickly traverses the table, with everyone taking a celebratory swig. When it reaches me, I allow a small stream of the liquid to pass my lips, just enough to make my swallow seem authentic. It takes mere seconds for the burn to lead down my oesophagus.

Conversation flows easily around the table, jumping from topic to topic. It starts innocently enough with discussion of wedding planning, but as the bottle of whisky tours the table more frequently, the conversation begins to veer into more risqué waters.

I'm squeezed between Neil and Greta. Occasionally, I feel Neil's leg brush against mine, intentionally or not, I can't tell. Either way it sends a thrill up my spine to feel his skin on mine. I would be lying if I said it was purely from my physical attraction. For a brief second, I allow myself to imagine what this could be. Neil, bringing me into this group as his girlfriend, his partner. Making me a Permanent, a person who belongs. The idea fizzes intoxicatingly inside me. This time, I don't pull away from his touch.

As Doug starts talking about a particular resort guest with whom he became intimately acquainted last week, my attention shifts to Cass, who's seated directly across from me. The glassiness from earlier has returned to her eyes, and she seems distracted, her gaze drifting beyond me, out on to the street. I turn around to follow her line of sight, but the street is completely empty. It's not surprising. Given the Full Moon Party down at the beach, there's no reason for any of the resort guests to come this far inland. By this time, they're all probably covered in neon paint – like the guy who pulled Lucy away was hours ago – dancing dangerously close to the fire and sipping fruit-flavoured concoctions out of fishbowls. I think back to my run-in with the girl – Lucy. I wonder what it was she could have wanted from me. The warning she carried in her eyes still tiptoes through my memory.

When I turn to Cass, her gaze is still glued to the street.

'Cass,' I whisper, just loud enough for her to hear.

'Hmm?'

'You all good?' I ask gently.

It's like my question flips a switch. Immediately, Cass's

gaze is alert and focused, and the smile she was wearing earlier is plastered back on her lips.

'Of course,' she says, as if my question is ridiculous.

Her tone is convincing, but I don't believe it.

'You're sure?' I try again, my voice laced with concern, but she just nods and places her hand over mine, crinkling her forehead in an expression of reassurance. We turn back to the end of the table just as Doug apparently reaches the punchline of his joke, some nonsense I don't understand but which elicits a groan from everyone else.

The whisky continues to circle the table, and I gradually notice the volume of voices growing louder, speech growing slower.

'Reckon I'll be hitting up the Full Moon tonight,' Doug says, when the conversation lulls. There's a noticeable slur to his speech. 'Who's coming with me? Neil? Logan?'

'You're not twenty any more. You do realize that, right?' Logan asks.

'Easy for you to say, mate. You're all shacked up.' Doug looks pointedly in Cass's direction. 'I'm still on the prowl. And you know how loose the tourists get at that shit. It's like open season.'

'Oh, those poor girls,' Greta says without a laugh.

'Come on,' Doug says, drawing out each word.

'I'm in.' Neil shrugs.

'It's up to you, Cass.' Logan turns to her. 'Should we go?'

I can think of a million things I'd rather do than go to the Full Moon Party, but as soon as Cass nods her head, I know my answer.

As we stand up from the table, picking up the discarded cups and bottles, Neil turns to me. 'So, what about you, Miss Brooke? Will you do me the honour of being my date to the Full Moon Party?'

He's close enough that I can feel his breath warm against my cheek, and his fingers brush my hand.

'I suppose so,' I say sheepishly.

'Good.' Neil's smile is wide. He grabs the near-empty whisky bottle from the table and hands it to me. 'You won't regret it.'

This time, I take a large gulp, finishing the rest of the bottle. As the liquid sears my throat, I hope he's right.

5

Saturday

Cass

The pulsating wail jars me awake. My eyes are gravelly, my throat dry. The alarm pulled me from yet another nightmare where I was back in that hotel room.

Even after I silence my phone, an incessant vibration continues, as if my brain is rattling around inside my skull. I stifle a groan, thinking of how stupid I've been. I never stay out late the night before a morning dive. Why did I have that glass of champagne? And those beers at Frangipani? And whatever else I may have drunk at the Full Moon Party . . .

But I know the answer to these questions. I plastered on my brightest smile, tried to be the cheeriest version of myself, not wanting anyone to suspect what's really going on.

I tried to put everything that happened yesterday out of my head: the threatening envelope on my doorstep, that weird interaction with my dive student, Ariel. And I think everyone bought the act. Except for Brooke. I kept catching her looking at me, throwing concerned glances in my direction. I assured her I was okay – I just got engaged, I'm over the moon! – but I couldn't shake the feeling that someone was watching me. It was the same sense I had yesterday as I left my house. And I could have sworn I heard a rustling coming from the jungle lining the road outside Frangipani. But as I peered out into the darkness of the trees, nothing moved.

I shake my head to clear away the memory, flinching at the sudden pain.

I wish I could blame my current state on the alcohol alone, but unfortunately there's more to it.

I reach over to my bedside table as quietly as I can to make sure Logan doesn't wake up. I feel around until my fingers brush against a cardboard box, buried under old ChapSticks and neglected paperbacks. A cocktail of shame and guilt washes over me as I pull out the box of little white pills that I hid last night.

I had promised myself I would never use them again. But that was before yesterday. I cautiously carry the box with me to the bathroom and push a pill through the thin foil of the blister pack. I don't bother finding a cup of water and instead position the Xanax on the centre of my tongue and draw up enough saliva to force it down. The rounded corners feel jagged on the dry sides of my throat, and I swallow several times before I'm sure it's down.

I've barely even made it two weeks without one. They've become something of a comfort when things start to derail, a way to dull the unnecessary noise. I first used them three years ago, to drown out the media circus and the world, eating up the stories about me spoonful by tabloid spoonful. I didn't want to, especially given what had happened, but the doctor assured me that, if used responsibly, they would help. And they did.

I thought that would be the last time I would need them,

but I was wrong. Three weeks ago, I found myself picking up the familiar box from the Kumvit pharmacy that sells prescription meds by the truckload, catering to all the partying backpackers. That time, I needed it to forget what I had seen, to help me believe that my life was still on track.

But last night was stupid. I knew better than to mix drinking and Xanax. And I'm paying for it now. I try to remember the Full Moon Party, but everything after Frangipani is hazed by a cloud of alcohol and pills. I struggle to piece together what happened on the beach or how I got home. But only a few scenes come back to me, like damaged strips of a film reel; jagged pieces that don't seem to form a whole. The feel of sand on my toes, the heat of flames being twirled by fire dancers standing way too close, teasing my flesh; the sight of neon bodies mashed against each other, limbs splayed, desperate for contact; the weight of something heavy in my pocket as I walked in the front door of our house; and a woman's voice. It hits me with the weight of a fist. Not exactly shouting, but talking firmly. 'No.' It comes again: 'No, no, no!'

Was it me making that sound? Or someone else? Brooke? Greta?

I shake my head again, glad to find that this time it feels an ounce less painful.

I walk into the bedroom, pull on my one-piece swimsuit and throw my hair into a messy bun, another question gnawing at me all the while. What did I have in my pocket last night?

I grab my shorts, discarded on the floor, and quickly check the pockets, but they are all empty. I then conduct a quick visual sweep of the surfaces of our bedroom, but I don't see anything unusual. I slide the ring from my finger and place it in its designated red box before hovering over the drawer, the Xanax box clutched in my hand. After a moment, I shut the drawer and shove the Xanax into my bag.

I stand at the side of the bed and look down at Logan. He's still fast asleep, his chestnut curls framing his face angelically, his tattooed arms stretched out on to my side of the bed, as if he's reaching for me. Suddenly I'm struck with a need to wake him, to tell him everything, to feel his arms around me. But I can't. Because that would mean explaining that I've lied to him about who and what I am for years. And he would never forgive me for that.

Instead, I stand there for a few minutes, listening to Logan's consistent deep breaths. Eventually, I bend down to delicately kiss his cheek. His eyes flutter but he doesn't wake.

'Ah mate, please tell me you brought some Berocca with you.'

Doug is flopped over the desk in the dive shop, wearing the same outfit from last night. I try to ignore the shame filling my stomach. He seems to be acting normal – hungover Doug is certainly not a unique experience – so I must not have done or said anything too awful last night, I assure myself, only half believing it.

'Whew, good thing we don't have an open flame in here,' I joke, waving my hand in front of my nose. 'The alcohol fumes coming off you could explode the whole island. No Berocca, unfortunately, but I do have this.' I toss him a Powerade I picked up on my way in. He looks like he could use it more than me.

As Doug chugs the drink, I busy myself with preparing the tanks and the BCD vests that will aid us with floating while we're in the water. I'm checking the sizes when the bell over the door chimes. Neil drags himself in, not bothering to remove his sunglasses once he's inside.

'I'm guessing you're not feeling so hot either,' I say. His eyes are downcast, and his quiet entrance departs drastically from his usual arrival in the shop, haloed by a cloud of energy, cracking jokes before he even says hello.

'Definitely not,' he says flatly, and I don't dare to push it. My 'hangxiety' returns with full force.

He joins me, pulling BCD vests from behind the tanks. While he doesn't have a dive group to supervise today, he's on the schedule to help me – an extra set of hands to prep and clean up and drive the boat.

I briefly wonder how the rest of the Permanents are pulling through today. Whether Greta and Brooke are as hungover as we are.

'Oh, by the way, you better do the Turtle Cove dive first and the shore dive in the afternoon,' Doug warns.

I jerk my head towards him, instantly regretting the sharp movement as a wave of pain hits my temple. 'Why?'

Doug's eyes flick to Neil, who seems less than concerned, barely even looking up. We always start with the shore dive and save Turtle Cove for the afternoon, after the students have worked through the exercises on their first dive. They tend to like the boat ride, plus there's more coral out there, and by extension more wildlife. It's like a reward for the guests for finishing the course.

'The visibility is pretty bad on the coast right now, but it's supposed to get better as the day goes on. Out by the cove, though, it seems to be fine, according to the tracker,' Doug explains.

'Got it,' I say, but I groan internally. I understand why we need to shift, but the last thing I need this morning is to deviate from routine. I check my watch and notice it's five minutes to eight. 'Well,' I say to Neil, 'may as well get this over with.'

As soon as we step back outside, the sun bites my skin. Ariel and Tamar are already here, waiting patiently. Ariel stares at me dead on, his eyes clear and unreadable, as if nothing out of the ordinary happened yesterday. Tamar, on the other hand, seems embarrassed, and she gives me a small smile before fixing her eyes on the ocean. I try to forget that strange interaction with Ariel, wish them both a good morning and proceed to stand awkwardly in front of them, unsure what more to say, as Neil busies himself getting the boat in order.

'Oi, wait!' Daniel runs to us from the hill leading up to the resort. 'Sorry I'm late. Wild night,' he says, hands on his knees, panting.

'Good morning.' I take him in: he's already drenched in sweat, despite the early-morning hour, and looking a bit worse for wear. A slice of panic hits me as I realize that he may have seen me at the Full Moon Party, doing God knows what. The broken scenes of last night's memories come back to me again. The lights, the sand, that woman's voice, her firm 'No, no, no!' I swallow hard, forcing my tone to remain normal. 'I'm guessing you didn't follow my advice against drinking last night?'

'Come on,' he says. 'We're in Thailand! I couldn't pass up a Full Moon Party. Besides, it's going to take more than a hangover to beat me.'

Daniel frowns slightly, as he apparently takes us in for the first time. 'Where's Lucy?' he asks.

All four of us look around, expecting to see her walking down the hill from the guestrooms or wandering somewhere further along the beach. But we all come up empty.

I check my watch. It's five past eight. Frederic has ingrained the schedule into us. We don't wait for anyone. If a guest is late, they need to come back and pay for an extra day at the end of their course. And despite Doug's easy-goingness in all other aspects of life, he doesn't deviate from Frederic's rules. In fact, his hangover is likely the only thing that has prevented him from coming out and enforcing Frederic's mandate already.

'Have you heard from her, Daniel?' I ask.

'Nah, not since last night. She partied with us on the beach for a bit. Couldn't stay away and all that.'

I find that a bit hard to believe. More like he didn't give her a choice to reject him. 'Do you have her number? Can you call her?'

I could go back to the shop, get her number from the paperwork and call her myself, but it would mean going inside and dealing with Doug. I can already hear what he would say, channelling Frederic's favourite slogan: 'We're not the guests' babysitters. If they can't be bothered to show up on time, that's on them.'

But there's no need. Daniel's already holding his phone to his ear. After a few suspenseful seconds, he puts it back into his pocket. He shrugs nonchalantly but his shoulders seem tense. 'No answer.'

Before I can respond, I hear Neil's voice from the boat behind me. 'Cass, you should come and look at this.'

'We've got a problem,' he says, once I reach the boat, just loud enough for me – but not the rest of the group – to hear. 'The boat won't start.'

It's not all that surprising. Even though the boats are fairly new, compared with most of the resort's equipment, they still give us trouble now and then. But my God, could just one thing go right today?

'Looks like we're going to have to start with the shore dive after all, poor visibility and all,' I say. 'Maybe Doug can fix it when we're out and have it ready for this afternoon?' I offer to head inside and clear it with him, but Neil is already walking towards the shop. Even with the relative chaos this morning, I feel my nerves from earlier return at Neil's uneasy quiet.

I turn back to the group. Selfishly, the boat problems actually work in my favour. This means we can do our final equipment check on the beach and give Lucy twenty or so more minutes to get here. It's not so much the idea of leaving Lucy behind – in fact, I'd be pretty grateful not to have to stare all day at those eyes, the same shade of cornflower blue as Robin's. But there's something about Lucy that I can't quite put my finger on. I think about how the envelope landed on my doorstep the day after she arrived on the island, how I've had the feeling of someone following me ever since. I don't know who's behind it all, but if there's even the smallest chance that it's Lucy, I want to know where she is, what she's doing. If she's skipping out on dives she's already paid for, she must have a reason.

'Okay,' I say, taking another unsuccessful look up the path for Lucy. 'Let's get started, shall we? Daniel, until Lucy shows up, you'll be my buddy for the equipment test.'

'Well, I certainly can't argue with that,' he says, not missing a beat.

We spend the better part of the next half-hour walking through the lessons we learned the day before. We test each part of our equipment – making sure the fins and masks are tight enough, checking the air in our tanks, practising breathing through our primary and alternative respirators, and confirming that our depth gauges are reading correctly.

'As we talked about yesterday,' I say, 'diving in Koh Sang is a bit unique. Unlike most other dive sites, you don't always have to take a boat out to the ocean to complete your dive. Instead, because the water drops off here so close to the coast, and one of the most beautiful reefs in the Thai islands is within sight of the beach, all we're going to do is walk on out into the water to start our dive.

'We'll be down on the ocean floor for about forty-five minutes. We'll stop a few times and practise some of the same exercises from yesterday. All the training you need to handle the worst-case scenarios.'

I was hoping that, by now, Lucy would have shown up. But she's still nowhere to be seen. I have Daniel try her mobile again, but it's the same result as earlier. We have no choice but to go on without her.

I take in the three students standing in front of me, trying to ignore the pungent smells of gasoline floating over from the boats parked further down the beach. All three of them share the same nervous look in their eye, even Daniel. This is always my favourite part of teaching. The moments before the first dive. Watching the students' faces painted over with anticipation and a healthy dose of anxiety. It always makes me think back to my first time, when I realized just how peaceful it can be underwater. A place where no one judges you, where you don't have to act, or think, or be what everyone expects you to be. It's easier underwater. My fears always seem to slip away as soon as I break the surface, as the salt water cleanses my skin.

I give them the warnings I can now say from memory.

'It's going to be very different from yesterday. If you encounter a problem, you won't simply be able to stand up and be above water. We'll be about ten metres below the surface, so if an issue comes up, we need to deal with it effectively. When we're down there, we can't have any joking around.' I cut a sharp glance at Daniel, who raises his arms in mock innocence. 'Do not panic if something goes wrong. Keep your breathing as routine as possible, otherwise, you'll rush through your tank of air. And, most importantly, do not – under any circumstances – panic and swim directly upwards.'

We talked extensively yesterday about the dangers of a rushed ascent. The broken eardrums, the nitrogen poisoning, the popped lungs. My warnings have done little to settle their fears.

'I envy you guys,' I say, straining my voice to sound comforting. 'You are about to have one of the most magical experiences of your whole lives. Your first time breathing below the ocean's surface. The world is different underwater, you'll see.'

I expect Daniel to come back with a witty remark about how cheesy I'm being, but he's silent, the nerves apparently getting to him.

Once I'm sure everyone is set, our group of four starts walking towards the water. Our toes touch it first, then our ankles, our knees, our legs. We continue to wade out, the tanks strapped tightly to our backs, like soldiers on a battle march. Slowly, as we gain ground, the water rises, eventually splashing against our necks, our toes no longer brushing the wet sand. The inflated vests keep us afloat, bobbing above the waves.

I check that everyone is ready, and then it's time to descend. It's painfully slow, stopping every few feet or so to check our depth, deflate our vests a bit more, and plug our noses and breathe sharply into our masks to clear our airways. The water lapping at our skin subtly transitions from bathwater to a temperature cool enough that it makes me thankful for my wetsuit. But the descent goes without a hitch, and eventually, we're on the ocean floor, the transparent water stretching above us, the surface now a glass ceiling.

Once we're all down, I check in again with Ariel, Tamar and Daniel individually, using the sign language we discussed in class. I see the same spark in their eyes that I remember having on my first time.

I indicate for them to follow me before I turn and start swimming, my hands clasped behind my back, propelled by my fins sluicing the water like a pair of sharpened scissors. Groups of fish, so small and white they're almost translucent, recoil when they feel the current from our bodies. All the worries I've had over the last day seem so insignificant now, as if they belong to someone else.

Doug certainly wasn't wrong about the visibility. The water is usually clear enough here to see a dozen or so metres in any direction, but today the waves are stronger, picking up the sediment on the ocean floor and blurring it into a soupy haze, granting us sight for only a few metres at a time. We pass a school of clownfish, and about eight minutes into the dive, we spot our resident sea turtle, Harold. I point him out to the others, placing one hand over the other and wiggling my thumbs as Harold swims by, looking at us through apathetic, wizened eyes. I watch my students' faces glow with a childish gleam behind their masks. Daniel makes some inaudible sound as a flurry of bubbles rises from his respirator, and giddiness fills my chest. The shame, the anxiety, the paranoia from earlier seems to wash away as the salt water laps against my skin. None of that can touch me down here, none of the problems that infiltrate every one of my thoughts on ground seem capable of penetrating the water's surface.

And seeing my students recognize the same feeling for the first time puts everything in perspective. These are the moments that make everything worth it. I would never have experienced this beauty, this calm, without all the horror that had to happen to lead me here.

Once the excitement calms, I stop the group near a familiar body of coral and gather the three of them in a circle, each of us hovering a few feet above the ocean floor. We start with the first exercise: taking out our respirator as if it's been ripped from our mouth, so that they know how to handle themselves if their source of air is suddenly cut off. I demonstrate, reminding them how it's done, before pointing to Daniel, signalling for him to execute the skill. He looks at me, shooting an 'OK' sign with his fingers before getting to work. He repeats my moves exactly: removing the respirator, throwing it behind him, blowing out the small trail of bubbles.

But as his arm reaches back to locate the respirator, he stops. His eyes grow wide, his limbs look as if they've turned to stone.

I pause a moment, frustration simmering. It's one thing to play his asinine games when we're in the pool, but this is different. Losing your source of air at this depth is not a joke. I snap in his direction, the friction between my thumb and index finger making no sound but producing a thread of bubbles designed to catch his attention.

But he remains unmoving, his eyes staring past me.

I turn, squinting to see what he's looking at through the impaired visibility, and slowly it comes into focus. An outline, a form silhouetted against the haziness of the water. I shift my body, edging closer to it. At first, I think it might be litter, some piece of discarded material thrown overboard from the boats that plough through here as if they own the place.

As I move closer, though, I see that it's certainly not trash.

It's a person.

The person isn't dressed in scuba gear. No fins, or vest, or even a mask. They're floating upright, as if standing with their feet glued to the ocean floor, coral arching above them, the backdrop for an eerie portrait. Strands of hair float delicately above their head in the current like human seaweed.

This isn't right, I realize, panic seeping in through my wetsuit, fear bubbling under my skin.

Behind me, I hear a flurry of noise. By the time I turn, Daniel's kicking straight upwards, his respirator trailing uselessly behind him. I move to grab him, to stop him from rushing to the surface and popping his eardrums – or worse. But for the first time beneath the water, my body feels weighted, anchored in place.

I look over at the others. Tamar's eyes are panicked, glued on the body behind me, the bubbles emerging from her respirator more and more rapidly. As for Ariel, that anxiety from after class yesterday seems to have returned, his body stiff, his grey eyes impenetrable behind his mask. His words from yesterday come back to me, inauspicious and unwelcomed.

It is not safe here.

I force myself to turn and shift closer to the body. And the face comes into focus. Lips separated slightly as if they're preparing to speak. And those eyes, open wide, as if in a scream. The blue has not yet faded, but tendrils of red close in from the sides.

Instantly, all motion around me stops. My underwater reprieve morphing into my worst nightmare.

Robin.

I can't move my eyes from her. I stare at that face I know so well, ultimately landing on her forehead, now marred by one red horizontal scratch. I move my sight lower, to her neck, and spot the ghostly blue marks on either side. I continue downwards, to her waist, where I note the string of fabric from her T-shirt snagged around a piece of the reef. And then to her foot, wedged into a crack in the rock-like coral, preventing her from rising to the surface. She's stationed there, motionless in the water aside from the current rippling her clothing.

Amid the pulsing dread, my mind takes a moment to refocus. This isn't Robin. It's Lucy.

Before I can fully register this conclusion, something sparkles in my peripheral vision, bright enough to distract me from the horror cresting like a wave above me. Following the light with my eyes, I spot a small piece of metal half buried in the sand several feet away from the body, glinting off the surface light. I inch even closer, the blood pounding in my ears like waves against my skull, and reach my hand down, pulling the object free from the sand.

I look down at what I'm holding. And with that realization, the wave of panic crashes down, enveloping me. A flurry of bubbles escapes from my respirator, as a blurred choking sound reaches my ears. A scream, I realize. My scream, muffled from the weight of the water.

And I finally let the panic pull me under.

6

Brooke

'*Kap khun ka*, Sengphet,' I say as he deposits the steaming coffee on the table in front of me. He bends forward, hands clasped in his signature sign of gratitude.

'You are welcome,' he says slowly. 'You need. Last night big party. Coffee will make you feel better.' He pauses between each word, punctuating them with his endearing smile.

I smile back, something that comes naturally whenever I talk with Sengphet. As I do, I notice the dark circles beneath his eyes. Looks like even he had a late night – or an early morning. I can only imagine what time Frederic makes his staff get up to get the restaurant restored after a party like the one last night and ready to open on time.

The Tiki Palms is still deserted, despite being nearly nine o'clock. It feels as though a collective hangover has settled over the island.

I check the engagement on my Instagram post from earlier this morning, which I timed perfectly for when my American followers would be getting off work and relaxing for the evening. I notice a new comment from @Travelbarbie, another travel influencer whose following makes mine look paltry in comparison. *Looks incredible!* she'd commented beneath one of last night's photos.

Wish you were here! I type in response.

I don't, of course. @Travelbarbie is just as heinous as her handle suggests. Platinum blonde, with every part of her enhanced – either surgically or through pounds of make-up – she's the type of influencer who will peddle anything from tampons to detox teas, the kind I never wanted to be. When our paths overlapped in Budapest during my early days of building @BrookeaTrip, I asked her to take a selfie with me. It resulted in me being forced to listen to her lecture me about how valuable her 'image' was and how people didn't want to go on social media to be ranted at about the world (as I apparently did), but to remember its beauty (as she was apparently so adept at leading them to do). But through more patience than I knew I was capable of exercising, I managed to convince her, and she posted the picture on her account that night. It did the trick. I woke up the next morning to no less than four hundred new followers. I push away the memory and read through a handful of other comments before taking a sip from the mug Sengphet delivered.

'Shit!' The word comes out louder than intended as the hot coffee burns my tongue, a blister forming almost instantly. The shock only adds to the pain growing behind my eyes. Contrary to Neil's promise at Frangipani, my hangover smears my scattered memories of the Full Moon Party in a film of regret. I survey the stretch of beach spread out in front of me, now empty of bodies and the trash they left behind. I think about Sengphet and the other resort staff members, walking along the sand just as the sun peeked above the horizon this morning. I picture them, bleary eyed and exhausted, trash bags billowing in the dawn breeze as they meticulously picked up every piece of detritus that had been casually discarded during the party, so that no guest has to see the precious beach in any state less than total perfection. The silence is almost jarring after last night. I can still feel the pulsing bass of the speakers, lodged like a painful rhythm in my back molars.

Suddenly, the still morning is broken by a muffled yell. I scan the beach again but see nothing. I turn to Sengphet, but he looks just as confused as I must. The sound comes again, this time accompanied by a familiar voice.

'We need to get you in. Now!' It's Cass.

And then I see them, a group of two bobbing on the water, about twenty metres from the beach. I watch Cass, mask flipped on to her forehead and loaded down with scuba gear, dragging the person next to her towards the beach.

Something is clearly wrong.

Two figures pop up on the surface behind them, and I realize they must be the two older students I spotted Cass teaching yesterday.

One of them swims forward, his arms slicing the water until he's next to Cass, relieving her of the person she's helping.

I get up and run out to the waterline to meet them. As I watch them steadily make their way back to land, the pulsing beat of blood in my ears quickens, a disturbing crescendo. When they get closer, I recognize the person the older male student is pulling in. It's the loud Brit from last night who dragged Lucy away from our conversation.

But now he's completely silent, his face pained, apparently relying entirely on the other student to get him to shore.

I wade out until the water reaches my knees and grab the Brit on his other side, helping the older student pull him further up the beach. Even with two of us, the Brit's weight is crushing, at least two hundred pounds of pure muscle, and it takes everything we have to get him only a few steps before we collapse on the sand.

'What the hell happened? Is he okay?' The questions come as rapidly as machine-gun fire, erupting from my mouth before my brain can even recognize the words.

'Daniel ascended too quickly,' Cass says through quick breaths, reaching the shore only a few steps behind us. As she pulls off her mask, I spot tears in her eyes. 'He panicked and swam straight upward.'

I breathe out, relieved. A diving injury. It's not great, sure. I've heard both Cass and Neil talk about the dangers associated with rapid ascents, but I'd been expecting worse. The other female student finally reaches the beach, her eyes as round as moons and her face paper-white. And that's when I realize who's missing. Lucy, the girl who had cornered me outside my room last night. The fourth student I spotted in the training pool yesterday.

Around the same time, Neil and Doug come running from the dive shop. They head straight towards Daniel, clearly identifying the injured party, but two words from Cass make them stop short.

'It's Lucy,' she says. It comes out like a croak.

'Lucy?' I turn her name into a question, my eyes desperately searching the beach as if there's been some misunderstanding, as if she'll pop out and surprise us at any minute.

Doug is busy taking Daniel's pulse, but Neil turns to me. 'Cass's fourth student. She didn't show up for the dive this morning.'

My stomach turns uneasily. And then Cass says words that make everything freeze.

'She's . . . she's dead.'

Time seems to stand still. A sob escapes Cass's mouth, but I barely register it.

She's dead. I replay the words over and over, my lips mouthing along silently, my tongue twisting around the syllables. My memory ricochets back to last night. Lucy's attempt to talk to me, the stark gaze she fixed on me as she walked away.

I feel my heart rate quicken, my fingers fold into themselves.

'We need to call the police.' It takes a moment for me to realize the unfamiliar, accented voice belongs to the older male student.

I nod, already pulling my phone from my pocket.

'We'll do that as soon as we get to the dive shop,' Doug says, having finished taking Daniel's pulse and apparently concluding that his condition isn't critical. Doug's voice is stunningly calm given the circumstances.

'I – I have my phone—' I start.

'No. We need to get back to the dive shop and take care of Ariel and Tamar. Get them out of these wet clothes,' Doug orders. 'We'll use the phone there to call. The service is more reliable from the landline.'

I clench my teeth together. Despite everything, I can tell how much Doug loves this. Being the one in charge.

'Daniel needs medical help,' Cass says, her voice nearly drowned out between sobs. I look over at Daniel, who's still on all fours, his chest heaving.

'Already on it,' Neil says. 'We saw you through the shop window, dragging Daniel in. We could tell something was wrong and called the medical centre just to be cautious. They're on their way.'

In an instant I realize how useless I am in this situation.

And just like that I'm on the outside again. There's no role for me to play in this group.

'I'll stay with him,' I say suddenly, clinging to a way that I can help, a means to claw my way back in. 'You go to the dive shop, call the police. I'll wait with Daniel.'

Doug barely acknowledges me, already turning on his heel and heading towards the dive shop. Cass nods her thanks and corrals the other two students, following Doug. Neil sticks around for a second longer and turns to me.

'Thank you,' he says, his dark eyes holding mine. Before I realize what he's doing, he's leaned in and given me a kiss on the cheek. The movement is so natural, yet so unexpected that despite the unromantic circumstances, I feel heat rise through my body. Before I have a chance to respond, Neil's gone, jogging to catch up with the group, leaving me alone with Daniel.

'So,' I say tentatively after a few minutes, once Daniel has rolled on to his back and up to a seated position and his breathing has finally returned to something resembling normal. 'Feeling better?'

He looks at me flatly, and I realize how out of my element I am. What is a person supposed to say to a stranger who has just found out his friend is dead?

'I'm Brooke,' I finally think to say, realizing I never introduced myself during our brief exchange last night.

'Daniel.' Unlike then, when his eyes roamed my body freely, this time he doesn't make eye contact. But he does begin to stir as if he's getting up.

'Whoa there, tiger.' I scramble up next to him, quickly grabbing his arm. Even with two hands, my fingers can't stretch around the perimeter of his biceps, but I try to guide him back to a seated position. 'People are coming to help you. We just need to sit tight until they arrive.'

Surprisingly, he obliges, and we fall back into an uncomfortable silence.

After what feels like an hour of nothing but the crash of the waves and Daniel's heavy breathing, my curiosity can't stand it any more. 'So,' I ask, 'do you, um, want to tell me what happened?'

He turns quickly, too quickly, and I cringe when I see him wince in pain.

'You heard her. Lucy's dead.'

I expect emotion with this statement, but his tone is so cold that it takes me by surprise. He seems like an entirely different person from the brash guy I met yesterday.

'But she wasn't diving with you guys, right?'

'No,' Daniel says coldly. 'She didn't show up this morning. But she was already . . . down there.'

I don't know how to respond. Eventually, he starts again, seemingly talking more to himself than to me. 'She was just floating there. At the bottom of the ocean. But it wasn't *really* her, you know what I mean?'

I pause for a moment, a bit taken aback by his response. Hadn't he just met her when the dive class began? I didn't expect Daniel to be so introspective, to form connections with fellow travellers that quickly.

But then I think of that girl I saw just yesterday. Those big blue eyes, so determined. That quiet confidence she seemed to exude. She was certainly one to make an impact. And it doesn't seem possible that all the life she carried could have been extinguished so quickly.

But I suppose that's the nature of death. It never seems possible.

'How could this have happened?' Daniel continues.

'I mean,' I say, brainstorming, 'maybe she had too much to drink at the Full Moon Party and—'

Daniel doesn't give me the chance to finish.

'Naw, I don't think so,' he interrupts. 'I saw her at the party. She wasn't pissed.'

I try to think back to last night on the beach, my memories smeared into flashing neon and the punching bass. It's possible I saw Lucy there, but with everyone's faces lined with green and pink paint, I can't be sure.

'Hm,' I muse, reflecting on how he and Lucy were on their way to pregame when I left them last night. Maybe Lucy was drunker than he noticed. 'Then that means it was an accident.'

Daniel turns to look at me, his expression concerned. 'But why would she get in the water alone? And how would she have got so far out from shore?'

His questions are valid. Why *would* Lucy have done that? Even if she had been intoxicated, what could possibly have convinced her to get into the ocean alone in the middle of the night, while a huge group was partying just down the beach?

'Well, if it wasn't an accident then . . .' I trail off, and I watch Daniel's eyes widen as we seem to reach the same conclusion. 'Someone did this to her,' I say, finally. I expect Daniel to laugh, to tell me my idea is ridiculous. But he stays quiet.

And then I think again of seeing Lucy last evening. How desperate she was to talk to me about the woman who fell from Khrum Yai. Lucy is now the second woman to die on this island in less than a month.

Suddenly, a commotion from behind makes me turn. Two staff members dressed in white polo shirts with the

Koh Sang Dive Resort logo emblazoned on the chest run towards us from a golf cart parked at the edge of the sand.

As they approach, Daniel starts to stand. I try to help him, but he shakes me off. He mumbles a 'thanks' as the two staff members take over, flanking him.

I watch as the trio shuffle towards the golf cart and lay Daniel in the back seat. And as I do, one thought plays on repeat through my mind.

It's happening again.

Because a guest is dead. And if our suspicions are right, someone on this island killed her.

7

Cass

The world moves around me as if I'm still underwater. Voices hit my ears as low murmurs, the clarity of the words lost to the ocean.

Because in my mind, I'm still there, staring at those big blue eyes, that fine, delicate hair, that familiar face. Doomed to meet the same fate as Robin.

'Cass.'

The voice is gentle, but insistent, as if this isn't the first time it's said my name. My eyes take several blinks to come into focus, but when they do, I register Neil, bent down, looking at me with concern.

'Are you okay?'

I want to laugh. I'm the furthest thing from okay. I just stared death in the face for the second time in my life. And for the second time, I can't fight the persistent thought that it was somehow my fault.

The message on my doorstep the other day. Someone on the island figuring out who I am, just as another innocent girl dies. It can't be a coincidence.

And then there's the object I found next to Lucy's body. The one I haven't told anyone about yet. How could it have ended up down there?

A fleeting panic strikes me at the realization that I may have said all this out loud, but Neil just stands there, forehead scrunched.

'Okay,' he says, 'I've got Tamar and Ariel set up at the restaurant for the time being, with orders to Sengphet to keep the free food and drinks coming. They seem like they're hanging in there.'

Neil's words still mean little to me, but, for the first time, I register where I am. My back is pressed against something hard that feels like wood, my wet legs sticking to a cushion beneath me. I twist my head around, taking in the octagonal room. The teak walls are barely visible, nearly every inch covered by hanging masks and fins, with tanks, vests and various tubes stacked precariously against them.

I'm sitting on the bench in the dive shop, but I have barely any memory of getting here.

'I just got off the phone with Frederic,' Doug interjects from behind the desk. 'I figured it was better to call him before the police. He okayed Tamar and Ariel's upgrade to the honeymoon suite and Daniel's upgrade to the second-best ocean room. We can reimburse them for their full stay and dive package and Daniel's medical expenses, of course.'

Neil nods, but I just continue to stare at them. They sound so normal. Like they're checking items off a to-do list. I want to scream. But I don't. I sit there quietly, staring.

'Frederic will be here tomorrow morning. He's catching a flight from Bangkok tonight and then getting on the first ferry from Koh Samui. We just need to keep it together until then.' Doug waits for our response. When none comes, he picks up the phone again, evidently calling the police.

A steady stream of Thai flows from his mouth within

seconds. My brain tries to grab hold of the syllables, but the words slip past – vowels my mouth has never been able to grasp, sounds that seem to originate far too deep in the throat for me to imitate.

As the door creaks open, I realize that my fingers are subconsciously stroking the scar that lies above my heart. With a jolt, I drop my hand as Brooke walks in, her face hesitant. 'I just wanted to let you know that Daniel made it to the medical centre.'

Neil places a hand on her shoulder to thank her, and when she turns to see me, an emotion I can't quite grasp flashes across her face. Then she's next to me, her arm on my shoulder. And for the first time since I saw Lucy, I feel some semblance of comfort.

'Oh, Cass. I'm so sorry.'

Her words prick at the back of my eyes, and before I know it, the floodgates open, tears rushing down my cheeks. Through it all, Brooke sits there, her T-shirt growing damp with my tears, her hand never straying from the circular pattern it rubs into my back.

The next several hours pass in a blur. Logan and Greta arrive at the dive shop together, Logan rushing to my side, forcing Brooke from her comforting duty. I bury my head in his shoulder, inhaling his familiar scent. The smell of home. I listen as he tells me everything is going to be okay, and I try to believe him. But I know better.

At some point, the police come. At first, it's difficult to cling to the passage of time. Everything seems to be happening all at once, yet hours apart. But eventually, with Logan whispering calming sounds in my ears, things begin to acquire a sequence, the world slowly adapts to normal.

'How about some air?' Logan asks eventually.

I nod silently and he helps me up. My legs feel sturdier beneath me than I expected, and with Logan's help, I make it the few steps to the door. The sun burns my retinas as we exit the shop, forcing me to blink several times. As the beach slowly comes into focus, it's completely unfamiliar. Yellow caution tape is looped around the perimeter of the dive shop and a few dozen metres of sand. Onlookers have sidled up as close as the tape allows, cautioned by black-clad men I've never seen before.

As if on cue, all heads turn in the direction of the water and a low murmur starts among the crowd, eventually growing into a din that seems to drape over the entire length of the beach.

'Maybe we should go back inside,' Logan says, nudging my arm towards the dive shop.

But I ignore him and turn in the direction where the crowd is looking. With a sharp inhale, I see a boat carrying three men – Doug in a dive shop-issued wetsuit, with two strangers dressed all in black – approach the beach. As they kill the engine and step out on to the sand, I can tell they aren't alone. They start to pull an object in a large black bag out of the boat. They're joined a few seconds later by more men dressed in black who are quick to cover the object, and I finally understand what it is.

Lucy's body.

The thought sends a shiver up my skin. Logan pulls me into his side, and we watch as the men lug Lucy's remains towards the run-down ambulance parked along the sand.

I don't remember going back into the dive shop, but some-how I do. Everyone is there. Logan, Greta, Doug, Neil, Brooke and someone else I don't recognize. A skinny, moustached man in an ill-fitting white shirt. When he talks, it's in stilted English, the thickness of his Thai accent making his words nearly incomprehensible. A drop of sweat inches down the scraggly hairs on his upper lip and I find myself transfixed, unable to look away.

'We take body back to office for now. Office have a . . .' He trails off, looking to Doug to help him, murmuring a word in Thai.

'Morgue,' Doug prompts.

'Morge.' The man's imitation lacks the hard G sound. 'We take girl there. We run tests to know why she die. We come back tomorrow to ask questions, once we get results,' he says without urgency.

When it's apparent that the man has no further information to provide, Doug leads him out of the shop, closing the door tightly behind him.

I feel the warmth of Logan's body next to me, his arm close to mine. I shift slightly, not enough to be noticeable, but enough to get some distance. On my other side sits Brooke, her fingers entwined with mine. She was quick to grab my hand as soon as I re-entered the shop, and despite all the horror surrounding us, I feel a warmth between our palms.

Several moments pass before anyone speaks.

'Wait,' Brooke says, as if she truly doesn't understand, 'the police aren't going to question anyone before they go? Not even Cass?'

She looks over at me, a sympathetic expression on her face, and I divert my eyes. I feel the muscles in Logan's arm tense.

Only Doug shakes his head, before clearing his throat, apparently putting a definitive end to Brooke's enquiry. He looks to the others.

'We should figure out how to handle this.' He pauses,

apparently waiting for someone to agree with him, but no one does. He checks his watch. 'Until Frederic arrives, we need to keep this as low key as possible.'

'But all of those crowds,' Greta says, her eyes bloodshot. 'Everyone knows *something* has happened. Shouldn't we make some type of announcement?'

'Frederic said to wait,' Doug says, shrugging. 'I guess if anyone asks, we just tell them there's been an accident.'

'An accident.' It takes me a moment to realize that the voice belongs to Brooke. Her words are laced with a hardness I've never heard from her. In an instant, she drops my hand from her clasp. A sudden coldness enters through my skin, and I can't tell if it comes from her disengaging fingers or from the words she speaks. 'Just like the other woman.'

I know who she's referring to, of course. The woman who fell from Khrum Yai a few days before Brooke arrived on Koh Sang. Brooke kept asking about her during our hike the other day. She wanted to know what the woman was like, whether I thought she killed herself, whether it was feasible that someone would stray so far off the hiking path that they could fall. Her questions conjured images of Jacinta. Her chestnut curls, her big brown eyes, the attention she seemed to command when she walked in a room, just like Brooke. They were more similar than Brooke could ever realize.

I didn't know how to answer Brooke's questions, so I didn't. I claimed I didn't know Jacinta, that I'd never met her. I hated lying to Brooke, of course, but it was easier than telling her the truth. Than getting tripped up by the follow-up questions she would inevitably have.

From the corner of my eye, I see Logan's head dart upwards, his eyes fixing on Brooke leaning against the desk.

'Yes, an accident,' he says coldly. 'You come to an island with strong currents and rocky cliffs, and you combine that with wee kids who don't know how to hold their booze travelling alone for the first time in their lives, and that's what you get. Accidents.'

My stomach muscles clench as I feel Logan's frustration bubbling inside him. He doesn't need to explain it. All of the Permanents understand what will happen if the police determine Lucy's death wasn't an accident. The salacious headlines, the cancelled bookings, the lost profits. The resort can't afford that. And neither can we.

'It just seems like quite the coincidence . . .' Brooke trails off, but I can hear the irritation in her voice. Brooke's never been one to shy away from expressing her opinion. It was something that drew me to her in the first place, the confidence with which she seemed to say whatever she thought, with no care as to whether people disagreed with her. But this is different, there's a new anger that edges beneath her words.

'I – I saw something,' I say, eager to end this growing confrontation. My words are so quiet that I'm not sure anyone has heard them until Greta turns to me.

'What did you see?'

My mind flashes to the metallic object glinting on the seabed. The feel of it, light but solid in my hand. I shake it off.

'She was hurt.' I feel everyone's eyes on me, prompting me to continue. 'She had a cut on her forehead,' I say quickly, the attention sending warmth to my cheeks. 'And it looked like bruises on her neck.'

Neil has been leaning against the shop desk, but upon hearing that, he shifts upright. 'What did they look like, the bruises?'

'I don't know for sure, but they were small lines on each side of her neck. Like . . . like . . .' I falter.

'Like handprints?' Brooke asks.

I nod. I hadn't thought it through until now, but the blue imprints on either side of Lucy's neck could definitely have been caused by fingers. Someone strangling her from behind or shoving her head into the water. I squeeze my eyes shut, trying to force out the images.

'Did you see them, Doug?' Greta asks, her voice rushed. 'When you were helping the police with her body?'

Doug shakes his head slowly, his mouth set in a firm line. 'No. But to be fair, I was trying not to look at her. I carried her to the surface from behind, so I didn't really see her face or neck.'

'Maybe the cut on her forehead was from something else,' Greta says. Her voice is quiet, and her face looks paler than usual. 'She could have gone swimming during the party. Maybe she was drunk or on drugs. She could have hit her head on something – a rock or coral – and lost consciousness.'

'But what about the bruises?' Brooke questions.

Greta shrugs. 'Maybe they were unrelated. Or . . .'

She trails off, and I feel eyes shift to me, the silent implication hitting me a moment later than the others.

Maybe they weren't really there. Maybe I imagined them.

'It's just that shock does weird things to the mind,' Greta rushes to say in an apologetic tone.

'She's got a point,' Neil says. 'When you're down there, the water can change how you see things, especially in low visibility. The marks could have been anything, a refraction from seaweed, a smudge on your mask.'

I nod. I know all this. I try to think back to that moment when I noticed the phantom fingerprints on Lucy's neck.

There was so much happening. The shock of seeing her body there, of finding the object next to her, of becoming aware of Daniel's rushed ascent. And then my mind returns to the pill I took this morning. I know the side effects of Xanax. I know how it can screw with your memory. And what if there really wasn't any bruising? What if I made it up?

'You're right,' I say finally, weighing my options. 'It could have been anything – her veins showing through her skin, maybe? I don't know.'

Neil nods encouragingly, and I feel Logan resume rubbing my back, but my eyes shift to Brooke, whose forehead is scrunched.

'This has been a traumatizing day for everyone, especially Cass,' Greta says, turning to Doug. 'Any chance we can get her back home?'

I shoot Greta a look of gratitude, which she returns with a kind smile.

Doug clears his throat and injects a note of authority into his voice. 'Of course. The police aren't going to have the autopsy results until tomorrow at least, and they said they wouldn't be back for questions tonight. We've all been here for hours.' I look through the small window of the dive shop and see the sun beginning to dip over the ocean, the sky growing a vibrant purple. 'Let's all go home and get some rest. We'll close the dive shop for now.'

'Good idea,' Logan says. 'I'll keep Frangipani closed too, out of respect. It's not like we'd get a big crowd the day after Full Moon anyway.' He turns to me. 'Let's get you home.'

We say our goodbyes and disperse as Doug locks up the shop, Brooke walking back to her room and the rest of us heading to our bikes.

85

'Come on, love,' Logan says, leading me to his motorbike. 'You shouldn't be driving. I'll pick up your bike later.'

I follow his lead and perch on the bike behind him, my arms wrapped around his solid torso. I lean my head against his back, suddenly exhausted.

As he drives out of the parking area, I pull my legs up. As I do, I feel something shift at my waist. A cold metal brushes against my flesh through the thin lining of my shorts pocket.

And instantly I'm underwater again. Next to Lucy's body, pulling the glinting object free from the seabed, my back turned away from Tamar and Ariel, my tank blocking their sight.

I brushed it free of sand, but even before it was clean, I knew what it was.

A perfect gold circle. I flipped it horizontally so I could see the words engraved inside, knowing already what they would be.

Forever Us Two.

The phrase Logan had engraved on our matching engagement rings. Our version of I love you.

As the wind whips against my face, I replay the one question I've been asking myself all day.

Why did I find Logan's ring next to Lucy's dead body?

8

Cass

Once we're home, Logan escorting me to the front door like I'm a patient recovering from surgery, we sit on the couch. He pulls my feet up on to his lap, gently massaging them. From the outside, it would look like any other night when Logan wasn't working. The two of us cuddled up on the couch, a Netflix documentary playing on the TV. But there's no documentary playing now, and this is no normal night, as the anxiety swirling around in my stomach keeps reminding me.

'I can't believe you had to go through that, that you had to – to find her like that,' he says, his face twisted in concern. 'I just wish it had been me.'

I place my hand on his arm, unsure what to say.

'I mean, it's crazy, isn't it?' Logan continues. 'That woman who fell from Khrum Yai –' I flinch when he references her '– and now this.'

The ring sits like a stone in my pocket, weighing me down so that I feel as though I may sink into the couch. I look at Logan, his face so earnest as he seems to be trying to piece together what's happened.

I should tell him that I found it. Our ring, *his* ring. The one he had made as a pair. I know it's his, I knew it as soon as I plucked it from the sand. I keep replaying this morning in my head, my decision to leave my ring at home, nestled in the red box in the drawer of my bedside table where it still sits. I figured it would be safer there; I didn't want to run the risk of losing it in the water. The irony hits me like a cold slap to the face.

I should just ask him. I think of Brooke, how direct she is. She wouldn't hesitate to confront him. She certainly wouldn't be avoiding the conversation, drumming up unrealistic explanations in her head like I have been. *Maybe he went for a swim early this morning and it fell off his chain. Maybe it belongs to someone else who just happens to have the same ring with the exact same engraving.* No, Brooke would come right out, point blank. *Logan, why did I find your ring next to a dead girl's body?*

But I'm not Brooke. The idea of confronting Logan ignites a wave of nausea in my stomach. Because I don't want to hear the truth. Not if it changes what we have. I've worked so hard for this – for him. And here we are, finally engaged. If I lose him, I don't know what I would do. He's the only thing that's got me through these last few years after I lost everything. My mother to breast cancer when I was thirteen, and then Robin and my father to that hotel room. I had nothing when I arrived on Koh Sang: no family, no friends, no future. Logan changed all of that.

I never knew what it was that first attracted him to me when we met two years ago, all wild limbs and awkward bones jutting every which way, barely able to string together a logical sentence. The year of grief and solitude had animalized me, and I was only just coming out of hibernation.

After everything that happened in that hotel room, no one knew what to do with me, especially after what

88

they'd thought I'd done. And the police didn't help things, letting me go for lack of evidence, but never clarifying to the public what really happened.

My grandmother was the only option. So I lived with her, each of us mostly avoiding the other in that old house upstate. Although I'm not sure you could technically classify what I was doing as living. Curled up on my bed, constantly thinking of Robin, periodically looking through the gap in my curtains at the reporters camped out at the end of the driveway, each trying to outlast the others for a peek at America's newest villain. They stayed for months, but eventually they lost interest, just as I hoped. So, I pulled the curtains slightly wider, and kept looking out into the world thinking of everything Robin had wanted to see but hadn't had the chance to. Because of me.

My mind kept going to one place in particular: Southeast Asia. Robin's dream destination ever since we watched *The Beach* with our babysitter, long before we were old enough to. I didn't have any particular feelings towards the place, but Robin's excitement was always contagious.

So when my grandmother finally died, almost a year to the day after her son's death, and her inheritance – a hefty sum when combined with the estate my father had left behind – transferred to my bank account, the first thing I did was book the ticket. One way to Phuket, followed by an eight-hour ferry to a place I remembered Robin mentioning once, as she pored over glossy websites about the Gulf of Thailand: Koh Sang.

Even as the ferry approached the island, as exhausted as I was from the multi-day trip, I couldn't take my tired eyes off the sight of it. The mountains, basking in a pinkish glow, rising serenely over the water. An island of colours so vivid they burned my eyes. It was like staring directly at the sun after spending a year in winter greys.

I forced myself to take the dive course. I was never interested in scuba, but Robin was. And this trip was for her. So I went, barely talking to anyone, avoiding eye contact with the other people in my group and my dive instructor, a charming red-headed Brit named Neil, who every female student – myself included – couldn't help but have a school-girl crush on. But as soon as I took that first breath under the water, it was as if something opened in me. Something I had kept closed since the day I lost Robin. There was a sort of freedom to being underwater. Who you were, what you'd done no longer mattered below the surface. All that did was the tempo with which you dragged in each breath, the second that passed before you released it.

By the end of that first dive, I was addicted.

As soon as I finished the beginner course, I signed up for another, and another, making a small dent in my inheritance. I spent my days training underwater, my nights in my closet-sized Terrace room, studying the textbook Neil had given me. At the end of that first week, Neil persuaded me to go with him to a bar his friend had just opened, and a few hours later, I was clinging to him on the back of his motorbike as he led me down palm-filled roads to a bar that was nothing more than a bit of open ground and a palapa situated next to the jungle.

'This is Frangipani,' Neil said after he parked near the chain-link fence surrounding the lot. 'My mate Logan just opened it. It's the main expat hangout here.'

My underarms were damp and my mouth sandy as we entered and a group of heads turned in our direction. A tall blonde Scandinavian-looking woman, a grungy surfer guy with hair so tangled it was halfway to becoming dreadlocks, a pale, dark-haired, severe woman who was the only one not to break into a smile, and Logan.

Their voices greeted me all at once, a mixture of accents and dialects hitting my ears simultaneously, none of the words comprehensible.

It was the most excitement I had received in response to my presence in years, and I felt a warmth grow deep in my stomach as I took in their eager faces. I realized instantly there was something special, something tightknit about this group. And for a moment, I felt like I was back in college, surrounded by people who accepted me. My roommate, her boyfriend, Eric, and their friends. People who made me feel like I was something more. Like I was special.

In response, I managed a feeble, 'Hi, I'm Cass.'

The name felt foreign in my mouth. I'd only said it a few times since I wrote it on my hotel registration, thankful that the woman at reception didn't insist on checking it against my passport. A new heat broke out through my chest, as I swallowed down the panic of being found out. I prepared for my lie to spark a flurry of accusations, of knowing eyes quick to label me a liar. Or worse.

But instead, all I heard was Logan's deep Scottish brogue.

'Well it is certainly a pleasure to meet you, Cass.' Hearing my name in his mouth was intoxicating, and when his dark blue eyes rested on me, I felt my temperature skyrocket. Bits of my vision turned to black, like a television screen on the blink. And as soon as I saw him, I knew. This was not just a place I would visit. Koh Sang was a place I would stay.

And stay I did. In the following months, Logan and I spent virtually all our free time together. He integrated me into his life, into the family he'd formed on this island. After I passed my divemaster training, Frederic took me on in the dive shop. I would spend every night sitting at the bar at Frangipani, as the female customers smiled at Logan coyly, watching their cheeks grow red as he'd lean in to kiss me across the counter. Knowing that he'd chosen me.

Frangipani struggled for that first year or so, being such a hike from the flurry of Pho Tau beach. Logan had spent pretty much all his savings buying it, so I helped him out for a few months when he couldn't make his mortgage payments. I didn't mind; I certainly had enough money to spare. And eventually, Logan found his footing as a manager. With some help from the other Permanents, he worked up a strong enough marketing campaign to convince the resort guests to make the hike out to the bar, even getting Frangipani listed as a permanent fixture on the island's official pub crawl.

But more business means I've seen him less lately. There's no longer a spot for me at the bar most nights; all the stools are occupied by customers, so I've been spending more nights at home or at the resort's fitness studio, doing a Pilates class with Greta. More time apart meant more distance for things to get between us. So much so, that a few weeks back, I thought I'd lost him. But that all changed again with the engagement, our vow to spend the rest of our lives together.

Suddenly, I'm struck with a panic, the thought of him leaving seizing me by the throat. The same way it did a few weeks ago. I've tried to keep these feelings buried, tried to forget about what happened. I can't let them come back, especially now. I give a little cough, which does nothing to help.

'You okay?' Logan looks over from his side of the couch,

concerned. I nod, although I'm about as far from okay as is humanly possible.

He yawns and stretches up his arms. 'Well, I'm knackered. And you must be, too. What do you say we have an early night? I'm sure there'll be loads for us to sort tomorrow once Frederic gets in.' As he gets up from the couch, I want to run after him, to beg him to tell me that nothing will change, that he had nothing to do with Lucy's death. But I sit there, stone still, until he reaches the bedroom door. 'Coming?' he asks.

I follow him into our bedroom, the sight of the dark sea through our floor-to-ceiling windows for once doing nothing to improve my mood. Logan's already stripping off his shirt and tossing it in the hamper. As he turns towards me, my eyes travel to his neck, flashing over the Scots Gaelic text inked across his clavicle. *Chan eil tuil air nach tig traoghadh.* I'd asked him what it meant the first time I'd seen him shirtless, less than a week after we met at Frangipani. 'It's an old proverb,' he murmured in my ear as I traced my fingers over the raised flesh. 'There isn't a flood which will not subside.' And I thought then that it all made sense. *I had made it through the worst.*

But now, as my eyes skirt over that same tattoo, coldness rushes in. It's not the words themselves, it's what's missing from the naked skin above them. The chain is still looped around his neck, but it's naked of the ring he vowed to keep attached to it only a few days ago.

The words escape before I can stop them. 'Logan, where's your ring?'

He looks down at his chest as if he's been shot. When he raises his eyes to me, they're filled with guilt. I take a step back, grasping on to our dresser to steady myself, bracing for his admission.

'Ah, Cass, I'm so sorry.'

'Logan,' I say, silently begging him to stop.

'I didn't mean to . . .'

'You don't . . .'

'Doug convinced me to put on that bloody neon paint when we got to the Full Moon Party.'

Huh? My heart is beating so hard that it feels like it's going to escape from my chest. What the hell is he talking about?

'I should have just said no, I mean it's a stupid thing to do. But you know Doug when he's pissed – you saw him last night, he was in rare form. So, I did it. I took off my shirt and drew some stupid designs on my chest. The chain must have come unclasped, and the ring must have fallen off somehow. When I got home, I found the chain wrapped up in my shirt, but no ring.'

I stand there, not sure I understand what he's saying.

He rushes over to me, cupping my elbows in his hand, his dark blue eyes inches from mine. 'I'm so sorry, you shouldn't need to be dealing with this, especially not tonight. But it was an accident, I promise. It'll be some-where on the beach. I'll get someone to help me search. We'll find it.'

Tears prick the back of my eyes, and before I can stop myself they fall, one by one.

'Oh, love. I'll find it, I promise.'

Logan pulls me into a hug, and I sob against his chest as I process everything: finding Lucy, then the ring, suspect-ing Logan was somehow involved, and now hating myself for ever thinking he was capable of that. *I'm* the one who should be sorry.

But there's one more thing I need to know. I push away from his chest.

'So, you never saw Lucy last night, right? Before she . . . you know.'

His forehead crinkles in confusion. 'Did I see Lucy?' He repeats. 'I – I don't think so. But I don't know what she looked like. You said she was tiny and had curly brown hair, right?' I nod and he pulls his top teeth over his lower lip, thinking. 'No, I don't remember seeing her. Why?'

I breathe an enormous sigh of relief. 'No reason,' I say, my voice almost giddy. I'll give the ring back to him tomorrow or the day after. I'll tell him that I found it somewhere on the beach. He doesn't ever need to know.

Because Lucy must have picked up Logan's ring when she was at the party. Maybe she was trying to find who it belonged to so she could return it. Or maybe she stole it. I realize I have no idea what kind of person she may have been. Either way, she must have had it in her hand or somewhere on her when she went swimming later that night. She could have dropped it as she drowned. That's how it landed in the sand. It all makes sense.

As the tension washes out of me, exhaustion floods in. I almost collapse in Logan's arms.

'Hey there. I think it's time we got you to bed.' In one swoop, he picks me up, carrying me like a baby over to my side of the bed. Once I'm under the sheet, he bends down, kissing me gently on the forehead.

'Forever us two,' he says.

'Forever us two,' I murmur, already closing my eyes.

Sleep comes fast, blocking out everything, including the pinprick of doubt lodged in the back of my mind.

9

Sunday

Brooke

I've been awake for hours – most of the night, really – when I receive the text. Late-morning light filters in through the one window of my Coral Bungalow room.

Despite the Permanents' insistence that Lucy's death was just another accident, I don't buy it. I think of how Cass mentioned the cut on Lucy's forehead and the bruising on her neck. How quickly she retreated on that point when she was challenged. There was a caginess there, something she wasn't quite saying. And then there's my run-in with Lucy. How she seemed to be waiting outside my room to confront me about that girl who jumped from Khrum Yai. How her eyes looked when they met mine, desperate and searching.

I knew there was a story here when I came to this island. But I could never have expected this. I've started to feel that familiar itch that runs just under my skin, the ache in my fingers for a keyboard to type on.

I haven't felt this since those early days in college when I joined the school paper as a freshman. I was only assigned the fluff pieces, of course – the opening of a new restaurant in the campus cafeteria, new vending machines in the sophomore dorms – but each assignment was a challenge, forcing me to weave words to bring life to these events, to show why they were worth caring about.

Back then, I had thought journalism was my future.

When I started travelling, my plan was to find freelance work with various media outlets to fund my travels throughout Eastern Europe. I longed to cover stories as they happened in real time: the border disputes, the ethnic crimes, the ongoing rivalries that outlived the end of the wars decades ago. But despite countless emails and uninvited visits to every newspaper office I could find in the former Soviet Bloc, I had no luck. No one wanted to hire a college dropout with no writing credits to her name.

That was how the @BrookeaTrip persona came about. People couldn't care less about the stories I told of all the places I visited, but they will pay good money to advertise their products through a scantily clad woman with a sizeable Instagram following and decent photography skills.

But this could be it. The story I had planned to write about this island just got a whole lot more interesting with Lucy's death. It would have emotion, suspense, everything a good story needs. It would surely get picked up on some regional – or maybe even national – outlet. This could be my big break.

So I've spent most of the morning – and a considerable portion of the night – scouring social media for any idea of who Lucy was. But despite my best efforts, working with just a first name and the image of Lucy's blue eyes burned into my brain, I've come up with nothing.

When my phone chirps, I lunge across the hotel desk for it, eager for any information. It's a message from Cass, and I feel my heart rate speed up.

*The police just told Doug the results of the autopsy.
They said Lucy died from drowning. No signs of foul
play.*

My grip tightens around the phone, and the rage rises in
my throat. I force myself to swallow it down and type out
my reply through tense fingers.

Can you meet me?

Ten minutes later, I'm waiting outside the dive shop, where
Cass joins me.

'So the police think it was an accident?' I ask as soon as
she's opened up the shop and we've taken our seats at the
bench that lines one wall.

Cass steps back defensively, and I force my hands to
unclasp. I can't come on so aggressively, especially after
what she's gone through. I noticed I was doing it yesterday
in the dive shop as well. Stepping over the boundary of
who this group wants me to be: the ditzy, fun influencer. I
was too loud, too opinionated. I could feel them pulling
away.

But even so, I can't sit by as they label Lucy's death an
accident, when all signs say there's more to the story.

'I didn't get too much information from Doug, other
than what I told you. He doesn't think the police have done
a full report – not that they would have shared it with us if
they had, since we're not Lucy's family. They just called
him and told him the conclusion to relay to Frederic. We
have a staff meeting later when Frederic gets in. We should
learn more then.'

'Did they say anything about the bruising on Lucy's neck?'

Cass looks down, her face sheepish. 'Doug said the

police didn't find any bruising. I guess it's like what the others said yesterday. I must have jumped to conclusions.'

'Well, what about the cut on her forehead? You saw that, right?'

Her mouth is a straight line. 'They think maybe she bumped her head against a rock. The current was bad on Friday night, and portions of the shore can be quite rocky.'

'Isn't this all a bit quick?' I ask. 'I mean, it's been less than twenty-four hours since they found her.'

Cass doesn't say anything. I shouldn't be surprised. It's not typical for Cass to speak her mind. Every other time I've heard one of the Permanents voice an idea, she's quick to go along with it. She's never one to rock the boat.

But even so, I know I'm right. I think back to the conversations I watched Doug having with the police officer in charge yesterday, the soft glances, the muffled exchanges. I think how eager they all were to label Lucy's death an accident.

Frederic must have paid them off. The police were never going to determine Lucy's death was murder because Frederic didn't want them to.

I feel it again. The rage from earlier this morning. My fingernails form crescent moons on the whites of my palms. I don't want Cass to notice, so I force my hands open and move my left hand over my right wrist, fingering the bracelets that rest there. Shifting them, one at a time, up and then down, swallowing the anger.

'They're still running tests to determine the level of alcohol in her system and whether she was on drugs,' Cass says softly. 'They said they should know the results later today.'

I barely hear her. I already know what the tests will say. Exactly what Frederic wants them to: that Lucy got drunk, or high, or whatever. That she decided to go for a swim but couldn't handle the current. She hit her head on a rock and drowned, sinking to the ocean floor, where Cass found her.

A simple, easy solution. One that works for everyone. Except Lucy, of course.

Cass's eyes meet mine, and I think I see a flicker of doubt there.

'You don't believe that, do you?' I ask, sensing an opportunity.

'I don't know. I mean, it does make sense . . .'

'Do we even know whether the police have called Lucy's parents? Whether they've notified her family?'

'I'm not sure,' Cass admits. 'It might be difficult. Doug checked this morning and Lucy never filled out the emergency contact portion of her dive forms. I don't know how I missed that. I'm usually so careful . . .'

'So, her family doesn't know,' I pretend to think aloud. 'They think she's still alive. It's not right. Someone needs to tell them.'

I hold my breath, waiting for her to respond, but her eyes remain glued to her hands. I recognize my chance.

'Cass, if you know Lucy's full name and the room she was staying in, I might be able to find her parents' contact information.' I've considered trying to get this myself from the front desk, but I know how strict Frederic is with the receptionists. They would never tell me Lucy's room number. But as an employee of the resort, Cass could get this information easily.

When she answers, her dark brown eyes meet mine.

'Her name was Lucy Dupin. And I know where she was staying.'

*

I thought I had explored the entire resort in the weeks I've been here, but I've never made it this far. We've been walking for fifteen minutes already, our skin damp from the fuzzy heaviness hanging in the air. By now we've long crossed over the road that bisects the resort and passed the resort's enormous party pool on the hill's summit.

'The Terrace rooms are free with the purchase of a dive course,' Cass explains. I had assumed she would just give me the room number, but she insisted on coming along. And I wasn't really in a position to turn her down.

'Since these rooms are free, they're obviously pretty bare bones and they're definitely a hike,' she continues. 'Once guests see how far away the rooms are, nine times out of ten, they choose to hand over the 1,500 baht per night it costs to upgrade from the Terrace to the Coral Bungalows, back down near the dive-training pools.'

By the time we finally reach the Terrace, a building that looks almost identical to the rooms on the south side of the resort minus the balconies, my hamstrings are on fire and a thick sheen covers my forehead. If Lucy decided to stay up here after seeing how excruciating the trek was, she must have had a damn good reason for doing so.

Cass pauses outside the building, twisting her head back and forth to make sure there's no one around. But this part of the resort seems utterly empty.

We head up a set of stairs to the third floor. Cass lets me lead the way, following silently. When we get to the door for Room 324 – the number Cass had found on Lucy's information sheet – I breathe a sigh of relief upon finding that, just like the other rooms, the Terrace rooms have actual locks, rather than a pad for a key card.

'I – I don't have a key,' Cass says, as if I hadn't already thought about that.

101

'Don't worry about it.' I pull two hairgrips from my hair, letting my messy bun fall down my back. I stick one in the bottom of the lock and open the other to make it as flat as possible before inserting it above. 'One of my mom's boyfriends taught me,' I explain, feeling Cass's curiosity.

Craig, Carl, something like that. His face has faded into the men who were universally present in our trailer, a round stomach, nondescript features. He was one of the few good ones. He didn't try anything.

I twist and pull, waiting for the telltale click, thinking as usual how disturbingly simple this is. And then I hear it.

Unfortunately, the door itself is more difficult to manoeuvre, the wood swollen from humidity. I shove my shoulder against it, feeling bone connect painfully with wood, but no movement. I try again, hard enough to bruise my skin, but still the force isn't enough.

'Here, let me,' Cass says, prompting me to step aside.

She swings her foot up quickly, connecting with the door, which flies open.

'Okay, girl,' I say, my surprise evident. I look over at Cass, her eyes innocent, her typical shy smile decorating her mouth, and I can't help but be impressed.

We walk in, pulling the door shut behind us.

The place is a mess. Stuff covers every inch of the closet-sized room. An assortment of clothes, shoes and papers are draped across the flat, hard-looking bed that reaches both walls, and a lone T-shirt hangs from the plastic fan in the corner. And all of it is illuminated by the afternoon sunlight filtering through the cheesecloth curtain covering the room's one window, which is bright enough to accentuate the dirty grout between the floor's tiles.

It's immediately clear that, despite the similarities from

the outside, these rooms are a far cry from the guestrooms back towards the beach.

'Wow, what a shithole,' I say, hoping Cass doesn't realize how close I came to staying in one of these rooms. If Frederic hadn't finally relented and given me a discount on my room in the Coral Bungalows, I would be out here in the resort's designated Siberia. I try to ignore how much Lucy's room reminds me of my mother's trailer back in our small town outside Lexington. Add in a bunch of run-down shelves overflowing with worthless knick-knacks and the thick stench of cigarette smoke that shrouds all my childhood memories, and it would be just like home.

'I actually stayed in one of these rooms the first few weeks I got to the island,' Cass says, 'when I was deciding whether to live on Koh Sang permanently. Looks like they haven't changed much.' Notes of nostalgia creep into her words, and for the second time in a matter of minutes, I try to hide my surprise. It's clear Cass has money. Even living on a remote island filled with backpackers, she can't hide that. It's in the way she carries herself. I never would have guessed that she would have slummed it in one of these rooms.

An enormous travel backpack is perched near the door. As I bend down to look at it, I realize someone's ripped it open at the seams, as though they lacked the patience to fiddle with the zipper. The backpack's innards stream across the dirty floor tiles.

'Someone's been in here,' Cass says softly, 'I can't imagine Lucy would leave her place in this condition.'

I nod, taking another look at the ripped seams, the discarded items flung about the room. Based on the very little I knew about Lucy, she didn't seem the type to needlessly shred her belongings.

103

Someone seems to have been looking for something in here. Someone in a rush.

'Maybe we shouldn't touch anything,' I think out loud. I've seen enough police procedurals to know that rubbing our fingerprints all over Lucy's stuff could compromise an investigation.

Cass shakes her head. 'The police aren't going to change their minds.'

And I know she's right. All they care about is Frederic's money.

'Okay,' I say, resigned. 'We better get started then.'

I told Cass that I wanted to find her parents' contact information – and I do. But I'm also looking for anything that tells me who Lucy really was, why she came here. Anything to indicate why she may have been killed – or why she appeared so desperate to talk to me the other day. I spend a few minutes rifling through the clothes left in and around the backpack. A handful of T-shirts, a set of pyjamas, one flip-flop – its partner likely strewn somewhere else in the room – three bikinis, and a pile of underwear and bras. Exactly what you'd expect.

'Find anything?' I ask Cass, who's holding a handful of papers in her hand. Her expression is unreadable.

'These are all printouts of pages from the resort website,' she says finally, handing the pile to me, and I flip through them. The papers are filled with information on the different dive courses offered, the types of rooms, even the bio pages of the shop's two dive instructors. Neil's face is first, his smile wide, those freckled lips open. Cass stares up at me from the second page, decked out in a red staff shirt, and a half-hearted smile, but there's an air of discomfort in her eyes, as if she'd rather have been doing anything in that moment than getting her photo taken.

'Why would she have these?' Cass asks.

I shake my head in confusion and hand them back to her. I take the few short steps to the bathroom, leaving Cass staring at the papers as though they're foreign objects.

The bathroom is no more than a toilet, sink, shower head and an insufficiently sized floor drain, all hidden from the rest of the room by a mildewed blue curtain.

I start with the sink. The small cosmetics bag that teeters on its ledge is filled with typical inexpensive mascara, eyeshadow, blush, and a tube of light pink lipstick.

I note a blue toothbrush on the left side of the sink and a towel hanging from a rack, still damp. As I scan the room, I spot something purple on the floor, discarded next to the small bin. I bend over and pick it up, my fingers brushing against the hard plastic, my mind working to understand what I'm holding.

Another toothbrush. Dark purple with white and lilac bristles. It was resting face down on the tiles, like it had been accidentally knocked off the sink. I look back at the blue toothbrush I spotted before. Why would Lucy need two?

I head out of the bathroom. 'I found—'

But before I can say another word, Cass grabs my hand, alarm in her eyes. She raises a finger to her mouth, urging me to be quiet.

I blink at her in confusion, and she points to the door to the room before pulling me down so that we're pressed to the floor, hidden by the bed.

I stay quiet for a moment, holding my breath as I hear the soft staccato of footsteps falling a few metres outside the door, barely muffled by the cheap plywood walls. We've kept the light off, and the room's single window is obscured by a sheer curtain, but still my heart rate speeds up, goaded on by panic. I look over at Cass. If it wasn't for her, the person outside would have heard me and known we were in here.

She saved us from whoever's out there.

'It can't be housekeeping,' Cass breathes in my ear. 'They only do the free rooms once a week, on Saturdays.'

I hold my breath as the footsteps come closer, until they sound as if they're right outside the door.

And then they stop.

10

Cass

There's no sound other than my rapid heartbeat, so loud and fast that I worry the intruder can hear it.

A slight jingle sounds as the door handle decompresses.

I can't remember if these doors lock automatically. If not, whoever is trying to get in is going to find us, hiding on the floor, covered in dirt and guilt.

The second it takes for the handle to stop stretches on for an eternity. I clench every muscle as I wait for the click to signify the intruder's entrance.

But it doesn't come.

The intruder seems as surprised as we are. They press down again and again, their movements becoming quicker and more forceful until they're rattling the doorknob back and forth as hard as they can.

I don't dare breathe out, as if doing so will provide the door with the movement it needs to swing open. I turn my head to Brooke. Her eyes are staring at mine, and I know she can see the terror plain on my face. We don't need to say anything. It's clear that whoever is on the other side of that door didn't come here with good intentions.

After what feels like hours – but realistically couldn't have been more than a few seconds – the intruder gives up. I hear an indecipherable mumble of what sounds like a four-letter word as the footsteps trail away.

We lie there, waiting for our heart rates to return to normal. I slowly start to unclench my muscles one by one, but only after a few minutes, once I'm sure the person is gone, do I begin to move.

Brooke is far ahead of me, already running the few steps towards the window before I'm off the floor.

'Don't!' I whisper-scream across the room, but she either doesn't hear or ignores me. She's already pulled the curtain back enough to see out.

'Come here, quick.'

I rush to her side, seeing what she does through the window. A person, walking briskly from the Terrace steps. They're already too far away to make out any features. The only thing visible is the black hooded sweatshirt obscuring the back of their head. No one in their right mind would be wearing a sweatshirt in this weather. Other than someone who didn't want to be seen.

I notice Brooke holding something in her hands, something important enough to draw her attention from the window.

'What is that?' I ask.

'I found it when we were down there, under the bed,' she explains. 'It was wedged in between the bedframe and the wall. It looks like it may have dropped through the crack.'

She slides it into my hand, which I notice is visibly shaking. A small rectangle of laminated plastic. In the light sneaking through the crack in the curtain, I see Lucy's face staring passively out from the front of the card. She's quite a few years younger than she seemed when I met her, and a small smile teases her lips, one that had been noticeably absent during class the other day.

A hologram creeps across the surface of the card, painting Lucy's face in wavering pinks that glint off the sunlight. Despite the suffocating heat in the room, I feel myself shiver as I realize what I'm looking at.

It's an identification card. Not for Lucy Dupin of Australia. But for Lucy Taylor, the eighteen-year-old resident of Greymouth, New Zealand.

We're both quiet as we walk away from the Terrace rooms, each apparently lost in our own thoughts. The air has grown even heavier than this morning and along the horizon, I see a crack of lightning splice the sky. These flash storms happen once a day in the rainy season, but they usually only last for about twenty minutes.

I break the silence as we walk past the party pool, which is, thankfully, quite subdued today – whether because of the coming rain or the news of Lucy's death is anyone's guess.

'Why would Lucy have been going by a fake name? And why did she have those printouts of the diving staff? And who was that person trying to get into her room?'

My questions only seem to be growing with each new piece of information. I have more, of course, questions I can't ask out loud. Like, is the person who killed Lucy the same person who's after me? And is all of this somehow connected? Could it be my fault that this girl is dead?

Brooke turns to answer, her mouth open, but before she can say anything, a crack of thunder rolls through the resort and the sky opens.

We sprint blindly down the path leading from the main road to the beach, the cold of the raindrops pounding at our backs a shocking contrast from the swollen heat of the air. Having taken this route hundreds of times over the last two years, I can easily do it with my eyes closed, and I lead Brooke back to the dive shop, where we'd left our bags before heading to Lucy's room. Once we're inside, I slam the door closed, and the roar of the rain diminishes to a muted rhythm against the shop's roof. I breathe a sigh of relief when I see that we have the place to ourselves; the dive shop isn't open on Sundays. But the memories of yesterday, the panic, the shock, still hang heavy in the air, so palpable I can almost taste them.

I grab two towels from the back of the shop and hand one to Brooke, which she uses to wipe her face.

'So what do we do now?' I ask, wrapping the other towel around me. With a prick of shame, I realize how much I've come to simply follow Brooke's lead. How even in the short time since she's arrived, I've naturally looked to her as the leader.

But now Brooke seems lost in thought, her eyes glued to the shop door, and I feel a flash of panic at her quiet. After a moment, though, she gives an almost imperceptible shake of her head and turns to face me with a tired smile.

'Well, now that we know her real name and address, we should try to find her on social media,' she says, taking back control. She's focused, her voice slightly different than usual. It's flatter, as if a different inflection is poking through her West Coast accent. There's something familiar about it that I can't quite place. The rain has also pooled mascara under her eyes, which she quickly swipes away with the towel, leaving her eyelashes bare. There's a vulnerability there that I rarely see, and again, something nudges my memory. 'Maybe get her phone number,' Brooke continues, before I can analyse the thought further. 'Figure out who we need to contact.'

110

I nod. Despite stating Lucy's full name, address and the fact that she is – or *was* – an organ donor, her identification card didn't give us any indication of how to reach her family. As much as I hate to admit it, social media probably *is* our best option.

'Okay,' Brooke says, pulling a laptop and her mobile from the canvas tote she'd left here earlier. She sits on the bench, the computer opened on the towel she's draped across her lap. 'I'll start with Google, Twitter and Instagram. Why don't you take Facebook? That old computer has an internet connection, right?' She nods to the rusty PC on the desk, which is probably as old as the resort itself.

I nod. 'It's slow, but it'll do the trick.'

I settle on to the stool and watch Brooke as the old computer slowly comes to life. Her fingers tap diligently on her keyboard, and she expertly alternates her focus between her laptop and phone.

I deleted all my social media accounts three years ago, when they were deluged with requests to be my 'friend', most of which were accompanied by messages that started with an expletive and only got nastier from there. Ironically, Frederic put me in charge of handling the dive shop's Facebook and Instagram accounts. My guess is that he figured the one woman in the shop would be the best suited for it. Unfortunately for him, I don't quite have Brooke's skill set. I go on the accounts every now and then to upload photos taken with the dive shop's underwater camera, all of which lack filters and any attempts at witty captions, and which usually fail to garner more than a handful of likes. But sometimes when I'm on there, I'll spend a few minutes searching names of people I no longer know. My college roommate, for one, who's now married to the captain of our university's swimming team, a muscled jock I'd had a hopeless crush on. I look at the photos they post – his arm wrapped around her waist, a baby cradled in her arms outside their home in Greenwich, Connecticut. A painful reminder of what I might have had if life had turned out differently.

I turn my attention back to the screen, which has finally booted up. A Facebook search for Lucy Taylor returns thirteen thousand results. Award-winning authors, famous actresses, professors, doctors, porn stars, you name it. Just about everyone but *our* Lucy Taylor. I narrow the results to users from Greymouth, New Zealand, the name of the city on Lucy's identification card. Nothing. I try again, filtering by the names of cities located close to Greymouth. Still nothing.

As if reading my thoughts, Brooke groans. 'Nothing on Instagram, Twitter or TikTok. I even checked LinkedIn, but no Lucy Taylor.'

'No luck on Facebook, either,' I say.

'What kind of eighteen-year-old girl doesn't leave an internet footprint?' I feel my cheeks grow hot at Brooke's question, thinking of my own noticeable lack of social media presence, but Brooke doesn't seem to notice. 'Then again, what kind of girl checks into a scuba-diving resort using a fake name?'

'Wait,' I say, her comment triggering a thought. 'Maybe she didn't just use the Lucy Dupin name for check-in. Maybe it's, like, her internet alias.'

'Hmm.' Brooke's typing before I've even finished the thought.

I input *Lucy Dupin* into the Facebook search bar. Twenty-five results. Much more manageable. But I feel my hope drain as I scroll through them. None of the profile pictures resemble the fair, blue-eyed dive student.

'She's on Instagram,' Brooke says, stopping me mid-scroll, her eyes not straying from her phone. 'Her handle is @LucyDupin1. I think I . . .' She pauses in thought.

I grab my phone, log into Instagram using the dive shop account, and quickly type her handle into the search bar. The search yields only one result.

Her profile is public, but as barebones as it gets. No information in the description under her handle and no pictures. Her profile picture is just the standard grey silhouette provided by the app. I click over to her connections. She has a grand total of five followers, all of whom appear to be bots, but she's following seventeen people. I start at the top: the official Koh Sang tourist page, the Koh Sang Dive Resort page that I curate, Frangipani Bar, the Sunset Restaurant. Clearly, she was planning for this trip. I keep scrolling, bristling as I see more familiar names pop up. Logan, Greta, Doug.

I'm mid-scroll when Brooke's voice interrupts me.

'I have to go.'

'What?' I say, not sure I fully understand. 'But you see who she's following, right?'

'Yeah, it looks like she had a reason to come here. Either that or she was just extremely overexcited for this trip.' Brooke's face is pale, her jaw set as she talks. 'But I just remembered I have a meeting with a company about promoting their product. It could be a big gig for me.'

I stare, open mouthed and more than a little disappointed, as Brooke quickly gathers up her things. She's never flaky like this. In all the times we've ever made plans, she's never cancelled, never even showed up a minute later than the meeting time we agreed upon. And while she's always working – responding to Instagram comments or editing photos – she's never used it as an excuse before. I always got the impression that her influencer responsibilities weren't something she was overly excited about. Certainly not more important than getting to the bottom of a mystery swirling around a dead guest.

I think of the rain, desperate to make her stay, but I realize that, as we worked, the storm must have diminished to a mere drizzle and then to nothing, leaving as fast as it came. Now, the only sound from the dive shop roof is the occasional beat of a stray raindrop from one of the palm trees overhead.

'I'll check in with you in a few hours,' she calls over her shoulder, an afterthought as she pulls the shop door open.

This isn't the first time Brooke has done something like this. I think of her dropping my hand as we sat here in the dive shop yesterday. Since we first met a few weeks ago, she's showered me with attention, making me feel like I'm her best friend. But then there are times like this when, without warning, she'll become distracted, distant. As if a switch flips and she's reminded that she has much more pressing concerns.

I usually try to ignore it, but this time it stings. In the past few hours, I've come to see us as a team. I wasn't fooled by her claim that she wanted to find a way to contact Lucy's family. She clearly didn't believe Lucy's death was an accident, and despite my best efforts, I can't shake the image of those ghostly blue fingerprints on Lucy's neck. The more I think about it, the more I *know* they were real. And now that I know how Logan's ring came to be by Lucy's body, there's no reason to protect him.

I don't believe this was an accident, either. As much as I want to deny it, I think somebody killed Lucy.

And this Instagram profile seems to finally be getting us somewhere, giving us some insight into what she was doing on Koh Sang in the first place. Lucy had clearly planned for something. First the dive shop printouts, and now the Instagram profile. Plus, she met me, Doug and Neil throughout the dive course, but never Greta or Logan. What possible reason would she have had to follow them?

Before I can dig into the thought any further, the bell over the shop door chimes.

It's Doug, his matted hair messier than usual, dark bags packed under his eyes.

'Oh good, you're here,' he says, rushed. 'Frederic just got in and he has news. Team meeting in ten.'

He exits the shop as swiftly as he entered, a ball of nervous energy, saying that he's going to help Frederic get settled into his office. As soon as he's gone, I reach for my backpack, rummaging around until my fingers find the beat-up box of Xanax I made sure to bring with me today. Checking the door to make sure no one is outside, I pop out a pill, swallowing it in one swift motion.

The guilt returns, quick and fierce. But I know what this meeting will entail: Frederic ordering me to recount everything that happened yesterday from start to finish. And the thought of having to relive finding Lucy's body, on top of everything else, is too much to handle. I feel the pill's effects working long before it's actually possible. An avalanche of calm creeping through my veins, destroying the anxiety that has built up over the last two days.

As I shove the blister pack into the box, it catches on something. Logan's ring. When I woke up this morning, I transferred it from my shorts pocket to the box, somewhere I knew he would never look. I intend to stick to the plan I came up with last night. I'll give it back to him in a few days, telling him I found it on the beach.

I hear a sudden noise outside. As I look up, a shadow

seems to pass over the window that faces out towards the beach. It's gone in a flash, a streak of black, but I instantly think of the hooded person that Brooke and I saw leaving Lucy's hotel room. Of whoever's been following me, who- ever left me that threatening note.

I'm out of my seat in a second, throwing open the door. I stifle a shout, recoiling with surprise as a body fills the door frame.

11

Brooke

Saliva groups thick in my mouth as I throw open the door to the dive shop. I gulp in breaths, but the heavy humidity does little to ease my nausea.

I want to scream, to yell in frustration, but I don't of course. I realized a long time ago that nothing good ever comes of that. A woman's anger makes it easy to paint her as crazy. I know from experience.

Instead, I force myself to swallow and walk back to my room in a haze, the reality of what I just discovered overwhelming.

A girl was just found dead at the bottom of the ocean, a girl who had come to me for help – twice. Once via social media, and when that failed, again in person. I think of her parents somewhere back in New Zealand who have absolutely no idea that their baby girl is gone for ever.

I breathe a sigh of relief when I shut the door of my rented hotel room. The room itself is fine. Simple, but certainly an improvement over Lucy's. White walls, a queen-size bed with a mattress that barely moves beneath my body, a nondescript desk, and a large, beige-coloured floor. I try not to think of how much it reminds me of the other place they put me in years ago, the one devoid of colour.

After a minute, I force myself to pull out my phone and look again at the accounts Lucy Dupin followed on Instagram – the Dive Shop, Greta, Logan, all names I recognize – until I see one I know better than the others. The one I saw minutes ago in the dive shop. Marked with a photo, hair tied up in a ballerina bun, lips pursed in a barely there smile, and a European mountain range in the background.

Lucy Dupin followed *me*.

I've gained so many followers since I've gotten to Koh Sang. The picturesque backdrops and – more importantly – the bikini pictures have rocketed up my Instagram engagement. I haven't bothered to track the messages they send me or the comments they're leaving on my page.

I navigate over to my message inbox. I get hundreds of direct messages from followers who I either don't – or refuse to – follow back. I scroll through them, starting with the most recent, images of sleazy men and budding influencers flying past, until I see her handle: @LucyDupin1. I open the message I saw for the first time in the dive shop. It's dated exactly a week ago, a few days before she checked into the resort. It's short, only a few words, but each one sinks me like a stone.

Hi. Can you help me? Please?

It's so innocent. So childlike. If I had spent even another moment inside after I saw it, I would have exploded. I needed to breathe fresh air, to process this new piece of information.

What did Lucy need my help with so badly that she'd approached me for it twice? Did it have something to do with the woman who fell from Khrum Yai? And, more importantly, would Lucy still be alive if I'd given her the help she needed?

The last question crushes me.

A thought breaks through the surging wave of guilt. Maybe she'd tried another way to get in touch with me when I didn't respond to her direct message. Maybe she commented on one of my posts.

I navigate to my meticulously curated profile, stopping on my most recent post – a photo from my hike with Cass. I told her I wanted to see the view from Khrum Yai, the tallest mountain on the island. But really, I had another reason.

I wanted to see how far off the beaten path Jacinta, the poor woman who fell from the mountain only a few weeks ago, would have had to go to fall. It was closer than any reasonable person would go towards the edge – especially given the magnificent view that could be seen from steps away – unless they wanted to jump, or unless they were pushed.

I asked Cass what she thought about it and her expression grew serious. 'It was a horrible accident. That poor girl.' I pressed her. 'Did you know her?' But she just shook her head. 'I never met her,' she said, 'but losing a hotel guest hit us all hard.'

I look now at the photo I had Cass take of me on that summit. My arm is cocked on my hip, the colours edited so that it's impossible to tell where the sky ends and the ocean begins. Fifteen thousand likes. A ridiculous number. A quick search shows me that Lucy is one of them. Despite the lack of ventilation in my small room, the sight of her name sends a shiver through me. I posted that the day of the Full Moon Party. The day Lucy died.

I start scrolling below the post, looking to see whether Lucy has left a comment. When I come up empty, I continue down my profile page, searching the comments of my other recent posts. I stop at a post from last week of me lounging in a bikini at the resort's infinity pool, my cleavage pouring out of my top. That one scored a record number of comments.

I flick at my screen, so that they whirl past in quick succession.

Get a fucking job, says @Christine472.

Nice tits. That one courtesy of @KasimXXX.

Why don't you come over here and I'll stick my— I stop reading that one halfway through, flag it as inappropriate, and delete all three comments. But nothing from Lucy.

I move to the next post – me again, holding a cocktail in front of a majestic sunset – and check the comments. Nothing from Lucy, but my eyes touch on another comment from @Christine472. *White privileged bitch.*

Comments like this used to bring me to my knees, but after two years, I've become fairly hardened to them, especially from trolls like @Christine472, women – and sometimes men – who channel their envy over my seemingly perfect life into anger and resentment. They all think they know me: the pretty, successful, carefree woman in skimpy clothes posted all over my page. But she isn't real.

I think of what that little girl from Monroe would think of these pictures and all the followers. She'd probably be in heaven, drowning in the attention that was almost entirely absent in her frigid Kentucky trailer. I knew what everyone there thought I was: the kids at school, my teachers, even my own mother. *Trash.* So, I made it my mission to prove them all wrong. I holed myself up in my bedroom, away from the leering eyes of my mother's revolving door of boyfriends, and dug into my dog-eared textbooks, breaking from my studying only to sneak out to the living-room television for the six o'clock news every night.

Eventually, I graduated second in my high-school class and earned a full scholarship to college. College was my way out, until it wasn't. Until it, along with everything else in my life, crashed and burned, sending me running straight into a hell worse than the one I had tried to escape.

No, I'm not the spoiled rich brat most of my followers think I am. I'm just an expert at looking like one. Underneath it all, I'm nothing more than Lucy, with secrets and an agenda, masquerading as someone I'm not.

The thought of her brings me back to the present, and as much as it hurts, I return my focus to Instagram. When it becomes clear that she hasn't commented on any of my recent posts, I switch back over to her profile page. But no matter how much I try, I glean no new information from it. She's never been tagged in any photos, nor has she ever posted anything.

Then an idea hits me. I return to the search bar and type in #FullMoonParty. I'm instantly swarmed with results, most of which are affiliated with the bigger Full Moon Party on Koh Phangan. But I scroll through them, stopping at the first one I see that's geotagged as Koh Sang.

It's a photo, two twenty-something women, both too old to be Lucy, their heads pushed together, joined at the cheeks, each sucking from a fishbowl filled to the brim with some unnaturally blue liquid. I keep scrolling to the next post with the correct location. It's a video depicting one of the resort's staff members – a local guy I've seen around the grounds – twirling a long stick lit with fire on both ends. He dances around, deftly jumping away each time the fire nearly kisses his skin. I continue scrolling, contemplating how useful this whole approach actually is as I pass through blurry selfies and bright neon clips drowned out by dance music.

I'm about to give up when the next post shows another video as part of a carousel of images from the party. It's silent, and for the first few seconds everything in the shot is blurry, but then the image begins to come into focus. Bodies pressed up against each other, streaks of neon-painted flesh flashing through the dark sky. The screen shakes, like the person taking the video is also moving – dancing, probably.

I'm about to close out and move to the next result, labelling this as unhelpful as the previous posts, until the image zooms in shakily on one figure standing apart from the dancing crowd. When the zoom function seems to narrow in as far as it possibly can, the image still comes closer, the person recording apparently walking towards their subject. After a few seconds, my breaths start coming in quick, jagged succession.

Because I recognize the person on the film. Her eyes dart from side to side, looking for someone. Her small hands are clenched into fists, and she looks frightened, but prepared. For what exactly I can't tell.

And all at once, her eyes land on the camera. Lucy's expression is unreadable but fixed with the same intensity I saw from her the other morning as she walked past the Tiki Palms. Before either of us knew what would happen to her.

The video ends abruptly, and I sit for a minute, my mind racing. This could be the last video ever taken of Lucy. In fact, if she died at the Full Moon Party, this could be one of the final moments of her life.

Once I recover from the shock, the questions come again, an avalanche of enquiries. Why was this person following Lucy around the party, filming her, apparently monitoring her every move?

On my screen, I navigate to the profile of the person who posted the video. Their handle is @dab2000, and their profile picture is the Arsenal Football Club logo. But as my eyes trail down the screen, I find the name of the person who followed Lucy around the other night, hours, or maybe even minutes, before she died.

Daniel Ayadebo.

12

Cass

'Whoa, love. What's got into you?'

Logan stands in the doorway to the dive shop and rests his hands on my shoulders. I try to calm my breathing, to process the fact that I must have imagined the man in the black hooded sweatshirt from earlier peering in the shop window. That it's just Logan.

Even so, I twist my head back and forth, looking for the person in the black sweatshirt. 'You didn't see anyone out here, did you?'

He looks around, apparently confused. 'Nope, just me. Sorry to disappoint.'

I know he's looking for me to respond, to assure him he could never disappoint me, but I'm too distracted.

'You were gone before I woke up this morning,' Logan says. 'What have you been getting up to?'

I mumble something about meeting Brooke for breakfast, adding yet another check to the tally of lies I've told over the last few days. Logan nods, but his jaw tightens at the mention of her name. I've never understood why, but there seems to be something about Brooke that irritates him. I've noticed his eyes narrow, his back stiffen whenever she speaks.

I suspect it has something to do with her being an influencer. He's protective of this island, our home. Even though word-of-mouth is undoubtedly what keeps the Resort and Frangipani afloat, he cringes every time he sees a post or story on social media hawking Koh Sang as the 'hidden jewel of Thailand'.

'Should we go inside?' Logan suggests. 'I just saw Doug talking to Frederic in the lobby, and Greta and Neil are on their way.'

Neil, Greta, Logan and I are all crowded into the dive shop when Frederic enters, Doug trailing behind him. Frederic's been gone for over a week, evidently negotiating land rights to build a new resort in Bangkok, right on the bank of the Chao Phraya, and, truthfully, we've all been a bit thankful for the freedom – especially Doug, who seems to come into himself whenever Frederic leaves him in charge. But Frederic's presence now in the small dive shop is so overpowering, it feels like he's never left. He's a short man, but what he lacks in height, he compensates for in width, his wide belly extending far beyond his loosely belted khaki shorts. The sight of him makes each of us sit up a bit straighter.

He's gathered all his most trusted workers here, including Logan, whom Frederic still considers an honorary resort staff member, even though he gave up his position as chief bartender at the Tiki Palms over two years ago.

'Tell me what happened,' Frederic orders as he takes his seat behind the desk. His eyes lock on me.

I clear my throat, trying to ignore my racing heart as I give him my first-hand account of yesterday. Logan's hand is laced in mine as I talk, and when I get to the part about finding Lucy's body (leaving out any reference to Logan's ring), he gives it a tight squeeze.

Frederic is silent for a moment when I finish, leaning back on the stool with his hands placed over his curved stomach as if he's digesting my words, before straightening up again.

'We need to control the narrative,' he says in his normal commandeering tone, each of his vowels extended by his French accent. 'As you have all heard, the police have deemed this an accident. They found no bruises on the victim's neck.' I feel my cheeks grow hot, but Frederic doesn't bother looking in my direction. 'That is good. But it is not enough. We need to make clear to our staff that this was not our fault, and keep this accident as quiet as possible. We are sad for this girl, yes, but it was her mistake. It could have just as easily happened on Koh Phangan or Koh Samui. It could have happened anywhere. It was. Not. Our. Fault.'

We all nod in agreement, knowing we have no other option.

'We will hold a meeting. Tonight. All the staff must be there.'

'Tonight?' Neil asks. He steals a glance out the window and we follow his gaze. The afternoon sun has already begun to grow heavy, and several of the guests who returned to the beach following the storm are packing up their belongings to head back to the hotel. 'Isn't that a bit last minute?'

'No,' Frederic responds, not one to mince words. 'It is good. I have talked to the lawyers. They said we cannot let this get out. And I have to return to Bangkok. We get this out of the way as soon as possible.'

None of us has the courage to question this decision. We've all seen him fire staff for much less.

'Neil and Greta,' Frederic orders, 'you make the rounds and alert everyone that we will be meeting on the upper level of the Tiki Palms in one hour. Cass –' he tosses a piece of paper in my direction '– here is the staff list. Call everyone else who is not on duty and make sure they get here. And Logan, I need you to take care of the bar during the meeting. I cannot find Sengphet anywhere. I have no idea where he's fucked off to. Doug, you come with me to my office and help me prepare my speech.'

Without waiting for a response, Frederic is out the door, Doug riding his coat-tails and the others not far behind him.

'See you after the meeting,' Logan says, stopping to give me a kiss before he heads towards the bar, leaving me alone in the dive shop.

I pick up the landline, about to start on my assigned list of calls, when my mobile dings. It's a message from Brooke.

I open my messaging app, expecting a text, but it's a video. A grainy, faraway film of Lucy, apparently at the Full Moon Party. Knowing what comes next for her is disturbing, and my first question is immediate. *Who took this?* But before I can type it, another message from Brooke comes sharp and fast on to the screen.

Daniel posted that. He was following Lucy. He might have had something to do with her death.

I think of Daniel's unreciprocated come-ons to Lucy before the Full Moon Party. Sure, he was joking around, but maybe he was more pissed off about her rejecting him than he let on. And then I remember his muscles cutting seamlessly through the pool, as if he were breaking glass. He would surely have been capable of overpowering her petite frame.

Rather than responding to Brooke, I boot up the old

dive shop PC for the second time today and plug *Daniel Ayadebo* into Google. Almost immediately, the page returns a litany of results, but it's the one at the very top that catches my eye – a link to an article posted by a small London-based newspaper.

I click on it, and Daniel's face fills my screen. While his face is familiar, in the photo there's a darkness about him I don't recognize from our time together. His features are hardened, the scar running across his cheek prominent and severe.

My eyes dart to the top of the screen, to the article's headline. Time seems to stand still as my brain processes the words.

HACKNEY MAN CONVICTED OF SEXUAL ASSAULT FLEES COUNTRY, VIOLATES PAROLE

13

Brooke

When I leave my room, the sun has just begun to dip behind the mountains, casting the entire island in shimmering pink rays. The beauty of this place is undeniable, but today it feels different. The grey of Lucy's death seems to dull the effect of the late-afternoon sky – although I seem to be the only one who notices.

The quiet and discomfort that seemed to run through the resort earlier today has already faded as the possibilities of the night draw nearer. A low excitement buzzes among the guests wandering through the grounds, a combination of hope for further partying, mixed with the salaciousness of yesterday's news – a guaranteed icebreaker for meeting fellow backpackers. I can already hear it: Lucy's death becoming nothing more than a pickup line. *Did you hear about that girl who died? Makes you want to live every minute to the fullest, doesn't it?*

As I walk out of my room, I check my phone. I initially didn't plan to text the video to Cass, but her eagerness from earlier convinced me. She seemed so invested as we searched Lucy's room, and later as we scoured social media, but how far is she willing to go? I figured the video could serve as a test of sorts. To see just how committed

Cass is to figuring out what really happened to Lucy. But she hasn't responded.

I hadn't pegged Daniel as a killer, but what other reason could he possibly have had to follow Lucy around the other night, filming her? Cass had mentioned off-hand that Daniel had seemed into Lucy, and that Lucy hadn't reciprocated. Could that have been enough to set Daniel off? I've known guys who've been drawn to violence for less.

I think back to our conversation after they found Lucy's body, how casually he led me to the conclusion that her death wasn't an accident. Could that have been part of his plan? Trying to shift the blame to cover up what he'd done?

I stop at the medical centre first, even though I know there's little chance Daniel's still being treated. When the cheerful receptionist at the front counter confirms as much, I head towards the Tiki Palms, but a quick glance around shows me Daniel's not here.

I turn down the beach until I reach the dive shop and then double back. Frustration simmers in my gut. I'm walking aimlessly now, with no idea where he could be. I don't even know what room he's in.

But just as I reach the first plateau, I see a figure coming towards me, and as I take in his gait, I know instantly that it's him. His face is shadowed by a hooded sweatshirt despite the oppressive evening heat, and my jaw drops when I notice the colour. Black. It's the same hoodie worn by the person I saw leaving Lucy's room earlier.

The realization hits me in an instant. Not only did Daniel spend his time at the Full Moon Party following Lucy, but he was also trying to break into her room earlier today.

What did he want to find? Or cover up?

I watch his head rise slowly and, without thinking, I throw myself behind one of the massive palm trees lining the walkway a moment before his eyes pass over the spot where I'd been standing.

I had planned to confront him, but a pulse of fear lodges in my chest.

I want to see where he's going, to catch him doing something that will give me enough evidence for this to all make sense, to smash this entire story open.

I watch him walk closer to my hiding place. I expect him to turn into the Tiki Palms, but instead, he takes a sharp right, heading on to the beach road that leads away from the resort and towards Kumvit.

I take a deep breath, and when Daniel's about twenty yards away, I step out from behind the palm tree to follow him.

I stay close enough to see which way he goes, but at a safe enough distance for him not to notice.

After a while, though, as we get closer to Kumvit, Daniel veers suddenly off the main road and into an alley I've never noticed. I look towards where he's heading, but the dark trees lining this stretch block out the dim light filtering in from the sunset, darkening the path. Even so, I can make out Daniel's form walking ahead of me.

With his head covered, walking down a nondescript alley, it's clear he doesn't want to be seen.

The thought further raises my already strong suspicions, but I don't pause to consider the potential ramifications.

After a few steps, I feel a vibration against my leg, the sound exploding against my eardrums. I scramble into my shorts pocket for my phone, fumbling until I find the switch on the side that stops the vibration. I hold my breath and force myself to lift my head and look upwards.

But Daniel doesn't seem to have noticed.

Cautiously, I pull out the phone. It could be Cass, and I

want to let her know where I am, in case something goes wrong.

I quickly change the settings to lower the brightness of the screen and, with my eyes flicking up regularly to trail Daniel, I pull up the message.

It *is* from Cass, but it's not at all the message I expected.

Where are you? Found something new about Daniel. He's dangerous, stay away.

Despite myself, I feel a warmth from her message. She's concerned about my safety. But the feeling is quickly dissolved by my curiosity. What does she mean *he's dangerous*? I click on the link she included at the end of her message, and for once on this island, the internet loads mercifully quickly. I inhale sharply as I take in the headline and Daniel's mugshot.

I glance upwards to check that Daniel hasn't noticed anything is amiss – he hasn't – and move to the side of the alley so that I'm in the shadows offered by the trees, before I feverishly read the article.

HACKNEY MAN CONVICTED OF SEXUAL ASSAULT FLEES COUNTRY, VIOLATES PAROLE

Daniel Ayadebo, a 22-year-old Hackney man, has reportedly fled the UK following his recent release from HMP Pentonville. Ayadebo was convicted by a London court on charges of sexual assault and actual bodily harm two years ago, following an incident in which he reportedly attacked his former girlfriend.

Ayadebo's accuser, who wishes to remain anonymous, claimed that Ayadebo followed her home from a London nightclub, forced his way into her apartment and sexually assaulted her. Evidence presented at trial, including the accuser's physical injuries in the form of a black eye and a sprained wrist, as well as testimony from witnesses confirming that Ayadebo and his accuser had argued at the nightclub that night, led to his conviction. Ayadebo served twenty-four months of a twenty-eight-month prison sentence and was released early for good behaviour.

According to Ayadebo's probation officer, he disappeared less than a month after his release, and the belief is that he has left the country. Ayadebo's flight from London constitutes a violation of his parole and warrants his return to prison.

Readers with knowledge of Ayadebo's whereabouts are encouraged to contact us at tips@hackneysun.com.

I stare at the words for a moment. Daniel is a convicted criminal. Of sexual assault.

He's more than capable of violence.

I'm so invested in the article, my mind racing with its implications, that I don't hear it: the sudden blanket of quiet that drapes the alley.

There are no more footsteps.

I look up, but the alley in front of me stands empty. I hurry to the end of it, ignoring the unemptied waste bins and discarded palm fronds lining its sides, until I reach a passage that is so narrow it's almost hidden. I follow it for a few seconds before it deposits me on to another road just outside of Kumvit, on the opposite side of the resort. But there's no sign of Daniel.

The road is busier in this area closer to town, backpackers and locals alike gearing up for the evening. I look frantically both ways – any attempts at furtiveness long discarded – but I don't see anyone in a black hoodie.

Daniel's gone.

There's a crowd gathered at the Tiki Palms when I arrive, and I'm surprised to see Logan behind the bar. Shoes aren't allowed inside – as per Thai custom – so I slip my sandals off and leave them in a pile with the other guests'. I wait until Logan's attention is focused on a group of girls placing a large drink order, then head to the staircase in the back corner of the restaurant. It's blocked by a sign that reads FIRST FLOOR CLOSED FOR STAFF MEETING, which I deftly skirt around before tiptoeing up the stairs.

I spent ten minutes searching every side road and alley weaving through Kumvit, trying to ignore the nerves fluttering in my stomach when I imagined how exactly I would confront Daniel. But ultimately, I didn't see any sign of him. Yet, I couldn't shake the feeling that he didn't want to be found.

I headed back to the resort, reading the additional texts from Cass that had come in as I walked. She told me about the staff meeting at the Tiki Palms and asked me to meet her in the lobby, where Frederic has her manning reception. But I told her I'll meet her afterwards. There's something I need to do first.

I know the meeting's just for staff, but if there's any chance that Frederic is going to share insider information about Lucy's death – especially information that may confirm my suspicions about Daniel – I have to know. My hands are still shaking with the adrenaline of following Daniel as I walk up the stairs, but I can't deny the buzz that vibrates just beneath it. The excitement of knowing I'm getting closer to the truth.

I reach the upper level to find that the meeting hasn't started. A cloud of chatter, conversations mingling in Thai and English, drapes the room, giving me the cover I need to sneak in and stand at the back, unseen.

I look over the crowd of thirty or so staff members seated in fold-up chairs in neat little rows. Greta is at the very front, apparently helping Frederic with his notes, but despite looking for them, I don't spot any of the other Permanents.

'*Sawadee krap, bonsoir*, good evening,' Frederic's voice bellows from the front of the room, and the conversations immediately cease.

I've only met Frederic once, on one of my first days on the island. I had sought him out, hoping to form some type of collaboration with the resort to help fund my stay here. At the front desk I'd been forced to schedule a meeting with him, and had to wait several days for him to become available. 'He's a busy man,' all the receptionists assured me.

'It's good of you to ask,' he said, once I finally had his attention, his fleshy face observing me from across his desk. 'But I am not interested in further advertising.' He rested his elbows on the desk and intertwined his piggish fingers. I couldn't help but notice how long his fingernails were, feminine but with a visible crescent of dirt under a few of them.

'It's just,' I started, hating how weak my voice sounded in the wake of his sharp rejection, 'I have more than fifty thousand followers and have collaborated with hotels, agencies and companies throughout Eastern Europe. I'm sure any of them would be happy to pass on a great recommend—'

'I will stop you there,' he said, holding up one meaty hand, his French accent thick and contemptuous. His eyes were far too small for his face, and his lips were a disturbing shade of purple, as if he'd been cut off from oxygen for too long. 'Do you know how many "travel influencers" –' he raised his swollen fingers in air quotes to show his disdain for my profession '– come through my resort every day?' He didn't wait for me to answer. 'No offence,' he said, drawing my attention to just how much offence he intended, 'but I could choose from influencers with far more experience and hundreds of thousands more followers than you have.'

He paused, as if waiting for me to react. Whether he wanted tears or anger was unclear, but I refused to give it to him. I didn't let my fear at the realization that there was little way I could fund my stay on Koh Sang without his help reach my face.

Instead, I plastered on the expression I typically reserve for TikToks and Instagram lives – my lips turned up softly, my chin tipped forward, so that I peer out from beneath my lashes.

'Terrible news about that woman's fall from Khrum Yai a few days ago . . .' I let my words hang between us for a moment before delivering the sucker punch. 'I was thinking of doing a few sentimental posts about it. My followers love that sort of thing. She was staying at your resort, wasn't she?'

To his credit, Frederic didn't flinch, but I spotted a flash in his eyes – not panic, as I expected, but something else. I shivered as I realized what it was. Kinship.

'Fine,' he said eventually, sighing. 'If you insist on receiving handouts for posting a couple of photos of yourself, then I suppose I can give you a discount, but this will require you to do real work, which I am sure you are not familiar with.'

Frederic spent nearly an hour after that iterating and reiterating all the posts and videos and highlights that were required of me in exchange for the room discount – far more than had ever been required by any other hotel I've promoted. The meeting ended with him threatening to revoke my discount should my posts fail to improve resort traffic. Through it all, I forced myself to wear a polite, grateful smile, while my insides burned with shame and rage.

Those same emotions flare again as I watch him address the crowd in front of me, his usual condescension replaced by a tone apparently attempting to mimic sincerity. 'By now, many of you have heard that we have lost one of our own. A special guest who we only welcomed to the Koh Sang Dive Resort three days ago. Her name was Lucy Dupin.'

A murmur rises from the staff members at the sound of her name, but Frederic continues, undeterred.

'On Friday night, at the Full Moon Party, an event that is supposed to inspire friendships, new beginnings and connection, Lucy experienced a horrible accident. She entered the ocean for a late-night swim, which you all know we regularly warn against here at the resort.' I can't think of any verbal or written warnings given to guests about the dangers of late-night swimming, but Frederic steamrolls on. 'Given the dangerous current in the water, and Lucy's intoxicated state, the police have confirmed that she drowned a short distance from the beach.

'We have also received additional news from the police just a few moments ago.' He pauses, savouring the suspense he's creating, and I want to scream. 'They informed us that they received test results which indicate Lucy was under the influence of alcohol and MDMA at the time of her death.'

The news isn't surprising – if the police did alter the autopsy results, as I certainly suspect they did, what was to stop them from falsifying some test results? But still, I find myself inhaling sharply. I think I see the whisper of a smirk on Frederic's lips. Of course, this is perfect for him. If Lucy was on drugs, it's even easier for him to paint this all as her fault.

'We are so sad to learn that Ms Dupin lost her life for such a mundane reason,' Frederic continues, quickly contorting his face into an expression that distantly resembles sympathy. 'She was a beautiful woman, with a world of possibilities ahead of her, and we here at the Koh Sang Dive Resort are so honoured that we got to know her, if only for a few short days.'

The superficiality of his words rings hollow throughout the room, and disgust rises in my throat.

'This is a tragic accident, but it is something that could have happened at any resort, on any island, anywhere in the world. No one here at the dive resort is culpable for Ms Dupin's regrettable decisions. We want to make that absolutely clear. As I have said, this was an *accident*.' He stresses the last word. 'Accordingly, we would like you all to refrain from discussing this in the presence of guests. We do not want this unfortunate news to detract from anyone's experience at our resort.

'With that in mind,' he continues, lifting a piece of paper in one hand, while using the other to pull a pair of reading glasses from his pocket, 'we have created a response for you to politely give to any guest who lodges such an enquiry. I ask that you please now refer to the handout under your seat.' He pauses, as the commotion of thirty people bending down and resituating themselves fills the room. 'Now, if we could all read this together . . .'

The voices speak in unison, like a congregation praying.

Thirty mouths move as the monotone speech fills every corner of the room. 'Ms Dupin suffered an unfortunate accident that could have been easily avoided should she have acted with more caution . . .'

Suddenly I can't take it any more. The canned response, the victim blaming. I need to be somewhere else, not listening to this bullshit. I head back down the stairs, not bothering to hide from view, knowing everyone is far too transfixed on their handouts to notice my departure.

I exhale deeply once I'm back on the ground floor of the Tiki Palms. I expect to feel better now that I'm removed from Frederic and his insincere bullshit, but after the stuffy silence upstairs, the din of the night-time bar crowd seems far too loud.

I'm about to head out on to the path that leads to the rest of the resort when I feel someone watching me. I turn, scanning the room, noting that Sengphet is back in his rightful place behind the bar, with Logan nowhere to be seen. I continue, until I spot someone in the far corner of the restaurant, removed from the rest of the crowd. She looks young, possibly still a teenager. Her thick, black hair is pulled back in a tight ponytail, and her dark, almond-shaped eyes are glued on me.

The intensity of her stare is jolting, and I jerk my eyes away. But when I look back a moment later, she's still looking at me pointedly. Perhaps it's the reminder of how Lucy stared at me on the day she died, of how I let her down, how badly I failed. Whatever it is, the emotion propels me towards this girl in a flurry of frustration. The adrenaline from earlier continues to pulse through my veins, and after everything that has happened today, I'm ready for a confrontation, to ask this girl what it is she wants. But at that moment, a group of guests chattering loudly in German pile into the bar, stepping in front of me. I try to move around them, but each time I do, another seems to pop up in my way. By the time I get past them, there's no longer any sign of the girl.

I try to shake it off, the uneasiness her stare has left in my gut, and turn back, slipping on my sandals and heading out of the restaurant.

Without the air circulating from the ceiling fans of the Tiki Palms, the night is heavy and humid. The waves crash against the beach, complementing the sounds of upbeat music wafting over from Kumvit. I breathe in deeply, forcing the salty air into my lungs. I start up the path away from the beach, but as I get closer to the Coral Bungalows, I can't quite bring myself to go back to my solitary room. I need to walk. To think through what I should do next. To figure out how to tell this story. To find a way to get justice for Lucy.

I veer off from the path, taking the beach road towards Kumvit, the exact route I travelled as I followed Daniel. I walk for a few minutes until I reach the alley where I last saw him. Instinctively I peer down it, expecting to see nothing but the bins and palm fronds from earlier.

But as I do, something further down catches my attention. There's a bundle lying against one of the bins, next to a puddle of water. A leaking rubbish bag left by someone who couldn't be bothered to throw it away properly, maybe? I rack my brain, but I can't remember it being there earlier. And something about the bundle, the length of it, draws me in. Before I can fully understand why, I'm walking towards it.

I hold my breath, blocking out the sweetly sour stench of rubbish that I was too distracted to notice earlier. As I walk further, the shadows grow darker, the streetlights from the main road doing little to illuminate this alley. No restaurants, no bars. Just abandoned trash and a rarely used shortcut.

But even without the lights, as my eyes adjust and I come closer, I can tell I was wrong about the puddle of water. It's not clear, but a dark, matte colour. I peer at it as I get closer. It's so dark, it's almost black. And there's a new smell now, something metallic in the undertones of the rubbish.

I draw close enough that I'm inches away. And as the realization starts to click, I shift my gaze to the object splayed out next to the puddle. The thing I mistook for a bag of rubbish is clearly anything but.

'Hello?' I ask quietly, the street swallowing the fear of my word and shouting it back to me in echoes.

As if my body is moving of its own volition, my knees bend, so that I'm crouched next to the object. I rest my fingers on it, pushing slightly. I pull away, the tips of my fingers damp and sticky.

As I do, the bundle slides, no longer supported by the bin, and topples on to its side. My breath catches in my throat with the shock of what I had suspected but hoped wasn't true.

This is a body.

As my eyes begin to adjust to take in its features, I observe the bright red line carved into the person's neck, droplets of blood clinging to it, seeking to join those that have already formed the puddle on the floor. I force my eyes upwards, to the pink scar on his cheek, to the wide, near-black eyes that stare out into nothing, to the shaved head.

The familiar features of the man I spoke with on the beach yesterday, the man I followed no less than an hour ago through this same street.

Daniel.

14

Cass

A sound, barely audible, slides through the night just after the meeting ends, as I head towards the Tiki Palms, fighting the current of staff members leaving the restaurant to head back to their posts.

Instantly, everything seems to speed up, as if someone's turned the world to fast forward. I hear one woman yell, 'That was a scream!' Guests and staff whip by in a blur, everyone apparently rerouted towards the source of the noise, eager to be the first to discover what's happened. People press around me, and I'm swept up in the wave until I feel the rough grip of fingers on my arm.

'Cass, come with me,' I hear Logan say, his mouth close to my ear.

I follow blindly, hearing Doug's faraway voice rise above the din.

'Everyone, please stay calm,' he yells into the crowd, his tone authoritative. 'Guests, we need you all to return to your rooms. Staff, please go back to your assigned posts.'

Logan leads me in the opposite direction of the rush. It's only once we're inside that I realize where we are. The dive shop.

Despite the sticky heat of the night, my skin is cold, the

hairs on my arms raised on end. Logan manages to find a blanket from the recesses of the shop and drapes it over my shoulders before joining me on the bench.

The door opens and Neil enters, followed by Greta, their faces stony.

'What's happened?' Logan demands.

'I don't know,' Greta responds, her voice faraway.

'It looks like something happened in one of the alleys off the beach road. Someone's hurt out there. I couldn't get close enough to tell who,' Neil explains.

The door opens again. This time it's Brooke and Doug, his arm holding her elbow. The unlikely pairing makes me pause until I notice her wide eyes, her mussed ponytail.

Logan and I abruptly stand, and Doug guides Brooke to sit down on the bench.

'It's Daniel,' she says. 'I found him in one of the alleys off the beach road. Someone slit his throat. He bled out. He's – he's dead.'

'But . . . he can't be,' I insist. It takes me a moment to realize I've spoken out loud, and I blush as I feel the room's eyes turn towards me. 'I mean, he killed her. Lucy.'

Neil, Greta and Logan all exchange glances.

'Cass, Lucy's death was an accident.' Logan speaks to me as if I'm a child who's misunderstood, and my frustration simmers.

'No,' I say more forcefully than I intended. I start to tell them about the article I found, but then the door opens yet again, letting a rush of humid air into the shop and interrupting me mid-sentence. Everyone falls silent when we see who it is.

'What a fucking nightmare,' Frederic mumbles, shaking his head. 'There's a whole mess down the beach road. Who did this?' He looks pointedly around the shop, apparently waiting for one of us to confess, but then barrels ahead, his voice rising. 'I can see it now, people calling us Death Island or something like that. The resort can't survive this. *I* can't survive it!'

Frederic's head whips around, searching for someone to blame. The only sound is our nervous breathing, until suddenly the shriek of distant sirens cuts through the air.

'*Merde*. I thought we had more time.' Frederic wrings his hands. I try to remember the last time I saw him nervous, but I draw a blank. 'I need to talk to the police. You figure out how we explain all this. And,' he says jutting his chin in Brooke's direction, 'someone get her out of here.'

As soon as Frederic is gone, Neil moves across the dive shop to stand next to Brooke, resting his hand on her shoulder.

'Brooke just had a huge shock,' he says to the rest of us. 'She should stay here for now until she's had a chance to recover.'

I steal a glance at Doug, expecting him to protest, to enforce Frederic's mandate, but he flicks his eyes towards the floor, avoiding Neil's pointed stare. Neil's proposal is met with a round of hesitant nods. Brooke shifts her gaze up to Neil, and I notice something pass between the two of them.

We sit in silence for a moment, our eyes on the shop's windows, our minds elsewhere.

'Look, are we sure Daniel was murdered? Could it have been an accident?' Doug asks finally, and it's difficult to ignore the pleading hope in his tone. I know what he's thinking; we all do. If Daniel was murdered, the resort is going to suffer. Two deaths in one week – three in a month if you count the woman who fell from Khrum Yai – is too much for the island's reputation to survive.

'Not unless he just happened to fall on a knife in a back alley,' Brooke responds monotonously.

Her response quickly shuts down that line of questioning.

'So,' she continues, her voice now clear, lacking any indication of the shock she was in moments before. 'Should we admit there's something happening here?'

Her question is met with silence.

'I mean, it could still be a coincidence,' Logan finally says, as if he's thinking out loud.

'Really?' Brooke asks.

'Yeah. There's nothing to suggest Daniel's death is tied to Lucy's, or the woman who fell from Khrum Yai . . .' He pauses as if he's trying to remember her name, and my frustration from earlier boils.

'Jacinta. Her name was Jacinta,' Brooke supplies stonily.

'Right,' Logan continues. 'I mean, Lucy and . . . Jacinta's deaths were both accidents. Maybe Daniel's is something different.' He looks around as if inviting us to back him up.

Greta takes him up on it. 'True. I mean if there's a killer out there responsible for Jacinta, Lucy and Daniel, wouldn't all three of their deaths look like accidents?'

I swallow nervously, remembering the bruises on Lucy's neck. But now doesn't seem like the time to remind them of this.

'Or the person who killed Daniel couldn't make his murder look like an accident,' Brooke suggests, undeterred. 'Maybe they ran out of time and that's why they left his body in the street.'

Brooke doesn't seem to understand what Greta and Logan are doing, but the rest of us do. They're clinging to any possibility that may save us from the repercussions of these deaths. If Daniel's murder is unrelated, maybe the resort can survive this. We need it to survive. Our lives are here, and without the resort and the tourism stemming from it, we have no way to live on the island. We would have to leave. We would lose everything

Doug acts as though he doesn't hear Brooke. 'Cass said Daniel's got a criminal record, right, that he's skipping parole. I reckon he just got wrapped up in some shady shit here. And . . .' He pauses for a moment, then pulls out his phone and taps at it, his face creased in thought. 'Remember that guy . . . what was his name? The one who was found with his throat slit a few years back in some alley over on Koh Samui. I can't find the story, but didn't the police reckon it was the Thai mafia, that he was running drugs for them?' He gives up on his phone but doesn't bother to wait for a response. 'I'm sure that was it. Maybe it's the same deal with Daniel. He looks the type to get caught up in drug dealing.'

Brooke turns on him sharply. 'So, we're going to throw some racial profiling into the mix on top of everything else?' Again, I can hear a different inflection creep into her voice, a somewhat familiar tone that scratches at my neck. But before I can dive into the thought further, Doug retorts.

'That's not what I meant, and you know it.' A flush creeps up the sides of his neck, and I cringe. I know what he gets like when he feels backed into a corner. 'Frederic was right, you shouldn't be here.' He points his phone at Brooke. 'You're not a staff member, you're not one of us. You'll probably be posting about this shit all over Instagram any minute.' His voice rises several octaves in an apparent impression of her. '*Koh Sang has perfect weather and fantastic cocktails, but they should really do something about the murder issue. It, like, dulls the whole vibe.*'

'Hey,' Neil says, his voice firm. 'Look, we're all stressed. Arguing with each other isn't going to help. Besides, we need to look at the facts. Three deaths in a month – one clearly a murder – is a bit too much of a coincidence.'

Everyone falls quiet as Neil's point sinks in.

'It just doesn't make sense,' I say, watching heads turn in my direction. 'I meant it. I really think Daniel had something to do with Lucy's death. I think . . . he killed her.'

Five sets of eyes stare at me blankly. I want to explain, to tell everyone the evidence that's led me to this logical conclusion, but it all suddenly seems fuzzy. Nothing makes sense any more. Every event of the past forty-eight hours is like a different puzzle piece and none of them fit together.

'Cass is right,' Brooke says, after what feels like an endless wait. 'Daniel was following Lucy during the Full Moon Party. He even took a video of her and was stupid enough to post it on Instagram.'

The news seems to come as a shock to everyone else. No one says anything, and Brooke continues. 'And I saw him, about an hour ago heading into Kumvit in the same alley where . . . where I found him later. He disappeared pretty quickly, as if he knew he was being followed . . .'

She trails off, leaving us with even more questions.

'Look, there's no question Daniel was murdered,' Brooke continues. 'You didn't see it. He had a huge gash in his neck and blood dripping everywhere.' Her throat catches on the last word, but she recovers. 'I saw Daniel alive around seven forty-five over near Kumvit. The last ferry out of Koh Sang is at eight p.m., and it takes about fifteen minutes to get to the ferry from the resort.'

The implication slowly dawns on us, but she says it anyway.

'So, the person who killed him is most likely still on the island.'

Hearing Brooke say it out loud feels like a spider crawling up my spine, and an uncomfortable silence falls on the group as we all look at each other.

The island is small, and the resort is the only hotel. Because of the Full Moon Party on Koh Phangan, we have less than seventy guests currently staying here. That, plus the island locals, doesn't leave us many options to choose from.

'So, I guess the first thing we should do is figure out where we all were when Daniel died,' Brooke says, capitalizing on the group's attention. 'You know, rule us out as suspects, so we can start figuring out who actually did this.'

'Oh, great, so now *we're* responsible?' The flush in Doug's neck is no longer creeping. It's fully arrived, a deep maroon burying itself in the apples of his cheeks. 'That's ripe coming from you, Brooke. We've lived here for years. You come to our home and you start pointing fingers at—'

'Doug, she's right,' Neil interjects. 'Frederic told us to fix this. Finding out who killed Daniel should be our first priority. Let's just get this part over with, and then we can start moving on to real suspects.'

'Well,' Greta says, acquiescing, 'it's an easy question, really. I was at the staff meeting helping Frederic. Logan was handling the Tiki Palms, Frederic had sent Neil and Doug to sort out paperwork in the dive shop, and Cass was in charge of manning reception during the meeting. Frederic had everyone on duty.'

'And what about Friday night?' Brooke asks, not ready to give in. 'Where did everyone go during and after the Full Moon Party? When Lucy was murdered?'

'Died,' Greta corrects. 'We don't know she was murdered.'

Brooke rolls her eyes, but apparently she's not interested

in resuming this argument. 'I'll start. I wasn't feeling great at the party. I needed some space, so I took a walk. Away from the group, down the beach. I stayed for a while, and then I went home.'

No one responds for a moment, everyone waiting for someone else to take the lead. Brooke sighs impatiently.

'Fine, I'll go,' Doug says. 'I don't really know what you want me to say. It was a party. I was partying. Had a few drinks, talked to heaps of guests. I was pretty loose, I guess. It's not a fucking crime, is it?'

'Yeah, me too,' Neil joins.

'Same,' Greta says.

I notice Logan has been quiet beside me. I rack my brain, trying to remember the end of that night, how I got home. Everything that happened after we left Frangipani is still fuzzy, the Xanax and alcohol erasing most of it. I can't recall anything other than those few strips of memory – the thumping bass, the sand between my toes, that unknown woman saying, 'No, no, no.' The regret hits me once more. How could I have been so stupid?

But I suddenly remember something from my conversation with Logan last night. I was so caught up in my suspicions that I didn't catch it when he explained how he lost his ring, but the words leap out at me now. *When I got home, I found the chain wrapped up in my shirt, but no ring.* When *I* got home. Not when *we* did.

Did Logan come home without me? If so, what was I doing? Was I there when Lucy died?

An uneasiness settles on me as I think through what this means.

'Cass,' Brooke nudges, and I remember I'm supposed to be answering her question.

'We came home together,' Logan says, saving me.

'Around eleven thirty, I think.' If I didn't know better, I would be confident Logan was telling the truth. But I notice the skin around his eyebrows crinkle slightly and he squeezes my hand.

'And what time did the rest of you go home?' Brooke asks.

'Around eleven or something like that,' Greta says. 'I had to teach a yoga class in the morning.'

'I don't know, Detective,' Doug says mockingly. 'I wasn't monitoring for a curfew. Probably around midnight.'

Neil nods. 'Yeah, same. I had to get up early to help Cass with the divers.'

The rest of them keep talking, but I'm barely listening. I'm starting to understand the enormity of what this means. The lapses in my memory from that night, the questions I can't answer.

What exactly *was* I doing when Lucy died?

15

Brooke

I make sure I'm gone from the dive shop before Frederic gets back. The last thing I need now is one of his brutal tongue lashings. It's only once I'm outside, breathing the night air, that I realize how claustrophobic it felt in there, so many bodies in such a tight room, compounded by the lies pressing in on us from every direction.

I overstepped, I know that. I was too forceful with the Permanents, too eager. I forgot any efforts at trying to fit in with them, fully distracted by getting to the bottom of Lucy's story.

But I'm not an idiot. I could see through everyone's apparent alibis for the Full Moon Party as soon as they opened their mouths. I watched their fidgeting hands, the flick of their eyes as they tried to recount the night of the party. Everyone just happened to be separated, with no one to back up their story.

And then there's Cass. I could tell how she blanked when I asked what time she got home that night. I'm sure she thinks that Logan's cover for her was artful, but the scrunch of his eyebrows when he said they left together couldn't have been a more obvious tell.

Once I'm in the safety of my room with the door shut

firmly behind me, I take a deep breath, savouring the quiet.

Slowly, I reach into my back pocket, as if whatever's in there might bite me. I consider wrapping my hand in a towel to prevent fingerprints, but it's too late for that.

Instead, I wrap my fingers around the object and pull it out.

Daniel's phone.

The scream erupted out of me when I realized I was standing over Daniel's body in the alley. But as I heard the footsteps rushing towards me down the beach road, I had a moment of clarity. I had seen where Daniel had kept his phone when I was following him: in the front pocket of his jeans; he occasionally took it out to check the screen as he walked. So, I reached into his front pocket, trying not to cringe as my hand brushed against his cold jeans. As soon as my fingertips made contact with the hard plastic, I felt a wave of relief. For whatever reason, whoever killed Daniel hadn't taken his phone. I yanked it out, stuffing the phone into my own pocket, just as I heard the footsteps of eager onlookers round the corner.

Because if Daniel didn't kill Lucy, then maybe he knew who did.

There's something there, I know it.

And one thing's for sure. I'll never know the truth if I leave the investigation up to Frederic and the corrupt Koh Sang police he keeps in his pocket.

I look at Daniel's phone now. I pause for a moment, trying to appreciate the solemnity of holding a dead man's phone in my hands before pressing the side button and bringing the screen to life.

'Oh, Daniel,' I mutter with a mix of relief and surprise as I see the home screen. No keypad appears for me to enter a password. Daniel had to be the only person under forty who didn't lock his phone. The realization strikes me with a stab of pity. Daniel would only have failed to lock his phone if he had nothing on it to hide.

I click the icon for his text messaging app and start scrolling. Names fly by on the screen – Sofia, Mum, Rod, Hamn – and I pause briefly to read the first few bits of each conversation. Everything is mundane: British-sounding slang to Rod and Hamn, a longer text to Mum, apologizing and telling her he's safe and not to worry, and a much sexier message to Sofia, which I click out of as quickly as possible.

Back on the home page, I search through the sea of apps on his screen for the green WhatsApp icon until I finally locate it.

The first message at the top of the screen is from an unknown number, identified only by a generic grey icon. The time stamp shows that the most recent message was delivered at six twenty-four p.m. I hold my breath as the message chain loads, expecting a lengthy conversation, or at least a few back-and-forth messages.

But there's only one.

I know who you are. Meet me at 7.50 or my next
message is to the UK Parole Board.

It ends with a precise location, which I realize with a jolt is the alley I followed Daniel down and where I later found him dead. And the confrontation happened only about ten minutes before the staff meeting started. Which means that when I saw Daniel, he was on his way to meet whoever sent this message. He must have noticed me following him and hidden until he could re-enter the alley unseen.

I read the message again. Then for a third time.

Whoever sent this message was willing to blackmail Daniel into meeting them. But why?

My brain whirs, images from the video of Lucy that Daniel posted on Instagram clouding my mind. And then it clicks.

If Daniel really had been following Lucy that night, then maybe he saw who killed her. Maybe he even caught it on camera.

I fumble with the phone, almost dropping it from my hands as I hurriedly navigate to Daniel's photo gallery. As I click on it, the screen is immediately flooded with thumbnail images, all blurry and streaked with neon lights. I start by enlarging the most recent image, a barely visible photo of the beach. I swipe my finger right, and now I'm looking at a grainy selfie, the same neon paint striped across Daniel's cheeks that I saw the other night, his arm looped around a twenty-something woman with a vibrant red-dye job. The five or so photos that follow are largely the same, shots of Daniel and this red-haired woman staring at the camera at different angles, the woman's lips pursed in some, open and smiling in others. I begin to swipe more rapidly, through photos of nothing more than sand or feet, clearly taken by drunken accident. But after a few more swipes, my finger freezes, hovering a few centimetres above the screen.

It's a video, the frame paused on a wide-set image of the beach. I recognize it immediately. It's the same frame that started the video Daniel had posted on Instagram.

But unlike the version on Instagram, this video has sound.

I press my thumb down, and the video comes to life. I've watched it so many times on Instagram since this afternoon that I could narrate as the video progresses. The only difference is Daniel's voice yelling from behind the camera. 'Oi, oi,' he shouts repeatedly to Lucy, despite her attempts to ignore him. 'Lucy, love, come dance!'

A weak bass comes tinnily through the phone's speaker, serving as a soundtrack to the initial blurry scenes of the dancefloor. But everything else about the video stays the same: Daniel, behind the camera, making his way through the dancefloor until he spots Lucy on the outskirts of the party. The camera lens zooming in, closer and closer, until she takes up the entire screen, her eyes darting nervously, her fingers clenched into fists. I brace myself for the jarring finale to the video, when Lucy stares straight at the camera.

And then it happens, her gaze fixates intensely on the screen. I wait for the video to end, like it did in the version I watched on Instagram, but this time it doesn't.

'Come on, Lucy. You know you want to!' Daniel yells through the speaker.

Lucy continues to stare at the screen for another moment or two, but then gives Daniel a weak smile and looks away.

'Oi, your loss then,' Daniel grumbles.

But I pause, freezing the screen on Lucy looking off into the distance, and check the timing on the video below. There are twenty-five seconds left.

I stare at it for a moment, puzzled, before it clicks. Instagram must have cut off part of the video Daniel posted.

Cautiously, I start it again and the video continues, the screen flipping upside down, making a bouncy retreat, as if Daniel began walking away and forgot he was recording. I flip the phone to follow along, and despite the distance, I can still see Lucy's head moving back and forth as she searches for something unknown, ignoring Daniel and his camera. And then she stops, looking at something off-screen.

I inhale sharply, holding my breath tightly in my chest as she appears to take a step towards whatever – or whomever – she sees. The camera follows her, zooming out to show her talking to someone.

The person is facing away from the camera, and the video shows only their back, but it's clear based on the broad shoulders and the matted hair that it's a man. He's nearly twice Lucy's height, and I watch, eyes wide, muscles taut, as he bends to whisper in her ear. When he separates from her, returning to his normal height, the video trains again on Lucy, a small smile on her lips, her head nodding in agreement.

I keep watching as he hands Lucy a drink, from which she obediently takes a sip. Then, he turns, and Lucy grabs his hand. He begins to lead her away from the dancefloor, towards the water, and as he does, he looks around him, as if making sure no one is watching, or following them.

'Aw, fuck it, the damn video's still go—' Daniel mutters.

And with that final commentary, the video ends.

I stare at the screen, my eyes glued to that final image, the man looking just beyond the camera, until a cough wracks my entire body. I'd forgotten I'd been holding my breath this whole time.

Quickly, I drag my finger along the bottom of the screen, rewinding the video several seconds, watching again as the man's face comes into focus. The man who pulled Lucy away from the party during which she apparently died. The man who could have been the last person to see her alive.

I register the matted hair, the yellow T-shirt I saw him wearing on Friday night, the crooked nose.

Doug.

16

Monday

Cass

Logan is still sleeping when I wake up the next morning, but for once, he doesn't seem peaceful. His forehead is scrunched, and one side of his lip keeps twitching.

We haven't talked since he covered for me at the dive shop last night. Once Frederic returned, Logan had to go straight to Frangipani to open the bar. Turns out the guests weren't going to let something as mundane as murder stop them from partying.

When I got home last night, I sat out on the patio for a while, thinking, an activity I continued in bed for several more hours, staring up at the ceiling, the thoughts and memories crashing against each other in my head.

The more I thought, the more I spiralled. Could all of this be connected? Could the killer be the same person who left that threatening note on my doorstep? Could I be next?

But one question stood out above the others: who is behind this?

I thought of Brooke's ardent questioning, her insistence

that we all clear our names. Like Greta told her, all of us were on duty during the staff meeting, which means none of us could have been behind Daniel's murder. So who else could it be?

I compiled a mental list of the other staff members, but I've never seen any of them even side-eye a guest, let alone do something that would give me reason to suspect they'd murdered one.

Which leaves either the locals or the resort guests.

My thoughts landed on a memory from the other day. The first floor of the Tiki Palms, the heat heavy around me, the sharp grip of fingers around my biceps.

Ariel.

I thought of how he flipped a switch from calm to violent in a matter of seconds. That horrible premonition he shouted.

It is not safe here. You are not safe.

Maybe it wasn't a premonition, but a warning.

I recalled Tamar's explanation. *My husband, he is not well.*

Ariel is sick. Sick enough to kill?

Ariel knew Lucy and Daniel from his dive class. To my knowledge he doesn't have an alibi for Friday night – he never admitted nor denied being at the Full Moon Party – or for the time of the staff meeting.

Ariel could be the killer. The thought hit me with a panic, an itch coursing just under my skin. I was overcome with restlessness, a need to act. But even in my frazzled state, I knew I couldn't confront him; Frederic would fire me in an instant if I stormed a guest's room in the middle of the night and accused him of murder.

Eventually, I came up with a plan. I would talk to them, find out whether Ariel really was sick, making sure to slide in questions that would help me determine whether he killed Lucy and Daniel.

After exhausting that train of thought, I shifted gears, my mind straying to the Full Moon Party. As hard as I tried to remember what happened – and I tried, squeezing my eyes as tightly as I could, retracing my steps after leaving Frangipani – even going so far as to google how to self-hypnotize to recover memories, which turned out to be a huge waste of time – that night remains elusive. The only clear recollection I have is of that woman's voice, repeating that one word over and over. 'No, no, no!'

I was still trying to remember when I heard Logan get home in the early-morning hours. I didn't know what exactly to tell him, how to explain why I didn't remember what happened that night. He saw what I was drinking, he would know I hadn't drunk enough to black out. And then I'd have two choices: come clean about the Xanax and everything that led to it or continue to weave more lies. Any way I looked at it, either option would end in the same result: Logan eventually leaving me.

I've told Logan small things about my past, breadcrumbs that carry just enough detail to hold the truth together. He knows my mother died of cancer when I was thirteen and Robin was ten. He knows about Robin and how close we were and how I lost both her and my father in an accident while I was in college. He's always assumed that was a car accident – the same one that gave me the scar above my heart – and I've gone along with it.

The past is just something we've never felt the need to talk about extensively. I know just as little of his history, only bits and pieces of his former life that have leaked out over the years. Like how his blue-collar family back in

Aberdeen had owned a struggling construction company and how it seemed like every decision he made in that town would lead to one option: spending his life working for the family company, married to a local girl he didn't love and would eventually come to despise. How he and his brother, Alec, used to daydream about getting out and seeing the world. And finally, the real reason why Logan left Scotland: when he found Alec dead in the passenger seat of his beat-up Peugeot parked in the family garage. The car had been running all night, the garage door tightly closed.

He lost someone he loved deeply, just as I did. It was a shared bond that no one else could understand. Even if I hadn't been entirely truthful about how that loss had happened.

I can't keep lying to him, I know that. At some point, I'm going to slip up and this house of cards is going to collapse, trapping me in the rubble. Tears prick at my eyes as I imagine what would happen. I'd have to move out, find somewhere else to live. If the others found out who I really am, no one on this island would want to take me in. I'd be forced to move somewhere new and start from scratch. Again. Without Logan and completely alone.

I can't do that.

So, I pretended to be asleep when Logan came in last night, impersonating the deep breathing he's now doing next to me. And in a similarly cowardly fashion, I'll leave before he wakes up. It's Monday, so I'm due to meet Greta for her morning yoga class, which we'll follow up with coffee, per tradition – although this week we certainly have more pressing things than usual to talk about.

I check my phone for updates on the investigation into Daniel's murder, but Doug hasn't texted. So, I slip out of bed as silently as I can, gather up my exercise clothes and my bag, making sure to remove one pill from the Xanax box before shoving it as far back as it will go in the drawer of my bedside table, and head out.

As I open our front door I'm hit by the weight of the morning's humidity, already clinging to my skin like a suffocating blanket. I try to be as quiet as possible as I lock the door behind me, but between the lack of sleep and the adrenaline still coursing through my veins, my hand trembles just enough for me to drop the key on to the doorstep.

'Shit,' I mumble under my breath.

It's as I'm reaching for the key that I see it.

An envelope, identical to the one I received a few days ago. As with the first envelope, this one bears my name, but it doesn't say *Cass*. Instead, *Meghan* is written in perfect typeface.

At first I stand there, stock-still, unable to look away from it. The name triggers a chorus of – mostly unwelcome – memories. I feel like I'm falling, and I have to reach my hand out to the side of the house to keep me upright.

Slowly, I put down everything and pick up the envelope using both shaking hands. An eternity passes as I unstick the label.

I know what it must be before I open it, but still my breath catches as I unfold the sheet of printer paper.

Another newspaper article.

It's the headline that first grabs my attention.

THE HUDSON MASSACRE KILLER: WHO IS SHE REALLY?

I don't bother reading the text filling the lines beneath it.

Instead, my eyes skirt down to the bottom of the page, where another personalized note lies waiting, in that red-inked handwriting I've come to know so well, as dark as blood.

This is all your fault, Meghan. And everyone is going to know the truth, soon.

17

Brooke

It's early, barely seven, and the beach is quiet. All the guests are probably still in their rooms, still sleeping off their hangovers from last night. The beach road looked empty when I passed, caution tape still looped around it near the alley where I found Daniel.

I look out now at the turquoise water stretching to eternity. Its beauty seems almost obscene considering everything that's happened in the last two days. I think of the greyness from that hospital a few years ago, the colour that still haunts me. I play distractedly with my bracelets, an amalgamation of vivid hues that intentionally could not be more different from that stale greyness, now forming an armour around my wrists, protecting me from those memories. Some of them are intricate, jade beads line up against rose-coloured metals and silver bangles that I picked up for cheap at a Bosnian market that are just shy of tarnishing. Others are much more simple, some nothing more than a loop of string, like the one given to me by a young Romanian girl. I'd stumbled upon her in a busy Bucharest street, crying over a spilled ice cream cone. After I bought her another one, she looped the bracelet from her own wrist on to mine and threw her arms around me in thanks. Now, my finger clutches that bracelet specifically, as if its touch could somehow transport me back to that moment and away from all this.

My mind has been racing all night, ever since I saw the end of Daniel's video. I watched it over and over, for hours, training my eyes on that final scene to make sure I was right, to confirm the face I thought I was seeing. I watched it until there was absolutely no question.

It was Doug.

The possibilities began to snowball as soon as I saw it. After he led Lucy away from the dancefloor, maybe he came on to her. Maybe she fought back, and he got angry. Or maybe he lured her away with the intent to kill her. Or maybe it was all more innocent than that and he just hooked up with her.

But whatever happened, Doug knows more than he's letting on.

I'm not surprised that Doug's involved. Even with Logan's coldness, Doug is the Permanent I've been most turned off by. He's always creeped me out, the way he hits on every female guest without fail, and regales everyone else with his successes at getting them into bed. I should have trusted my instincts.

I'll admit I spiralled a bit, the rage in my stomach growing stronger with each view of the video. So, I went for a short walk early this morning, to clear my head, remember why I came to the island in the first place.

'How's your coffee?' The question drags me from my thoughts.

'It's good, how's your sugar and cream?'

Neil looks at me from across the table in mock outrage and gestures to the Thai iced coffee in front of him. 'This is a Thai delicacy I will have you know. I'm simply appreciating the culture.'

I laugh and then immediately stop, remembering what's brought us here.

I texted him as I walked. I told myself it was to get his perspective on Doug, to figure out what he's really capable of. Neil's been on the island longer than Doug; he even lives with him. But as I typed out the text inviting Neil to coffee, it wasn't Doug I was thinking about. It was the heat of Neil's leg against mine at Frangipani, the light touch of his kiss on my cheek amid the chaos on Pho Tau beach two days ago.

I cringed at the realization, my thoughts of Neil soaking through the armour I've built over the years. But as he smiles at me now from across the table of the Monkey Bungalow, one of the open-air cafes lining the sand of Pho Tau beach, I feel it again. That sense of possibility. The desire to feel his body against mine. My gaze, as always, is drawn to those freckled lips.

I force away these intrusive thoughts with the one question I know will put an end to my giddiness.

'Have you heard any more news about Daniel's murder? Do the police have any idea who did it?' I ask. Although, given what I know of the Koh Sang police, I can already predict the answer.

Neil shakes his head slowly, confirming my suspicion.

'Listen, I'm sorry you had to witness . . .' he trails off, his face suddenly serious, 'well, everything that's happened. I don't want you to think this is normal. That guests just . . . die out here.'

I sit quietly, considering how to respond, but Neil jumps in again. 'Sorry, that was insensitive. I guess I'm just a bit nervous,' he says, fiddling with his straw.

'Nervous?' I ask. Neil is always goofy and charming and extroverted. I've never seen him look even remotely nervous.

'Yeah,' he says with a chuckle. 'You make me nervous.'

I wrap my hand around my coffee mug, fixating on the small bubbles forming on the surface, trying to ignore the heat rising in my cheeks.

'You know, I was looking for you at the Full Moon Party the other night. I thought maybe we could . . . spend some time together,' he says.

'Me too,' I say quietly, meaning it.

'So, you weren't feeling well, huh? Based on what you said to the group last night?'

'Yeah,' I say looking back down at my coffee. 'I don't know what happened, but I just felt off.'

He nods, and when I don't elaborate, we lapse into a few seconds of comfortable silence.

After a while, Neil's smile fades, a look of concern shading his face.

'Look, I know the last few days have been a lot. And I know you've probably noticed how strangely everyone is acting over what happened to Lucy and Daniel.' He stares off at the water, his face growing uncharacteristically stony, before returning his gaze to me. 'You've got to understand, my life before I came here was pretty bleak. I've never told anyone this, not even Doug or the others. Something about you just makes me want to open up I guess . . .' He sighs, trailing off. It's not at all what I expected him to say, and as his pause extends, I worry I've lost him, but he starts again hesitantly. 'I tried to end it a few times.'

'End what?'

'My life, Brooke,' he says more forcefully. 'Once with pills and once with smack. Neither time took, just landed me in hospital. Looking back, I guess I just didn't want to die enough. If I did, I would have found a way to make it stick. But back then, it was like I couldn't even kill myself right.'

The news strikes me hard. I can't reconcile the man in front of me: Neil – silly, pink-cocktail-drinking Neil – with someone who would ever even consider taking his own life. But I'm sure that's what people have said about me. Without thinking, I place my hand over his. He lifts his head and locks his eyes on mine.

'When I finally got out of England, it was like I'd started a different life. I came here, and I could actually imagine a future. A world away from the hell that I had lived in for twenty years. I was happy for – well – the first time. I found the ocean, I made friends. I had spent my life looking at people from the outside, jealous of their ability to simply carry on. Once I started building a life here, I felt like I'd finally been let into that club, like I actually deserved to be one of those people who could be happy.'

He pauses, nostalgia glittering in his eyes. 'They brought me back, you know,' he continues. 'The Permanents. As soon as I met them, I felt like I finally found my family. My real family. People who would do anything for me, who would love me no matter what shit I got myself into.'

I feel that same crack cut through my heart as I did at Frangipani. A crevasse of longing that has yet to be filled.

I take a deep breath, wondering if I should really do this. If I should finally share why I ran away from everything I knew back in Kentucky. I contemplate whether it's time to actually open up, to let someone else in.

'Sorry, that was a lot,' Neil says, pulling his hand back with a laugh devoid of humour, mistaking my silence for rejection.

'No, it's not that.' I pause. 'I did, too.'

He looks at me curiously, and I realize I'm not making any sense.

'I tried to end it, too.' I'm fiddling with my bracelets again. I can feel him lean forward, our coffees long forgotten, but I can't bring myself to meet his eye. 'In college, I – something happened. Something I had a hard time coming back from. So, I, uh, coped the only way I knew how.'

'Brooke, I'm so sorry.' His hand is back on mine, but I turn my head so he can't see the tears forming. I don't tell him the rest of it. First, the stay in the hospital, the physical recovery. And then, just when I thought I was going home, back to my mom's filthy trailer, the subsequent surprise. The transfer to the hospital next-door. 'I just don't know what to do with you,' my mother had said. 'What if you try something like this again? I won't survive it.'

She said this as if she couldn't see the irony in her words. I shouldn't have been surprised. She hadn't been there for me before that; why should she start then? So, I stayed for weeks in that hospital, with its grey walls, and grey floors, and grey patients. I drifted off to sleep every night to the screams ricocheting throughout the building. I spent my days on that horrible bed, the mattress springs poking at my spine, and I thought of the person who had landed me there. Not my mother, but the person who was really responsible. And I swallowed spoonful upon spoonful of anger, the rage eventually growing in my stomach, turning me into a person I no longer recognized. I lay there and waited, counting the seconds until I got out. Planning how I would get as far away as I could from that place, from my mother, from all of it. And then, when I got out, I made good on my plan. I got as far away as I could.

'I think most of us here have gone through something similar.' Neil's voice jars me back to the present. 'There aren't too many well-adjusted adults running away to live on a remote party island. But it's worked for us. Koh Sang is kind of our safe haven. A place where we can finally fit in, start over.'

I nod.

'Everyone's just worried that if news gets out about all this, the island will be finished. And we have nothing else. Nowhere to go.'

He puts his head in his hands, his elbows resting on the table, and my heart breaks for him. I get it. I know how it feels not to have a home to return to. I rest my hand against the side of his face, and he raises his eyes to look at me. For the first time in as long as I can remember, the feel of someone else's skin feels right.

I hate having to ruin this moment, but I have no choice.

'Neil. I think I might know who killed Lucy.'

My mind flashes back to the video, to the suspicious way Doug looked around as he led Lucy from the dancefloor. There was something happening there. Something that holds the key to this. I know it.

Neil immediately jerks upward, the intimacy vanishing, those freckled lips pursed into an 'o' of surprise.

'I think it was Doug.'

I don't know what I expect. Maybe for him to break down with the realization that he doesn't know the friend he's lived with for years, or maybe to react with obstinate denial. But I certainly don't expect him to laugh.

It starts with a mild giggle and evolves into something near hysteria. Loud gasps, rocking shoulders.

'I'm sorry,' he says eventually, trying to control himself. 'I really shouldn't be laughing. But Doug? Really?'

I nod, rushing to tell him about the video of Doug and Lucy, certain that will convince him.

'That's just Doug,' Neil responds. 'He hits on anything that moves, you know that.'

I fumble. I expected Neil, of everyone, to understand. 'Yeah, but Lucy died that night. If anything, he was the last person to see her. He gave her a drink and the police said Lucy had MDMA in her system, right? Maybe he spiked it. And then he leads her away from a crowd and the next morning she's dead? I mean, come on, that can't be a *coincidence*.' I cringe at how whiny my voice sounds. But how am I the only one who can see it?

'Listen,' Neil says, finally composed. 'I'm sorry. It's just, you don't know Doug like I do. Yeah, he can be a bit of a creep when it comes to the ladies, but he's struggling.' He pauses, taking a sip from his coffee. 'If you tell him this, I'll have to kill you – sorry, too soon – but the thing with Doug is that he's insecure. He's still trying to find himself really. He's kind of split between this Frederic persona that he's striving for – the big boss of the resort and all that – but at the same time he's still stuck in his early twenties. He had it rough growing up, like we all did, and I think he's trying to relive the youth that he missed out on. And part of that is finding a woman who understands him. He just goes about it the wrong way.'

'Yeah, but I watched him, Neil. I saw a video of him leading Lucy away.'

Neil shrugs. 'He was probably just trying to pick her up.'

'Then why would he say that he didn't see Lucy at the party?' I think about how seamlessly he lied last night in the dive shop, shaking his head along with the others.

Neil sighs. 'Ah, come on. I mean, if you had a romantic

moment with someone hours before they were killed, wouldn't you keep it quiet?'

I realize I'm not getting anywhere. Neil thinks he can tell what Doug is capable of, but I know better than anyone how well people can hide their true selves. I decide to switch tactics.

'Did you ever meet Jacinta?'

Neil's head darts up again, his eyes blurring in confusion.

'Jacinta?'

'The woman who 'fell' from Khrum Yai,' I clarify.

'Oh, right,' Neil mumbles. 'I met her briefly. She stopped by Frangipani one night when we were all there. I guess it was actually the night before she . . .'

He doesn't need to finish the sentence; we both know what he means. The night before she died. Or the night before she was killed.

'Did Doug know her?'

The question seems to surprise him, and as he looks at me I see understanding slowly creep into his face.

After a long while, he nods once.

'We were all pissed, so a lot of that night is pretty hazy. I honestly don't remember how she got to Frangipani. Maybe it was one of those bar crawls or maybe someone brought her. But yeah, Doug fancied her.'

The words hang between us for a moment.

'But she left alone, that I'm sure of. Because Doug was fuming . . .' Neil trails off.

'I went up to Khrum Yai with Cass a few days ago,' I say. 'It's not really a place that people just fall from. The ledge is a solid ten steps from the path. And the papers said some tourists found her body in the early morning. What would she have been doing hiking that trail when it was still dark out?'

'Maybe she wanted to see the sunrise,' Neil offers. But his tone is muted, and I can tell he doesn't really believe it.

'I don't think so. I think she was pushed. And I'm pretty positive Lucy was killed, too, maybe by the same person. And then Daniel, well, maybe he was killed because he knew something.'

'Why are you so sure?' Neil asks.

'I've just – I've been looking into it, that's all.' I don't mean to go further than that, but suddenly the words start pouring out of me. It's as if opening up to Neil about my past has loosened something inside me. I tell him how Cass and I searched Lucy's room and social media pages. How Lucy had thoroughly researched all of us and used a fake identity to check in. I stop short of telling him how I stole Daniel's phone – claiming I saw the video of Doug and Lucy on a guest's Instagram. I'm not ready to share that piece of information with anyone, even Neil.

He watches, eyes wide, taking it all in.

'Do you think Doug could be behind all of this?' I ask.

Neil shakes his head vehemently. 'It's not Doug.'

'Then what is going on? What is it with this island?'

His face carries a new emotion now, one it takes me a moment to recognize. But then it clicks.

Fear.

'Look,' he says with a deep sigh. 'I agree. Something's going on here that runs deep in the island. A reason tourists have died. But you need to trust me, I really don't think Doug's behind it.'

'Then who is it?'

'I don't know, it's just . . .' Neil looks behind him, checking to make sure no one's listening in on our conversation.

But other than the two of us and a bored waiter lounging on the front counter and playing on his phone, we're alone. 'There are rumours that it could be a group of locals. People who are resentful of the *farangs* who come in and act like they own the place. Others think it's the Thai mafia, like Doug mentioned last night. They sell drugs on the island – they bribe the police to look the other way – and I know that they own at least one or two of the bars on Pho Tau beach.

'But the moral of the story is that you need to stop looking into this. Whoever's involved, they're dangerous. And I'm worried that if you try to get in the way, they'll come after you.'

I nod, but I'm not fully convinced. Neil must see it, too, because he wraps his hands around my forearms. I feel my breath catch as he gently pulls me towards him across the table, so that our faces are mere inches from one another.

'I'm serious,' Neil says, his dark eyes round with kindness, and I feel the warmth from earlier return to my cheeks. 'Since you came here, I've felt . . . I don't know. It just seems like there are suddenly all these opportunities here on Koh Sang that I never noticed before. Things I didn't think were possible.' He laughs, a small sheepish chuckle, but thankfully his hands don't leave my arms. 'Listen to me, I sound like a right git. I just don't want you to get wrapped up in all this. If you got hurt – or, God forbid, worse – I'm not sure what I would do . . .'

Neil trails off, and before I even realize what I'm doing, before I can stop myself or think of the millions of reasons why I shouldn't, I've leaned in closer to him, pulling my arms out of his grasp, placing my hands on either side of his face and resting my lips on his.

18

Cass

'Lift your right leg behind you and raise it high towards the sky. And now reach that left arm back for it. That's it.'

I'm still shaking as I arrive at the fitness centre on the far side of the resort, Greta's melodic accent floating out to meet me as I walk up the stairs to the yoga studio. I've spent an inordinate amount of time processing the note – first staring at it in the kitchen, and then, when I realized Logan would be getting up soon, shoving it in my pocket and rushing out to my bike, to drive in circles around the island, thinking. So by the time I arrive, Greta's already wrapping up her class.

I expected the studio to be empty after what happened last night, but it's packed. Yoga mats litter the floor between the room's two mirrored walls, the guests separated from each other by only an arm's length. At the far side, the windows have been pulled open, and morning sun drapes the entire studio in incandescent light. The gentle breeze from the wood ceiling fans shakes the fragile flames of the candles Greta's placed in each corner of the room, engulfing the studio in scents of lavender and eucalyptus.

The entire setting radiates calm, but it does little to slow my racing heart. The words from the note keep screaming in my head. *This is all your fault.*

I watch the guests in front of me gracefully balance on one leg as they follow Greta's directions. I wish for a moment that I could be any of them, so removed from the outside world that they can turn off their brains long enough to mould their bodies in pretzel-like positions.

But I can't.

Everyone is going to know the truth, soon.

'Hopefully this flow leaves you feeling re-engaged and ready to tackle the day,' Greta concludes. 'Namaste.'

I start to walk towards Greta, but before I can reach her, she's rushed by guests. Adoring yogis, I assume, but as I drift closer, I realize why the class was so crowded.

'So, do you know who did it? Do the police have any ideas?' asks a girl with a large, shiny forehead in a pink sports bra.

'Yeah, I mean, I got close enough to see him. His throat was slit – like how you see on TV – and there was blood everywhere. Is the person who did it still on the island?' A skinny guy, with a hint of acne along his hairline, looks up at Greta imploringly. The others nod along. Greta maintains her smile, but I notice her eyebrows move slightly together, a line forming in the middle of her forehead the only indication of her irritation.

Anger rips through me, incongruent to the atmosphere of the studio. I want to charge at them, pummel them with my fists, claw with my nails, anything I can to cause harm. I know these people. These attention-grubbing, greedy rubberneckers, falling over themselves to be closest to a tragedy, but not close enough to be actually affected. They're always the same: my college roommate crying fake tears for the reporters as she told them she always thought there was something 'off' about me; the 'friends' who hadn't bothered to reach out to Robin when our mother died all trying to outdo each other by posting the most sentimental RIP message on her posthumous Facebook wall; and now these people.

'I'm sorry, everyone, but I don't have any information,' Greta answers. 'I'm as in the dark as you all. But as soon as I learn more, I will be sure to share. So make sure to come to our ninety-minute Bikram session this afternoon.'

I stare at the disappointed guests as they walk past. My hands clench into fists, but they're oblivious, consumed instead by the importance of their own lives, their shallow desires.

'Cass, love!' Greta's voice plucks me from my anger. 'Come take a seat.' She pulls out a yoga mat from the corner and expertly shakes it so that it lands flat against the floor a few feet away from hers. 'I'll grab us some water.'

I take a seat on the mat, tucking my legs up beneath me, and Greta returns a minute later with the waters, two cold glasses garnished with slices of cucumber. She's dressed in a matching leggings and sports bra set that shows off her toned abs, and her hair is pulled back into a ballerina bun. She gracefully slides down to her mat, her legs crossed in front of her, before leaning towards me and wrapping both of her hands around mine.

'Oh, my sweet thing,' she says, noticing the concern on my face, her expression instantly filling with empathy. 'I figured something was wrong when you missed the class. How are you?'

Her words are enough for me to break down, the tears barely having time to form before they flood down my face in waves. Everything rushes out: the fear of being exposed, the paranoia, my sadness over losing Lucy, the shock of

Daniel's murder. Greta, still seated, wraps me in her arms, rocking me back and forth.

As I drove around the island this morning trying to process the note and its implications, I realized that Greta was the exact person I needed. The speech she gave at our engagement party the other night was spot on. If the Permanents are a family, then Greta is the mother. It's a bit ridiculous, given that she's only ten years older than me, but she's a nurturer. Ever since I met her that first night at Frangipani two years ago, she's taken me under her wing, looked after me in a way. I've been thinking of telling her about my past for months now. Every week at our post-yoga coffee date, I consider it, even coming so close as to open my mouth to let it all spill. But something always stops me.

I rub my head against her arm, enjoying the feeling of her caress, convincing myself she'll fix this. Greta will know what to do. She'll know how to handle all of this.

'That poor girl didn't deserve to die like that, and neither did that man. You've been so strong through all of this. I'm so proud of you.'

I look up at Greta's dark eyes, brimming with compassion. I try to answer, but it's as if my throat has been filled with medical gauze. The tears keep coming faster, and soon, greedy sobs rack my chest, soaking up all the air. After a minute, Greta's voice breaks through the chaos, helping me focus on my breathing. *In for two.* I feel her hand rubbing delicate circles into my back. I can't remember when that started. I stay there for a few more minutes, enjoying the Scandinavian lilt of her voice, as gentle as a lullaby, directing me when to breathe. *Out for two.*

When I finally regain a semblance of control, my breath eventually regulating itself, I turn to look at Greta. And I'm struck with an overwhelming urge to tell her, stronger than any I've felt before. I think how easy it would be. To confess about the threatening letters, the pills, the things I can't remember from the Full Moon Party, all of it. To finally put my complete trust in someone.

But if Greta – nurturing, kind-hearted Greta – rejects me, what would I do? She would certainly tell Logan; I couldn't make her keep a secret like that. And then he would know I've been lying to him – to all of them.

'We don't need to talk about it just yet,' Greta says carefully, as if she can hear my inner dialogue.

I nod, thankful for the change of subject, and I let the scents of the candles and the lull of the fan wash over me.

'I'm so sorry,' I finally say when my voice nears something resembling normal.

'What could you possibly be sorry for?' she asks, her forehead scrunched.

'With everything that's happened, first the engagement and now –' I raise my hands outward, gesturing around me '– all this, I haven't checked in with you. It's only been a few weeks since Alice left. How are you doing?'

A shadow falls over her face, and it's as if something inside her crumples.

'I'm . . .' She falters. 'I'm getting through it. It will just take some time.'

She gives me a small smile, a knife to the heart. Greta is the only person I've met on this island who has been upfront about her past from day one. After the first night we met at Frangipani, Greta invited me for a walk on Pho Tau beach, just the two of us. As we walked, she didn't pry into why I came to Koh Sang – thank God – but she was more than willing to share her own story.

She told me all about Alice, the quiet, dark-haired

woman I'd seen at Frangipani that first night and a few times since then, Greta's arm always protectively looped around her waist. 'I met Alice in high school in a town outside of Stockholm. I knew she was the one, instantly, as soon as I saw her. I'd never felt anything like it before.' The memories glistened in Greta's eyes.

'Alice's parents didn't understand. They were old fashioned, originally from far up in the northern part of the country. They couldn't imagine their daughter dating another woman. And Alice, well, she couldn't get over it. In her mind, her parents had tainted the entire country. We needed to go, far away, somewhere we would be accepted. We went to a lot of places – India, Indonesia, Laos. But something happened when we got to Koh Sang. We felt so much love, both of us. We could picture a future here. I would teach yoga and she would cook at one of the beachside restaurants.'

Greta smiles at me now from her yoga mat with the same wistfulness she had when she talked about Alice on our first beach walk. 'We were good here for a while, me managing the studio, Alice basically running the kitchen at *Aroy Mak* . . .' She trails off. 'I mean, we were better than good. You saw it.'

I did. Greta showered Alice with love at every opportunity. Her mothering nature turned up to full blast whenever they were together. But Alice was different, colder. She was a bit shy and seemed young – even though she had to be the same age as Greta – and I was never able to get a good read on her. While Greta was always the centre of the group, Alice stayed more on the periphery, removed from the rest of the Permanents as if she didn't want to be a part of what we had. Truthfully, I never really understood what Greta saw in her.

179

One night a few weeks ago, just before Brooke arrived on the island, I showed up to Frangipani to find Neil, Doug and Logan all crowded around Greta. Her shoulders shook as she sobbed into her hands. Alice had left. Greta had come back from teaching a Pilates class to find her apartment empty, Alice's portion of the closet deserted, with no note and no explanation.

'I just never saw it coming,' Greta says now. 'I think I lulled myself into this false sense of security. It seemed like there was nothing to worry about.'

I shiver, her words hitting a bit too close to home. I force myself to nod, understandingly.

Our conversation lulls, but it's a comfortable silence. It always has been with Greta. She's the one person I feel like I can talk to without judgement, the only one with whom I can have conversations that I won't recite back to myself for hours, searching for the things I shouldn't have said, or mentally slapping myself for using the wrong tone.

And finally, it feels like the time to confide in her. The words are out of my mouth before I can stop them.

'Greta, I need your advice. I . . . I haven't been fully truthful,' I say, the emotion thick in my throat. 'I've been lying to Logan . . . about my past.'

She's quiet for a moment, and I squeeze my eyes shut, for once afraid to look at her. Afraid of the judgement I might see.

'And now that . . .' I trail off, swallowing the words I really want to say. *Now that someone's threatening to expose me for who – for what – I really am, he's bound to find out.* 'Now that we're getting married, I need to tell him everything. I can't keep lying to him any more.'

I wait for Greta to respond, an endless chasm of time that twists my stomach.

'Oh, Cass,' she says, and I feel my muscles loosen. She understands. When I finally open my eyes, her face is awash with sympathy. I expect her to ask questions – she has to be curious – but she doesn't. Instead, she takes me back in her arms, murmuring nothings in my ear.

'My sweet girl,' she says when we separate. 'You need to tell him the truth. Start your marriage off on a clean slate. No lies.'

I knew she would say this because it *is* what I need to do.

'But how do I know that he won't leave me?'

The question clenches my heart in a vice grip.

'That will never, ever happen,' Greta promises, her tone compassionate. 'I've never seen Logan look at anyone the way he looks at you. He has so much love for you, unconditional love. That will never change.'

I cling to her words, desperately wanting to believe her, but she wasn't there in that hotel room. She doesn't know what I did. She doesn't know the real me, just like Logan doesn't. And she doesn't know how difficult things were for us before the engagement.

There's one more thing I need to tell her. Something that might change her mind completely.

'Logan cheated on me, Greta,' I blurt out.

She draws back as if she's been burned, but I continue, laying the flame into flesh. 'Not so long ago. With that woman. Jacinta. The one who fell from Khrum Yai.'

The shock of my statement seems to fade from Greta's face, and she remains still.

'You knew?' I ask her, accusation seeping into the question.

She nods, ruefully. 'He told me after. He said it only happened once, that it was a mistake. I didn't think you knew.'

Neither does he. But I'd seen them.

Logan had told me he was going to the gym with Doug, just like he usually does each afternoon before opening Frangipani. I finished work early that day and figured I would surprise him, swing by the gym on my way home from work. But when I did there was no Doug, no Logan. Only a handful of tourists there on guest passes. So, I continued home on my bike, driving down the street filled with overpriced tourist-driven restaurants that no self-respecting local would ever enter.

I had turned my head to check for cars at the intersection, and that's when I saw them. Logan, his curls pulled back in his typical bun, his shoulder inches away from *her* – Jacinta – as they left one of the restaurants. And then, as they reached the corner of the street, he turned to her, pulled her head close to his, and kissed her. I watched until I heard a tentative honk from behind me.

Instead of going home, I drove straight to the Kumvit pharmacy. And for the first time in three years, I purchased Xanax. I needed the pills to drown out the image I had seen of Logan's betrayal. I needed it to force myself to believe it was a one-time thing, that it wouldn't evolve into more.

I didn't have to worry about that for long. Because the next morning, Jacinta was dead.

'The kiss didn't mean anything,' Greta assures me. 'Just pre-engagement jitters. And it never went further than that. He wanted to commit to you, but he was scared. Typical man. But it will never, ever happen again. He's promised me. He loves you, more than anything. In all the time I've known him, I never saw him truly happy until you arrived here.'

I nod, trying to believe her.

'I know Logan,' Greta continues. 'He was the first person who came to live in Koh Sang after Alice and I got here.

We've been friends now for years. That kiss was a fluke. That's not the type of man he is. Tell him the truth. He loves you, and nothing about your past will change that.'

I nod, but her words are hollow by the time they reach my ear. Because she can't know everything I've done, she can't even begin to imagine.

19

Brooke

Back in my room, I collapse on the firm hotel mattress, the touch of Neil's lips still fresh on mine. A giddiness flutters in my stomach that I haven't experienced since those few, short-lived days of excitement in college.

His comments from earlier come back to me, and the memory deepens the smile that's been plastered on my face since I left the Monkey Bungalow. But my mind flicks to what else he said, the warning wrapped in affection. *You need to stop looking into this . . . If you got hurt – or, God forbid, worse – I'm not sure what I would do.*

Can I do that?

For the first time since I've arrived, I'm questioning my reason for being here. For once, the anger I've been holding in my stomach is faint, drowned out by this new wave of excitement. Could I move on? Let it all go? Drop the story and make a life here with Neil? After everything that I've been through, don't I deserve to be happy?

Before I can deliberate any further, I feel my phone vibrate in my back pocket. I've been so distracted that I haven't even bothered to check Instagram since yesterday. I can only imagine how many messages and comments await my response. With a sigh, I flick on the fan by my bed, pull out my phone and roll over on to my stomach.

I'm met with thirty-seven new direct message requests and fifteen hundred notifications about various likes and comments on my posts. I hover my finger over the message icon, reluctant to see what awaits me. The chill of Lucy's unbearably innocent message yesterday – *Hi. Can you help me? Please?* – hasn't yet worn off, that last, desperate 'please' sitting hauntingly in my chest. And on top of that, I'm certain that the usual onslaught of overtly sexual advances and cruel attacks that fill my inbox will dull the thrill of this morning.

Still, I force myself to check. I scroll past the litany of insults and pick-up lines that I've grown accustomed to and breathe a huge sigh of relief when I reach the end. It's short-lived, though, as my phone flashes with another message notification just as I finish the task.

I scroll back up to the one new message request and click on it.

A small icon identifies the sender, a woman with eyes so dark they're almost black against her ivory skin and straight brown hair. The name next to the photo is limited to one word. *Alice.*

Her name scratches at my brain. Since Instagram labelled the message as a 'request', that means I don't follow her, and I don't otherwise recall interacting with her on this app before.

With a growing sense of dread, I click on the message, which is only a photo, no text. As I enlarge it, my phone screen fills with a group seated at a long table, a familiar-looking sunset looming behind them.

I recognize the setting immediately. The Sunset

Restaurant, perched atop the summit of one of the highest mountains on Koh Sang. And as I look more closely, I begin to make out the people. This woman, Alice apparently, towards the end of the table, Greta next to her, her arm draped over Alice's shoulders. And then it comes to me. *Alice.* Cass mentioned an Alice. Greta's ex. The one who left the island right before I got here.

I continue scanning the photo she's sent, dragging my eyes along both sides of the table. Cass sits on the other side of Greta, her lips pressed together, gaze diverted away from the camera. Neil, Doug and Logan sit across from them, seemingly mid-laugh.

But why would Alice send this to me, a stranger? With no explanation, just a photo of a good memory from her time on the island? Maybe she's jealous? She could feel that I'm encroaching on her territory since I've been posting photos on Instagram with the Permanents.

Before I can process this theory, my phone flashes with another message from Alice. I click on it greedily, seeing a second image, this time accompanied by a short sentence. I freeze as soon as I see the words.

Her death was not an accident.

My heart stops as I process the message. I take a deep breath before clicking on the new image she's sent.

It's two women. The one on the right is in her early twenties, standing on what I recognize as Pho Tau beach, the water lapping at her toes. Her hair is pulled back off her face, but brown curls fall over her shoulders. She's tall and thin and beautiful. A dimple dots her cheek as she smiles directly at the camera, a dive mask perched on her forehead. I recognize her instantly from the posts I've seen on various websites and travel blogs. They only ever used her first name, but it's enough to identify her now. Jacinta, the woman who fell from Khrum Yai.

I look at the person she's standing next to. A blonde woman with a scuba mask over her face, and the snorkel still in her mouth. But I know who it is. I can see the brown eyes through the mask, opened wide, as if the photo had caught her by surprise.

Cass.

I think back to our hike on Khrum Yai the other day, the questions I peppered her with about Jacinta. And her non-committal answers. *I never met her.*

Another lie.

Cass knew Jacinta. Well enough to be in a photo – albeit reluctantly – with her, and she lied about it. Just like she lied about where she was the night Lucy died. Just like she's lied about everything.

I turn the words from Alice's message over and over in my mind. Jacinta's death wasn't an accident. It's what I've suspected ever since I first heard of Jacinta, but now that suspicion is solidifying, turning hard and rough.

I dash off a quick message to Alice, asking why she's sending me these messages, what exactly it is that she knows, hoping to catch her while she's still online. And indeed, within seconds, my message is underlined by a grey 'read' confirmation. I wait several moments for her to respond, or at least to see a notification that she's begun typing. But nothing more appears.

When I click over to her profile, it's marked as private. Hastily, I click the request to follow her, eager to see if there's any more information I can glean from past photos she's posted. I check our message chain again, but Alice still hasn't responded.

Impatient, I grab Daniel's phone from where I've kept it on the side of my desk, turn it on and bring it back to the bed. Once the phone comes to life, I'm startled by the notification alerting me that only 2 per cent of his battery remains. His phone is a Samsung, which means my iPhone charger won't work with it, and there's no one I could ask for one without arousing suspicion. But it needs to last long enough for me to check this one last thing.

I spent hours last night going through Daniel's phone, meticulously checking his apps and messages and missed calls. But other than the video and the WhatsApp message from the anonymous sender telling Daniel to meet them in Kumvit, the phone was largely unhelpful. So I'd given up on it. But back then I was looking for evidence that nailed Doug as the killer. Now I have another motive.

I start back at the top of Daniel's photo gallery with the most recent photos, paying closer attention to the backgrounds, combing through everything with fresh eyes. He took a handful after the video that caught Lucy and Doug together. I scroll carefully through the first few blurry shots, but nothing new sticks out. Then I'm on the series featuring Daniel and the red-headed girl. I flip through them quickly, until I reach the third in the set. In that one, Daniel's looking straight at the camera, but the girl's head is bent down as if she's doubled over with laughter, revealing overgrown brown roots of hair. Behind her, a flash of something in the background catches my eye.

I zoom in with my fingers, stretching the image as far as it will go, until it confirms what I suspected. Blonde hair, the same colour as Cass's. She's turned away from the camera, facing out to the water, so that I can't see her face, but it's clear she's talking to someone. I shift my fingers to move the screen, bringing into focus the person next to her. The fine, curly hair. The petite frame.

My fingers clench around the phone, just in time for the screen to turn black.

The phone is dead, but I'm sure of what I saw. Cass was talking to Lucy after Doug led her off the dancefloor. Despite Cass's lies, this photo proves she was with Lucy that night. And she – not Doug – could have been the last person to see Lucy alive.

The anger floods back, hot and furious. A searing rage, deep in my gut.

'That lying bitch,' I mutter, my teeth clenched.

I should have trusted my instincts from the get-go. I knew from the moment I heard about Lucy's body that Cass was behind this. Self-hatred seeps in as I think how stupid I was, letting her convince me that she wanted to help find out why Lucy really came here, breaking into her room with me, looking into her on social media. And I ate it all up. Despite knowing better.

My thoughts from earlier are gone. Even with these growing feelings for Neil, I can't let it go. My reason for coming here. The story I was planning to write even before Lucy and Daniel's murders.

I'm off the bed, phone in hand, before I can let the guilt seep in, before I can acknowledge the reality of what I might be jeopardizing with Neil, everything I might be giving up.

I grab the keys to my motorbike from my bedside table, and I'm out the door instantly, with one goal in mind.

It's time to figure out what else Cass is lying about.

20

Cass

I can't keep lying.

If there's one thing I take away from my conversation with Greta it's that I need to come clean to Logan. If the mystery person leaving me these threatening notes is true to their word, then I need to tell him the truth about my past before they do.

I leave Greta to prep for her next class, her words giving me a new sense of resolve. I'm going to tell Logan everything: what happened in that hotel room, the pills, the threats I've been getting. There will be no more secrets. Greta's right. Logan will understand; he'll love me no matter what. And then we'll find the person behind this, as a team.

I rush to the parking area outside the studio, eager to get this over with, to put the lies behind us. Logan should be at the gym now with Doug. I'll head there directly.

But just as I pull out the key to my motorbike, I hear a familiar voice from across the parking area.

'Miss Cass!'

I turn, trying to compose myself. With everything that's happened this morning, I completely lost sight of my plan to confront Ariel.

'Good morning, Tamar,' I say as she and her husband walk towards me. Her pale skin is sun-kissed, but the concern etched into her face indicates that her time on the island has not been the relaxing getaway she must have envisioned when they'd booked this trip. 'Ariel.' I take him in. His face is as stoic and hard as ever, the vibrating tension hovering around him like an aura. His words from the other day strike at me.

It is not safe here.

I force my voice to sound pleasant, authoritative; the typical tone I use with guests. 'I need to apologize again for the other day. I assure you, things are not usually like this.'

'We understand,' Tamar says in her quiet voice. 'But we are very frightened. We heard what happened. First Lucy, now Daniel. Should we be concerned?'

I realize this is my chance to figure out whether Ariel is behind this.

'No, of course not,' I say carefully. 'Have the police spoken with you?'

Tamar shakes her head, her eyes wide.

'That's good, I thought they might disturb your holiday.' I think quickly. 'Did you end up going to the Full Moon Party the other night?'

Tamar shakes her head again, her husband barely acknowledging my question. 'We did not go. And we went to bed early yesterday. We did not learn anything about poor Daniel until this morning. *Zikhrono livrakha.*'

These questions aren't getting me anywhere. I think of what Brooke would do, how she would get to the bottom of this.

'Ariel,' I say, turning to face him directly before I can think better of it. 'I need to ask you about the other day. When you ... said those things after class. About how there was something wrong on Koh Sang. How did you know?'

He hesitates for so long that for a moment I think he'll refuse to answer. 'I do not know what you are talking about,' he says eventually, in that weird, gravelly voice.

My muscles clench, frustration growing.

'You said there was something wrong here,' I say more insistently. 'That it wasn't safe. That *I* wasn't safe. What did you mean?'

He stares at me blankly before shaking his head, and frustration and defiance run through me.

'You said it. You did,' I demand, in a voice I realize is much too loud. But this time, he doesn't react at all.

'I can explain,' Tamar says.

But I ignore her, because suddenly I'm hit with a furious need for my suspicions to be true, for Ariel to be the killer. It would make it all so easy. He would be arrested, and everything would go back to normal. Koh Sang may receive some bad press for a time, but it would blow over. We could all stay here, as a family. With this realization and the stress from the deaths, the notes, the lies, all of it combining in a potent mixture, I explode.

Before I realize what I'm doing, I've grabbed Ariel's wrist, which is so wide that I can barely wrap my fingers halfway around it.

'It was you, wasn't it?' I'm shouting, inches from his face.

'Please,' Tamar says, taking a step forward, trying to position herself between me and Ariel, but I barely hear her.

'You knew it wasn't safe here because you planned to kill Lucy. But why? Tell me why you—'

There's a sharp pressure on my arm, and the next thing I hear is my tailbone striking the pavement with a sickening crack.

I expect the shove to have come from Ariel, but when I look up, Tamar is standing over me. 'How dare you!' she spits.

Her eyes are no longer wide and scared; there's a toughness to her now that I haven't seen before.

'Why won't you listen to me? My husband had nothing to do with this,' she says through gritted teeth. 'I told you, he is sick. He has PTSD.'

I try to take in what she's saying, but it doesn't make sense.

'Ariel was in the IDF,' she says, her voice cold, and I vaguely remember a news article I read a few months ago about the conflict in the Middle East. IDF, the Israeli Defence Forces. 'Do you have any idea what it is like for him? When he hears loud noises or experiences shock it is like he is right back there, in that war zone. It is torture for him.'

My attention jerks to Ariel, whose stare is fixed on the ground, as if he's ashamed. I think back to the other day in the upper level of the Tiki Palms. The slam of the bathroom door right before Ariel grabbed me, his shaking hands. And I know immediately that Tamar is telling the truth. He wasn't behind this; neither of them had anything to do with it.

'We came here to escape all that. To have a break. And this is how you treat us? You should be ashamed.'

Tamar grabs Ariel by the arm and hurries him down the path, back towards their room. Neither of them looks at me, sitting on the hard ground, tears pricking at my eyes.

I sit there for a while, ignoring the strange looks from the guests walking past. What is happening to me? It feels like everything is beginning to slip through my fingers. The feeling is uncomfortably familiar, a reminder of the days and weeks following my time in that hotel room years ago.

Eventually, I force myself up and on to my motorbike, wincing as my tailbone touches the leather of the seat. I try to relish the sun on my face as I drive the familiar path home, but I barely register it.

My resolve from earlier has melted back into uncertainty. There's no way I can confess everything to Logan in this state. I'll fall to pieces as soon as I open my mouth. I need to get a grip on myself, and there's one place I know where I can do that.

Thankful to be certain of at least one thing, I drive straight past the gym, failing to even brake. Minutes later, I'm on the winding hill leading up to our house.

I pass a motorbike parked on the side of the road that looks like Brooke's, and for a moment I have an almost unbearable craving to talk to her. She's always so strong, even last night after she found Daniel. I don't know what it is exactly that I want to say to her – whether I'm ready to admit what just happened with Ariel – but I need to hear her voice, to have some of her strength rub off on me. Once I'm parked in our driveway, I pull out my phone and call her. I hold my breath while it rings, anticipating Brooke's voice answering.

But other than the incessant ringing, there's nothing. The wind rustles the trees around me, and from somewhere far off I hear a high-pitched trill. Birdsong, most likely.

When her message tone beeps, I hang up, because what am I going to say? Instead, I look up at our house, the home Logan and I have built together.

For a second, I think I see something dark blur the front

window, but it's gone almost as soon as my mind registers it. I squint, but the half-closed blinds make it impossible to see anything. I don't want to risk going inside if there's a chance Logan's already home from the gym. I'm not ready to face him.

I spin, looking down the road. The feeling of eyes on me has returned, pricking up the hairs on the back of my neck. I look up and down the street before glancing again at the living-room window, which remains unmoving.

I don't wait a second longer. I head out towards the road, turning left at the end of the driveway.

After a short walk uphill, the road ends, blocked by a wall of dense trees. I find the opening to the Khrum Yai trail, the one I've used for years, and squeeze through the gap between two trees, just slightly larger than the rest, unnoticeable to anyone who doesn't know what they're looking for. Once I'm inside, I look up. I'm surrounded by lush, dense greenery. The noise is different in here, everything is muted. The air is different, too. Still.

As I walk up the steady incline of the trail, I force myself to think of something other than my confrontation with Ariel. Or that handwritten note. Or the seconds ticking down until the stranger makes good on their threat. *Everyone is going to know the truth, soon.*

But the only other thing my mind can settle upon is Logan and Jacinta, his lips on hers, his hand resting on the back of her chestnut curls. I'd managed to force it out of my head after a while, to convince myself it was nothing, especially once Logan proposed. But now the image has come rushing back.

She was beautiful, Jacinta. Long tan limbs, her dark brown hair streaked with strands of red. Doug couldn't resist himself, touching her arm any chance he could, making sure he was always occupying the seat next to her. Even Neil kept stealing glances at her. But it was Logan's gaze I couldn't tear myself away from. The way his eyes stayed trained on Jacinta, as if I wasn't even there.

The rest of that night at Frangipani is a bit of a blur. I had taken two – maybe three – Xanax that afternoon after seeing them together, enough that I could pretend to act normal.

And the next morning Jacinta was dead.

I tried to raise the topic with Logan in the days that followed, to see whether he would admit to kissing her. To determine whether there was more to it than that. 'It's such a shame what happened with that poor girl,' I'd say as we were eating dinner or sitting on the couch, and a cloud would pass over his face. But he'd always find a way to shut it down. 'Yeah, it's sad. But she shouldn't have been walking so close to the ledge. What was she thinking?'

And then things started to return to normal. In fact, Logan was more affectionate than ever, taking any excuse to rub my shoulders or touch my hair. And was it really worth talking about it? It was only a kiss. So, I followed his lead and pretended it had never happened. Pretending is something I'm especially good at, after all, having spent years honing my skills.

I've done it ever since Mom died, back in that old house in New York, the one that quickly stopped feeling like a home. I did it on the days the house was still, when trash would pile up in the kitchen and the doorbell would ring unanswered. Those were the safe days, when my father would hide in his bedroom, without any memory of his two children roaming the house. Those days were much better than the others, when the stillness would break into frenzied, hysterical episodes, as if his hibernation had fuelled up an uncontrollable energy. He would start something – a house project, or an assignment for work, or a plan for a family vacation – with unrelenting vigour. Materials strewn throughout the house, his limbs moving so fast that he looked like a cartoon. That energy was potent, often boiling over into violence. A black eye for Robin, a sprained wrist for me.

Afterwards, my father would be inconsolable. He would grab at us, hard, pushing our skin against his, as if the feeling of our flesh would bring him back to normality. He would tend to our injuries furiously. Fixing gauze on our cuts, holding ice to our bruises. And then the apologies would start, a running stream of excuses, all of which tied back to Mom. As if he deserved a free pass from the grief that had destroyed all three of us. As if the burden was on us, his two adolescent daughters, to fix this. To fix him.

So I tried. And in doing so, I destroyed everything.

I can't risk doing the same with Logan.

I breach the Khrum Yai summit and see the island spreading out below me. I take a few steps from the path and sit, my legs straight out in front of me, my feet just brushing the edge of the cliff.

I barely register the view. Instead, despite my best efforts, my thoughts return to the threatening notes. Who is leaving them? I think about all the times over the last few days that I've felt someone following me, watching me.

I imagine what Robin would say if she was here.

It isn't the first time I've done this, far from it. I'll choose a secluded spot on the island, somewhere I think she would have loved, and pretend she's next to me. I like to imagine what she would think of me and the life I'm living, whether she'd be proud.

I've never told anyone about this. Not Brooke and

especially not Logan. He wouldn't understand. None of them would.

I look out on the sprawling waters in front of us, a view that Robin never saw in life, and try to breathe. But the anxiety has contracted my chest so tightly I feel I might explode.

And then I realize. This is what they want. The person who's been leaving me these threatening notes, who's been following me around the island, who's been threatening me in my own home. They want me to suffer.

I think of Robin, of everything she never got to see during her short life. And I feel the anxiety change shape, hardening into something else. Anger.

I stand up abruptly, the decision coursing throughout my body.

No more. I'm not going to let this stranger win. I'm not going to give them the satisfaction of watching me squirm as I wait for them to act.

I look out at the beauty of Koh Sang, at this perfect island that I've made my home, at this life that some stranger now wants to steal from me, and I'm certain.

I'm going to find them, and I'm going to do everything in my power to stop them.

21

Brooke

The silence that follows my scramble to turn off my ringtone stretches interminably. I hold my breath, crouched beneath Cass and Logan's living-room window.

Up until now, things had been going smoothly. I'd used the same hairgrip trick that had worked on the door to Lucy's guestroom, and the lock had clicked open without a struggle. Clearly the security systems in Koh Sang could use some work. Even though I'd knocked before resorting to the hairgrip, I still paused in the doorway, listening. I knew from Cass that Logan spent most afternoons at the island gym before starting his shifts at Frangipani, but I had no idea where Cass could be. I called out their names gently, prepared with an excuse in case either of them happened to be home – their door was already open a crack, and I just wanted to make sure nothing was wrong – but I was met with silence.

I started with the desk in the living room, and I was in the process of rifling through its top drawer when I heard it. A soft purring from outside, an engine easing up the drive. Before I could process the implications – Logan returning early from the gym, Cass getting back from wherever she may be – my high-pitched ringtone flooded the room. I scrambled for my phone, my fingers fumbling to silence it, Cass's name left flashing mutely on the screen.

I slid over to the side of the room and ducked beneath the window, holding my breath.

Now, letting my muscles relax, I inch up slowly and flick at the cheap blinds lying horizontally against the window-pane.

Cass is staring right at me.

I immediately drop to the floor, clasping my hand over my mouth. I stay there for a moment, my back hunched, my head buried. Finally, after an endless moment, I lift myself up just enough to see out of the very bottom of the window.

I let out a deep sigh. She's left her motorbike and is walking towards the trees at the start of the Khrum Yai trail. The thought provides only temporary relief. The hike is short, and she'll be back soon.

I flip down the blinds, blocking out the sun, and get back to work. The desk has proven useless so far, so I tidy it up as much as I can and head back to the bedroom.

It only takes me a second to figure out which side of the bed is Cass's. On the left-hand bedside table are several protein bar wrappers and a water bottle, its sides stained with the residue of pink-coloured powder. There's nothing on the one on the right, however, apart from a small, framed photograph of Cass and Logan smiling at the camera.

I pick it up and look at it for a second, my skin burning as I take in her smiling face, before setting it back down on the bedside table, a bit more forcefully than I should.

The drawer is tightly packed with what appear to be all of Cass's residual belongings. I pick through it until my fingers brush against something that feels like cardboard at the back. I pull out all the stuff on top to reveal a white box with red lettering. Xanax. The familiar name jolts me. I open the box, quickly surveying the three blister packs, one of which is almost completely empty, before my fingers rest on something heavier. A small, gold band tucked at the bottom. I flip it in my fingers, noticing the engraving. *Forever Us Two*. Their engagement band. But why would Cass keep it here? As if she didn't want someone to find it?

Despite these questions, the sight of the oblong white pills, each tidily suctioned in its own little bubble, is temporarily distracting, blurring my vision with memories. I can almost taste their chalky texture on my tongue, after the apathetic nurse at the college infirmary prescribed them. For a minute I'm back in my dorm room, collapsed on my bed – where I stayed for weeks. Long enough for my roommate to request a room change and for the school to place me on academic probation. Every day, another handful of pills. Every day, wondering how many I would need to end it all. Always stopping just short of enough, waking up with a dry mouth, a pounding head and a sense of regret for not forcing down one more.

I don't know how long I stand there with the box in my hand, allowing the hazy memories to take over. Even now, the sight of those pills invigorates that need from years ago. I force myself to toss the box on the bed and get back to my search of the drawer, finding Cass's passport buried beneath a half-full bottle of sunscreen and a mildewed paperback detective novel. I open it, knowing exactly what I'll find, and snap a photo of the identification page with my iPhone.

In a final desperate attempt, I decide to check under the bed, dropping to my knees. The bedframe is too low for me to get a good look, so I lean my arm in the crack, swinging it back and forth.

It connects hard with something. The sound of plastic scraping against the wood floor rings out as the object skids a few inches. I reach in further, blindly searching for the mystery object, until I feel my fingers grasp it.

I pull it out, and I'm staring at a model of mobile phone that I haven't seen in years. One of those old Nokias that no one other than cheating spouses and drug dealers still uses.

But before I can wonder why Cass would have a burner phone under her bed, I hear something from the front of the house. My ears prick and my spine goes ramrod straight. It comes again, the rattle of metal against metal. A key in the door.

Logan must be home. Or Cass has come back again.

Either way I'm screwed.

I shove the stuff back into the drawer as quickly as I can and slip the phone into the front pocket of my shorts. I whip my head around, trying to size up my options. There's the bathroom, which is likely the first stop they'll make. Or the closet, which is filled to the brim with clothes and shoes. Or the patio, with a steep drop to the rocky beach below.

I'm trapped.

22

Cass

I know before I turn the front door handle that Logan is back. The light's on in our living room, and the window blinds are flicked fully closed. I look down at the doorstep as I approach the house, bracing myself, expecting to see a new envelope there. But it's empty.

I take a deep breath. I know what I have to do.

Logan walks out from the bedroom when he hears the door. He's wearing a towel tied loosely around his waist and a T-shirt patterned with droplets of water left from the shower. Without a word, he wraps his arms around me in a big bear hug, and the water on his skin soaks through the thin fabric of my shirt.

His face is laced with concern when we separate.

'I think we need to talk.' His tone is gentle, but firm.

I nod. 'We do.'

We take a seat on the living-room couch. It feels like something has changed in here, but I can't put my finger on exactly what. It's as if there's a current in the air that wasn't there before. I let Logan start, because I know what I need to tell him will change everything.

'Cass,' he says, his brow furrowed, his dark blue eyes

staring into mine. 'What happened the night of the Full Moon Party? Why did I have to cover for you yesterday?'

I take a beat and breathe. 'I don't remember.'

It's not the response he was expecting. 'What do you mean?' he asks. And then it clicks. 'Wait. Did you black out?'

'Logan—' I start, but he cuts me off.

'You did? My God, how much did you drink? And then you taught the next day?'

His disappointment is palpable.

'It wasn't just—' I try, but he doesn't let me finish.

'And you don't even know what you did? That was the night Lucy died. You know how bad this looks, right? And I had to cover for you.'

I feel my shoulders straighten, my back muscles clench. The anger that seeped in while I was up on Khrum Yai starts to solidify, heavy in my veins. Where does Logan get off on judging me for drinking too much? He's a bartender, for God's sake. He serves shots to inebriated tourists – not to mention Doug – day in and day out. And I distinctly remember him taking generous swallows from that bottle of Thai whisky being passed around the picnic table at Frangipani that night. And now he's mad about having to cover for *me*? I found his damn engagement ring next to Lucy's dead body and I sure as hell didn't tell anyone about *that*.

I should pause and control my breathing. I should explain to him about the Xanax. But the bitter words sneak through my lips before I can stop them.

'Like you're so perfect.'

'What does that mean?' Logan counters.

I clench my fists, the fury and disappointment and sadness that I felt when I saw him those weeks ago with Jacinta mixing with my new-found anger. All of it whirling in my gut like a tornado.

'I saw you,' I spit.

He scrunches his forehead, confused.

'With her. With Jacinta.'

It's like I've pulled a knife on him. He backs up on the couch. 'Cass, it wasn't what it looked—'

'You were kissing her. It was exactly what it looked like.'

I can see how far off course this conversation has derailed but I can't stop.

'And then I found your engagement ring next to Lucy. It was buried in the sand on the sea floor, right next to her dead body. Were you lying about losing that, too?' I rush forward, before he has a chance to answer. 'Were you hooking up with Lucy before she died? Is that why she had your ring? Or was it worse than that? Did *you* kill her?'

The venom pools out of me, the jealous accusations leaving my mouth half-formed. I don't know what I'm saying. I've never thought Logan was responsible for Lucy's death or even that he was interested in her. But all of a sudden I'm in that hotel room again, my back to the wall. I'm reaching for anything to deflect his anger, his disappointment.

Before either of us can say any more, I hear something. A small bang from the back of the house.

'What is that? Is someone here?' I ask frantically.

Within seconds, I'm in the bedroom. The doors to the closet and the bathroom are still open, humidity clinging to the air from Logan's shower. I throw open the door to the patio and stick my head out, but the balcony is empty.

I don't know who I'm looking for or what I'm expecting, but the feeling from the last few days returns with full force. Eyes on me, following me. Someone tracing my movements. And now that person is here. In my home.

I frantically rummage through the closet and get on all fours to check under the bed. Nothing. If someone is hiding in here, they're doing a damn good job of it.

'There's no one here, all right?' Logan says cautiously. 'It was probably just a branch hitting the side of the house or something. You need to calm down.'

I ignore him, but he's right. I do need to calm down. This anger isn't accomplishing anything.

I give the room one last glance and settle on my bedside table. Everything is as it should be, except for the picture I keep turned to the bed of me and Logan. Now it's turned away, our smiles facing the room as if on display.

'Did you move that?' The accusatory inflection in my tone isn't lost on Logan.

'The picture? Why would I do that?'

'I always keep it facing the other way. You were snooping through my drawer?' I think of the Xanax I've hidden in there. He can't know about it.

'Of course I wasn't. Love, what's going on?' Logan pulls me down to a seated position next to him on our bed, his forehead threaded with lines of concern.

I don't know where to start. I haven't had a pill since this morning, and my mouth waters. I glance back to the drawer. Only a short reach away.

'Cass, sit down, please.' He says it gently, pointing to the spot next to him on the bed. Once I'm seated, he turns his body towards me, his hands clasping mine, and despite everything, I feel warmth radiating through them.

'You're right about Jacinta,' he says, and I feel something inside me break. Despite seeing it with my own eyes, I wanted him to convince me I was wrong. That it was all some big mistake. Instead, he maintains eye contact, his voice soft. 'I had lunch with her one day. I shouldn't have even gone, but I met her the night before at the bar, and when lunch was over, she – she kissed me. I don't know, Cass, I can't explain it. I had just bought the rings – our engagement rings – the day before, and I was planning to propose that week. But all of it just seemed so real, so permanent. I got scared. What do people call it? Cold feet?'

He doesn't wait for me to answer. 'I have no excuse for it. All I can say is, she – Jacinta – tried to do more after that, but once we left the restaurant, I stopped it. It was like I finally came to my senses. I realized how much I was sacrificing, everything I could be throwing away. And I couldn't lose you. You're everything to me. This life we've built – it's everything.'

His voice breaks on the last word, and he stops, bending his head forward as if trying to regain his composure. When he looks back at me, a strand of curls rests against his forehead and there are tears in his eyes.

'I don't know how I could have been so stupid. But after that, I was certain. More certain than I've ever been about anything. You're the person I want to spend my life with. The person I love.'

My tears are coming quicker now.

'And about the ring,' he says. I move to stop him. He doesn't need to explain. I was being ridiculous. I believe him. Lucy must have found his ring and had it with her when she went swimming. I was wrong about all of it.

But before I can, he shifts away from me, reaches his hands into the neck of his T-shirt and pulls something out.

I suck in a harsh breath.

It's his ring. Resting on the delicate gold chain around his neck, right where he promised to keep it.

'Cass, Sengphet gave this to me this morning. He said he

found it on the beach the morning after the Full Moon Party when he was cleaning up.'

'B-but . . .'

This can't be true. I have his ring. I stuffed it into the box of Xanax. I was planning on giving it to him in a few days, pretending like I had found it while I was on the beach. My eyes dart guiltily to the bedside table.

'You might have found a ring,' Logan says. 'But it wasn't mine.' He sighs again, preparing himself. 'I know you've been going through a lot these last few days, so I didn't want to say this.'

He looks down, and my breath catches in my throat as I wait for what he'll say next.

'You need to stop taking the Xanax.'

The words are a punch to the stomach. He shouldn't know about that.

'You were going through my things.' The coldness in my tone is palpable.

'I was worried about you. First the nightmare, and then all the stress you've been under. You haven't been yourself. On edge. I just looked quickly in your drawer and saw the box.'

I don't know what to say. It's not as if I can deny taking the pills.

'That bloody stuff isn't good for you. It fucks with your mind. I looked up the side effects and they're crazy. Mood swings, sleep deprivation, paranoia, issues with your memory, even hallucinations.' He ticks them off on his fingers as he goes.

I know the side effects, of course. I'd read them thoroughly when the doctor prescribed the pills three years ago. But I never experienced any of them. Back then, my mood was never stable enough to notice a change, and I didn't want to remember. Plus, I don't think it qualifies as paranoia when the entire country has turned against you.

But now it's different. I think of the feeling I've had the last few days, that gnawing sensation that someone's been watching me.

One question keeps niggling at me, though. 'If it wasn't your ring that I found, then whose was it?'

We both know the answer before I finish asking the question.

'Cass,' Logan holds my hand up between us. 'Where is *your* ring?'

I look down at the thin, pale strip on my fourth finger. I startle for a moment, but then remember. 'I took it off before my dive on Saturday morning. I didn't want to lose it. I put it in the ring box in my drawer.' I did, I know I did. I remember standing before the bedside table, pulling open the drawer as Logan slept beside me. There was never a question that my ring was there, safe in the confines of that small red box.

But I think of the words Logan just said, the side effects. *Issues with your memory, hallucinations.*

I yank the drawer open and begin rummaging through it until I find the ring box. But even before I open it, a small part of me knows what I'll find.

I stare at the open box, at the thin divot where the ring should be. It's empty.

Frantically, I reach for the Xanax box, buried under some other detritus that I relegated to the drawer, and wrench it out. I dump the contents on to my bed, and sure enough, a slender gold ring tumbles out amid the stacks of blister packs. The ring that I found near Lucy.

And then everything falls into place.

I must not have put my ring back into its box the morning before the dive. I couldn't have.

Because it wasn't Logan's ring I found near Lucy's body. It was mine.

'Cass,' Logan says, his hand tentatively touching my shoulder. 'We should talk about this.'

23

Brooke

A drop of blood sneaks through the crack in my lip, the coppery taste filling my mouth. Still, I keep my teeth clenched on to my lower lip. The pain has been a useful distraction from the growing cramps solidifying in my leg muscles. The one time I tried to move, my foot hit the side of the balcony, ringing out like a shot and piercing the quiet of the hills. The sound was enough to send Cass flying through the patio door.

I held my breath as the door sailed open, biting into my lip even further as it ricocheted against my shin bone. I'd contorted myself into the small crevice in the side of the balcony, right behind the patio door, which shielded me from Cass's view. If she had hung around a second longer or glanced slightly downward, she would have seen me, my feet visible in the few inches beneath the door. But she didn't, and when she returned inside, she failed to pull the door completely shut behind her. It stays now where she left it, resting gently against its frame, the voices from inside the bedroom drifting out on to the balcony.

I've heard everything. Logan's kiss with Jacinta, and then Cass finding a ring near Lucy's body. A fact that even as she tried to get me to believe we were investigating Lucy's death together, as a team, she failed to mention.

And of course, the Xanax.

'How could my ring have gotten there? Just sitting near her body like that?' Cass's voice trickles through the door, weepy and weak. It's clear all the fight she had moments ago has left her. 'I couldn't have done it,' she says.

'I know, love, I know.' Logan's voice is low and reassuring. 'We'll fix this, whatever happened. But I need to ask you something important.' Logan's voice grows soft, and I crane my ear towards the door to make out his question. 'Do you really not remember anything about the Full Moon Party? Nothing at all?'

She's silent for a moment. When she speaks, her voice is so quiet that I have to strain to hear her.

'Just flashes. I remember the fire twirlers and the music and . . .' She trails off.

'And something else?' Logan prompts.

She's quiet, and I picture her shaking her head. 'I should never have been so stupid to mix the Xanax with the drinks.'

Logan is quiet for a minute, and I picture him comforting her. 'It's okay, it's okay.' He pauses. 'But why did you need the Xanax? Is something going on that I don't know about?'

She's quiet for a long while. I want so badly to peer in the window, but I can't risk it.

'No, it's just stress,' she says finally. 'Everything with the engagement and all that, I just felt a bit overwhelmed.' Logan must react silently in some way, because Cass jumps in again. 'No, babe, it's not like that. I've never been happier. It's just . . . it's a lot of change.'

After a moment, I hear Logan's voice again, a soft, gentle murmur. 'Cass, there's something I need to tell you.'

I tighten my body, straining to hear every syllable of whatever confession Logan's about to make.

'I lied to Brooke last night. When she asked about where we were the night of the Full Moon Party.'

My heart stops. Biting my lip is no longer cutting it. I claw my fingers into the palms of my hands, bracing myself for what else he has to say.

'I *did* see Lucy that night. I talked to her. Nothing flirtatious,' he rushes to add, 'just normal talk about how her stay was going and whether she liked the island. It's just that . . . well . . . do you think you might have seen me talking to her?'

'I'm not sure,' Cass says meekly. 'Maybe. Why?'

'Nothing, nothing, love,' Logan says, but he sounds distracted, as if he's running through possibilities in his head.

Cass responds with a sob.

'It's okay,' I hear him say again, as Cass's breathing becomes louder and more ragged. It sounds as if Logan's trying to reassure himself as much as Cass.

I'm not expecting her to say any more, so I'm shocked when I hear her voice.

'Logan, I – I haven't been myself lately.' She pauses, and I feel like my legs will snap from clenching them so hard. 'I lost control earlier . . .' She trails off, and I wait for her to say more, but my anticipation is met only with muffled sobs, as if Cass is crying into her hands.

'Shh, love. Whatever happened here we'll sort it out,' Logan says, in the same comforting tone.

They're quiet for another moment, until Logan speaks again. 'Look, I'm so sorry but I have to go and open Frangipani. I would give anything in the world to stay here with you right now, but there's no one to cover for me, and there's a bar crawl tonight, so it's bound to be busy.' He pauses for a moment, as if thinking. 'Why don't you come with me?'

'No,' I hear Cass say quietly. 'You go. I'll be fine here.'

Logan sighs. 'Okay. Try to relax. Take a long shower, get into bed and get some sleep.' I hear the crinkle of cardboard. 'I'm going to take this with me, so there's no temptation.'

The Xanax, I imagine. He's cutting her off.

Their voices recede, and I picture them walking towards the front of the house. A few minutes later, I hear the front door latch. Logan must have left. I listen for Cass's footsteps coming back to the bedroom, but it's quiet.

I wait for a few minutes, trying to process everything I've heard. Did Cass do this? Did she really kill Lucy? Was I right all along?

I sit there, waiting for some sense of validation, but instead, I feel an overly familiar emotion course through me, one I've felt so often throughout my life. Disappointment.

I continue to plod through my muddled thoughts until I hear Cass's footsteps, followed by the trickle of water running from inside the bedroom, eventually turning into a steady stream. Cass must be showering. I wait another minute or so, until the heat begins to fog up the glass of the patio door, and then I take my chance.

I steal back into the bedroom, opening the patio door as quietly as I can, bracing myself for the creak that will give me away. But it doesn't come. I peek quickly towards the sound of water, where a thin curtain shields me from Cass's sight, before scurrying past into the living room, through the front door, and down the stairs. When my feet hit the pavement, I open my stride into a full sprint back towards my bike. The burner phone I found beneath

Cass's bed rubs against my leg from where it rests in my shorts pocket.

By the time I'm back at the resort, most of the adrenaline has worn off. I push open the door to my room, the familiar damp air hitting my nose, and pull out the burner phone.

Why would Cass have this? And why would she leave it half-hidden under her bed?

I process these questions as I locate the power button, bringing the phone slowly to life. I pull up the call log first. It's full of past calls. Most outgoing, but some incoming as well. There are two incoming calls from a number saved as 'Dan', and I realize with a jolt that those must be from Daniel, although I've never heard Cass refer to him by a nickname. I look hurriedly at the time of the calls, thinking I may have found the person Daniel was meeting last night, but both are from Saturday morning, when he should have been at the dive course. I remember seeing him there on the beach, standing with Cass and the Israeli couple as I waited for Sengphet to deliver my coffee at the Tiki Palms. If he was with Cass at that time, what reason would he have to call her?

The realization hits me like a bullet.

Unless this phone doesn't belong to Cass.

The rest of the calls in the log – both those outgoing and incoming – are to one unnamed number. Ten digits, starting with a country code I don't recognize. I consider calling it, but I have no idea what I would say if someone answered. I need more information first.

I move on to the text messages. There's one message chain, an exchange with the same unidentified number that appears in the call log.

215

It's clear that a large portion of the message chain has been deleted. All that's left are a handful of incoming messages that came in three nights ago, the night of the Full Moon Party. The owner of the phone has read them but not responded.

Are you okay? Where did you go?

Please answer.

I have a bad feeling about this. I shouldn't have let you go off with her alone. She lives here. She has the upper hand.

Just come back to the party. We can talk this through. Tell her you've changed your mind. I don't trust her.

The messages come in short bursts, each sent only a few minutes apart. I can feel the sender's panic bubbling through the phone as I read them, leaving me with a dull pain in my gut. If this phone does belong to Cass, who was she texting with and who was she planning on meeting the night Lucy was killed?

The dull pain turns to fire when I scroll down to the last message. One final plea for information, a last-ditch effort to confirm the reader's safety.

Please just tell me you're okay, Lucy.

The last word hits me square in the chest.

This was Lucy's phone.

She was planning to meet someone the night she was killed. A female. Who lives on Koh Sang.

I think of this phone sitting discarded beneath Cass's bed less than an hour ago. And then I think of how Cass couldn't account for where she was the night Lucy was killed. And the image of the blonde woman talking to Lucy that I saw in Daniel's photos. And the anger, the jealousy she felt when she saw Logan and Jacinta together. How that must have resurfaced when she saw him talking to Lucy at the Full Moon Party.

And just like that, the pieces finally fall into place.

Cass killed Lucy.

24

Tuesday

Cass

One benefit of not sleeping is that it destroys any chance of nightmares. I stare at the wooden blades of our ceiling fan, rotating steadily. I've been watching them for hours, waiting for one of them to go awry, to stray from their monotonous cycle and choose their own path. But they remain contained, responsible. Unlike me.

I've spent the night replaying my conversation with Logan and what it all could mean. Thinking back to his gentle tone sends a plunging shiver through me, the guilt and regret commingling.

Despite everything, I find myself craving a pill. I want to reach into my bedside table drawer, but I know it's futile. Logan took them, removing the ring – *my* ring – from the Xanax box where I'd stored it and hiding the pills from me like I'm some crazy addict. But I suppose it's for the best. The Xanax is the reason why I can't remember the Full Moon Party. It's probably why I keep feeling as though I'm being watched, and it must be why I feel so out of control lately, as if I'm watching a movie of my life unfold in front of me that I can't seem to pause or rewind.

Logan came home late last night, later than usual. I pretended to be asleep again when he got in, a habit that's becoming all too familiar. But I couldn't handle more lies.

I had planned to tell him everything yesterday, to confess it all. But things went sideways so quickly. And when he asked me about the Xanax, why I needed it, the truth stuck in my throat like a pill that wouldn't go down. I couldn't tell him then, not after everything else he'd found out – the pills, my ring. It would be too much. Too many lies to ever put us back together again.

I shared the few things I remembered from the Full Moon Party. But I didn't tell him about the feeling of carrying something in my pocket or the other memory, the sound that keeps hitting my skull, jerking me back to that night whenever it hits.

That woman's voice, desperate and loud, familiar yet unidentifiable. 'No, no, no!'

How did this all happen?

As much as I rack my brain, I can't make the pieces fit together. Unless . . .

You killed her.

The whisper comes from the back of my brain before I can shut it out. I squeeze my eyes shut, but the echo lingers.

I think of how angry I was when I saw Logan with Jacinta, how betrayed I felt. How much hate I had for her in that moment. And then how easily I lost control when confronting Ariel.

Could I have become so enraged that I killed Lucy?

The idea sounds ridiculous, and I try to push it away.

But you've done it before. The voice comes again, the truth smearing my mind, slick and sinister.

I force myself to ignore it and grab my phone from the bedside table, desperate for a distraction. The first thing I notice is a message from Doug, sent nineteen minutes ago.

The police figured out who killed Daniel.

I sit up in the bed, gripping my phone, and force myself to read the message again carefully. The text doesn't change.

I type as quickly as I can. One word, but I have to correct myself several times, deleting errant letters that sneak into the message courtesy of my shaking hands.

Who?

I stare at the phone, hoping for an immediate response, but it doesn't come. Suddenly, I'm suffocating. I need to be out of here, away from this bed. I need to know who did this. I need Doug to tell me that it's the same person who killed Lucy. I need him to say that person wasn't me.

I open the door to the patio as quietly as I can, pressing the call button next to Doug's name on my phone before I'm even fully outside. The phone rings endlessly, each trill hitting my eardrum with a bolt of anxiety.

As I wait for Doug to answer, I look out over the ocean. It's early still, but already light. The sun hangs heavy in the red sky above me. That can't be good.

From the far recesses of my mind, I hear my mother's voice. *Red sky at morning, sailors take warning.* She used the same sing-song rhyme whenever the day began with a pink sky. And without fail, by the time nightfall had hit, our town would be blanketed in rain.

Looks like the island is in for a big storm today.

This is something I should know. It's part of my job to track the weather and to adjust dives accordingly. But with everything else going on, I haven't even bothered to check.

'How ya going, Cass?'

Doug's voice startles me. I was so distracted that I had completely forgotten I'd called him. His tone is light, free of concern, completely disconnected from the hell I'm experiencing. I force myself to swallow, stale bile flooding my throat.

'Doug, what's going on?' I aim for the words to sound as calm as possible, but the question comes out tight and wavering, like a vibrating string.

'The police came here yesterday evening. I called Logan after it happened, and he said you were ill and not to bother you, so I figured I'd wait until this morning. You feelin' any better?'

Despite the kindness of his question, irritation lifts the tiny hairs up off my arms. How can he be interested in anything besides the news of the investigation?

'I'm fine. So, what happened?' The words come out clipped, impatient.

Still, he pauses.

'Doug!'

'Ah yeah, my bad. I'm checking the radar. We've got a ripper of a storm coming in.' And then finally, he tells me. 'The police said that Sengphet confessed.'

Suddenly, the patio rocks beneath me like the deck of a boat tossed in rough waters. I grasp on to the railing in front of me in a futile attempt to steady myself.

I should be relieved at hearing someone else named as the killer. But this doesn't make sense. There's no way Sengphet is capable of killing Daniel.

'Sengphet?' I force my lips around his name, which comes out shakily. 'As in the waiter at the Tiki Palms?'

'Yeah, can you believe it? I wouldn't have pegged him for the type. Frederic is mad as a cut snake, understandably.'

The image of Sengphet's face flashes across my mind. That perpetual smile as he darts around the restaurant, delivering every order with his palms pressed together and a small bow in the customers' direction. Always so gentle, so kind. The only time I've ever seen his brow even furrow is when he's stretching to understand a guest's English.

'But wh-why? Why would they think he did this?'

'The police said it was a drug deal gone wrong. I guess Sengphet was dealing. Daniel must have tried to rip him off or something.'

'They're sure?' I ask. There's no part of me that can reconcile cheerful Sengphet with a drug dealer turned murderer.

'Yeah, they said he confessed,' Doug assures me. 'I mean it makes sense. Remember how Frederic couldn't find Sengphet before the staff meeting? Apparently that was when Daniel was killed.'

I think back to the other night. Brooke suggested that Daniel might have been meeting someone. I just never thought it would be Sengphet.

'But he has a family back in Laos.' I recall one morning at the Tiki Palms when he explained to me in broken English how he sent money home to his wife and kid.

'I guess Frederic wasn't paying him enough,' Doug suggests. 'He had to find cash somehow.'

It makes sense, at least at surface level. But Sengphet, really? I just can't make it fit in my mind.

'Wait,' I say, as a thought clicks in my brain, 'Sengphet

doesn't speak Thai, right? And his English barely extends beyond the dishes and drinks on the Tiki Palms's menu. How could he have possibly confessed everything to the police?'

I can almost hear Doug's shrug down the line. 'Dunno, but I guess he did.'

But who was he working for? And what went so wrong between him and Daniel that he needed to kill him? And how – if at all – does this connect back to Lucy?

I'm about to voice these questions, but Doug has started making a clicking noise with his tongue. I've worked with him long enough to know that tic. He's distracted, probably engrossed in the radar map again.

'Damn, this storm is looking really intense. It just keeps building. Anyway, Frederic and I are going to talk through this today. Try to figure out the best way for us to frame it so this doesn't blow back on the resort. We might have to hire outside PR.'

I barely register his words. My mind is still locked on an image of Sengphet, smiling and cheerful.

'We're not opening the shop today, so don't worry about coming in. We can't dive in this weather. Oh, and did you hear they've stopped the ferries to and from the island?'

I make a sound in response that I suppose could be mistaken for agreement. The news isn't surprising. It's not safe to take people out on the water during a storm like this. The island has stopped the ferry routes many times since I've been here, and it's never been too much of a concern. I never had anywhere else to go. But this time, with everything that's happened and now Sengphet's arrest, it feels different. Like we're isolated from the rest of the world.

Or trapped.

I look out again over the water that just a moment ago

was basking in the glow of the red morning sky. But in the few minutes I've been on the phone, that glimmer has faded, the air now coated in a darker tint, the previously translucent waves now opaque, masking whatever the ocean hides below.

'You should stay home and prepare the house,' Doug says, breaking back into my thoughts. 'Just keep your phone on. Frederic might need to call an "all hands on deck" meeting later this morning to talk through ideas.'

I nod, as if he can hear me through the phone.

'Tell Logan to lock up the bar. We've still got time. The rain isn't supposed to start till late arvo.'

We exchange goodbyes, and a few seconds later the line goes dead.

I should be relieved. If Sengphet killed Daniel, then Daniel's murder isn't connected to Lucy and Jacinta. The women's deaths were just accidents. I had nothing to do with them. My ring ended up next to Lucy's body by mistake. It's all just a bunch of unfortunate coincidences.

But I don't believe a word of it.

I know Sengphet isn't behind this. My stomach turns at the thought of this poor man, who moved here and gave up everything in the hope of giving his family a better life, now blamed for a murder he didn't commit. An easy scapegoat to make the tourists more comfortable, to keep the guests coming in.

But that's not the only thought whirling in my gut.

Because if I'm right, that means the killer could still be walking free on the island.

25

Brooke

Sun filters through my window as I lay my phone on my desk. Exhaustion settles dense in my muscles, but anxiety buzzes just underneath, carbonating my veins. I tilt my neck first to the right, then to the left, relishing the satisfying popping sound.

It's done.

For a moment last night I considered confronting Cass. About Lucy and everything else that came before. But something stopped me. I could already hear the excuses she would fall back on, the lies she would continue to weave.

Everyone will let you down if you allow them. And some will do it over and over if they get the chance.

No, this is the only way.

I pick up my phone again and read through the lengthy Instagram caption I've written for the umpteenth time. No typos. It's ready to go. But as my finger hovers over the 'post' button, I change my mind, saving the draft and closing the app. One more read-through with fresh eyes, I tell myself, and then I'll publish it.

But I know it's not my concern over typos that's causing me to procrastinate. I think back to yesterday morning, my kiss with Neil, and consider what I would be doing to him by posting this. All the possibilities that seemed like potential realities for a short while yesterday – building a relationship, settling down with him on this island, even becoming one of the Permanents and finding the family I never had – will go up in smoke as soon as my finger touches that button.

I navigate back to my inbox, but there's still no response to the message I sent Alice yesterday, nor has she accepted my follow request.

I push my chair back from the desk and immediately feel a hollowness, an aching emptiness in my carved-out gut. I realize I haven't eaten since last night – I've been so deep in the story I've pieced together, making sure it all fits perfectly, that I never even recognized my hunger. As tired as I am, I feel an urgent need for food, a manic desire to fill the emptiness. I grab my canvas tote and stuff my laptop in it, along with my wallet.

But there's one thing I need to do first.

I grab my phone and navigate to the call log. The number I'm looking for is the first listed, and my phone notifies me that I've called it no less than a dozen times since last night.

It's the number I found in Lucy's phone, the one from which all those urgent text messages came. The first time I called it, it rang three times before someone answered. Or, more accurately, the call connected. Because whoever picked up the phone said nothing. All I heard was rapid breathing coming down the line. Before I could formulate a greeting, the line disconnected.

Since then, my calls have gone directly to voicemail – an automated message that recites the number I called back to me. I call one more time, but it does the same. Whoever was looking out for Lucy has turned off their phone. Either that, or Lucy's killer has already got to them, too.

I order a full breakfast from one of the British-owned restaurants on Kumvit Road, paying with my last wad of baht, and check my email on my phone as I wait. The commission I'm owed for a hotel post in the Czech Republic still hasn't come in. I try to force away the worry; I have much bigger things to deal with at the moment. But the concern lingers. Without that deposit in my account, I have barely enough to cover another week of accommodation on Koh Sang, let alone a flight out of Thailand.

I get the food to go, hoping to avoid a chance run-in with any of the Permanents, and as I begin to walk, I'm daydreaming of the breakfast I plan to inhale as soon as I get to my room. I turn on to a small side street that connects back to the beach road, but as I round the corner, I stop short.

Someone is watching me.

I turn around. A few early risers are wandering down the street but, beyond them, I spot one person standing still, her gaze glued on me.

It takes me a moment to recognize her: the girl I saw the other night at the Tiki Palms after the staff meeting. The young, dark-haired girl whom I had caught staring at me, just as she is now.

Her tanned legs peek out from a rumpled T-shirt and khaki shorts, and her now-familiar eyes are lined with dark circles. Even so, they're filled with the same uneasy intensity I noticed the other night at the Tiki Palms. There's something about this girl, the way she looks at me like she needs something, that makes me uncomfortable. I realize with a start that it's the same look I'd seen on

Lucy's face the day she confronted me, the day of her death.

I take a step towards her, planning to ask her what she wants. But as soon as I do, she darts away, as deftly as she did on Sunday night. I try to follow her, hurrying back towards the street where I ordered breakfast, but by the time I round the corner, she's nowhere to be found. I notice a small break in the trees behind the restaurant that I think leads into the other winding roads of Kumvit, and I briefly consider entering it. But I know it's no use. She's had too much of a head start. I'll never catch up with her.

I turn back around and keep walking, but my thoughts stay with that girl.

I know something's wrong by the time I get back. The door to my hotel room is open a crack. I rack my brain, retracing my hurried steps out of the room. I know I pulled it shut and locked it. I always do.

I press my palm against the door gingerly, bracing myself.

It's utter chaos. My clothes have been pulled from my drawers and strewn everywhere. The sole lamp lies shattered on the floor, and the sheets have been pulled off the bed, the mattress askew on its frame.

I clutch my tote bag, feeling the weight of my laptop against my hip and breathe a sigh of relief. I have my laptop and my phone. I scan the room, but my chargers for both are gone.

I think of something else and hurry to the desk, pulling open the top drawer.

There's a space where I'd stored both Daniel's phone and the burner phone I'd found under Cass's bed.

I look around the room again, searching for anything to

suggest who could have done this. There's no note but the intent is as clear as if it'd been written on the wall: *Leave this alone. Mind your business. Or else.*

Words I've been told over and over in my life.

I feel something light in me, a flame kissing the powder keg of rage in my abdomen. Despite everything, I smile. Do they think this will stop me?

They don't know how far I've come, everything I've sacrificed. They can't know the real reason I've come to Koh Sang.

I sit down on the mattress, pulling out my phone. I know I don't have too much time – without a charger, I've got only a few hours of battery life at most.

I pull up the Instagram post I had drafted before, skimming it one more time.

It's time to clear the air. For me to confess my true motive for coming to Koh Sang. It wasn't the sun, or the diving, or the hype of island living.

It was for a person. A woman.

And before you start thinking something salacious – no, it wasn't for sex or romance or any of that.

Most of you – my American followers, at least – probably remember Meghan Morris. Meghan the Murderer. The Hudson Massacre Killer. The person who ruthlessly murdered her own father and little sister a few years ago. You may recall that the tabloids painted her as a villain out for blood. And I can tell you it's all true. Meghan doesn't care about anyone but herself. I know from personal experience.

Even in the aftermath of the murders, which gained the attention of the whole country – hell, even the world – Meghan declined to give us any answers for why she did what she did. She refused all interviews, holed up in her grandmother's home for nearly a year, and left us all wondering how a seemingly normal girl could be so evil.

When the tabloids finally died down, Meghan saw her chance for escape. No one knew where she went to or where she's been hiding out for the last few years.

Until now . . .

Meghan came here, to Koh Sang, the island where I've been staying for the last few weeks. She started going by the name Cass Morris, took up scuba, and began living the life that neither her sister nor her father was apparently entitled to.

But it seems like Meghan is back on her bullshit. Because wherever she goes, people get hurt. Or, in this case, killed.

I skim over the rest of the post, which details all the evidence I've collected on the island: Cass's connection to the three deaths, her convenient little drug problem, the phone I found in her room.

The words lie beneath an album. Four photos in all. A still frame from Daniel's video that shows Lucy talking to Cass at the Full Moon Party; a screenshot of the text messages the mystery sender sent to Lucy on the night of her death; and a zoomed-in photo of Cass's passport, with all information blocked out aside from her passport photo and her name – Meghan Morris. But the coup d'état is the first photo, the cover of the album. A photo of Cass that I persuaded her to reluctantly allow me to take as we hiked Khrum Yai days ago. I've layered it in a black and white filter that amplifies the plain discomfort on her face and makes her eyes look too dark against the bright sun, almost scared. She had begged me not to put the photo on Instagram, and I had promised her I wouldn't. Until now.

Because I came to Koh Sang with one goal in mind: to find Cass. To confront her. And to destroy her.

I just didn't predict that I'd find a trail of dead bodies in her wake.

I've been following her as often as I can since I've arrived, watching her tiptoe through life, as if one wrong move will bring everything down. I've been choosing places, like my favourite table at the Tiki Palms, where I can monitor her as she teaches classes, noting her schedule, who she talks to, what she does, going after her whenever she hops on her motorbike, always keeping a safe distance so she won't ever suspect.

I've been the one leaving her little notes on her doorstep. Letting her know she hasn't changed. That she's still the same girl from years ago. The one who hurt me. The one who ruined me.

I think of the promise I made her yesterday.

Everyone is going to know the truth, soon.

I take a deep breath and press my finger down hard on the 'post' button, all of my hesitations from earlier long gone. I can't let anything get in the way of why I came here.

It's time I made good on my threat.

26

Cass

The sky has morphed from a harsh pink to the beginnings of a bruise as I speed down the hill, away from my house. Despite Doug's recommendation to stay home, I need to get out. It's not just avoiding Logan – though that's certainly part of it. I need to feel the water on my skin, the sea stretching up above me. I need to dive.

It's been a while since I've had a craving this intense to be underwater. Lately, I've been dulling any urges with the pills. But for the first time in days, my head finally seems clear of chemicals, dirtied now only by the thousands of anxieties rushing through my mind. And diving is my one sure way to silence them.

It's a twenty-minute drive across the island. It would be much quicker to go to Pho Tau beach, but I can't bear the thought of running into anyone. I'm not prepared for the avalanche of images the sight of the Tiki Palms would unleash: Sengphet smiling as he delivered my coffee; Sengphet waving to me cheerily from behind the bar; Sengphet bruised and bloodied, alone in a nondescript cell.

I've seen first-hand what the police are capable of. Last year, my dive student went and tried to fight an off-duty cop while on a midday bender. The police didn't take kindly to that, so they tracked my student down in his Terrace room, dragged him away from the resort and locked him up in the Koh Sang jail, a narrow hallway of cells connected to the police station. Frederic sent me there with a crumpled envelope filled with American dollars. The handover was easy, cash in exchange for the guest, a South African tourist in his early twenties. He was cocky, reluctant to listen to any of my instructions during class, just like Daniel was at the beginning. But when I picked him up from the jail, he was someone else entirely. Blood had dried in a crusty mess along his lips and chin, cigarette burns lined his shoulders and he was missing a fingernail.

And that was just for an assault. I can't begin to imagine what they would do for a murder.

I push the thought from my mind as I pull up to Lamphan beach. As I hoped, the sand is empty aside from one long-tail boat tied up at the far end of the shore. This part of the island has none of the tourist draws of Pho Tau: no beach bars or water-sport stands. Only silky, white sand and turquoise waters that stretch on for ever.

I pause, reminding myself how lucky I am – despite everything – to call this my home. I inhale deeply, relishing the fresh, salty smell of the air, and peer across the water. This beach is usually calm, protected by the cliffs that surround it. But today, as the storm nears, the waves have started to pick up, a handful of white caps marring the placid surface.

After parking, I walk out on the sand and pull the tank and the BCD vest I dragged from the house – my personal back-ups – off my back. I empty the bag I have looped over my arm, removing fins, a mask, my respirators and my wetsuit, and leave the rest of my things on the beach. I don't worry that anyone will take it. This part of the island is – has always been – a safe haven. Within minutes I'm at the water's edge, savouring the easy comfort of the water filtering over my feet.

And for the first time in days, I relax. My muscles loosen, the thoughts subside and I let myself enjoy this. The sun is absent today; dark clouds and the growing winds cast a murky glow over the water. But still, it's beautiful. Small fish skitter away as I approach them, basking in the beautiful glow of the coral that lives on this side of the island. But the views aren't why I came here. It's the reprieve I'm after, the temporary pause of the real world around me.

I stay down for far longer than I should. Whenever I try to ascend, I'm stopped by an all-encompassing reluctance to surface.

Finally, when my air gauge reads close to empty, I break the waterline. I allow myself to float there a moment, buoyed by my inflated vest, and spin, taking in the full 360-degree view. The sky has darkened since I got in the water, a growing wind pushing the sand down the empty beach, spotted only with the occasional palm tree, its branches bending precariously.

When I can't put it off any longer, I swim back to shore, ultimately collapsing on to the sand next to where I left my bag. I sit there for a while, long enough to feel a few light drops of rain fall from the sky. When the unease starts to return, eradicating the calm like a virus, I finally pull my phone from my bag.

My screen flashes before I can even press a button, warning of seventeen notifications.

I was hoping to acclimatize back into the anxiety of the real world, but it hits me like a wave, taking me under. I open my messaging app and scroll. Panic thumps in my chest as I take in the number of different senders: Greta, Neil, Doug, Logan and Brooke.

Something is clearly wrong.

I decide to start with Brooke's message. As I click on it, I realize how much I've missed talking to her, and for the first time, I wonder why she never returned my call from yesterday afternoon. Until I see it.

Maybe now you'll rethink what you did.

A thrum of dread races through me, and at the tail end, confusion. What did I do – or more importantly, what does Brooke *think* I did? What does she know? I squeeze my eyes shut, as if that will stop the text from existing, but the words burn into the back of my eyelids. *What you did.*

Suddenly, the moment I've feared since I first stepped on to this island two years ago, since I first realized I had a second chance at life, feels imminent.

I force myself to confront what Brooke is talking about, to get that confirmation, and open the new messages from Logan.

Please answer.
Tell me this isn't true.
Cass, these are lies, right?

They all follow the same theme. Something terrible has happened. Something that involves me.

And I know. Without having to look, I know that it's time. Whoever left those envelopes on my doorstep has finally made good on their threat.

Still, I scroll up the thread, finding the first message from Logan.

I click on it, my hands shaking so hard that it takes several attempts for my finger to land precisely on the link. The internet loads slowly so far away from the bustle of Kumvit and Pho Tau beach, and I realize I'm holding my breath.

The link connects to my Instagram app, pulling up a profile I know almost by heart. A beautiful woman stares out at me from the upper left corner of the screen, her shiny hair pulled back in a tight bun. I click on her most recent post, recognizing it before it even enlarges on the screen. And then everything makes sense.

Why Brooke, this beautiful, confident influencer took such an interest in me when she got to the island. Why someone of her popularity would be drawn to a quiet, inconsequential dive instructor.

We never had the instant connection I thought we did. She was never the friend or the mentor I believed she was.

She was my betrayer.

All this time, it's been Brooke. She's the one who has been leaving those notes, who's been threatening to expose me. The only reason she got close to me was to use me.

I pause briefly on the photo she's posted of me on the top of Khrum Yai. I told her not to, lying that it was because I didn't like the way I looked, not because I didn't want any one of her thousands of followers to recognize me as *Meghan*. Now with the eerie filter she's laid on it and paired with the words beneath, it's haunting. Exactly what she intended, I'm sure.

I read the caption as quickly as possible, my mind tripping over my name – the real one – paired with the ones the papers had so kindly gifted me: Meghan the Murderer;

The Hudson Massacre Killer. But the words Brooke's typed under those names hurt even more.

I hold the phone, staring at the post for so long that the screen goes black, reflecting my own face back to me. My hair is wild, my cheeks raw from the salt water.

I look like a person who could kill.

Who *has* killed.

My heart skids against my chest, and I feel as if I'm being buried alive. I picture sand filling my lungs like the bulb of an hourglass. Gasping, I suck in as much of the hot, humid air as I can. *In for two.* I try to regulate my breathing as I would underwater, standing in case it will help.

But this time it doesn't work. I try again, but it's as if my airway has closed entirely. I drop to my knees.

Black dots begin to flicker at the corners of my eyes, my vision curling up at the edges like the damaged film of the home movies we used to watch on Dad's old projector.

The memory floods back. Robin and me, probably in sixth and fourth grade at the time, and Mom, running along the beach, Dad off screen, handling the camera as it bounced with each stride. 'I can't keep up,' I yelled at Robin and Mom. They stopped. Robin turned around and walked back to me, her voice sweet. 'Of course you can. You're my big sister. You can do anything.'

I try again to breathe, flaring my nostrils as wide as they go, desperate for air. *I can do this. I'm your big sister.*

And I force myself back to standing. It's time to confront what I've done. To make this right as much as I can.

But the question still pulses deep within me. What could I have possibly done to Brooke to deserve this?

27

Brooke

It happened three years ago. I was a freshman in college. Only eighteen, the same age Lucy was when she was murdered.

The plan was to meet him in the library.

I tried to calm myself down as I trekked up the barely used back staircase. He's just a guy, I told myself, a few years older than you. And it was just a stupid story.

But I knew it was more than that. It was my first big piece for the *Hudson Herald*. The first time the editors had trusted me with anything more than a one-paragraph segment they would hide in the back pages. This was my big break, or as big as a break can be for a college paper in Upstate New York. An interview with Eric Verrino, the captain of Hudson's swimming team, which was predicted to win the division championships that year.

I followed the directions in the text he'd sent me after my editor gave me his number and weaved through stacks of old, obsolete books to a collection of three study carrels I'd never known existed. And there he was.

He had olive skin topped with jet-black hair and gleaming dark eyes, and was dressed in maroon workout pants and a black zip-up windbreaker, the swimming team's unofficial campus uniform. His smile formed a charming divot in one cheek, revealing a line of straight, ultra-white teeth.

'You must be Brooke.' His voice was kind, his beautiful smile laced through it.

I nodded, too eagerly. 'Nice to meet you, Eric,' I said shakily, flinching at how thick my Kentucky accent sounded in the quiet library.

I'd never been this person, someone who lost their mind over a guy. But good lord, this was like seeing a Greek god in the flesh. I cursed myself silently. I was already nervous about the interview, I didn't need this on top of it.

He gestured to the chair at the carrel beside him, and I sat. As I pulled out my second-hand laptop to take notes and my phone to record, I tried not to think of how close his arm was to mine or how the sound of his breathing made the little blonde hairs on my arm stick up.

'So, let's talk about how you won the 800-metre freestyle at the semi-finals last week. That was huge, and you were so—'

He held up his hands, laughing in a way that made his eyes sparkle.

'Why don't we get to know each other before we start?'

My cheeks grew hot, and I cursed myself again. How could I be fucking this up so quickly?

'Sorry,' I mumbled sheepishly.

'No need to apologize,' Eric said, and I could feel him looking at me, even as I kept my gaze locked on the table. 'I just want to get to know you a bit first.'

I had prepared all last night for this interview, thinking up questions, identifying conversation starters, but I hadn't prepared for that. What about *me* could he possibly be interested in getting to know?

'You're a freshman, right?' he asked. I nodded, realizing how effortlessly he'd taken control of the interview I was supposed to be leading. But I didn't mind. I could listen to his voice all day. 'What do you think of Hudson so far?'

I wouldn't say I was enjoying myself at Hudson University. I had a roommate I barely spoke to, bullish professors, and omnipresent anxiety that I wouldn't make the grades necessary to keep my full academic scholarship.

But it was what I didn't have that bothered me the most. I hadn't met a single person I felt like I connected with. It was as if the stigma of my mother's trailer park had followed me all the way from Kentucky, clinging to me like a stench I couldn't shower off. All the other female students, clad in their Lululemon leggings and perfect contour make-up, seemed to smell it on me, knowing immediately I wasn't worth their time.

I planned to respond with a non-answer: 'Good', 'Fine', or even 'A lot of fun'. So I was shocked when my voice turned on me. 'It's been a bit of an adjustment,' I heard myself say.

'I get it,' he said, his words woven with understanding. 'I had some trouble when I first got here, too.'

I shot him a look that made my disbelief clear. I couldn't imagine Eric Verrino feeling uncomfortable in any setting. He laughed, a sound that sent a flutter to my chest.

'It's true. I didn't click with the other guys on the swim team right away. I was so used to my friends and my team back home in Connecticut. It took me a few months to figure out where I fit in here.' As if I wasn't taken enough with him before, his vulnerability made me want to melt into the library carpet. 'Have you picked a major yet?' he asked, deftly changing the subject.

'Yup, journalism,' I said. There was never any question that's what I would study.

'Journalism,' he said, raising his eyebrows. 'That's a respectable profession.'

'I spent a lot of time watching the news when I was growing up. My mom raised me and she . . . worked a lot, so usually it was just me and the TV at night. I kind of became obsessed with it.'

I didn't tell him how much I came to rely on the people who reported to me from my screen, how they became the closest thing I had to friends back then. Some of the only regulars I could rely on. Instead, I felt my cheeks grow hot, realizing how much unsolicited information I was sharing. But Eric didn't seem to mind. Instead, he listened, really listened, his eyes growing wide at the right times as I talked. And as we kept talking, he began sharing, too, telling me about his family back in Greenwich, his friends on the team, the finance major he felt his parents had forced him into.

We'd been there an hour before I realized I hadn't asked him a single question about the swimming team. But for the first time since I'd arrived at Hudson, it felt like everything would be okay.

The text came in when I got back to my dorm that night, hours after Eric, in a flurry of apologies, had ended our conversation, admitting he had to get to class.

Want to finish that interview at my place tomorrow night?

The first thing I noticed when I stepped out of the cab the next night was how quiet it was. There was no house music pumping from speakers, no kegs in the backyard, no scantily clad girls laughing on the front lawn. Just one light glowing from the ground floor of the house.

I know Eric had said he wanted to finish the interview, but I had expected that was just pretext; I had predicted a party. Isn't that what seniors did on Friday nights?

I rang the doorbell, forcing myself to remember to breathe as I waited for someone to open the door. After what felt like several minutes, someone finally did. A girl with long brown hair that had been straightened to the brink of death. Her fringe clung to her forehead. She looked me up and down, clearly unimpressed.

'Can I help you?'

'Um, I'm here to see Eric?' Suddenly, I was sure I'd made a mistake. Maybe I was meant to come over earlier or maybe we were supposed to meet on campus. Did I misread his text?

'It's for me!'

I relaxed as soon as I heard his voice. He appeared behind the girl and placed a hand on her shoulder. Her face warmed when she heard him, but her gaze still regarded me coolly.

'Brooke, come on in. You need to meet everyone!' Eric said, grabbing my hand and bringing me into the living room. A handful of people lounged on the couches, limbs intertwined, but the girl who opened the door sat by herself on an armchair. She and some of the other girls were holding red Solo cups, but the guys didn't seem to be drinking.

'Everyone, this is Brooke,' Eric announced to the room, drawing none of the guys' attention. Some of the girls looked up, intrigued, but returned to their drinks after an apathetic glance, except for the brunette from the door who hadn't stopped looking at me. 'Brooke, this is everyone. Can I get you something to drink?'

I told him sure in a voice that didn't sound like mine. He disappeared and returned a moment later with a single can of Natural Light, which he handed to me.

'You're not drinking?' I asked.

'Nah, it's dry season for us. Our coach doesn't want us drinking or partying for a month before championships. We've got two weeks left to go, and it's torture.'

'It'll be worth it,' one of the guys volunteered from the couch, a redhead with full, dark eyebrows. I recognized him from the photos on Eric's Facebook page.

His comment sparked a conversation about the impending swimming competition. After a few minutes of lively discussion – none of which I participated in – Eric finally turned to me.

'Do you want a tour of the house?' He asked it quietly enough so that no one else would hear.

I knew what this was. It was what I'd been waiting for. An excuse to go up to his bedroom.

'Sure,' I said almost before he could finish asking. Because I *was* sure. I wanted to go upstairs with him. I ached to touch him, to feel his lips on mine. But still, my heart rate accelerated as I stood.

The guys whooped and cheered as we left the living room. The girls stayed silent.

At the top of the stairs, Eric led me down a narrow, wood-panelled hallway. The walls were empty of decoration except for a big whiteboard. I could see Eric's name written on it in marker, along with the names of his roommates and some others I recognized from my research on the swimming team. Each name had a flurry of lines next to it. I tried to stop to look at it, but Eric pressed his hand against my back.

'Come on,' he murmured. 'My room is down here.'

We stopped at the last door in the hall, which Eric opened to a dimly lit room with wood floors and walls covered in posters and stray clothes. It smelled damp and slightly chlorinated, the source of which I guessed was the pile of crunchy-looking Speedos in the far corner of the room.

He guided me towards the bed, and I sat down, seeing nothing but him. His face. That beautiful face.

And soon it was on mine. His lips soft at first, fleetingly so. Quickly, his tongue pushed my lips apart, exploring my mouth. I could feel the lipstick I had so meticulously applied smearing as his hands snaked around to my back and under my shirt, searching for my bra clasp.

What was happening? This wasn't how it was supposed to be.

I pulled my head back, pressing my palms against his chest.

'What's the matter?' His tone was hard, cold. It didn't sound like the voice I'd grown accustomed to in the library yesterday. 'Isn't this what you want?'

'Yes, but—'

Before I could finish, his mouth was back on mine. Once he succeeded in loosening the clasp of my bra, he grabbed my hand hard, shoving it between his legs.

'Eric, stop.' It came out garbled. His tongue was still in my mouth.

'Jesus.' Now he was angry. 'What?'

I didn't know what to say, so I said nothing. He moved his face back close to mine, as if he was going to kiss me. Instead, he spoke.

'Look, you were all over me yesterday. I didn't waste all that time in the library for you to decide at the last minute that this isn't what you want.'

I stared at him, my mind struggling to process his words.

My emotions ping-ponged from shock, to sadness, to anger, and my thoughts wouldn't calm down enough to figure out which one I felt most.

He didn't wait for me to respond. Instead, he covered my mouth with his hand and whipped me around. I felt his other hand yanking my pants down. I tried to cry out, or at least I think I did. To this day, I'm not sure if I made a sound.

And then came the pain.

Every thrust brought a hot, searing flash behind my eyelids, as if he was ripping further and further inside of me. I had stopped taking in breath, his hand blocking my mouth and one of my nostrils. It was as if my body refused to do anything other than focus on the pain.

His hand twisted around my hair, yanking my head back. Heat burned through my scalp, a welcome distraction from the agony between my legs. I focused on it, picturing every little hair being broken, leaving behind ragged roots.

And as suddenly as it started, it was done. I felt him crawl off me, but I couldn't move.

'That was good,' he said over the scratchy sound of metal on metal as he pulled up his zipper. 'I'll see you downstairs.'

And then he was gone.

I lay there for a minute, terrified. Wondering if he would come back or whether I was free to go. I knew every second I spent in his bed I was begging for it to happen again. But it was as if I was frozen there, stuck to those crusty sheets, the smell of blood and something more sour flooding my nose.

I heard him clomp down the stairs. Then a few seconds later, his voice, jubilant.

'Twenty-six!'

Cheers followed. A mix of male and female voices. I had no idea what that meant, but I knew it had to have something to do with me.

When I finally got up, I didn't have anything to wipe myself off with. I looked down at the sheets. They were covered in what looked like rust. It took me a minute to realize it was blood, and then another to figure out where it was coming from. I collected my jeans from the ground and pulled them back up, thanking God they were dark, that they wouldn't show anything.

I tiptoed out of the room, trying to make as little noise as possible. I could hear sounds from downstairs, laughing and muffled conversation.

I headed toward the stairs, stopping in front of the whiteboard. Eric's name was listed at the top. Underneath were five groupings of lines, each of which had a diagonal line struck through it. Twenty-five.

My brain was cloudy. But not enough to prevent me from understanding what this was. I was number twenty-six.

When had the contest started? The school year? That month? Not that it mattered. I was just a number to him, and in a way, he was the same to me.

He was my first.

I stopped being quiet. Instead, I ran down the stairs, hitting each one as hard as I could. I turned my head towards the living room before reaching the front door.

And in that moment, I saw the girl who had opened it for me. Her eyes were locked on me without any sign of emotion. As if she were empty.

I've thought about those eyes constantly. Despite all the rage I felt towards Eric, what that girl did seemed even worse. Opening the door, welcoming me in, knowing full well what was about to happen. She sat there as Eric led me upstairs, aware of what he planned to do to me. And then she ignored it, denied any effort to help.

And the rage is relentless. I try to dampen it, but even at my happiest, it's always there. A sour taste in the back of my throat. A dull ache in my abdomen. Waiting for me to lower my guard, so that it can crawl like dark ivy through my veins, choking out every other feeling.

Even years later, I spent nights awake, staring up at the ceiling of yet another Eastern European hotel, fantasizing about how I would ruin them – both Eric and the girl who let it happen. But that was all it was, fantasies. I knew I would never be able to touch Eric. I'd monitored him on social media, his six-figure starting salary at the finance firm on Wall Street, his happy marriage – to Cass's old roommate, no less – a newborn baby rounding out their perfect family of three. He has enough charm, enough money, enough pull to get away with anything, especially when his accuser is a mildly successful travel blogger with a penchant for bikini photos. And he has friends, like the girl in the swim house that night, who will do whatever it takes to cover for him.

I'd kept tabs on her, too, of course. I watched the stories come out about her, her family. Thrilled she was going to get her comeuppance; that she was being named every-thing I had called her in my own head. But then after everything that happened – everything that she did – she got off free. I was enraged, sickened that she manipulated her way out of the terrible things she had done. And soon enough, it became impossible to find her.

Until several months ago. I was in a hotel room in Roma-nia, scrolling through past blog posts by another travel influencer I follow, when something made me stop. It was a mundane post, filled with photos the influencer had taken of her first scuba experience. But there was one picture squeezed in at the bottom that seized my attention in a chokehold. It was a photo of the influencer and three others, gathered around a small table loaded with drinks, a beautiful landscape of white sand and turquoise waves in the background. 'Celebrating being scuba certified with the amazing staff at the Koh Sang Dive Resort!' she had captioned the photo, geotagging it as the Tiki Palms Restaurant. I skimmed over the two men at the table – one with a mashed-up nose and dirty-looking hair, the other a redhead with a kind smile – to the only other woman, her expression surprised as if she wasn't expecting the flash. She was different, of course: the blonde hair, the tanned skin, the new name. But her eyes were the exact same as they'd been three years ago.

Empty.

It was the girl from the swim house. The girl from the newspapers. Her.

I spent weeks learning everything I could about her, scouring the resort website and social media pages for any crumbs of information I could gather, each realization expounding my anger. She'd left New York, started over. She had a brand-new life, a boyfriend, a job, a set of close friends on this paradise island. The unfairness of it cut me to my core. She didn't deserve this, any of it.

So, after a few months of saving and researching and planning, I spent everything I had to come to this island to find her. To see if she'd changed. And if not, to get revenge.

I went to the Tiki Palms the morning after I first arrived on Koh Sang, knowing we would cross paths eventually. I was so jittery I could barely sit still, my heart beating so hard I expected she would hear it as soon as she entered the restaurant. I thought for certain she would recognize me, convinced my plan would be destroyed before it even started. Despite rounding out my Kentucky drawl, my new hair colour, and learning how to use make-up – thanks, Instagram – I still look like the girl I was back at Hudson University. But Cass was so guileless she never even questioned it, which only made my rage burn brighter. She's the same person she was back then, desperate for the attention of those who shine bright, no matter the cost to others. And, as a glittering new Instagram celebrity, I fit the mould pretty well.

I sit now, at the top of the hill leading to her house, because I'm consumed by the need to see those eyes that have haunted me every day since I entered that swim house. I need to see that she understands. I need to see that I've broken her as much as she did me.

28

Cass

As soon as the shock of reading the post wears off, I'm back on my motorbike, speeding away from Lamphan beach. Anger and betrayal lap at the back of my mind like waves, but I'm fully consumed with one task: finding Logan.

The words of his text sawed at the few threads holding me together these last few days. *Tell me this isn't true.* I need to see him, to explain everything I should have told him yesterday. The things I should have confessed to years ago, when we first became serious. I need to make this right.

Nausea clings to my throat, cloying and threatening as I think about what all this could mean for us. The desperation from yesterday returns in full form, clutching at my throat and pressing tighter and tighter. I need him. For the first time, it starts to sink in. I barely survived losing Robin. I wouldn't make it through losing Logan, too.

I drive like my life depends on it – which it very well might – my resolve growing with every rotation of my bike wheels against the road. I'll tell him everything. I'll make him understand. We'll get through this. We have to.

I barely see her as I near the house, so focused am I on

the crushing disappointment that comes when I realize Logan's bike isn't parked in the driveway.

I look around, expecting him to walk into view. And that's when I notice her. Her motorbike parked at the mouth of the Khrum Yai trail, her lips contorted into a smug smile.

I barely manage to park my bike before I'm running towards her, fists balled. I don't know what it is I plan to do with them. I manage to stop with my face inches from hers, and a small pulse of satisfaction thrums in my muscles when I notice her flinch.

'How could you.' The words come out as a growl, more demand for an explanation than question.

This close, Brooke looks as if she hasn't slept in days. Her face is awash with dark circles and broken capillaries, and the whites of her eyes are tinged red, though not enough to dampen her disdain. I suppose there's no longer a reason for her to hide her real feelings for me.

'You really don't remember me, do you?' Brooke asks slyly. I open my mouth to claim she's mistaken, that we've never met. But before I can, I note yet again the echo of something familiar in her voice. The flattened vowels, the slight twang. A sound I've only noticed in a few of our most recent conversations, when Brooke was focused or irritated.

'What accent is that – where are you even from?' I ask with trepidation. 'You said you were from out west.'

Brooke puts a mocking finger to her mouth.

'Guess that Hudson education really did wonders for you, huh?' She begins pacing, swinging her arms at her sides casually. 'By the way, have you kept up with your friends there, your old roomie? Eric, perhaps?' Her voice is razor sharp, eyes poisonous.

And then it comes to me. I *have* met her before.

It was one time, years ago, and only for a few minutes.

That skinny girl in her clearly second-hand clothes and badly dyed hair. The quiet one who spoke with a heavy drawl, her insecurity painted across her face.

The swim house, three years ago. A night that would otherwise have blended in with hundreds of others if not for the fact that it happened only weeks before my life imploded. That girl, showing up at the house, smiling eagerly at everyone. I watched her with distaste, as she drowned in Eric's attention, thinking she was actually special enough to deserve it. I knew she'd find out eventually that she wasn't, that Eric was just using her for that stupid contest over which guy could sleep with the most women during their dry month. It was appalling, in retrospect, but at the time, I laughed along with them. I did what I needed to do for Eric and my roommate to keep me around. They, in their infinite popularity, made me feel special, the same way Brooke has in these last few weeks. Until now.

That night, after the girl went up to Eric's room and he came back down to the living room victorious, she caused a scene. Pounding her way down the stairs, slamming the door behind her. I remember watching as she ran out of the house, embarrassed for her. She looked at me as if I did something wrong. I didn't understand it, and I barely thought of her again.

The Brooke I know bears no similarities to that girl. She's changed everything about herself, swapping her second-hand clothes for more flattering styles, trading her terrible black hair for soft honey waves, her bony limbs expanding into appealing curves.

But as she stares at me now through those red-rimmed eyes, her bracelets jangling as she runs her hand through her hair, I can see a flash of it in her face. That same eagerness to be accepted that wafted off her at the swim house. I think back to the few times I brought her along to hang out with the Permanents, before Lucy and all the chaos that unfolded with her death. How quick she was to laugh at a joke or throw a compliment in Greta's direction. She may have suppressed her desire to fit in – she certainly wasn't as obvious as that girl at the swim house – but now I can see the times when her need for acceptance poked through.

'Should we go inside?' Brooke says now, three years older and much more vindictive than that freshman girl in the swim house. She nods back down the hill to where one of my neighbours is cleaning out his gutters in preparation for the impending storm while indiscreetly shooting glances in our direction. 'Wouldn't want to cause a scene, would you?'

Normally, I would agree with her. Normal Cass would invite her in, offer her a drink and wait for her to tell her side of the story. But that's what got me in this trouble to begin with. My willingness to please.

That Cass is done.

'What, do you think someone will overhear what you just shared with the whole goddamn world? No, this is exactly where we'll do it.' My hands shake, and I stuff them in my pockets. But, unlike usual, the tremors aren't from nerves; they're from fury.

Brooke raises her eyebrows slightly, and a small part of me is proud that I've finally been able to surprise her, which just infuriates me even more.

'So, she's finally found her voice after all,' Brooke says in an indifferent tone I've never heard her use. I don't even recognize her. This person isn't Brooke. The woman who made me feel special, even loved. The person who I was too nervous to admit had become my best friend in only a matter of weeks.

But I guess that's the point. She is – and always has been – a complete stranger.

'Who the fuck are you? What kind of person does this?'

Brooke's response is immediate. 'The kind of person you will never have the balls to be, clearly. One who doesn't let bad people get away with bad things.'

Her tone is scathing, fury radiating off her.

'And now I know, your sister and your father, all that from the past, that wasn't all you've been capable of, was it?' Brooke continues, venom dripping from her voice. 'I heard your conversation with Logan about the Xanax and his little indiscretion. And I found Lucy's phone. That was really smart, Cass, keeping it under your bed. I mean, how dumb can you be?'

Her fury seems to dissipate as she says this, replaced with a smugness that's somehow worse. I feel my forehead scrunch in confusion. It was the one part of her post I couldn't piece together – why she claimed I had Lucy's phone, why she lied – but she rushes on before I can question it.

'So was that it?' Brooke continues. 'Is that why you pushed Jacinta from Khrum Yai? Because your boyfriend was cheating with her? And Lucy? All he did was talk to her, but you were too jealous to even stand that. Daniel – I bet you were just covering your tracks with him. Gotta give it to you, murdering him was ballsy. But how exactly did you do that? I mean, he was so much bigger than you. Did you surprise him from behind and slit his throat? I've noticed those scuba knives you keep in the dive shop. Is that what you used?' She leans towards me, mockingly, her fist beneath her chin as if she's begging for gossip. 'Do tell. I would love to know.'

I shouldn't be surprised by these questions. I know her suspicions. She made them quite clear in her post. But my mind halts on one thing she said. *I heard your conversation with Logan.*

I knew there was someone in our house last night. I don't know where she could have been hiding, but she *was* there, watching and listening to all the things I didn't want anyone to know. And it all makes sense.

'You've been following me.' This time, there's a waver in my voice that I can't attribute to anger. Despite everything – the post, the threatening notes she left on my doorstep – this realization seems like the worst thing she's done to me. I've felt crazy these last few days, feeling eyes on me everywhere I've walked, the stifling paranoia that I could never verify. All that time it was Brooke following me, the woman I thought was my friend.

'Wow, you really are slow. Welcome to the party, Cass.' Brooke's lips are turned upwards in a self-satisfied smile that makes the nausea return with full force.

'But why?' I force the words out, laced with frustrated confusion.

'Why? Really?' That harsh laugh comes again, but then Brooke's tone changes, as hard and sharp as a knife. 'He raped me, Cass. Eric Verrino, your friend. And you just sat there and let it happen.'

'No-no,' I stammer. That didn't happen. I would have known. Sure, the game Eric and the other swim guys were playing was disgusting, horrifying even. But he wasn't a *rapist*.

'Y-yes,' Brooke stutters, mockingly. But despite the sarcasm, I can sense something has changed in her. 'You could have stopped him. Warned me from going up to his room, but that wasn't even the worst part! Afterwards, you lied about it. You covered for him.'

I stand there, stunned, not fully grasping what she's implying.

'You know how hard it was for me to get a lawyer? How many people I had to call and tell my story to over and over and over, just to have them tell me it was my fault? How horrible that was? And then, when I finally found her, the one lawyer willing to go to bat for me, she came to you directly, Meghan.' She spits out my name – my real name – like a curse word. 'She asked you point blank if you knew what happened that night. And you lied. You fucking lied.' A sob rises in her throat, her anger bubbling into sorrow. She tries to overcompensate for it, her voice getting louder and louder. 'You told her I was obsessed with him. That I came over there for sex. That I was only mad because I realized I had been a number in a stupid game.'

I remember now, a moment that was quickly replaced in my memory by the events that happened in that hotel room soon after. A stern-looking woman in a black trouser suit cornering me and my roommate outside our dorm. She asked us both rapid-fire questions about where we were the weekend before, how well we knew Eric. It was clear she was trying to pin something on him. And then she asked if he raped that girl from the swim house. That made me and my roommate stop walking.

My roommate turned to the woman, her voice steely. 'Eric is a good guy. If that girl is saying that he raped her, then she's probably just jealous.'

The words sounded wrong as they hit my ear, but my roommate looked over in my direction, silently urging me to back her up. So I did. 'Yeah, that girl came over for one reason. She wanted to have sex with Eric. She was just mad because she realized that he didn't really like her.'

The memory hits me like a slap in the face.

'You told her I *wanted* it.' Brooke is yelling now, and I see my neighbour out of the corner of my eye. He's given up all pretence of clearing his gutters and is staring at us, open-mouthed. 'What kind of woman are you? What kind of *person* are you?'

I try to grasp her questions, but the answers slip through my fingers.

They're the same questions I've been asking myself since my conversation with Logan last night. What kind of person am I? Why would my ring be next to Lucy's body?

'Look,' I say, my voice shakier than I would like. 'I'm sorry I did that, but we were in college. And I didn't know what he did to you. How could I? And why me? Eric is out there living his best life.' I think of all the times I've wandered to Eric's profile after posting an Instagram photo on the dive shop's account. Scrolling through the endless shots of him and my roommate and their perfect life. 'You talk about what kind of woman I am, but what kind of woman are you?' I'm gaining momentum now. Her story threw me, but my anger comes rushing back. 'You target me and what? Dedicate years of your life to tracking me down and ruining me? You don't think I already went through enough hell after college? You know what happened to me, you know what everyone said about me. But you don't see me hunting down the people who said it, do you? God, you really are crazy.'

Brooke's eyes flash and I prepare for her to yell, to scream. But when she finally speaks it's steady, with an icy rage.

'Yeah, that's what they said at the hospital.' She looks down at her wrists. 'You asked me about my bracelets when we first met.' The words aren't what I expected, and I feel myself pull back. I watch as Brooke pushes the bracelets up her arm, raising her arms to expose her wrists.

I suck in a mouthful of air as I realize what she's showing me. Ghostly white slices cut diagonally across both of her wrists, fragile, puckered skin stretched together like two ethereal bracelets.

'You,' she says. 'You did this.'

29

Brooke

I feel a sick pleasure in watching Cass's face contort as she sees the scars.

I don't tell her what ultimately led me to do it. The days I spent after that night at the swim house, refusing to claw myself away from the dirty sheets of my dorm-room bed out of fear that I might run into Eric, or her, or any of the others who sat silent in that living room while it happened. The dozens of calls I made to lawyers who refused to help me. Finally convincing one to take my case, only to hear from her a week later, telling me that she couldn't find a single witness to support my story, informing me that the girl I'd identified to her on Facebook had said that I'd willingly hooked up with Eric. I sat at my desk after the lawyer hung up, staring at my phone. And then, without fanfare or deliberation, I dug two clean lines along the length of each wrist with a pair of scissors, cleaving my skin into two curtain-like folds.

The next thing I remember is waking up in the hospital, my mother next to me, looking more annoyed that she'd had to drive all the way from Kentucky to Hudson than saddened to discover that her only child had tried to kill herself. And then, when I didn't think it could get any worse, came the transfer to the psych ward. Those three weeks filled with colourless pain, my world reduced to nothing more than grey and the echoes of screams filtering down the halls.

When I was finally released, I took what little money I had in my bank account and booked a one-way flight to Prague, the cheapest to Europe that I could find. I needed to go, to get as far away from everything as possible. In the few days before my flight was scheduled to leave, I stopped at the Dollar Store and bought stacks of bracelets to cover the two over-sized Band-Aids on my wrists. As I travelled, I traded them out for others, souvenirs I gathered in the many cities I worked my way through, always looking for something to help mask the scars.

I watch Cass's mouth gape open and closed like a fish, and I feel another wave of revulsion run through me.

'Brooke,' she starts, and I know she's going to try to concoct some half-ass pitiful apology for what I had to go through.

'Stop, just stop,' I snap at her. 'Just tell me the truth about Lucy. Why did you kill her?'

'I didn't. You of all people should know that.' I watch her spine straighten, the fight in her return. 'If I did, why would I have ever agreed to search her room with you? And why would I have helped you hide from whoever was trying to break in?'

I've already thought this through, at least her reason for agreeing to the search. 'You wanted to be inside the investigation. To make sure I was only finding the things you wanted me to.'

She stands silent for a second, as if running through her options. 'But what possible reason would I have to kill her?'

'I heard you, remember? I heard you tell Logan that you saw him cheat. With Jacinta, who just happened to drop dead hours later. And then you see your precious fiancé talking to another girl at the Full Moon Party. You lose it. You manage to get her a far enough distance down the beach so that no one will notice what you're doing, and then you strangle her and leave her body in the ocean. Did I get that right?'

Her eyes fill with confusion.

'Oh, right. You don't remember. How convenient.' I pause. 'I mean, come on,' I say, leaning towards her conspiratorially. 'There's really nothing about that night that's come back to you? Not a thing? You can tell me, we're friends.' I draw out the last word so that it drips with sarcasm.

I watch her eyes dart quickly to the side, and I know there's something she's hiding. There's something she remembers that she hasn't told me or Logan or anyone else.

'I don't remember anything,' she says finally. 'But I didn't kill Lucy. I couldn't have. I was the one who found her body the next morning. I – I wouldn't have.'

'Sounds like you're trying to convince yourself,' I say, my anger returning. 'I just wish you hadn't been such a cliché. I mean, the jealous girlfriend, really? Personally, I can't imagine killing someone for *any* reason, let alone one so mundane. But you're pretty used to that, right? I mean, you've done it before. To your own family, no less.'

I watch her cheeks flush and her hands ball up. For a second, I really think she might punch me.

'You have no fucking idea.'

'So tell me,' I order. 'Tell me what I'm missing.' I've dropped the act. I want to know. Or more than that. I *need* to know. Looking into all this started as a story, one that

261

would serve the dual purpose of getting revenge on Cass and finally starting my career as a journalist. But Lucy's got under my skin. Those big blue eyes she locked on me that night when she came to me for help. The strength she carried in her delicate frame. Her unwavering confidence. All of that, just thrown away, left to rot in the sea.

Cass stands there, shaking her head, her eyes stone. 'Robin was an accident,' she says finally, her voice so quiet it's barely audible. 'My dad was sick. I tried to fix him, to get him the meds he needed. But it all went wrong.'

Something unclenches inside me. I'm getting somewhere, finally. She's going to confess.

'So, what about Lucy?' I ask eagerly. 'Was that an accident, too? Why else would your ring be near her body? And why did you have her phone under your bed?'

'I never took her phone,' Cass says quietly.

'There's no use denying it. I found it under your bed.' Cass stays silent, her forehead wrinkled, so I switch tactics. 'And what about Jacinta? What were you doing the night she died?'

'I was at Frangipani. She was there. But . . . but then I went home. I'm sure I did.'

Wait. She's *sure* she did? 'You don't remember?'

Her face drops. 'I started taking Xanax that day. I think I took too many of them at first . . .'

She trails off, and I process what she's saying. Despite all the evidence, a small part of me didn't *really* think my theories could be right, but what Cass is saying basically confirms them.

'Cass, *you* killed Jacinta. You lured her up to Khrum Yai and pushed her. And then you strangled Lucy, leaving those bruises on her neck.'

Her gaze slides off me and up the trail to Khrum Yai. As if she's remembering.

She opens her mouth, and I brace myself for her confession.

And then the rev of an engine ricochets off the trees lining the hill, the sound deafening amid the silence.

Logan is home.

30

Cass

'Leave, now. Before I call the police.'
'Oh right, you have them all in your pocket, don't you,' Brooke retorts. 'That must be convenient, you know, now that you're getting married to a murderer and all.'

I feel emotion flood my lungs, forcing in a breath at Brooke's comment. At the noticeable flinch I see in Logan's face as he's confronted for the first time with what I actually am. *A murderer.*

'But you don't know anything about her really,' Brooke continues. 'You don't know what—'

'I said, leave.'

Logan's voice is gruff, a tone I've never heard him use before. I watch as his hands ball up, his muscles tense. The only time I've seen him this angry was when he found out an employee at Frangipani had been stealing money from the bar. He'd come home that night with rage on his face and bruises on his knuckles.

Brooke notices it too, and I see a flash of fear in her eyes as she takes a step back. She opens her mouth again, but Logan beats her to it.

'Come inside,' he says to me.

And I do, but first, I steal a glance back at Brooke. She's

still standing there, her lips parted slightly, the anger flashing in her eyes.

I turn, following Logan in, my mind playing Brooke's accusations on a loop. *You killed Jacinta . . . You strangled Lucy.*

I try to deny it, but I'm not sure I can any longer. I was so jealous, so hurt when I saw Logan and Jacinta together. It threw my entire life off course.

And everything Brooke said makes sense. All the evidence adds up.

I barely register once we're inside. For once, this house doesn't feel like home.

Logan takes a seat in the armchair at the far side of the living room and buries his head in his hands. A portrait of a man defeated.

'Logan,' I say, going to him. But when I place my hand on his shoulder he recoils, as if I've burnt him.

I can feel the life I've built here crumble around me. It started when I saw Logan with Jacinta, a few pieces of sand breaking off. And then a wall fell when I found that first envelope on my doorstep, and now, all of it has turned to dust, a sturdy sandcastle washed away in the waves.

With that realization comes the panic that's been lapping at my toes the last few days. I've built everything around Logan, this man who loved me, who wanted to spend his life with me. I have nowhere to go, no idea who I am without him. Compulsive need engulfs me, squeezing tight.

'Please. I love you.' The panic laces my words, but Logan doesn't even turn. 'Let me explain.'

'Explain?' That does it. Logan spits out the word as if I've cursed him, twisting his body towards me. 'Explain what? That you lied to me about who you are this whole time?

265

That you said your father and sister died in a car accident? That I know bugger all about you? Not even your name?'

'Please,' I try again.

'I thought Brooke was lying. When Doug told me about her Instagram post, I didn't even want to look at it. I told him that it was a load of shite, that you would never lie to me. I thought I knew you . . .' He trails off, clears his throat. 'But then I thought of the paper I found in the drawer the other day when I was looking for a takeaway menu. It said something about a massacre and had a picture of a girl on it. I thought it was rubbish and I tossed it. God, I didn't even recognize you in that picture. My own fiancée. You must have thought I was so stupid.'

'No, Logan, never. You have to understand, I couldn't tell you who I really was. You never would have loved me.'

Logan makes a noise that falls somewhere between a cough and a laugh. 'But I did, Cass – Meghan, whoever you are. I loved you so much.'

Apparently not enough to stop you from cheating with Jacinta. The words come from nowhere, rising up my throat like acid, hot and mean. I force them down with a swallow that feels like needles sticking into my throat.

'I've protected you from so much here that you don't even know about. I've made it my job to keep you safe. I lied for you about where you were the night Lucy died, and I was prepared to keep lying for you.' Logan's use of the past tense causes my muscles to stiffen. 'And then I find out that it wasn't the first time you killed. You murdered your own father *and* sister for God's sake. I googled it. None of it makes any sense.' His voice breaks. I move forward to comfort him, but I stop when I see him flinch. 'You told me they died in a car accident. A car accident!' He shakes his head, as if he still can't believe it. 'Honestly, it makes me sick to think I've been sleeping next to you all these years.'

'Logan, please,' I cry. Every one of his words slices my skin.

He turns his head, but he's quiet. And I realize this is my chance. The only one I may have left. I need to make him understand. I take a deep breath, and I finally let out the words I've been holding in for so long.

'My father was sick,' I start. Logan's head is still turned away from me. 'It was likely undiagnosed bipolar disorder. He seemed to have it under control when I was young, at least from what I remember. But when my mother died when I was a teenager . . . I think the grief triggered it. He had these, like, manic episodes. He would be violent towards me and Robin. He would hurt us.

'The injuries were never too serious. We could usually cover the bruises and scrapes easily enough, so no one would know. When I left for college, Robin had to bear the brunt of my dad by herself. I thought he was getting better by then, we both did. I wouldn't have left her behind if I thought otherwise.

'But then, during the beginning of my sophomore year of college, he lost his job. After that, he spiralled. Robin's injuries became more frequent, more severe. We tried to get him to a doctor, but he wouldn't go. During fall break, I requested that he go see our local practitioner, and I ended up with a dislocated shoulder. And it wasn't like we had any other options. Both our parents were only children, my mom's parents were long since dead, and my dad's mother didn't want anything to do with us.

'I needed to help Robin. But she was still seventeen. Underage. If I called Child Protective Services, they would have put her in foster care. It would have killed my father. And I was only nineteen and in college. I wasn't ready to take care of her on my own.' I squeeze my eyes shut, working up the nerve to tell the worst part of the story. 'So, I did the only thing I could think that would work. That would save them. Robin *and* my dad.'

All this time, Logan's had his eyes glued to the floor, but this statement finally prompts him to turn towards me, giving me the reassurance I need to continue.

'I knew my father would never get better without medical help. But there was no way Robin and I would ever be able to get him to go to a doctor. So, I decided to bring the medicine to him.'

I remember when the thought came to me as I was tossing and turning in my dorm-room bed. It was so simple it made me sit upright. If this worked, everyone would win. My dad would get better, Robin would be safe and everything would go back to normal. Like it was before my mom died.

'I started going to the school medical centre, telling them I had all of Dad's conditions. I explained my periods of hyperactivity, which would boil over into violence, along with weeks where it was impossible to get out of bed. I included just enough second-hand details to make it believable. And it worked. The doctor prescribed me Xanax.'

I feel Logan's attention prick up at the sound of the drug.

'I started stockpiling it. My father and Robin were planning to come visit me at school for Thanksgiving that year. I figured I would slip my dad the drugs during the visit. If it made him calmer, more like our old dad, I would give the rest to Robin with instructions to start putting the crushed-up pills in his food and drinks. I thought I'd figured everything out. Thinking back on it now, I can't believe I thought it would work. It was stupid really – so many things could have gone wrong. The doctor could have stopped prescribing me the Xanax, maybe it wasn't even the type of medication my dad needed after all. He could have noticed or felt the difference and panicked. But I didn't think that far ahead – I was just happy to have found what I thought was a solution, a way to help Robin after leaving her in that mess.'

I cough, trying to cover the emotional chokehold the memory has over me. The anger at my naivety.

'I barely slept the few days before my father and Robin came to visit. But when they did arrive, Dad didn't notice anything was off. He didn't stop talking long enough to. He'd booked us this huge room at the hotel down the street from school, a suite with two separate bedrooms, a living room, and a makeshift kitchen. More space than we needed by far.

'When we were unpacking, he pulled out a cooler I hadn't noticed in the car. It had a bottle of Moët and a Tupperware of strawberries. He said he was proud of us and wanted to celebrate . . .' Tears prick the backs of my eyes and I feel my throat grow thick.

'That's why you seemed so off when we had the champagne at our engagement party,' Logan says, and I nod frantically, feeling a small prick of hope that I can make him understand.

'Dad popped the bottle and started pouring, and he had Robin use one of the hotel knives to cut up the strawberries to put in our glasses. When he turned around to supervise her, I knew that was my chance. I pulled out a Ziploc bag of two crushed Xanax pills I'd prepared the night before and shoved in my pocket, and dropped the contents into one of the glasses, using my finger to stir it as quickly and quietly as I could. Neither of them noticed.'

I look over to Logan, who's still staring at me with wide eyes. I want desperately for him to reach for my hand. To give me the comfort he usually does. But he doesn't move.

'They came back from the kitchen with the strawberries, my dad picking up each glass and plunking them in. I made sure Dad got the right flute, and after we all clinked our glasses, I watched him take a sip. I was so relieved, so sure that everything was going to work.

'I hadn't told Robin about any of it. I didn't want her to be involved if my father found out what we were doing. I wanted all the blame to be mine.

'My dad was on a high, talking a mile a minute. And then he grabbed us, one by one, twirling us around the room, dancing, despite there being no music. He took the glasses, handing each of us one to drink. I tried to follow them, I really did, but I didn't see which one he picked up. I couldn't be sure that he'd grabbed the right one.'

I pause again, my breath growing thin as I get closer to the end.

'I should have found a way to confirm that Dad had the right glass. I should have knocked it out of Robin's hand or warned her in some way. But I couldn't move. It was as if I was frozen. And she drank it so quickly. In two gulps. She was so excited, her first glass of champagne.'

Despite everything, a sad, wet-sounding laugh erupts from my lips, quickly evolving into a sob. I swallow it, forcing myself to continue.

'And then Robin started saying that she felt sick. She staggered into the closest bedroom, barely making it on to the bed. And she never moved again.'

I hear Logan's breathing stop, just like Robin's did all

those years ago. I force myself through it, as I feel the tears on my cheeks, rushing to get to the end as quickly as possible.

'Dad knew something was wrong immediately. He ran to her, shaking her body, screaming her name, but she didn't move. He checked her breathing, took her pulse, but I could already tell she was gone. And then, he snapped. Just like he always used to.'

The tears pool at my eyelids as I remember his voice, deep and hateful, a tone I had never heard him use even at his most manic. '*You*. You did this. What did you give her? Her heart, Meghan!'

'Apparently, my sister had a heart condition I didn't know about,' I continue. 'She had been diagnosed a few months before, but she never told me. I guess she didn't want me to worry. She wasn't supposed to drink, something my father clearly ignored. And the Xanax mixed with the champagne was too much for her to take.' I pinch the bridge of my nose and feel a tear sneak down my cheek.

'My dad started coming at me across the living room,' I say, forcing myself to finish. 'I could tell in his eyes, Logan, he was going to kill me. I've never seen such pure rage before. So I backed up, away from him, until my legs hit the kitchen counter. And he grabbed my throat, squeezing, squeezing. I don't know how he didn't break my neck.'

Instinctively, my fingers rise to my throat, and I can feel my father's hands there. As if, in some way, they've never left. My mind flicks back to the ghostly bruises I saw on Lucy's neck, and I shake my head to rid it of the memory. I can't think of her right now.

'I tried to grab anything I could to fend him off. Anything that would get his hands off me. And then my finger brushed against the knife Robin had been using to chop

271

the strawberries. I grabbed at it and raised it above me, but Dad saw it first. He released his hand from my throat and took it. I never had a chance.'

As if on cue, the overhead lights flicker. I pause, listening to the steady thrum of rain against the roof. I've been so absorbed in my story I hadn't noticed that the storm had finally started.

'He didn't even pause. I didn't feel it when the knife went in. It was like watching a movie. When he realized what he'd done, Dad just dropped his hands and backed away, like he was in shock.'

I realize my fingers have moved from my throat and are now tracing the scar above my chest. Logan's eyes dart there too.

'That's what the scar is from. Not a car accident,' he says, understanding breaking through the sorrow in his eyes. All I can do is nod.

The doctor told me later it was a miracle, that the knife had missed my aorta by less than a centimetre. He told me I should be grateful. I couldn't even comprehend the meaning of the word.

'Somehow I managed to pull the knife out with both hands,' I tell Logan. 'I swear, it was like it was all happening to someone else. I didn't feel anything. And before I knew it, the knife was in my hand, and then it wasn't any more. It was in my father's stomach.'

I trail off then, exhausted. I want to collapse, to sleep for ever. But I can't. I need to see what Logan feels after hearing this, the story I was never prepared to tell him. I brace myself for his anger, his disgust from earlier.

But his eyes carry none of those emotions. Instead, he looks at me with a mix of shame and pity. He shakes his head solemnly, and for the first time since I saw Brooke's letter on my doorstep days ago, I cautiously let myself believe that everything will be okay between us.

'Cass,' Logan says, and I feel my heart rate accelerate. 'I'm so sorry that happened to you. I can't believe you had to go through that.'

I want to reach for him but wait for him to give me the signal to do so.

'But I can't process this all right now.' His words make me shrink back. 'Why wouldn't you just tell me at the beginning? Why all the lies?'

'I just didn't—'

'You never gave me a chance,' he interrupts. 'You didn't trust how much I love you.'

I cling to that word, the present tense. 'We can still fix this, Logan. We can put all this behind us.'

Logan shakes his head once, and it feels like a bullet to the chest. 'Brooke's post is all over Instagram. It's bloody viral.' He looks down at his hands. 'It puts everything we have here at risk.'

He stands up and I want to cling to him. He starts walking towards the door.

'You're not ... leaving?' I manage to ask through the tears stuck in my throat.

I see him open the front door and I feel so far away, so helpless.

'I just need some time to think this through,' he says. 'I'm sorry, but I think it's better if you find somewhere else to stay tonight. I . . . I need some space right now. I'm going to take a drive. Please don't be here when I get back.'

And then he's gone, closing the door behind him, and all of my worst nightmares have become real. He's leaving. And I'm completely alone.

I rush to the door and fling it open. I want to stop him,

but I have nothing more to say. Instead, I watch from the doorway as he pulls on his helmet. As his bike weaves down the hill, the wind whips raindrops on to my arm, the force of it hitting my skin like a dozen fists.

I barely feel it.

31

Brooke

I pretend to leave when Logan comes home. Confronting him is different to arguing with Cass. I've seen the thinly veiled dislike he has for me. As if he's waiting for me to take one wrong step, so that his feelings will be justified. And now I've given him that – and so much more – on a silver platter.

The muscles he spends hours working on each day ripple beneath his shirt as he yells, reminding me of exactly what he has the power to do to me. I remember the feel of Eric's muscles pushing me down flat on his bed. Despite the strength I'm trying to project for Cass, I wince.

So, I do what he says – or at least start to. I return to my motorbike and put on my helmet.

It's begun to rain, a steady drizzle foreshadowing just a taste of the torrential storm the internet has predicted. I should go back to my room. I've done everything I've needed to do here on Koh Sang. It's over. I should take advantage of this time before the storm gets going to start drafting a full-length article on the island and plan my next steps. To follow up with the Czech hotel that owes me money. To make sure I have the cash I need so I can be the first off the island when the ferries start running again.

But where do I go now?

The question sits deep in my gut, and I realize I have absolutely no idea how to answer it. I've got nothing left to work for, nothing to plan. No future.

This makes no sense. I should be on top of the world. I'm victorious, after all. I did what I had been waiting years to do.

Yet all I feel is that same hollowness from earlier expanding like a balloon in my gut. An empty void where the rage used to reside, leaving me almost nostalgic for it. And slowly, drop by drop, the guilt trickles in.

I think of calling Neil, remembering that fleeting moment of happiness yesterday morning as he kissed me. But as soon as I pull out my phone, I remember. I betrayed him.

I imagine his reaction when he sees the post, his shock when he realizes what I've done. My Instagram post has the capability of ruining – or at least severely damaging – tourism for the island. It will force Neil and Cass and the rest of them to move somewhere new, to start over. And still I posted it, even after Neil confessed to me why he'd come here, everything he'd run from, and how Koh Sang is the only place he's ever been truly happy. He confided in me, and I threw his trust away.

And I know what I gave up in doing so. I chose revenge over a potentially happy future.

I start walking away from Cass and Logan's house. I need to do something, to distract myself. I can't bear the thought of returning to that empty hotel room just yet. I walk past the motorbike and keep going. The rain is coming down faster now, hitting my shoulders, my calves, my head, slicking my hair to each side of my face. But I continue to the break in the trees, the same route Cass and I hiked just a week ago. The Khrum Yai trail.

As soon as I duck into the jungle, it's as if I've stepped into another world. The deluge has turned into a trickle, most of the rain caught in the thick canopy overhead. The birds have fallen quiet, disappearing God knows where for shelter; the only sound is the rhythmic hum of the rain against the trees' heavy branches. Water has begun seeping into the dirt of the trail, filtering a fresh, earthy smell into the air.

I'm not dressed for a trail hike, and my flip-flops sink into the thick quicksand-like mud. Each step is a fight between me and the earth, bringing a moment of suspense before my sandal breaks free, reuniting with my foot in a satisfying squelch.

I don't mind. I've always liked a struggle, never shied away from it. Maybe that's my problem. I yearn for confrontation, for wrongs to right. I was never left with a choice not to. If I had been like Cass, appeasing and pleasant, I would have ended up like my mother, living in that squalid trailer, trading disgusting men and the drugs we needed to put up with them.

Ending up like her wasn't an option. I had to fight. Didn't I?

Maybe I could have simply talked with Cass, confronted her individually about how much she hurt me in college, without involving the entire world in our mess. But that wasn't enough. I wanted more. I wanted her to suffer like I did.

By the time Logan interrupted us, I was entirely positive that I had trapped Cass in her lies. That she killed Lucy, and Jacinta, and – God knows how – Daniel. But with every step I take, my certainty fades, little by little.

Because it doesn't make sense. Sure, maybe Cass pushed Jacinta from Khrum Yai, but would she really do that after learning that Jacinta kissed Logan only once? And would

Xanax be enough for her to completely forget luring Jacinta up this mountain in the middle of the night to push her to her death?

And then there's Daniel. He was huge. How could he not have fought back against her? And even if she did kill him, wouldn't she have been covered in blood after the staff meeting? But she showed up at the dive shop that night without even a hair out of place.

And, of course, Lucy. Cass had her phone and she admitted to finding her own ring by Lucy's body. It's all incriminating, sure, but things just don't add up. Why would she have claimed to Logan that it was *his* ring? And something she said a few minutes ago sticks with me. If she did kill Lucy, then why would she have helped me search her room? Why would she have been so genuinely scared when we heard that person trying to break in? Why would she have helped me hide?

I replay the words she said a few minutes ago, the attempts at explanations that I threw away as useless excuses. But one claws at the side of my brain, refusing to leave.

I was the one who found her body the next morning.

It didn't register at first, why Cass was clinging to that to prove her innocence. The fact that Cass allegedly found Lucy didn't mean she didn't murder her.

But now I think of what I've accused her of. Strangling Lucy and leaving her body in the shallow water.

If that was true, Lucy's body would have easily washed ashore, leaving some traumatized guest to find her during an early-morning beach walk. But that's not what happened. Cass found Lucy's body the next morning at the very bottom of the ocean, affixed to the coral, at least a hundred yards from the shore. For Cass to have killed

Lucy, she would have had to swim out and dive down several metres, dragging Lucy's body with her.

That's a lot of strength for anyone to have – especially after killing someone with their bare hands. And an almost inconceivable amount for someone as doped up on Xanax as Cass apparently was that night.

I think back to how fragile she seemed by the end of our confrontation, as she apparently grappled with the possibility that she really did kill Lucy. I had expected her to deny everything, to have some sort of excuse to explain it all away. But her response seemed completely genuine. Which leaves me with one question.

Could Cass really be behind this?

No matter how I spin it, the only answer I can come up with now is *no*.

I realize I never gave her a chance to explain the other evidence I used to jump to my quick conclusions. To tell me why she had Lucy's phone or what had happened in that hotel room all those years ago, the deaths the police would barely comment on, that the press speculated so wildly about. I was just so excited to finally have revenge, and to do it in a way that would propel me forward, back into the life I had dreamed of. Because I know what will happen if this post gets enough press. Forget about reaching out to news outlets and offering to write a story; they'll be running to me, throwing money in my direction for a first-hand account of my experience with the Hudson Massacre Killer, especially one filled with salacious musings linking her to more murders. It will get me the journalism career I've always believed I deserve. The one I might have had if Cass had just spoken up after Eric raped me.

It had all seemed so noble since my arrival on the island, this crusade to confront Cass, to then stand up for the three people who were so mercilessly killed on Koh Sang. But now, it seems tainted with a selfishness I hadn't noticed before.

I hear something crack behind me. A branch, loud enough to break through the thrum of the rain.

I spin around, but it's silent. The trees are close together, close enough to obscure someone hiding behind them. I stay still for a few seconds, squinting, but all I see beyond the trees is darkness. I pause, waiting for the noise to come again, but other than the drumroll of the rain on the canopy, there's only quiet.

I continue walking up the trail, not stopping until I reach the summit. The path opens up to a plateau, the trees no longer providing cover. The wind slaps my face as I leave the confines of the jungle. I step carefully towards the edge of the cliff, where the footing breaks off at jagged angles, giving way to the long drop to the sea and rocks below. The same place I stood just days ago with Cass. The same place Jacinta must have stood seconds before her body crashed on to the rocks.

Rain pummels down as I inch my foot towards the ledge, until my toes are dangling off. It would be so easy to take one more step, to make all these thoughts just stop. To not have to think about the new guilt lying fresh in my stomach, about everything I've done wrong in this life, everything I should have done differently. I wouldn't have to figure out where to go from here, how to start over.

I tried it once before. I could do it again. Better this time, with no room for error.

The sound comes again from behind me, audible over the wind. This time it's louder than the cracking of a stick, more human.

I spin around, and my foot slips, sending small pebbles

tumbling over the cliff. The rain drowns out their collision with the rocks below.

'Who's there?' I shout, but the wind seems to hurl my words over the edge as well.

I wait.

'Who's there?!' I say it louder this time. Peering through the rain, I think I spot something shift behind one of the trees lining the trail, but I can't tell if it's human or animal or just a figment of my paranoia. I realize with a jolt that this must be what Cass has been feeling these past few weeks as I followed her around the island.

'Cass?' I yell.

At first, I find myself hoping it *is* her, that she's followed me to give me another chance. A chance to apologize for how I got it so wrong. But even as the thought bubbles into my head, it pops with the reality of the situation. After what I just did, she's certainly not here to help me.

Whoever is following me has darker intentions.

I pull my phone from my pocket, before remembering I have no one to call for help.

I look frantically in all directions, trying to pinpoint the source of the sound. But there's nothing but dense trees on one side and the cliff on the other. No way to escape. Nowhere to go but down. I peek over the side. The sharp points of the rocks reach skywards, barely visible through the rain.

My thoughts from moments ago are long gone. With a sudden burst of clarity, I realize I don't want to end up like Jacinta, lying broken and alone at the bottom of this cliff.

The sound comes again.

And with it, a realization. If Cass really isn't behind the three deaths, then whoever killed Jacinta, Lucy and Daniel is still out there. And likely still on this island.

I want to yell, to scream. But I know it wouldn't do any good. Who would hear me? Who would even care after what I've done?

Still, my throat seizes, ready to make as loud a sound as I can muster. But the scream lies stagnant in my throat. I turn back around, cautiously, as if one misstep could throw off whatever delicate balance I'm hanging in.

And then I see it. A shadowed mass stepping out from behind a tree.

Approaching, closer and closer. Until slowly, unbearably slowly, it comes into view, close enough for me to make out the shape. To recognize who it is. But it doesn't make sense.

The figure keeps walking towards me.

And finally, I scream.

32

Cass

I want nothing more than to take a pill and lie down. To find solace under my covers and stay there for eternity.

But that's not an option – Logan made that abundantly clear. And he's right. If we're ever going to work this out – a possibility I cling to with all the hope in the world – then I need to give him space.

So I throw a change of clothes into my backpack, force myself out of the house and drive. The red from this morning's sky is nothing more than a memory. Slivers of silver peek through the massive grey storm clouds that blanket the island, the streetlights doing little to illuminate the road. The wind has picked up incrementally since I went into the house with Logan, and I grip the handles of my bike tightly as I go, barely avoiding hydroplaning on the puddles that have begun to form. Despite the daily storms, the island isn't equipped for a long, sustained deluge like this, and flooding is a near certainty. Just as I near the turn to my destination, the island vibrates with a huge *boom* and the streetlights all extinguish in unison. The power's gone out, and the island is awash in darkness.

The wind whips at my face and the rain spits, and by the

time I arrive, standing outside the one place where some-one may still accept me, I'm drenched to the bone.

'Oh my sweet thing,' Greta says as she answers the door. 'You're soaking wet. Come in, come in.'

As soon as I see her, emotion floods out of me. Hyster-ical sobs shake my body and leave me gasping for breath.

We stand there in her doorway, where I find myself unable to move. I fall to the floor, my knees skinning on the cement of her doorstep, and she stays with me, rub-bing my back in the motherly way she does. Between the sobs, I try to tell her everything. The story falls out in jag-ged, incoherent chunks, jumbled by the mess of my mind and the sound of the rain pelting furiously around us.

'I've ruined everything. I think I may have killed Lucy. And Logan's gone . . .'

My explanation devolves into incomprehensible sobs, but Greta doesn't seem to mind. Nor does she appear turned off by my confession, as I feared.

'Shh, shh,' she mumbles, her hand never straying from my back. 'Come on, love. Let's get you inside. Then we'll figure out what exactly to do about this mess.'

Greta helps me into her apartment, a small one-bedroom located a few blocks over from Frangipani. I lean against her, my breath coming in ragged peals, and allow her weight to support me.

When we're inside, she grabs me a towel, ushering me into a chair. She's already lit candles to combat the power outage and has placed them around the living room, cast-ing the apartment in a soft glow.

'Wait here one second.'

Greta disappears briefly into the adjacent kitchen, returning with a cold glass of water, which she places ten-tatively in my trembling hands.

'You sip on that,' she orders. 'I'm going to grab some dry clothes so we can get you out of these soaking wet things.'

She's gone again, this time disappearing down the hallway back to her bedroom.

I sit and look around at the familiar living room. Every time I've been here, the apartment has always been tidy and organized, but it seems like in the last few weeks – at least since Alice left – it has deteriorated. Their once pristine coffee table is now littered with food wrappers, magazines and scratch paper.

As I shift the mess aside to set down my glass, careful not to spill a drop with my shaking hands, my eye is drawn to an object beneath a stack of Styrofoam takeaway containers. I move them to the floor, revealing a heavy, hardcover book, spread open at the spine. As I lean closer to look, the pages come into view, showing rows of glossy headshots.

The minimal text on the open page is in a different language, but it's still clear what this is. Greta's yearbook. She must have been feeling sentimental after Alice's departure and probably lugged this out from wherever she stored it, looking for a return to better days.

I spot Greta's photo at the top centre of the page. She looks younger, but mostly the same. Her ice-blonde hair curls around her chin in a chic bob, and she smiles, closed lipped at the camera. Underneath the photo, in small, italicized font, is a word: *Engelskalärare*. Maybe she won some type of award to claim pride of place at the top of the page. Not surprising, given how smart she is.

I scan the rest of the layout as I hear Greta rifling around in her bedroom. Most of the other students beneath Greta's picture are also blonde and smiling, but they all look a bit younger. Greta has always seemed mature for her age.

My eyes eventually come to rest on a girl who looks different from the rest of her class. Dark brown hair and familiar coal eyes. Alice. I forgot she and Greta had met and fallen in love in high school.

But the photos stir something at the back of my brain, a memory that's just out of reach.

Hearing Greta coming down the hallway, I close the book and lean back from the table, not wanting her to think I've been rifling through her things. Her arms are filled with clothes, which she places on the couch next to me.

'Here you go, honey,' she says, before kneeling in front of me, her hands resting on my legs, the sides of her dark eyes crinkled with a sad smile. 'I'm so sorry this happened to you, Cass. We all are. I want you to know Brooke's post doesn't change how we think of you. We all have things we're hiding from. We'll be here for you, no matter what.'

I want to thank her, to show her how much I appreciate her kindness even when I've potentially ruined this island for everyone. But there's only one thing I can think of.

I feel the emotion I've finally begun to control rise again in my throat. 'Unfortunately, Logan doesn't seem to feel the same way.'

She grabs hold of my left hand. 'He'll come around. I know he will. He just needs time. It will all be okay.'

And in the soft glow, with the rain pattering down outside, I try to believe Greta might be right. Maybe this doesn't mean the end. Maybe there's a way back for me and Logan, for all of us.

I feel her palm roam over mine, her fingers tracing my ring finger.

'Oh no, tell me you didn't lose your ring, too,' Greta says. I'm so lost in my thoughts that I don't understand her words. 'Logan was devastated yesterday, when he told me how he'd lost his so soon after the engagement,' she continues.

'What?' I ask, as a pulse of anxiety thrums through my body. 'He told you this yesterday?'

'Yes, yesterday afternoon. We met for coffee after he and Doug went to the gym.' She catches the look of shock that crosses my face. 'Oh no. Did he not tell you? God, me and my big mouth. I didn't mean to get him in trouble!' Greta covers her face with her hands.

I try to process what this means.

Sengphet didn't give Logan's ring back yesterday morning as Logan claimed. It was still missing last night, when I confronted him about it.

And then he convinced me that it was mine. He told me I had lost my ring, when really he must have taken it from the ring box where I kept it in my bedside table and pretended it was his. And he convinced me that *my* ring – not his – was next to Lucy's dead body.

But why?

The question strikes me from all sides, but the answer is always the same: because he had something to do with Lucy's death.

The room seems to come crashing down around me.

'Cass? Are you okay?' I don't know how long Greta has been saying my name, but this clearly isn't her first attempt. 'Oh, love, you're white as a ghost.'

I open my mouth, trying to figure out how to tell her everything, but all that comes out is one short sentence.

'I think Logan might have killed Lucy.'

Greta's eyes grow wide, and I open my mouth to explain more, to tell her all about the ring and the lies. But before I can, she's handing me the pile of clothes she'd brought out moments earlier.

'Why don't you go and change? We'll sort all this out once you're in dry clothes.'

I want to protest, to tell her everything as I process it myself, but as a shiver racks my body, I know she's right. I nod, taking the clothes from her, and walk out of the living room as if on autopilot.

As I head down the hallway I feel the familiar weight of eyes on me. I turn around, but Greta hasn't moved from her spot on the floor. She's still looking at me with an expression on her face that I can't read.

But I barely register it. Because I can only think about one thing.

Logan lied.

33

Brooke

'Why are you here?'

The figure keeps coming, step by cautious step.

'Don't come any closer.' I hear my voice waver, and I know this person does, too. They pause briefly and then return to their slow stride.

I search frantically, looking for anything I can use as a makeshift weapon to defend myself. I grab a rock nearby, only to realize it's more like a pebble. Whatever, it will have to do. I raise it above my head and prepare to chuck it.

'What are you doing? Stop!'

The figure raises her arms in protection. When she lowers them, I see that her long, dark hair is soaked like mine. Her almond-shaped eyes are awash with concern, and her forehead is scrunched, predicting the wrinkles that won't be visible for many years. Her features are familiar, now that I'm seeing them for the third time.

'Who are you? Why have you been following me?'

She steps forward again. 'Before I tell you, d'ya mind putting that down?' Her accent is familiar. It sounds Australian, but slightly off.

I look up. I forgot I was still holding the stone. I lower my arm, my terror from a few seconds ago now seeming ridiculous. 'Sorry,' I mumble, before regaining my composure. 'But what do you want? Why did you follow me up here?'

'One question at a time please.' There's a look on her face that I can only describe as haunted. 'Can we step back on to the trail, so we don't have to have this conversation on the side of a cliff? I've been yelling at ya to step back from it. One wrong move and you're over.'

She's right. I've inched back almost as far as I can. That must have been what she was doing. Walking towards me carefully to warn me to step away. It was too hard to hear her over the rain.

I waver for a minute, not sure who to trust any more. This could be a trap. Maybe this girl is the killer. But I look again at her dark eyes and my curiosity wins out over fear.

I drop the stone and walk towards her.

We take a seat on a rock off to the side of the trail, back under the canopy of trees. As we sit, I register how wet I'd become while standing on the cliffside. Sodden clothes hang from me, and as the shock of seeing the girl wears off, they begin to feel heavy on my limbs. The damp sends a chill through my body, and I realize with surprise that this is the first time I've been cold since arriving on the island. The girl is drier, having mostly stayed beneath the confines of the canopy, but only marginally so. The rock on which we sit is small, barely wide enough to accommodate both of us, and I can feel the body heat radiating off her.

We've been sitting in silence for a few seconds, each of us waiting for the other to start.

'So, who are you?' I ask finally, breaking the stillness.

'My name is Alani,' she answers. 'I was friends with Lucy. I came here with her.'

My heart rate has finally slowed since my flirtation with the edge of the cliff, but this news sends it ratcheting up again. Amid everything else, I'd forgotten about the second toothbrush I'd found in Lucy's bathroom, but now I realize it must have belonged to Alani. Her accent suddenly makes sense. She must be from the same town as Lucy: Greymouth, New Zealand.

'Why have you been following me?'

'I thought I could trust you,' Alani says. 'So did Lucy. I mean, you weren't on the island when Jacinta died. And we watched you around them, the Permanents. We picked up on how you'd look at them when they weren't looking. Lucy thought maybe you knew more than you were letting on, and I kind of agreed,' Alani explains. A memory flashes from the other night. Lucy, waiting outside my room, confirming when I'd arrived on the island.

'But after Lucy, I couldn't risk it,' Alani continued. 'I needed to know for sure that you would help me. So I followed you, trying to figure out what side you were on. When I saw the post you published today, that's when I knew I could trust you. I watched as you confronted that woman, Cass. But I didn't interrupt. After she went inside, I came up here after you. I waited in the trees until I was sure you weren't meeting anyone before I tried to get your attention.'

Her words make sense separately, but woven together, it's as if she's speaking a different language. I settle on the first of many questions.

'What do you mean, what side I was on? Side of what?'

She barely lets me finish. It's as if after all these days of staying silent, she's opened the floodgates.

'They killed her.'

I swallow, forcing myself to stay composed. 'Okay, okay. Calm down and start from the beginning.'

Alani takes a deep breath.

'A few weeks ago, Lucy's sister came here, to Koh Sang. She was amazing. Always kind to me and Lucy, always including us. Never acting like we were a burden or too young to hang out with her. Nothing like my older sisters.' There's a familiar grief on Alani's face, the same kind I wear when I think of my mother.

'Anyway, she was travelling through Southeast Asia, working her way through Thailand. She called home every day to update us. Lucy and I loved it. Lucy would put the phone on speaker, and her sister would tell us everything about what she had been seeing and eating. And best of all, about the hot boys she was meeting. She was gorgeous, so obviously they were tripping over themselves to get to her. Honestly, hearing her stories was better than watching *Love Island.*'

Alani wears a sad smile. I rest my hand on her elbow, and she looks up at me, returning to the present.

'The calls stopped two days after she got to Koh Sang.'

I nod, bracing myself for the rest of the story.

'She arrived late on a Wednesday. She called us early Thursday morning. She was excited because she was going to try scuba diving for the first time. She was staying in a free room at the dive hotel. She called us the next day, too – Friday – to fill us in on dive school. She loved everything about it, the diving, the school, the island. She told us a little about the dive training from that day, but she mostly talked about this guy she had met. An expat who lived on the island. She was straight-up giddy.

'She said they were planning to go out again that night. That the guy had something special planned, but she didn't know what.' Alani's voice breaks. 'And then, nothing. We didn't hear from her again. Lucy called non-stop, but eventually her sister's phone just went straight to voice-mail. Turned off. A full week later, the Koh Sang police called her parents. Told them that Jacinta had died. That she'd taken an early-morning hike alone and had fallen off the side of the cliff.'

'Jacinta Taylor,' I say. I suspected it as soon as Alani started telling her story, but I willed it not to be true. Jacinta, the girl whose mangled body was found on the rocks below Khrum Yai, was Lucy's sister.

'Yes,' Alani confirms, her voice catching. 'She fell right there.' She raises her finger, pointing to the spot that I was standing at just moments ago, and I shiver from a coldness entirely unrelated to the rain.

'It didn't make sense,' Alani continues. 'Jacinta was a night owl. She would never have woken up early if she didn't have to – especially for physical activity. And there was never any question about suicide. She loved life too much to even consider it. Lucy's parents accepted the police's story; they were too heartbroken not to. They couldn't bear the thought of coming here, so they had her remains shipped to New Zealand. But Lucy and I, we just couldn't let it go. It didn't seem right.

'We spent days rereading her texts and listening to her voicemails. We learned everything we could about the island. We tried to find the guy Jacinta had been dating on social media, but the only information she had given us was that he was an expat and "totally gorgeous".' Alani stops, a sad smile playing at her lips thinking of Jacinta's words. 'She usually took a few days to post pictures on Instagram, so we had no photographs of him. It didn't really give us much to work with. We'd gotten as far as we could through our online investigation. So, Lucy decided we needed to come here and figure it out ourselves.'

Alani shivers now, and I remember that despite every-thing she's done, all the risks she's taken, she's just a girl.

'Lucy and I had taken a year off between high school and college,' Alani continues, 'and we'd been working for a few months, so we put together all the money we had saved and bought the cheapest flights we could find. We told our parents we were road-tripping through New Zealand's North Island, y'know, a way to break through the grief . . .' Alani trails off, and when she looks up at me, tears well in her eyes.

'Once we got here, we decided to retrace Jacinta's steps. We came prepared. We'd researched everyone at the dive shop.' I think of all the printouts Cass and I found in Lucy's room, and how Lucy was following all the Permanents – and me – on Instagram. 'Lucy signed up for the dive class. She got a free room like Jacinta stayed in, and I snuck in. It was awful. I thought summer was bad in New Zealand, but a room without air conditioning in Thailand, with the two of us in that little bed . . . it was torture.'

Alani laughs, a throaty noise that seems to surprise her. She sniffs it away.

'We split up the morning after Lucy checked in. She went to her dive class, and I walked around the island, try-ing to get as familiar with the place as I could. I found the dive bar where Jacinta had said all the expats hang out – Frangipani, I guess they call it.

'Lucy and I met down at the Tiki Palms that evening, after she was done with class. She was with a couple other people, including that guy Daniel –' I suck in a breath at the mention of his name '– but she pulled me away so that we could debrief. She said she'd met someone who remem-bered her sister. The woman told Lucy that she knew something, and they agreed to meet that night during the

Full Moon Party to talk about it further. Lucy and I agreed that I would go with her, that we would confront this woman together.' Regret seems to seep into her words.

'When the party started, it was so crazy down at the beach, so chaotic,' Alani explains.

I think back to that night, the bodies grinding against each other, the heat from the fire dancers close enough to singe flesh.

'I saw you at one point, too,' Alani says.

'At the party?' I ask cautiously. The thought is jarring.

Alani nods solemnly. 'I recognized you from Instagram. Lucy had followed your profile. I think she might have even sent you a message or something.'

Hot shame floods every inch of my body as I remember Lucy's innocent plea for help sitting in my inbox, ignored.

'But when I saw you at the party,' Alani continues, 'you didn't look like you wanted to be bothered.' She diverts her eyes away as if she's embarrassed.

I think back to the night of the Full Moon Party, when we arrived as a group from Frangipani. My memory flashes to Neil's hand, warm and safe in mine as we wandered on to the beach, and I force it away. It's too painful. As he and the others had gone to get drinks, I'd headed to the bathroom, but amid the flashing lights and the painted, camouflaged skin and the bone-shaking bass of the speakers, my body returned to that night three years ago. I stumbled to a secluded area far away enough from the party so that no one would see me – or so I thought – trying to get as much distance from the writhing bodies as possible, just as the feeling hit. It felt like fingers reaching into my core, strangling me from the inside out. My heart beating so fast it seemed like it would detach itself and rip out my chest at any moment, my breathing so jagged that more air was rushing out than coming in. And the memories, coming in spurts. The smell of Eric's pillow, a mix of cheap hair gel and chlorine. The pain reverberating through my scalp. The shame.

'I had a panic attack,' I admit. 'I get them sometimes. I didn't think anyone saw me.'

I hadn't told any of the Permanents about it. I didn't want them to know how easy it was for me to lose control.

Alani nods. 'I thought so.'

I find I'm holding my breath, silently begging for her to continue.

'Somehow, I'd lost track of Lucy. I don't know how. I turned around for one second and when I turned back she wasn't there. I looked everywhere, but with all the people pushing against me . . . I just . . . I couldn't find her.'

A sob sneaks out of Alani's throat, and she clasps a hand around her mouth to prevent another from following. I hold her other hand in silence for a minute until she recovers enough to continue the story.

'I found Daniel. He'd been following Lucy and I for most of the party. He kept trying to get Lucy to dance with him, although it was clear she was not at all interested.' She smiles, a sad, slight upturn to her mouth as she remembers, and suddenly Daniel's video makes sense. He had been following Lucy in a desperate, drunken ploy to get her attention. It wasn't anything sinister, it was just annoying and a tad creepy. Daniel being Daniel.

'But by that time in the night, Daniel had become distracted by some other girl,' Alani continues. My thoughts go to the redhead I saw in the dozens of selfies he had taken that night. 'It was a bit difficult to get anything coherent out of him, but he eventually said that he'd seen Lucy talking to Doug, that Australian guy from the dive shop, and later to one of the other expats. And I knew instantly it was the expat Lucy had mentioned, the woman she planned to meet at the party. She wasn't supposed to meet her alone. I was supposed to be there, to protect her . . .'

She sobs again, and instinctively I shuffle closer to her.

'I finally spotted two figures, way down on the far side of the beach, barely visible, and I just knew something was wrong. I had this feeling in my gut that Lucy wasn't safe. That the woman was going to do something to her. I sent Lucy a few messages, trying to get her to come back to the party, but she didn't respond.'

I remember the messages I'd found on Lucy's burner phone. They were from Alani.

'I started running as fast as I could. But by the time I got close enough, it was too late.'

She falls quiet, as if she can't bear to finish the story. 'Alani.' I say her name gently. 'What happened?'

She responds without a pause. 'She killed her.' Her voice is clear and convinced, absent of the emotion in which it was wrapped mere seconds ago.

'Who did?'

She ignores the question. 'They're not who they say they are. They're all in on it.' Her words lose their meaning, tumbled together among all the questions racing through my mind.

'It was the woman Lucy met that night who killed her,' Alani continues, and the sound of it turns my bones to ice. 'The blonde one.'

'Cass?' The name shoots out of my mouth. I recall the blonde woman I had seen in the background of Daniel's photo. The woman talking to Lucy, who I was sure was Cass. If it *was* Cass, then my instincts were right. Everything I've done would have been worth it. But I know before her name is out of my mouth that I'm wrong.

'No,' Alani says, and my shoulders slump. 'The other blonde. The Swedish one.'

I stare at her, processing, before the name bubbles to my lips.

'Greta.'

34

Cass

I can hear Greta rustling around the kitchen as I thread my arms through the zip-up hoodie she's lent me, knocking my elbow against the wall of her tiny bathroom in the process.

Then the rustling stops. Like most of the island's apartments, the walls are thin, and after a moment of silence, I hear Greta's voice, too quiet for me to make out what she's saying. Curious, I lean my ear against the door, straining to hear. Is someone else here? Is it Logan?

Carefully, I depress the handle to the bathroom door and push. It opens with a squeak that echoes off the tiled walls of the bathroom. I freeze, waiting for Greta to turn down the hallway to come check on me. But she doesn't.

It's silent, and I consider returning to the bathroom. But then Greta's voice starts again, faint, as if she's intentionally trying to shield her conversation from me.

Slowly, I take a step down the hallway, towards the kitchen. I feel a bit ridiculous, spying on Greta, the one person who I can turn to in a time like this. But why is she being so quiet?

I continue walking until I'm almost at the kitchen. But

as I take another tiptoed step, the floorboard beneath me lets out a betraying squeak.

Greta's head whips around. In the light of the candles around the kitchen, she looks unfamiliar, and for a moment I feel as though I'm standing with a stranger.

'Sorry,' I mouth, thinking fast. 'I'm done changing, and I heard you on the phone. I didn't want to interrupt.'

Greta shoos my apology away, smiling now. And just like that, the old Greta is back.

'That's great,' she says into the phone, her voice now a normal volume. 'We'll be right there. She'll be happy to see you.'

She hangs up, walks over to me. 'That was Logan. I hope you don't mind that I called him, but I wanted to help make this right.'

She rubs my arm, and my face grows warm, a mixture of gratitude and shame commingling in my chest. What was I doing spying on one of my closest friends?

'Come on, love,' she says, already heading towards the door. I follow her, still lost in thought.

Greta pauses at the door to slip on her rain jacket. As I wait, I look around the tiny living room, my eyes landing back on the coffee table and the yearbook I'd seen earlier. That same thought from earlier niggles at the back of my mind, an idea just out of reach.

'Greta?'

'Hmm?' she asks, head down as she zips her jacket.

'What does *engelskalärare* mean in Swedish?' I ask, my tongue tripping awkwardly over the unfamiliar consonants.

'English teacher,' she responds, distractedly. 'Why?'

And then it all clicks. The connection that's been nudging at me since I saw her yearbook. I remember the conversation I had with Greta when I first got to the island.

How she told me that she'd fallen in love with Alice at school and how Alice's parents had disapproved. *They couldn't imagine their daughter dating another woman.*

Greta wasn't Alice's classmate. She was her teacher.

I think about how unhappy Alice always seemed, constantly reminiscing about Sweden. She never wanted to come here. That was Greta. What Greta did, having – or forcing – a relationship with Alice, was illegal. Greta didn't bring Alice here because she wanted to get away, she did it because it was the only way they could be together.

I realize I never answered Greta's question, and she's eyeing me curiously.

'No reason,' I say, but my lie comes out stiff.

If Greta lied about her relationship with Alice, what else did she lie about?

I think back to the mumbled conversation I overheard Greta having on the phone. If she was talking to Logan like she said, then why was she being so quiet? What didn't she want me to overhear?

Unless she wasn't talking to Logan.

I think of Brooke's post, how it didn't just expose me, but everyone else on the island. How Logan was so concerned about it. *It puts us all at risk.* Especially Greta.

I watch as Greta's eyes follow the path of my own to the yearbook on the coffee table, the smile slowly fading from her face. When she looks back at me, her features are painted with a coldness that tightens my throat.

35

Brooke

'I saw it from down the beach as I ran towards them,' Alani explains. 'By the time I got close enough, I could see that blonde woman – Greta – knock Lucy down and . . . then she wrapped her hands around Lucy's neck and held her head under the water.'

I think of the blue marks Cass had seen on Lucy's neck. And then I think of Greta's thin, sinewy muscles, hardened from years of yoga practice. I don't doubt she had the strength to kill Lucy. I just never expected she would.

'I wanted to scream. To attack Greta, but it was like I couldn't move.' Alani turns to me, her eyes filled with tears, her face awash in guilt.

'You were in shock,' I tell her, remembering my inability to remove myself from Eric's bed three years ago. 'It's not your fault.'

Alani looks away, and I can tell she doesn't believe me. 'By the time I tried to run back to the party and get help, there were more people headed our way. I guess Greta called them. When I realized who they were, I ducked behind a line of trees so they wouldn't see me. It was three guys I recognized from our research. Logan, Doug and . . .' Alani ticks the names off on her fingers.

'Neil.' I breathe out his name, finishing her thought. The realization that he's involved in all of this drops the ground out from beneath me. I thought he was different, the complete opposite of Eric. But under all the charm, he was just the same.

'Right, the English one,' Alani continues. 'Once he figured out what had happened, he jogged back to the dive shop and came out a few minutes later with his arms full of scuba equipment. He handed it over to the other two guys, and they put it on. They picked Lucy up, one grabbing her by her feet, the other by her shoulders, and carried her into the water. I don't know what they were doing down there, I guess hiding her body? But they didn't resurface for like twenty minutes. The whole time Neil and Greta kept watch on the beach. Greta kept saying, 'No, no, no,' over and over, like she couldn't believe what she'd done. She was pretty loud – I'm surprised no one heard her.

'Eventually the two guys came out of the water, and after a while, all four of them left. But I stayed there for most of the night. I couldn't believe it. My best friend was dead. Killed by the same people who murdered Jacinta. We should never have come here . . .' Alani drops her head in her hands.

'Was Cass there?' I ask. 'Was she with them?'

Alani looks up, shaking her head. 'She wasn't there. I never saw her that night.'

I exhale sharply. Cass didn't kill Lucy. And if she didn't kill Lucy, then she likely didn't have anything to do with the other deaths either.

'But what about Daniel?' I ask. 'Who killed him?'

Alani shakes her head. 'I don't know,' she says, dejected. 'I was at the Tiki Palms that night, hiding in the back, remember?' I nod. 'I talked to him the day after Lucy died.

He came and found me after he got released from the medical centre.'

'What did he say?' I ask eagerly, hanging on her words.

'He'd been going through his phone and came across the video he had of Lucy from the Full Moon Party. He said he had posted it on Instagram in good fun – to give his followers a taste of what they were missing and to show off all the "fit birds" he'd been meeting.' Despite everything, I find myself smiling at Alani's dramatic impersonation of Daniel, including the – quite bad – cockney accent.

'But he said that when he watched it again, after finding Lucy, he realized that it connected Lucy to the expats. He thought he could use it against them, to make them confess. He told me he'd sort it. But, the next thing I knew, he was dead. Another person lost to this goddamn island.'

There's a flash in Alani's eyes as she says it, the first time I've noticed her anger. 'I don't know for sure who killed him,' she continues, 'but it must have been Greta or someone covering for her. It was one of them, that's for sure.'

I let what she says sink in, as I rearrange the pieces of the story in my mind. But there are still some things that don't make sense.

'Why would Lucy check in under a fake name and write on her scuba form that she was from Australia? And what about you? Why is there no record of you ever staying at the hotel?' I feel bad interrogating this girl after everything she's gone through, but I need to be sure she's telling the truth.

'I guess we got a little too into it,' Alani says sheepishly. 'We didn't take any chances. Lucy didn't want anyone on the island to recognize her connection to Jacinta, so she used her mother's maiden name and pretended she was from a different country. She lied about losing her passport to the receptionist at check-in, so they wouldn't double check. Lucy's room was free with the dive course, and we knew that if the resort was aware I was staying there too, they would make me sign up for the course or pay for the room. And I mean –' she shrugs '– we didn't have that much money to spare.'

'And what was with the burner phones?' I ask, remembering Lucy's old-school Nokia and Alani's text messages.

'Lucy's parents paid her phone bill,' Alani said. 'If they saw international charges, they would have suspected what we were up to and they'd have been on the first plane here to stop us. So, we bought burner phones at the local shop before we left New Zealand. We loaded them with pre-paid travel minutes and used them when we got here. I don't know what happened to Lucy's phone the night she ...' Alani trails off, as if she can't bring herself to say the word. 'I tried to find it on the beach, even called it a million times, but it always went straight to voicemail. It must have turned off.' She hesitates, her eyes glazing with concern. 'But I had a number call me yesterday. I don't know who it was.'

'That was me,' I say, remembering the incessant calls I made to that number as soon as I found Lucy's phone last night.

Suddenly, everything seems to be making sense, all the incongruent puzzle pieces shifting together.

'So, what happened after the Full Moon Party? Why didn't you just go to the New Zealand Embassy for help?'

Alani swallows. 'After I saw what the expats did, how easily they got rid of Lucy's body, I knew these people were dangerous. I wasn't sure if they knew I was here, but I couldn't take any chances. And I knew the police were useless. I could tell from how they handled Jacinta's death. I considered calling the embassy, but even if they came to investigate, it would be my word against the expats and the police. I didn't know who to trust. It was better if I just disappeared and waited to report Lucy's death until I was away from the island. Safe.'

I nod. The girls had littered a trail of lies behind them that would have smeared any truthful story Alani had tried to tell.

'Later that night,' Alani continued, 'I snuck back to our room. I tried to get rid of anything that would suggest who we were. I packed up all the stuff I could carry and tossed the rest. I couldn't find Lucy's ID, though. I knew she'd hidden it somewhere in the room, but I tore that place apart.'

I think of the mess in Lucy's room when we broke in, the ripped zipper on her backpack, the ID card I'd found wedged between the bedframe and the wall, as if it had fallen down through the crack in the bed without Lucy realizing.

'It's okay,' I say. 'Cass and I found it.'

Alani looks at me for a moment, confused, but keeps going. 'I wasn't sure how far the expats' influence reached. I thought they may have had people keeping a lookout for me at the ferry. I figured my best bet was to wait a while until things died down. I couldn't stay in Lucy's hotel room, and I couldn't risk checking into the resort under my name, so I found a dingy apartment in the middle of Kumvit to rent the last few days – near where I saw you this morning. I've used up basically all the money Lucy and I brought with us. And now they've shut down the ferries, and . . . I'm stuck.'

I sit there for a minute, taking in the similarity of our predicaments, and piecing it all together. Until one thought springs out above all the rest.

Cass is innocent. And I exposed her and this entire island.

I think of how far the Permanents have gone to protect themselves and what they would do to stop us from exposing any more of their secrets. Cass could so easily be caught in the crossfire. I consider calling the American Embassy, but as soon as I pull out my phone, it notifies me that I have no connection. I watch Alani do the same. Despite the awful service on the island, I usually manage to get at least one bar. The storm must have knocked out the signal on the entire island.

I check the time, alarmed to see that an hour has passed as I've listened to Alani. I look around, noticing that the darkness sifting through the cracks in the canopy is from more than just the storm. Whatever weak sunlight had managed to poke through the clouds earlier is now long gone.

'We need to find Cass,' I decide.

Alani recoils in surprise. 'Cass?'

'She's innocent in all of this. She didn't know about Lucy or Jacinta. By exposing her, I've put her in danger.' Alani's eyes are full of questions, but I don't have time to explain.

'Please. I have to make this right.'

I can almost see the thoughts whir through her head. I understand her hesitation. She saw these people murder her friend and cover it up. She's been hiding from them for days, alone.

'You've got me now,' I tell her. 'I won't let anything happen to you.'

Eventually, she gives one short nod. And within seconds we have a plan. We'll find Cass and we'll hide out at the apartment where Alani's been staying. We'll wait until mobile service is back up and running on the island, and then we'll call the American Embassy and get help.

I pull Alani up from the rock, and we begin to run.

After a few minutes, we emerge from the dense jungle cover and back out on to Cass's street. As soon as we reach the break in the trees, it's clear the storm is in full force. The wind pummels us from both sides, and the rain beats down furiously, attacking our arms like needles, but I barely feel it. We run past where my motorbike is parked by the edge of the jungle and head straight for Cass's house. My heart sinks when I see how dark it is, but then I realize the whole street is pitch-black. The power must have gone out on the whole island.

I bang on the door several times, praying Cass is alone, that I won't need to confront Logan. But there's no response. No one is here.

'She's gone,' I say to Alani as we huddle under the narrow cover of Cass's doorway. She either left or . . .'

'They've already got to her,' Alani says, finishing my thought.

I try to think logically about where she might go or where they might take her, but my thoughts swarm like insects.

'Should we check the bar?' Alani proposes.

'You mean Frangipani?' I ask. Alani nods. I think there's little chance they'd be there in this weather, but it's worth checking. Plus, Frangipani is close enough to Greta's apartment and in the vicinity of where Neil and Doug live. If we're right, and she really is in danger, there's a solid chance she's in that area. 'Let's go.'

We head back to my motorbike.

Alani climbs on behind me, and I shove my key in the ignition. The ripple of the engine rises above the din of the rain, shaking the seat beneath us.

*

With each turn, I pray there's no one else on the road. Between the darkness of the night and the sheets of rain, I can barely see more than a few feet ahead. The rented motorbike that has come to feel so comfortable over the last few weeks now feels dangerous beneath me. The raindrops have merged into a wall of water, and my tyres slip over the mud as Alani tightens her grip around my waist.

Despite the conditions, I take the long way to Frangipani, using the beach road to check for any signs of life at the dive shop, in case Cass has found her way there. The weak light from my headlight illuminates a small part of the beach, and the unfamiliarity of the sight takes my breath away.

Dark clouds hover over the usually meticulous sand, which is now littered with palm tree limbs and seaweed that the ocean has coughed up. The once flat surface of the water is scoured with crevasses of waves, each of which slam against the shore with a brutality that matches the island's residents. As we near the dive shop, I notice the long-tail boats that are usually safely tied up on the shore now smashed into the rocks.

The shop, along with the Tiki Palms and the surrounding bars is all boarded up, the regular evening bustle along Pho Tau beach nothing more than a memory. And within seconds, it's clear that this detour was futile. The resort is empty.

As we circle back on to the main road, winding on to the smaller street that leads to Frangipani, we skid over a slippery patch, and the bike handles momentarily rip from my hands. I hear Alani yell as she loses her balance behind me, but I manage to correct the bike at the last moment, saving us from toppling to the road.

'Sorry. We're almost there,' I yell, although there's little chance Alani will hear me over the wind and rain.

As I take the final turn on to the dirt road where Frangipani lies, a bright light shines at us from the side of the road, blinding me. I assumed the entire island was at home, waiting out the storm.

I squint, pulling one hand from the handles to shield my eyes. And just as I do so, I make out the shape of something flying into our path.

I swerve to avoid it, yanking the handles as far as they'll go, veering off the road.

'Brooke!' Alani yells and grabs at my waist, just as we're about to collide with the trees lining the street. I swerve again, trying to recorrect, and feel my front tyre hit whatever it is that flew in front of us.

The world whirls as I fly over the handlebars, the ground rushing up to meet me.

And then everything stops.

36

Cass

Slowly, Greta's features morph. Her face washes clean of emotion, her eyes hardening into two beads. Focused, like an animal ready to pounce.

She lunges towards me.

I turn and throw myself down the hallway. Almost immediately, Greta's behind me, close enough that her outstretched fingers graze the skin of my neck. I force my body towards the bathroom door, the only thing in the hallway that can offer any protection.

And then I feel her. Her hand clenches around the fabric of the sweatshirt that I'd thrown on. And pulls it clean off me. In my haste to eavesdrop on her phone conversation, I never zipped it.

The unexpected movement is enough to propel Greta backwards, and I reach the door a step before her, whirling myself around and back into the confined bathroom. I pull the door towards me to close it, but she gets to it first. She yanks the door back, her fingers grasped around its side. And I pull. As hard as I possibly can. I channel the anger that has been piling up in me throughout this day. First at Brooke, then at Logan, and now at Greta. All people I trusted completely, only to have them betray me.

My biceps flush with pain, and it feels as though my tendons might rip from the strain. But I keep at it, until I feel the door press against Greta's fingers. And when she rips them out amid a shout of pain, I slam the door so hard that the whole house seems to vibrate. The lock turns quickly in my hand, cheap and light. Easily breakable.

I don't have much time.

I hear Greta's footsteps retreat, but I know she'll be back. I search feverishly for anything in the minuscule bathroom that I can use to defend myself. My wet clothes strewn across the floor, a plastic soap dispenser and toothbrush holder that rest on the sink beside a candle that throws shadows across the tiled walls.

And then I see it. A window in the upper edge of the wall, just above the toilet. My only means of getting out of here.

Suddenly, a banging comes from behind me, forceful enough to shake the entire bathroom. It sounds as if Greta is throwing her body against the door. With each slam, it creaks, the wood bending beneath her weight. The candle teeters precariously on the edge of the sink before crashing to the floor, plunging the bathroom into darkness.

It's now or never.

As my eyes adjust, I grab my soaking wet T-shirt off the floor and wrap it around my elbow as many times as the fabric allows. I try to clear my mind but, as usual, it returns to her.

Robin.

With the pressure bearing down on me from all sides, the memory forms like a diamond, rushing back in one forceful shot. The beach during the Full Moon Party. Making some excuse to the others, walking far enough away from the crowds so that the music was nothing more than a distant memory, allowing the Xanax to bathe me in a sentimental haze. Finding a spot up near the trees that separate the beach from the road. Digging my toes in the sand and pretending that Robin was there with me, living out the life she'd always dreamed of, the one she deserved. Before I fell into sleep, I remember a woman's voice drifting past me, riding on the faint night breeze. 'No, no, no.'

It wasn't me who made that sound. And it wasn't Lucy. Or if it was, I didn't cause her to say it.

I remember waking up, disorientated and dry-mouthed. Walking back to my bike and tripping over something left on the beach. A phone. Slipping it in my shorts pocket to bring to the dive shop's lost and found the next morning. It must have fallen out when I changed into my pyjamas that night, and by the time I woke the next morning, the memory had been completely erased. All that remained was the fragmented feeling of carrying something home in my pocket. That must be how Brooke found Lucy's phone under my bed.

Despite everything happening outside the bathroom door, I feel a small release. I didn't kill Lucy.

I flip down the toilet seat and step on top of it, praying it will hold. And before I can think about what I'm doing, I throw all my weight into my elbow as it connects with the glass in the window. It doesn't budge, and I propel backward, pain coursing up my arm.

The memory of Robin urging me on in that faded home video of us running behind our mother at the beach comes rushing back to me. 'You're my big sister. You can do anything.'

I ignore the pain and pull my elbow back again, my fingers coiled around themselves, nails digging into my palm. And I throw all the force I have against that window.

313

This time the impact is immediate.

Shards fly around me, and I instinctively squeeze my eyes shut. Splinters of glass land on my face and naked arms, and when I finally open my eyes, slivers fall from my eyelashes. I shift the bundled T-shirt around my hand and run it around the border of the window, trying to clear as much glass as I can.

This is it.

The toilet teeters under my weight, but I have no choice. My fingers grip the side of the window, and the remaining shards clinging to the windowpane dig into the flesh on my palms. I begin to hoist myself up with my biceps, thankful for the days I've spent hauling tanks from the dive shop to the pool.

And then I realize just how quiet it's been. I haven't heard anything from Greta in nearly a minute.

As if on cue, a crack echoes throughout the bathroom. I'm perched on the edge of the window like a gymnast preparing to start her uneven bars routine, but I steal a glance back towards the door. A slice runs through the middle of it, broken wood splintering from each side.

And then the sound comes again. This time the gap appears almost directly next to the first slice, creating a wider hole. I notice a flash of metal before it retreats. A knife, inches away from my calf.

Greta is cutting through the door.

I'm only halfway out of the window, trying to ignore the shards of glass digging into my torso, when she gets in.

I don't dare turn around. Even if I tried, I wouldn't be able to position myself to see. Instead, I shoot my leg back.

It meets only air. I swear under my breath, clawing my fingernails into the windowpane to try to steady myself when I hear the clatter of metal on tile. My kick didn't connect, but it must have surprised Greta enough to make her drop the knife.

My relief doesn't last long.

Almost immediately her hands are around my ankle. And Greta yanks. The force pulls me back, and the shards scrape against my stomach, digging deeper into my flesh.

She pulls again.

I'm not getting out of here. I'm hurt. Bleeding. Lying on broken glass halfway out of a window positioned a metre or so off the ground.

And then I think of Lucy. Abandoned at the bottom of the ocean. And Jacinta, her body broken on those rocks beneath Khrum Yai. And Daniel, his throat slit, never able to make another joke again.

And of course, I think of Robin on that hotel bed.

And I kick again. For them. For me.

This time, I hear a crunch as my foot connects with Greta's face, followed by a small yelp. Her hands are no longer on my ankle.

I take advantage and continue scrambling. The glass cuts through my torso, then my hips, and finally down my upper thighs.

And then I'm free. Falling, tumbling to the ground.

I crash on to the pavement with a sickening crunch.

I lie still for a minute, gauging the extent of my injuries. I try repositioning myself and red-hot pain sears through my shin. Several deep gashes trail up my thigh, courtesy of the glass left along the window's edges. I watch, stunned as the pavement around me turns a dark red. Quickly, far too quickly. But as soon as it appears, the rain sends it rushing down the street. I should wrap something around my leg to stop the bleeding, but there's no time.

I need to get up. I need to move.

It won't take Greta long to recover. And she can make it from the bathroom to the road outside her door in a matter of seconds. I crane my neck both ways. It's hard to tell with the constant stream of water, but it doesn't look like there's anyone else out here. Which means no witnesses.

The thought alone is enough to get me up. Every movement feels as though I'm being sliced, pulled apart at the seams, but I move anyway. After what feels like an eternity, I'm upright. Just in time to hear a noise. Something slamming open.

The front door.

I turn around, and Greta is on the street. Close enough for me to see the trail of red flowing from her nose. She'll be on me in seconds.

I run. My right leg drags, each step sending a shooting pain through my core. But my adrenaline wins out.

I make it to the end of the street, hearing her coming closer with each step. I turn the corner without thinking, cutting through the empty intersection and heading left. I'm running blindly, the pain blurring my sight with flashes of black and red.

After a few steps, I realize I don't hear her any more. Have I lost her?

That doesn't make sense. She has to be faster than me.

I turn around to see where she is, but I can't spot anything through the sheet of rain. I keep moving, blinking hard and trying to clear the blood and water from my eyes.

I look up, just in time to crash into something.

I hit it with the force of a truck. The impact sends explosions of pain through every inch of my body, propelling me to the ground. My vision goes dark as I land on my back, but I cling to consciousness.

Slowly, my sight returns. Pixelated, as if I'm recording through my phone.

The colours form into the image I know so well, and I realize why Greta stopped chasing me. As my eyes lift upwards, they take in the muscled, tattooed calves, the board shorts faded from years of sun, the slicked-back curls, wet from the rain.

'I'm so sorry, love.' The voice is so familiar, a part of me. Logan.

37

Brooke

When I come to, something wet is leaking into my eyes. Everything comes back slowly: the storm, the light, the crash. I wipe my hands across my face, but when I pull them away, they're covered in something much thicker and darker than rainwater.

I'm bleeding. I can't tell where it's coming from or even what hurts. But then I remember.

Alani.

'I'm okay, Brooke,' she says. Her voice is pained, and I realize I must have been screaming her name. She's close, having landed only a few feet from me. I turn to look, but my vision is still blurred. The rain and blood aren't helping things.

Then I hear something else, footsteps coming from my opposite side.

'Well, hello again, Brooke. And who is this?' The voice is familiar, but in the tumult of the rain I can't quite place it. My eyes finally focus on dirty tennis shoes as I try to lift myself up.

The same voice *tsks* at me. 'Not so fast there. Let me help you.'

The next thing I know, I'm being pulled up to my bare feet – my flip flops lost during the crash. The pressure is so great it feels like my shoulder might rip from my torso. I cry out, but it does no good. Once I'm up, an arm wrapped around my back to support me, I look over at the face next to me. The dirty-looking hair, wet and snarled, hidden beneath the black hood of a sweatshirt. The hazel eyes and the short yellow hairs breaking through the flesh on his chin.

'Doug,' I manage to say through my dry mouth. I turn my head slightly, enough for the pain to radiate down my neck, and see the trunk-like branch of a palm tree spread out across the street. That was what caused the accident. Doug must have thrown it in front of my bike when he saw us coming. He wanted us to crash.

'Shut the fuck up, bitch.' The playful tone from before is long gone. I think about how often I've seen words like that written in the comments beneath my Instagram photos. But this is different. It takes me a moment to understand Doug's hostility, but then I remember my post, the secrets I shared about Koh Sang. I've invited the world's attention into this haven, where people only stay to escape. And Doug is no different from the rest of them.

My gaze moves to his broad chest, clothed in a black zip-up hoodie. I take it in with sudden horror. I assumed the person I saw in the hooded sweatshirt leaving Lucy's room the other day was Daniel. But it wasn't. It was Doug.

Before I can voice this, Doug pulls me along next to him, my limp toes dragging thin lines in the mud.

'Whoever the fuck you are, come on,' he commands Alani.

She cries out, and I realize he must be strong enough to pull her with his other arm.

'Where are you taking us?' I say, but I barely hear myself. Everything sounds like it's coming from miles away.

His response sends cold flooding through my bones.

'You'll find out soon enough.'

38

Cass

Logan hauls me up off the ground, his hands wrapped around my arms like they have so many times before.

I hadn't thought through how I would confront him when I saw him, but I expected I would be furious. Not only did he lie to me about his ring, but he tried to make me believe I killed Lucy.

But when I realize it's him who I've run into, I can't help but feel rescued. He's saving me from Greta, just like he saved me from the life I had ruined back in Hudson. This is Logan, my fiancé, the man I love.

A flash of panic strikes me as I remember Greta behind me. But when I turn, she's nowhere in sight.

Logan props me up against him and I cling there, my hands grasping on to his shirt.

'Logan, what is going on?' I can hear the desperation in my voice, how much I need the same reassurance he gave me the other night, promising me that everything would be okay.

But my question is loaded, and his response answers nothing.

'I'm sorry. I didn't want this to happen.'

My mind is awash with confusion, but before he can try

to explain, I rush to defend myself. 'Logan, I remembered where I was the night Lucy died. I was on the beach, but I didn't kill her. And I didn't kill the others.' My voice sounds weak.

'I know,' Logan says. His tone is gentle, but something about his words pricks at my skin.

'But you said . . .' I plead for it not to be true.

He stares at me for a moment, not responding, his eyes tracing my face, and suddenly I feel like a child, urging their parents to explain how they could lie about something like Santa Claus for so long. But Logan's lies are different. He's made me think I've committed murder.

He readjusts, propping me against him. And my anger begins to build as the shock of escaping Greta wears off. Everything starts to click together. I can see our entire relationship through new eyes.

He was so furious at me for lying to him about my past. But what about him? Everything he's told me has been a lie.

'*You.* You killed Lucy. And Jacinta. Didn't you? How could you?' My voice is cold, unrecognizable, and Logan flinches.

'I didn't kill them,' he says, eyes flashing.

'Then what was your ring doing where Lucy's body was found?' He opens his mouth to protest, but I stop him before he has the chance to. 'I know it was your ring. I know you swapped mine with yours. I know you killed them.'

Because I do now. I think a part of me has known ever since I heard about Jacinta's death. But I wouldn't allow myself to believe it. I ate up his lies in heaping spoonfuls, always the patient girlfriend, the easily deceived partner.

He sighs. 'I didn't kill them,' he repeats, resignedly. 'But

I did help get rid of Lucy's body. That's why my ring was there. The chain must have come unclasped at some point. I found it that night in my clothes, but the ring was long gone. And later, I switched our rings to make it seem like it was yours.'

None of this seems real. Just a few nights ago I was accepting this man's proposal, vowing to spend the rest of my life with him. And now, it turns out, I never knew him at all. The realization blurs with the dizziness. I steal a glance down at my leg, the blood still gushing out.

'But why?' I finally manage, forcing coherence. 'Why do it? And, God, what did that poor girl do to deserve to die?'

He pauses and flicks his eyes downwards, as if he's ashamed to meet mine. Good. He should be.

'You have to understand. We didn't mean for this to happen. It wasn't planned. Greta thought she would be able to handle it with a warning. She planned to meet the girl—'

'Lucy,' I correct him. 'Her name was Lucy.'

'Erm, right,' he says, a flash of surprise darting across his face. 'Greta was going to tell *Lucy* to stop poking around. She was asking questions about . . . things—'

'What things?'

He doesn't answer, but I know what he's referring to. The other death. Jacinta's.

'It got out of hand,' Logan continues.

'So Greta killed her.' I almost laugh at how absurd the statement would have sounded just an hour ago, back when Greta could do no wrong.

But when Logan nods, I'm not surprised.

'Greta needed our help. We didn't know what else to do with the girl – Lucy. The Full Moon Party was going on, and we couldn't just carry her past everyone. So, we left her in the water. Doug and I dived down and brought her with us, securing her to the coral so her body wouldn't float. It was just supposed to be temporary. Somewhere she could be peaceful until we moved her.'

Peaceful. The word turns my stomach. Greta killed Lucy, and Logan helped cover it up. There was nothing peaceful about that.

'You weren't supposed to find her,' Logan continues. 'Doug had shifted around the dives for the next morning so you would take your group out to Turtle Cove first. We were going to move her when you were out, when it was still too early for anyone to come sniffing around the dive shop. But then things, you know . . .'

I think back to that morning. About how Doug told me at the last minute that we would be diving Turtle Cove, but how the boat wouldn't start, forcing us to stick with our original plan: the offshore dive. It would have been so much easier, in so many ways if that boat had just started. I never would have found Lucy. Logan and Greta and Doug could have made up some elaborate, more realistic story about what happened to her. I wouldn't be here, confronting the man I thought I loved, waiting for what could be the final minutes of my life to tick by.

'If everything had gone to plan –' I force the question through the bile rising in my throat '– what would you have done with Lucy's body?'

Logan sighs again. 'Cass, you don't need to know, it's not—'

'Tell me.'

Logan pauses, but reluctantly answers. 'Doug and I had planned to dive down and get her while you were out at Turtle Cove. We were going to wrap her in one of the tarps we use to cover the Frangipani courtyard when it rains. And we were going to bring her to – out to the middle of the island. There were a few fires lit. The locals burning

324

trash and all that. So, we . . .' He clears his throat. 'We were going to dispose of her there.'

My mind tries unsuccessfully to process what he's saying.

'We were planning to report her as a missing guest,' he says when I don't respond. 'Let the police draw their own conclusions.' He pauses and looks at me. But this time, his dark blue eyes don't make me feel warm and loved. Instead, I feel cold. So cold. 'You were never supposed to be involved, I promise.'

I think of his hands, the hands that have grasped my face as we kissed, that have traced my body countless times, that I wanted to hold in mine until we grew old. And then I think of those hands dragging Lucy's lifeless body out to sea, planning to toss her away, to burn. Discarding her like trash.

There are so many things I want to say to him. I want to yell and scream, and tear him limb from limb, not only for what he did to Lucy, but for how he's treated me. He cheated on me, gaslit me, lied to me. But when I finally open my mouth to speak, there's only one thing I can think of to say, one statement that encompasses everything I'm feeling.

'I don't know you at all.'

His face contorts as if he's been wounded. 'You don't understand. I did this for you. For *us*. So that we could continue our lives together. I didn't want you to have to play a part in all of this. I protected you so that you would never have to be involved. And I was hurt, Cass, really, when I saw Brooke's post. All those lies, you've got to understand . . .' He trails off, and I wonder whether he notices the hypocrisy in his statement. 'All I've ever wanted was you. To live a peaceful life on this island with *you*.'

'No,' I say, the rage bubbling in my chest, a strength

returning to my muscles despite all the blood rushing from my leg. 'You didn't do this for me. You never even thought of me. You did all of this for yourself.'

'Believe what you want,' he says, the pain in his face hardening, his jewelled eyes turning to stone. 'You shouldn't have gone digging into things you have no business knowing. Why couldn't you just let it be? And then you befriended that girl, Brooke.' He says her name like a curse word. 'If you hadn't brought her around, maybe she never would have published that post. Maybe things would still be the same.'

'No,' I say. 'You are not going to pin this on me, again. And it's not Brooke's fault, either.'

I feel the ground shift beneath me, and I realize Logan's arm is still looped around my waist. If he wasn't supporting me, I would collapse to the ground. But isn't that how it's always been with him? I've relied on him for everything since I first moved here. I set out to try to figure out who I was and find a life of my own. Instead, I found Logan.

Part of me wants to keep asking him questions, wants to understand why these three people had to die. But another part wants to run, to get away from this place and never have to see Logan or Greta or any of them again.

Logan begins walking, pulling me towards the end of the street. I try to stop him, using all my body weight to resist, but it has no effect. He drags me along as if I'm nothing, and I notice the faint line of red left in my wake.

I look up at him. His chin is clenched, his jaw set in a rigid line. And I realize he doesn't know me, either.

He only saw my weakness, my complacency. That's what all of them have always seen. Greta, Brooke, my father. None of them have ever known who I really am, who I could be if I just gave myself the chance.

326

Ever since Jacinta's fall, I've been too scared to confront Logan about the deaths. I didn't want to know and I didn't want to upset anyone or draw unnecessary attention. So I stayed quiet. I kept my suspicions to myself. I was the good girl this island family expected me to be, the quiet one.

But I'm done with that. That girl is dead.

I open my mouth wide, drawing on whatever little energy I have left. And I scream.

39

Brooke

My bones mash together as Doug drops me in the mud. I hear Alani crumple beside me, and I reach out my hand to her. She grabs it and gives it a small squeeze.

I blink several times, trying to clarify the familiar sights through my blurred eyes. Logan has draped a tarp above the wooden posts in Frangipani's courtyard, providing a covering, but the wind forces rain in from all sides.

I look around at the ramshackle bar, which now looks like nothing more than a piece of abandoned waste ground. The storm has tossed over leaves and branches from the jungle across the street, littering the area with detritus, and the wind has toppled over the lone picnic table. The fairy lights that are usually lit this late at night remain dark, and a harsh fluorescent glow comes from generator-operated industrial lamps I've never noticed, situated at all four corners of the courtyard. They illuminate the two people standing in front of us. Doug and Greta. Blood cakes her nose, and the makings of a bruise bloom along her cheekbone.

Doug walks over to me, and seconds later, I feel his hands on me, making me stifle a cringe. The scruffiness of rope burns my skin as he draws my ankles together and my wrists behind my back.

I try to kick as he does this, but he holds me down easily with one hand. I watch as he does the same to Alani, who is only a few metres away, seated in the mud. Guilt forces its way through my skin. I should have driven her back to her apartment and gone to find Cass myself. After everything this poor girl has been through, I've dragged her into even more danger. I think of the promise I made to keep her safe, and my stomach turns. I want to throw Doug off her, to run over and protect her. But tied up like this, there's no way for me to reach her.

I worry for a second that he may gag us to stop us from screaming, but then I realize that's not necessary. No one will be out in the storm. And even if they are, they wouldn't hear anything through the rain.

A moment later, I see a third person arrive, scurrying in as if he's late. I recognize his bulky build from behind, but when he whips off the hood of his windbreaker to reveal the mop of reddish hair resting above his freckles, I feel myself sink further into the mud.

The sense of disappointment that washes over me is unrivalled. The only thing that comes close is how I felt after Eric. But Neil's betrayal bothers me more. I thought he was different, that I was finally safe to have feelings for someone. But I was wrong.

He stands there next to Greta, his head down, refusing to meet my eye.

I hear a scream, a piercing wail that comes from mere feet away. I turn to see Logan deposit a broken hulk on the ground, next to the overturned picnic table, and it takes me a moment to realize it's Cass. Blood stains the ground around her and leaves Logan's shirt streaked with red. Her clothes are drenched from the rain, suctioned to her skin. She looks so small and beaten. I wonder how I could have ever thought she was behind all of this.

I watch uselessly as Doug ties her arms behind her, just like he did to me and Alani. But with Cass, he forgoes tying her ankles, apparently concluding, as I did, that she won't get far with the amount of blood seeping from her leg.

I stare at her. Her face is paler than I've ever seen. As if sensing my gaze, she turns her head, taking me in. Despite the blood loss, her eyes are clear and lucid.

'I'm sorry,' I say quietly. 'For all of it.'

'Me too,' she says, her eyes never leaving mine. And I know, more than anything I've ever known, that we both mean it.

I want to say more, but before I can formulate the words, my attention is drawn to the others. They've moved away from us to talk. The rain's percussive beat against the tarp drowns out their words, but Greta is waving her arms in anger. I watch Doug cut a sharp glance at Alani.

What are they planning?

I don't have to wait long for the answer. I see Logan reach his hand behind him as he pulls something from his waistband. As he shifts his arm back in front of him, the object in his hand gleams, the silver refracting off the harsh generator-fuelled lights.

Logan has a gun.

I have no idea where he got it from, but by now I'm not surprised by any of the shady shit these people get into.

Doug reaches for the gun, as if he has a sense of owner-ship, and Logan hands it to him easily.

Doug starts talking again, animatedly, and as the wind blows in our direction, I make out two words over the din of the rain that stick in my gut with alarming sharpness. *Murder-suicide.*

And it all makes sense. They're planning to blame this on Cass. To make it look like she took revenge on me and then killed herself. They just hadn't planned for Alani.

Every muscle in my body clenches. I can't die here, because of these people. I won't.

And I won't let Cass and Alani, either.

I shift, inching the thumb of my right hand up so that it connects with the rope looped around my wrists. Over the course of the last three days, my perfectly self-manicured fingernails have become jagged, my right thumb worse than all of them. I start to work it against the rope, realizing as I do that it's much less substantial than I originally thought. Closer to string than rope, really. Doug probably thought that through as well. Stronger rope could leave marks on our wrists, evidence that would make it hard for even the Koh Sang police to conclude our deaths were a murder-suicide. Plus, even if we did escape, it's not like we would make it far with four people barrelling after us.

I can already feel several threads of the rope break off under my fingernail, but it's not enough.

Apparently reaching some resolution, the others turn to face us. I see Doug's fingers tighten around the gun, and I know I have to buy time.

'We called the American Embassy,' I bluff. 'We told them everything. If you kill us, they'll know it was you.'

Greta's laugh cuts through the night, a crude bark. 'The storm has knocked everything out. The phones have been down for hours. No one is coming for you.'

I pause for a moment, desperation making me change tactics.

'You don't have to do this.' I say it to all of them, but the statement is directed to one person in particular. Neil.

Despite him standing in front of me now and all the

evidence pointing to the contrary, something tells me he wasn't involved in this. I can't believe that after the conversations we've had, the time we've spent together, the intimate kiss we shared just yesterday, that he would have helped kill Lucy or Jacinta or Daniel. And something about the way he's standing now – shoulders hunched, eyes downcast, as if he's ashamed or scared – makes me cling to that belief.

But I suppose Cass thought the same thing about Logan. She wouldn't have promised her future to him if she really believed he was a murderer.

I will Neil to raise his head, to look me in the eyes, but he refuses, his neck steadfastly craned down.

'You really haven't left us much choice,' Doug says. 'You should have kept your pretty little nose out of things. If you'd just minded your own bloody business, I reckon you could've moved on, kept posting all your sweet titty pics for the world to see.'

'Stupid girls,' Greta says, a wisp of sadness in her voice. 'You brought this on yourselves. We told you to stop, but you kept prodding. Including you.' She points dismissively towards Alani. 'How the hell are you tied up in this?'

'Lucy was my best friend.' Alani's voice is cold, with no hint of fear. A swell of pride rises in me.

'Lucy knew what she was getting into,' Doug says. 'She came here to expose us. She knew the risks. And you should have, too.'

'So that's why Greta killed her?' I ask, forcing my voice to be stronger than I feel, although I already know the answer.

At this, Greta's eyes dart to me. I feel a thrill thrum through my abdomen.

'Oh, yeah, Greta. I know all about what you did. You

met Lucy at the Full Moon Party and convinced her to take a walk down the beach with you. And when you tried to talk to her, to explain that Jacinta's death was an accident, she didn't buy it. She wasn't going to stop asking questions, and you couldn't have that. Because you all have something to hide, don't you? So, what's your secret?'

Greta's cold eyes stay on me, but she remains silent.

'Alice wasn't in love with Greta. Greta was her teacher.' I'm shocked to hear Cass's voice rise up next to me. When I look over, she's still on the ground. Her teeth are gritted, her hands clutching her leg. 'Greta must have tricked her into coming here.'

I try to nod away my surprise. 'So that's it. Makes sense.' Greta stares at me, her mouth contorted in spite, her eyes narrowed.

'And one of you killed Daniel, too,' Alani says, only a slight waver in her voice.

None of them bothers to correct her, and I see Neil's eyes flick to Doug.

'It was you, Doug. Wasn't it?' I ask. 'I saw you on Daniel's video. Talking to her, handing her a drink. Was that how she got the MDMA in her system?'

I notice a flush creep into Doug's neck. 'He tried to blackmail us, that dickhead. He tried to fleece us.'

'So you slit his throat. The only option, right?'

Doug's face turns even redder, and I swallow back disgust.

'But why Jacinta?' I hear Alani ask, her tone pleading. 'What could she have possibly done?'

'It was Logan.' My head whips around to where Cass is seated, her skin painted in rain-streaked mud. Her voice sounds softer than the last time she spoke, and I notice with alarm that the bleeding from the cuts in her leg hasn't slowed. But despite her broken limbs and battered skin, she looks stronger than I've ever seen her. There's a fierce determination in her eyes. 'You thought I was so stupid, that I wouldn't put two and two together,' she continues, her gaze locked on him. 'Did you kill her because of the affair, so she wouldn't say anything? Or was it something else?'

I think of what Alani told me earlier. How Jacinta was planning to go out on a date with the handsome expat she'd been seeing before she died. I wonder how far Logan would have gone to stop Jacinta from telling Cass about their affair.

For once Logan's face is contorted in pain. I always thought his privileged arrogance was why I never liked him. But now I see what it really is that's always irked me: the long, dark hair, the muscular build, the mischievous grin. He's just like Eric. Another man who thinks he can do whatever he wants to women and get away with it.

'I never said anything,' Cass continues. 'Because I thought I loved you. But now I know I didn't. I couldn't have.'

'Cass . . .' Logan starts.

'No, Logan. You didn't love me, either. We used each other. A fake family to replace the ones we left behind. Let's just be honest for once.'

Logan looks as if he's been struck. For a moment, I think he may crumple to the ground. Maybe he thought he loved her after all. But soon enough, his face contorts, shedding the emotion from seconds before. His lips roll upwards, and his gaze switches from Cass to me, his eyes filled with rage. I know what he's going to say before he opens his mouth. He's found someone other than Cass to serve as the target of his fury.

'This is all your fault, Brooke. You and that fucking Instagram post. We were happy before you came here. This was our home. And you destroyed it. I could tell there was something off about you from the first day you got here. Always there, always watching. Turns out I was right. You were sneaking around behind our backs the entire time. Trying to ruin us.'

Logan grabs the gun back from Doug's hand in one quick motion.

'Well, it's about time we return the favour,' he says.

I feel my chest tighten as he raises the gun, points it directly at my heart.

I close my eyes and prepare for him to shoot.

40

Cass

The accusations fell from my mouth, each of them confirming what I've known was true but could never acknowledge.

Was Jacinta the first time Logan cheated, or was that just the first time I caught him? And how many other women has he hurt since we've been together?

But the anger I feel burning in my chest isn't just for Logan's lies. It's how I've reacted to them. I've eaten them up, forcing myself to believe him, swallowing my doubts along with the pills. The same thing I did all those years ago for Eric. Brooke was right. How many lives have I ruined by failing to stand up for myself?

No more.

I watch Logan raise his arms out in front of him, his fingers firm around the gun, aimed steadfastly at Brooke. A threatening growl escapes from his lips, a sound I've never heard from his mouth before.

I look briefly down at my leg, the blood leaking from several deep cuts, and feel another wave of dizziness. I know what's coming. Even if they let me live, I wouldn't make it far in this state. And with the storm in full swing, none of the medical clinics on the island will be open.

My time is running out.

I wonder if Robin had the same realization after she drank that glass of champagne. I wonder if it's what Lucy felt as she waited for the water to flood her lungs, or Jacinta, as the rocks rushed up to meet her. Or Daniel, as he felt the knife puncture his throat. So many people who didn't have to die. Who shouldn't have.

I've trusted people I shouldn't, and in doing so, I've let down so many others.

But maybe there's a way that I can fix some of this. A way that I can prevent these people – my so-called family – from taking another person's life. A way that I can make up for letting Brooke down all those years ago.

I bend my palms flat against the muddy ground, giving me just enough support to work myself up to standing. Doug hadn't even bothered tying my legs. Underestimating me yet again.

I conjure up my last ounce of energy, and before my mind can fully acknowledge what I'm doing, my legs are moving. I no longer feel the pain that accompanied each step before. It's as if my body is functioning on its own.

I don't hear the noise, the screams that come at me from all sides as the gun fires from Logan's hands. I don't feel the pain that I've prepared myself for as I throw myself in front of Brooke. Instead, I spiral towards the darkness before I can even register the bullet that slices through my chest.

41

Brooke

I squeeze my eyes shut as I hear the gun erupt and brace for the hot pain that's about to flood my body. But after a moment, there's nothing apart from a terrible ringing in my ears and the distant sounds of screams. I must be in shock, I realize – my body's method of protecting me from Logan's bullet.

The first thing I see when I lift my eyelids is the crumpled mass in front of me, dark liquid pooling around her. The blonde hair, the skinny legs.

How did Cass get here? She was tied up over by the picnic table just moments before. But through the confusion, the thoughts come at me half-formed and abstract. Her untied legs. She must have run towards me when Logan raised the gun. The bullet hit her, not me.

And then I hear it. A wail, guttural and garbled, as if rising from the depths. I try to focus my blurred eyes, and when I finally do, I find its source. Logan, running directly at me.

I watch Greta try to stop him, but he easily breaks free from her grasp. Within seconds he's dropped to the ground, inches from Cass's lifeless body. He pulls her head into his lap, heaving sobs shaking his entire body.

A red plume blossoms across Cass's pink tank top, the rainwater blurring it at the edges like some grotesque watercolour painting. Her eyes stare up at the sky, registering nothing. Her chest is still.

In that moment, I know, just as Logan does, that Cass is gone. She threw herself in front of the bullet meant for me.

'It was for us, it was all for us,' he mumbles over and over into Cass's ear.

And that's when I finally feel the rope break free beneath my fingers. I shimmy my hands out of it, going to work on loosening the rope around my legs while everyone is distracted.

I need to get to Alani. To help her.

But before I can stand, Logan's eyes shoot to me, as if he's only just remembered that I'm here.

'You.' Vines of emotion crawl around the word like ivy. The menace of it solidifies in my bones, nailing my feet to the muddied ground. One thought pierces my skull, a phrase my brain sounds out backwards and forwards in the split second it takes Logan to get to his feet.

The gun.

The thought ricochets through my brain. Logan still has the gun in his hands.

I'm running across the courtyard before he can raise it, and then I'm diving, flying through the air. As the pistol blasts so close to me that I can feel the vibration from the barrel, I fall to the ground behind the picnic table.

The bullet lands just to my left, exploding the mud around me like a firework.

I duck behind the table, bracing myself for him to fire again, but the gun is silent; all I hear are yells and groans.

When I open my eyes, the chaos in the courtyard pauses in freeze frame. I see Logan with the gun, but it's no longer

339

pointed at me. And he's not standing, but lying in the mud, just metres away from his dead fiancée. I blink, forcing my eyes to come into focus.

When they do, I see a man standing over Logan. I take in his reddish hair, his freckled skin. I see the blood covering his hand, and that's when I notice the small knife sticking from the side of Logan's neck.

My brain registers it in flashes.

Neil stabbed Logan. To protect me.

I watch as Doug and Greta rush towards them, Greta dropping to the ground next to Logan, Doug attacking Neil, fists flying.

I want to do something to stop Doug. To protect Neil just like he did me. But I know it's futile. I know I can't fend off Doug, especially when he's in such close proximity to the gun.

Instead, I run back to Alani, frantically trying to loosen the rope around her hands. Just as the knot comes free, I hear her scream.

'Brooke!' My name comes out garbled from her mouth, and when I lift my head to process why, I see Greta running towards us, her hair – almost white in the light – flying behind her, witchlike.

And then she's on me. The force knocks me to the ground, the air exploding out of me, leaving me gasping. One of her hands is on my throat, crushing my oesophagus, her face knotted in a purgatory between grief and rage. The other hand is pulled back, preparing to make contact with my cheek. She's strong. But it's a strength that's built in studios, on cushy yoga mats. She's never had to fight. She didn't have one of her mother's boyfriends teach her self-defence so that she wouldn't keep getting the shit beaten out of her in junior high.

I did.

I manage to shift my head just in time for Greta's fist to impact the mud next to me. The contact catches her off guard, and her hand unclenches from my throat for a moment, which is all I need.

I flip her easily and crawl atop her so that she's pinned face down. I pull her wrists back behind her, securing them with my left hand, and I wrap my other hand around her hair. And then, as hard as I can, I shove her head down, as far as possible into the mud. And I hold it there. Just like she held Lucy's head under the water.

Her body squirms and shudders beneath me, but I don't let go. I grasp her hair tight in my hand, channelling all the anger that's flooded my body for years. I don't know how much time passes. Two seconds? Five? Ten? I imagine the dirt invading her mouth, clinging in clumps to her tongue. I picture her swallowing it, filling up her trachea like an earthy grave.

Time seems to stop in that moment. Nothing is real other than the feel of Greta's hair wrapped around my fingers, everything else fading into a blur.

Until a sharp sound drags me back to reality.

The gunshot reverberates throughout the courtyard, the deafening blast turning my blood to concrete.

I whip my head towards the source of the sound, my fingers reflexively loosening around Greta's hair. The next thing I see is blood. I didn't think it was possible for there to be more. But now it's coming from Neil's leg, which he's on the ground clutching.

'Get off her.'

Doug is mere feet from me. And in his hands is Logan's gun.

He shot Neil.

And again, the gun is pointed at me, this time at close enough range to blow my head clean off my neck. I drop Greta, feeling her body clench beneath me as she lifts up, desperate for air. Slowly, I raise my dirt-encrusted hands above my head, facing towards Doug.

I surrender.

I look to Neil, who's still on the ground. His one free hand – the one not clutched around his wounded leg – is also raised.

'Get on the ground,' Doug commands. 'You too.' He nods towards Alani.

And I know it's over. For real this time.

I drop, my knees hitting the ground with a wet *thwomp*. The sound of defeat. I hear Alani do the same, joining Neil and me in the mud, a trio of victims lined up before the firing squad.

I try to prepare myself again for what's coming. Scenes from the last few weeks flash before my eyes. I expect them to be filled with anger, the rage that's been following me for the last three years. But to my surprise, I see Cass. My arm wrapped around her on the summit of Khrum Yai. And Neil and me laughing into our drinks in the Tiki Palms.

'Drop it!'

This time I'm sure it's a voice I don't recognize. My eyes flick back and forth, ultimately realizing the command didn't come from any of us.

'Drop the gun, now!'

I watch the indecision play out on Doug's face as he weighs his options. I'm too nervous to risk taking my eyes off him for the second it will take to identify the source of the voice.

After an interminable pause, Doug obeys, bending down to deposit the gun in the mud. Within seconds, a swarm of black is on him and Greta. I register the uniforms, so much more official than the Koh Sang police, the guns in their hands, other weapons holstered to their waistbands.

Who are these men? How did they know we were here? Can they really be on our side?

But none of the answers matter as much as the man to my left. I crawl the few metres to Neil, pressing my hands over the wound in his leg. He's clearly in pain, but still coherent. I position my mouth near his face, close enough for him to hear me over the chaos around us.

'You saved me,' I say.

42

Two Weeks Later

Brooke

My hands grasp the wooden bar as my body jolts. The impact catches me unprepared, and I'm barely able to maintain my balance as the whirring of the engine cuts through the island air. I watch from the deck of the ferry as the mountains slowly recede, their imposing stature diminishing as we pull further from the shore. Away from Koh Sang, away from the island that has claimed so much.

The last two weeks have been a blur of police officers, reporters, and hospital rooms. And one visit to the island's morgue.

Two dead. Cass was pronounced dead on site; Logan died from blood loss in the makeshift ICU that had been established in the rickety Koh Sang hospital.

And I would have joined them had it not been for the police.

When I had checked the statistics on my Instagram post the afternoon it had been posted, it was clear that it would do well. But just how well, I had no idea.

It was reposted by a number of my followers and other travel influencers, some with pretty sizeable followings.

And it ultimately managed to attract the attention of the British Consulate in Bangkok, which threatened political action should the Thai police choose not to properly investigate Daniel's murder and bring his body home. Despite skipping parole, at the end of the day, Daniel was still a British citizen, and the UK government wouldn't stand for his murder to go unpunished. The Thai police were left with no option but to send a team of trained officers from Bangkok to Koh Sang to investigate.

Had the team waited even a few more minutes to fly out, they would never have made it. They landed their helicopter on Lamphan beach just minutes before the storm rendered air traffic impossible.

When they arrived, the team split up – two officers heading to question Frederic at the resort, the other two deployed to the police station. But when the latter cohort found the station without power and abandoned, all Koh Sang police having left long before to join their families for the storm, they decided to patrol the island. When they heard the gunshots coming from Frangipani, it took the officers only minutes to descend on the courtyard.

The police arrested Doug and Greta on site. Doug resisted, of course, surrendering only after being struck unconscious by the butt of an officer's gun. Greta went much more willingly.

She admitted to everything, starting with her relationship with Alice, which Cass had somehow discovered. I reached out to Alice again on Instagram after everything happened, and she filled in the gaps that had been missing. Greta, twenty-three, freshly graduated with a master's degree in education, had been one of Alice's secondary school teachers when she was only fourteen. Alice explained how Greta had groomed her, ultimately blackmailing Alice by threatening to report the relationship to her parents until Alice agreed to accompany her on a trip out of town. Greta never told Alice where they were going, and once they'd left the country, it was too late for Alice to get away. Greta kept her passport under lock and key, forcing Alice to play house with her on this island thousands of miles from home. But last month, in the chaos following Jacinta's murder, Greta must have become less vigilant, giving Alice the opportunity to find her passport and escape.

Alice told me that she never reported Greta once she returned to Sweden. Despite everything that Greta had done to her, Alice couldn't bring herself to hate her. In fact, in some strange way – despite working extensively with a therapist on this point – Alice still loved Greta.

But Alice knew her silence could cost others. So she kept tabs on the Permanents and the other individuals joining them, like me. When she saw the photos I was posting with the group, she sent me those Instagram messages as a sort of warning. She wanted me to know of the connection between Jacinta and the Permanents, but as soon as she did it, she felt conflicted, as if she had betrayed Greta. So she didn't respond to my subsequent messages and tried to ignore the guilt that gnawed at her, until she saw the news of what happened at Frangipani.

When the police confronted Greta with Alice's account of what had happened, she confessed. To all of it. To taking Alice, murdering Lucy and helping to cover up the other deaths.

But Greta and Cass weren't the only ones who came here to get away from what they'd done. Koh Sang is – or was – a place people go to hide, after all.

Logan was a prime example. After his death, the Scottish media tripped over themselves to be the first to expose the information they had dug up on him. Logan's brother, Alec, had died in Logan's car, but only after Logan rammed it into a tree while driving drunk. Most of Aberdeen believed the crash was deliberate, intended by Logan to kill – or at least injure – his brother, who had been hooking up with a girl Logan was interested in. Logan skipped town without a word to anyone while his charges for drink-driving and Alec's death remained pending.

And Doug. Doug of the small town of Bendigo, Australia, whose real name was actually Michael Williams. Who had an outstanding warrant for the rape of an underage girl and was suspected of having been involved in several other sexual assaults.

Doug refused to admit it, of course, just as he denied his involvement in covering up the murders of Jacinta and Lucy. He denied murdering Daniel, too, even when the police found the burner phone with messages to Daniel requesting that meeting under Doug's mattress.

Doug was quick to shove the blame on everyone else: Logan, Greta, even Neil. But after days of beatings and God knows what else at the hands of the Thai police, he finally confessed to killing Daniel. And he explained how this all started.

He told the police about Logan and Jacinta's affair. When Jacinta found out that Logan was in a relationship, she threatened to out Logan to Cass. Somehow, Logan calmed her down and convinced her to take a morning hike with him up to Khrum Yai. Just as the sun began to rise above the Gulf of Thailand's glittering surface, he pushed her and watched her body tumble to the rocks hundreds of feet below.

When people began to question Jacinta's death, Logan recruited the other Permanents to help him. They were each willing to do whatever was needed to avoid unnecessary attention. Doug confirmed that Greta took care of Lucy by drowning her at the Full Moon Party. And, finally, Doug admitted that Daniel had attempted to blackmail him with the video, trying to get enough money so that he could escape permanently, never having to return to London. Doug arranged to meet him, but rather than turning over the cash, Doug took Daniel by surprise, slitting his throat with a knife he'd taken from the dive shop.

The saddest part was that Daniel was innocent of the sexual assault crime he had been convicted of in London. No doubt seeing an opportunity for her fifteen minutes of fame, Daniel's ex-girlfriend came clean to one of the UK's trashier tabloids, explaining how she had accused Daniel of assaulting her only after he had abruptly ended their relationship.

I didn't get all the answers I wanted – for instance, who broke into my room the day I published the post. But given all that Doug's done, I can't help but lay that crime at his feet as well.

As soon as the police dragged Doug and Greta to the station, they released a very bruised and black-eyed Sengphet. In exchange for the mishap, and in return for Sengphet's agreement not to report his predicament to the media, the Thai government agreed to transport his wife and young son to Thailand with the requisite immigration papers, and to relocate them all to Koh Phi Phi, an island a few hours away.

Doug and Greta weren't the only ones to be arrested on the night of the storm. By the time they arrived at the Koh Sang police station, Frederic was already there. He eventually admitted to doing everything in his power to cover up what was happening on the island. But the police also recently released a statement revealing that Frederic had been involved in a long list of financial crimes on Koh Sang and in Bangkok, where he was in the process of opening a second resort. Always one to save himself at others' expense, Frederic was quick to hand over to the Thai National Anti-Corruption Commission a list of the Koh Sang police whom he had routinely bribed.

Alani escaped it all, relatively uninjured – physically, at least. Lucy's parents had flown to Koh Sang to recover their daughter's body and to accompany Alani home. They didn't blame her for Lucy's death as she feared; instead, they told her how indebted they were to her for finding out the truth behind what had happened to Jacinta and for trying to protect their younger daughter. I met them, too. The four of us – Lucy's parents, Alani and myself – spent several nights together on the beach as well as a few sunrise mornings on the summit of Khrum Yai, paying tribute to their daughters in the way they would have wanted.

I was released from the Koh Sang hospital ten days ago. My physical wounds are still healing; the doctors promised the stitches holding together the cut on my head would dissolve in time, and the bruises covering my legs have already begun to fade.

But a minute hasn't passed since Cass's death that I haven't thought about her. I cling to our moment in the mud of Frangipani, her apology. I'm struggling to come to terms with the guilt I have for exposing her and the fact that she gave her life for mine. I'm not sure I ever will.

On the day I was released, I was able to see Cass one final time. With no next of kin in the United States and no will, Thai law provided for a state-funded cremation. Given the circumstances, the police made an exception and let me visit her the day before.

Lying on the gurney, with her eyes closed and her hair pulled back from her face, she looked like a child, remarkably like the photographs of Robin in the newspapers years ago. I stood beside her for several minutes, telling her everything I'd never had the chance to while she was alive. The apologies, the explanations, how much I had got wrong about her. Because there was quite a lot. Ever since I had arrived on Koh Sang, there had been part of me, deep down, that knew Cass was a good person, even if I had tried my hardest to ignore it.

In the days following the showdown at Frangipani, a tenacious reporter broke the emotional story of what really happened in that hotel room in Upstate New York, correcting the years of lies painting Cass as the Hudson Massacre Killer. That reporter somehow got her hands on the statement Cass had made to the police back then, detailing the real story about what happened. The switched glasses, her sister's heart condition, Cass's self-defence.

And despite all the news stations villainizing her as a murderer in the wake of the incident, Cass never corrected them. She endured the claims, the ostracization, the pain, all by herself, as if she assumed she deserved it. She was stronger than I could have ever known.

As I stood there next to her body, between tearful sobs, I forgave her again for that night at the swim house and everything that happened afterwards. I realized I had been using her as a vessel for my rage whenever the hatred I held for Eric overflowed. But she was just a girl back then. A girl with struggles I never knew about. And she more than made up for it in the end.

The sight of Koh Sang fades in front of me now. Despite

everything, I can still make out people lounging on the beach, a handful of others on stand-up paddleboards. The tourism didn't take a hit as everyone expected. If anything, the news has given Koh Sang a new, dark allure for backpackers.

It's turned the resort into a place where everyone wants to stay.

I hear something behind me now, the sound of wood underfoot interrupting my memories. I feel the grasp of a hand on my waist and clench instinctively, before my fleeting panic is replaced with pleasure from the touch of light kisses on my shoulder.

'Hey, you,' I say softly, teasing my fingers through his tousled hair. Neil snuggles closer, the scratchiness of his cast brushing against the side of my leg. His colour has finally returned, a peachiness replacing the stark white in the gaps between his freckles that had stained his face for days after that night at Frangipani. After the arrests were made, the police rushed him to the makeshift medical clinic on the island. Until the electricity returned the next day, there wasn't much the doctors could do other than wrap his gunshot wound to try to stop the bleeding.

In the end, a doctor splinted Neil's leg and removed the bullet. He was lucky, the doctor reminded him repeatedly. The bullet missed any major arteries or ligaments and was easy to remove. He would struggle with walking for a while, but there would be no lasting damage.

I begged the nurses to let me out of my hospital room, and I sat next to him through all of it, shocked to see how scared it made me. Even knowing how I betrayed him, I hadn't fully processed the risk of losing him until I saw the bullet in his leg, and the fear that gripped my heart – clenched it tightly and refused to let it go – bled into another kind of emotion. Maybe not yet love, but deep affection.

When Neil's doctor finally broke the news that he would be okay, I pulled my chair as close as the bulky hospital bed would allow, and I listened to Neil tell me the whole story of his time on the island.

'Everything I told you before about my past was true,' he explained. 'About my rough upbringing, the attempted suicides, and about finding my family on the island. I was scared to give it all up, but I tried, over and over. I told Logan, Doug and Greta that I was planning on reporting the first murder, that I wanted to tell the police exactly what happened to Jacinta. But they swore that if I did, they would frame me for it. And when the bodies kept piling up, I repeated my threats, but they wouldn't let me say anything. You saw what they tried to do to you at Frangipani. I had been in that position, with no one else to protect me. They knew what they could do to me, and they reminded me often.

'I could never leave. Greta even took my passport and hid it somewhere in her house, exactly like she did with Alice. But even after everything, I still loved them,' he choked through tears. 'It's hard to explain, but they were still my family.'

I can only imagine how hard this has been for him. Losing two of his best friends to death, two to prison, realizing he never really knew any of them. I watched him call Greta's name at Frangipani as he lay waiting for his stretcher to be hauled into the ambulance. The police allowed her to go to his side, the rest of us giving them privacy. I was several steps away, too far to hear what they said over the rush of the rain, but I watched their short exchange, saw the glint of tears in Neil's eye as Greta walked away from him for ever.

I had been terrified that he would never be able to forgive me for publishing my post, but as we sat there in the hospital he looked clearly into my eyes and squeezed my hand. 'If you hadn't done what you did, I never would have left. You saved me.' And every piece of me believed him.

He'll be okay, and so will I. We can move forward now, no longer surrounded by ghosts. We can travel, work, live. Together.

The police questioned him extensively, pulling up a chair to his hospital bed, just like I did, and ordering me out of the room for hours at a time. After several anxiety-ridden days, the police finally explained that they wouldn't be pressing charges. Because he had provided so much information implicating Greta, Doug and Frederic, Neil was free to go. He and I both cried that night, my arms wrapped around his, until his lips touched mine again. And in that moment, it felt like everything we had been through had been worth it.

Neil and I agreed that we would take things slow. I knew I wanted to keep moving and so did he. After all the media attention around the island, offers from outlets flooded my email, and I decided to take a position with an American magazine that offered me a semi-permanent post specializing in travel. The only catch was that my beat would be Southeast Asia. But even so, I found myself excited. Something about this place had burrowed under my skin. I felt like I owed myself more time to explore. And Neil agreed.

We would travel and room together, saving money as we went, but our relationship would otherwise move at its own pace. It isn't conventional, but neither are we.

We watch in silence as the mountains retreat further. I feel a prick at the back of my eyes as I think of all the lives I'm leaving here and the women who will never be able to move on. But I feel a warmth radiating from the Ziploc bag inside my pocket. Cass's ashes.

The police had reluctantly turned them over to me when they realized they had no legal relatives or next of kin to contact. I promised Cass I would bring her on my adventures. I'd take her away from this island to other countries, leaving her scattered on the beaches and mountain ridges she and her sister only ever dreamed of visiting.

A tear escapes from the corner of my eye, and I feel Neil squeeze my hand.

'We'll be okay,' I say aloud, and he nods, understanding what I mean. It's a promise. To him and me.

And for the first time, I actually believe it.

Epilogue

Neil

I run my tongue along my lips, savouring the salt that the sea air has deposited there.

'You go and get some sleep. It's going to be a long ride to the mainland,' I say, stroking her hair. Brooke reaches up on her toes and gives me a small kiss before heading back inside the ferry cabin. A small spark shoots through me as I watch her. Not happiness, exactly, but something close. Victory.

Even in my wildest dreams, I couldn't have asked for a better outcome, everything wrapped up so tight and perfect, all leaking holes dammed. The police bought it, hook line and sinker, and so did the doctors. So did Brooke.

I had told Doug and Greta to take the lead that night at Frangipani. I knew I had to be extra cautious in the wake of Brooke's Instagram post. I'd hold back, I told them, until they needed me. But things got out of hand fast, too fast. They underestimated Brooke – we all did – and who would have thought Cass had it in her to take a bullet for someone? As soon as I saw that, I knew the tide had turned. And while all the others were consumed with Cass, bleeding out in front of us, I spotted lights from the courtyard, and I knew what that meant. It was time for the rats to leave the ship. I'd come prepared, of course, bringing one of the scuba knives we kept at the shop. It was a risk, stabbing Logan. But I did what I had to do, just like always.

And just like always, it worked out.

I didn't correct Cass or Brooke that night when they spouted their conclusions about the deaths. I nodded when they accused Logan of killing Jacinta. And I made sure to look over at Doug when Brooke asked about who killed Daniel. That didn't take much persuasion.

It was almost *too* easy. Logan kissing Jacinta while Cass looked on. This shit could write itself! How pathetic. The bastard was about to be engaged, but as soon as he saw Jacinta he couldn't keep his dick in his pants. I mean, yeah, she was gorgeous, but Logan's always been weak. She told me about the kiss later that day, how Logan had asked her to lunch, how he tried to slide his tongue into her mouth, how she was too shocked to act at first, but then came to her senses and pushed him away.

She told me all that during our dinner date that night, both of us laughing over how stupid Logan was, how he couldn't tell that Jacinta only had eyes for me.

And then, after a few hours of drinking at Frangipani, I promised her the most romantic sunrise of her life if she'd go for a pre-dawn hike with me. By then she was eating out of my hand. And once we were up on Khrum Yai, the sun just barely breaking over the water, I pushed her.

I know I'm not supposed to shit where I eat, but I had been good for so long.

And it was all just so damn easy. All it took was one quick shove, and that was that, finally feeding the impulse that vibrated through me. I watched as her body flipped over the cliff, as her bones cracked against the jagged rocks below. It really was beautiful.

Then that little bitch came to the island asking questions. Lucy. I made it clear to the others how bad this was for all of us. It didn't take much persuading. Hell, Greta even handled Lucy on her own. I couldn't help but beam with pride when I saw her down at the beach, Lucy's cooling body beside her.

Logan took a bit more work. He didn't want anyone to get hurt, he told me. Pussy. So, I told him what I knew. That he had kissed Jacinta less than twelve hours before her body was found and he had no alibi for the time of her death. I reminded him how it would look to the police, a spurned man getting revenge.

It was the opportunity I needed. After that, Logan felt indebted to me, and I used it. I had him do my dirty work: I loaned him Doug's black sweatshirt to break into Lucy's hotel room to get us any information we could use to help cover this up. He botched that, of course. And in exchange for keeping Cass out of everything, he promised to keep tabs on her. To plant the idea that *she* might be the one behind the murders, so she would stay quiet. And when I realized Brooke was poking around, asking questions even when she promised me she wouldn't, I had him break into her room too. He protested, of course, to all of it. But all it took was a gentle reminder of what I held over him.

Of course, I was the one to take care of Daniel. I wanted to. The shithead had tried to blackmail us, so I set up a little meeting, using a burner phone that I later stuck under Doug's mattress. I met him in that alley. As we started talking, he glanced down at his phone. I used that moment of distraction to my advantage. Just as he returned his phone to his pocket, I pulled out the knife I had brought from the dive shop, the same one I later used on Logan, and dragged it across his throat. Made it look just like that guy's murder on Koh Samui; the one who crossed the Thai Mafia. A nice touch if I do say so myself. But then I heard footsteps coming from behind me. I took off, thankfully remembering the slight curve at the end of the alley that leads to a bigger road near Kumvit, where I changed my shirt, before heading back out on to the street and dumping the bloody one in a kebab shop waste bin. I didn't dare go back to the alley to grab Daniel's phone, lest someone see me over his corpse. Instead, I risked it, hoping that without Daniel's guiding hand, the police wouldn't realize the incriminating evidence he had on his videos from the Full Moon Party. Not a big risk, really, given how bloody incompetent they are. So, I hoofed it back to the dive shop just as all the others were arriving.

I never imagined Brooke would be stealthy enough to steal Daniel's phone from his front pocket, but hey, that's my girl.

And she bought all of it, including the sob story about my rough childhood in Bristol. The basis of it was true, even if I did lie about trying to off myself – I could tell just by glancing at her bracelets what they were hiding, and what better way for her to trust me? I did leave out some of the more lurid details of my upbringing, though. My parents' double murder, which the police tried so badly to tie to me but never could. The home I was transferred to after, where the other kids just happened to start sporting new injuries after my arrival. A broken arm here, a black eye there. Until I got out of that dump.

I forced the tears to come the night everything happened at Frangipani, but I really didn't have to try much. The doctors back at that home in Bristol told me I was incapable of feeling emotions, but they were wrong. That night I was happy. The tears of triumph dropped one by one, just when I needed them. I made Greta come over to the stretcher before the police packed me up into the ambulance. I kept the tears flowing, so it looked like we were having a sentimental conversation. I'd already made her look guilty enough by planting my passport in her house, and I told her that if she ever decided to come clean and speak of my role in any of the murders, if she ever questioned any of it, I would track down Alice back in Sweden: the only person Greta ever seemed capable of loving. And I would kill her.

And she knew I was right.

I didn't have to worry about Doug. The police wouldn't believe a word that came out of that degenerate's mouth anyway. And the rest of them were dead. Easy as pie.

I'll miss it here, on this island. It's been good to me. A haven of sorts, where I could really be myself. Where I didn't have to hide my urges. But I'm optimistic. Brooke and I have a load of countries ahead of us. Countless unsuspecting women who don't know better and corrupt police who are easily dissuaded from investigating. And now I have the picture-perfect boyfriend façade to hide behind.

So, goodbye for now, Koh Sang. But hello, world of opportunities.

Acknowledgements

The idea of writing a novel – let alone becoming a published author – has always seemed like a fantasy to me. And it would have remained that way without the support, skill and encouragement I received from so many people.

Finn Cotton, my brilliant editor at Transworld, you turned this book into something I could only have dreamt of. Thank you so much for your passion for *The Dive* and your engaging and creative ideas. I could not have asked for a more intuitive and supportive editor. Also, a massive thank you to my incredible agent, Kate Burke, who saw something in my manuscript and helped polish it into *The Dive*. The amount of time and support you've devoted to this book is honestly mind-blowing, and I have so much gratitude for your endless encouragement! How did I get so lucky?!

Thank you also to the wider team at Transworld. Julia Teece, Hayley Barnes and Becky Hunter have been the best people to assist this self-promotionally challenged author with marketing and publicity. A huge thanks to Laura Ricchetti, Tom Chicken and Emily Harvey for all your behind-the-scenes hard work, and a special thank you to Charley Chapman, Barbara Thompson, Josh Benn, Bella Bosworth, Georgie Polhill and Joanne Hill for your eagle-eyed edits. I couldn't be happier to work with such a talented and brilliant group!

I am so grateful to the entire team at Blake Friedmann for taking a chance on me, especially to Sian Ellis Martin for her incredible edits and support, to Julian Friedmann and Anna Myrmus for their excitement in bringing this book to the screen, and to James Pusey and Hana Murrell for working tirelessly so that *The Dive* may reach as many parts of the world as possible.

Thank you also to everyone at Sourcebooks, my publisher across the pond, and especially to MJ Johnston, my amazing American editor.

I would be remiss if I didn't express my gratitude to the amazing book bloggers, Instagrammers and reviewers, as well as all the other authors who have helped get *The Dive* out in the world. I am so honoured to have been welcomed into such a supportive and friendly community!

The Dive is a work of fiction, but it was heavily influenced by my travels to Thailand in 2015. That trip would not have been as memorable – or nearly as fun – without my good friends Patrick Reagin and Bobby Ross. Memories from our travels will fuel stories for the rest of my life.

There are so many different stages to writing a debut novel. There's the *Is this ever going to get published?* stage, the *Who the hell is ever going to want to read this?* stage, then, once it is accepted for publication, the *What in God's name have I done, how am I going to deal with people actually reading my secret thoughts?* stage, and – the worst of all worsts – the *Contemplating never writing again after reading a bad review* stage!

I am so thankful to all my friends, family and colleagues who have been there through it all, talking me down by email, or over Zoom, or around the dinner table, constantly reassuring me, despite my neuroses, and – in the case of my adorable nephew – even making me a homemade stress ball emblazoned with *The Dive*, which proved especially helpful while editing!

A special thank you to my parents. You've given me endless opportunities and I am so lucky to always have you in my corner. Thank you for fuelling this nerdy child's imagination and love for reading, for teaching me the importance of travel and for being an endless source of love and support. As I put in the dedication, you have made everything possible, and I love you more than I can ever say.

To Erin Cruz, my sister and friend. You inspire me every day, and you are the reason why I focus so heavily on the bond between sisters in this novel. No one can make me laugh quite like you can, and there is no one I would rather discuss potential plotlines with during late-night Target runs or on the couch with Bravo playing in the background. To Marvin Cruz, my bro, for his extraordinary photography skills (shout-out for the author photo) and allowing me to show up out of the blue at his house and stay for a week. To my niece and nephew, Harper and Mason, for being my biggest (and cutest) cheerleaders. I love you all so much.

And to Filip Holmqvist, my travel partner, my scuba buddy, and the original lover of pink drinks. You make this life so exciting and support me in all my crazy ideas and hare-brained schemes. I love you, and I cannot wait to see what the future holds for us.

And of course, I want to thank you, the reader. You are the one who has turned this author's fantasy into a reality, and none of this would be possible without you.

About the Author

A self-admitted travel addict, Sara Ochs has built a life around visiting beautiful and sometimes dangerous destinations. While learning to scuba dive on a remote island off the coast of Thailand, Sara heard that two backpackers had recently been murdered not far from her hotel. Horrified that something so terrible could happen in such an idyllic location, she knew she had found the inspiration for her debut novel, *The Dive*.

As well as being an author, Sara is an attorney and law professor who splits her time between the United States and Sweden. You can find Sara on Twitter @OchsWrites and on Instagram @saraochsauthor.